# The Loved and Envied

BOOKS BY ENID BAGNOLD

THE LOVED AND ENVIED

DOOR OF LIFE • NATIONAL VELVET

SERENA BLANDISH

ENID BAGNOLD

# The Loved and Envied

DOUBLEDAY & COMPANY, INC., GARDEN CITY, N.Y.

1951

*The characters and incidents in this book*
*are entirely*
*the work of the author's imagination*
*and have no relation to any person or event in real life.*

# Cast of Characters

Sir Gynt and Lady Maclean.
Rose and Edouard de Bas-Pouilly: *old lovers.*
Miranda: *Lady Maclean's daughter.*
Tuxie: *her husband.*
Rudi Holbein: *an old playwright.*
Cora Holbein: *his ex-wife.*
James Edouard Goethe de Bas-Pouilly: *the heir after Edouard, Vicomte de Bas-Pouilly.*
Fanny and Ursula: *the mother and aunt of Lady Maclean.*
Sir Beddoes Thomas: *once the Public Prosecutor.*
Duke: *a dog.*
Piffle: *a nurse.*
Cacki: *a Chinese footman.*

Part One

# CHAPTER ONE

"Very handsome," said Rose.

"Less."

"You think less? That's not what you believe! After all, for fifteen years haven't I been jealous of her!"

The Vicomte de Bas-Pouilly smiled, taking this as a tribute.

"What does 'after all' mean?"

"It means that I have a right that she should be handsome after all the trouble I've taken to be jealous."

"Hush! The curtain's going up!"

In the first interval Rose looked again at Lady Maclean, who sat in the front of the author's box.

"Fifty? Do you think?" (She spoke as though the first act had been an insignificant interruption.)

"I think more," said Edouard.

"She sits magnificently."

"A straight back."

"And then do you see what it is that renders her immune to age? It's the clench of her teeth."

"My dear Rose!"

"I who was a painter—you don't often see such locked formation. When the top teeth come down upon the bottom teeth nothing moves. The muscles running round the jaw are as fresh as a girl's. The whole *mâchoire*, the whole muzzle is intact, as in youth. See— when she turns."

"She always had beautiful cheeks."

"You've noticed that? With us, alas, it's the mouth that goes. The mouth, and the bridle of muscle that runs to the ears."

He held her knee with his hand, for comfort, to keep in touch, to remind her that they were together. Rose stared past him at the box.

"There's Rudi come in again. Stooping to talk to her."

"I'm not going to look round."

"What do you think she can possibly find to say that's kind to him, to Rudi Holbein, after such an act? Look, she's saying something—perhaps severe!"

"Not severe," said Edouard. "She has no severity. That's merely her unsmiling face."

Rose recrossed her knees so that his hand fell from the satin slide of her skirt. She did not like to be reminded that Lady Maclean's friends never spoke of her as they spoke of other people.

"She has a curious stare," she said in her final tone, and changed the conversation to a discussion of the play. They agreed that it was machine-made and that they could have written it for Rudi, taking a handful of his seventy plays and impacting the acts together. But before the curtain went up again on the second act Rose could not resist flicking the duster out of her spirit's window. On it were the grains of jealousy.

"Of course one is at one's best in a theatre box. Are those enormous things diamonds?"

"Why not?"

"I thought you insist they're now poor."

"As poor as we all are, hardly knowing which is income and what capital, what we still have that's salable, how soon we're going to need it. She hasn't had to sell her diamonds, because perhaps she hasn't thought of it."

In the second interval Edouard went out into the foyer. He always asked Rose to accompany him but it was understood that she would never leave her seat. While he was away she watched everything. On his return she said:

"I saw Rudi speak to you. What did he say?"

"I didn't much like what he said."

"Tell me though."

"He made out to be inviting people right and left to his usual supper party. But one knows with Rudi he keeps his head. His carefree invitations were from some careful list. He stared at me suddenly and screamed in his cackle of a voice—'Tiens! Edouard! Tu es encore beau!'"

"I shouldn't have minded that."

"I objected, for I understood him. It was a kind of crow of what he thinks is his triumphant age. Coming from him it was like being accosted in the tomb, as though he took pains to admire the purple and bruises of my decay. One man of seventy doesn't say that to another without malice."

"Seventy! Nearer eighty."

"No. We're the same age."

"What an ugly man! That is what makes him seem older—his appearance. Are you leaving me for his supper party?"

"You know I shan't. And he didn't ask me. We have our old quarrel, years ago, too dull to remember."

"That's what upset you then? That he didn't ask you?"

"Do me justice—Rose."

There was no length Rose might not go with Edouard, no liberty she might not take, no temper she must conceal, nothing to him was unknown. Though the marks of his family breeding had proved too insistent for his private expression, and, to a man who had hardly spoken a cross word in his life, had given a narrow-built, elegant, and seemingly ill-tempered face, nevertheless he was endlessly indulgent. With his Pouilly eyes too close either side of his nose he observed. With his lips of thinnest skin, lifted against his will by Pouilly muscles into a sneer, he forbore to chastise. Only his close friends loved him. Rose's bad behaviour was one of the luxuries which he allowed her. He never had made her behave herself. Now that she was a spoilt old woman she behaved as she liked. He took the little claw, decorated with his rings, under his arm, and the curtain went up again.

"Where's Roccafergolo?" she whispered, continuing, indisci-plined, in the dark. "He's such a first-nighter." Though she knew nobody and only came out like a night owl with Edouard on the rarest occasions, she always talked as though in the thick of society.

"He's not well enough. I hear this illness he has is dropsy."

"Good God! Is it that then?"

"What?"

"Dropsy."

"So they say."

The neighbouring seatholders psshed and glared. Two more acts, and the play, having reached its climax, diminuendoed, like a ballet, like someone who falls asleep after tears. The lights went up. The noise was tremendous, from friends and foes. Eyes in the stalls met each other, laughs and unkind whispers were exchanged. Rudi Holbein, unable to distinguish failure, hallucinated by the culminatory moment after the months of work, risked his speech of thanks from his own box, standing behind Lady Maclean, speaking over her head. All eyes, watching him, took in her face as well, the diamonds at her breast nodding, trembling, like carnival lights, while she looked on unmoved. Behind and above her Rudi's walnut skull was canted back in the shadow, and one could see as he spoke how the jaws snapped—topping the white carnation which he wore, white tie, too large silk facings. How many first-night speeches he had made, all, naturally, from the stage! And now, so leisurely and easily he thought he held his Paris, he had the presumption to make this one from his box. It would deepen the gall in the pens and the typewriters tomorrow. He was a very tall man, very lean, very yellow, bony, a Jew of an unusual type—and so long famous that fame had given his face a cracked brown varnish like one of the world's pictures.

"What he must have looked like in the cradle!" whispered Rose as the crowds began to move. "What doubts his mother must have felt!"

They forged out together, Rose holding to Edouard's sleeve with her hand, Edouard nodding to acquaintances. It was a Friday night in a hot summer. In five minutes they entered the gardens of the Palais Royale at the bottom and walked up the left-hand arcade, Rose's high heels tapping, her hand through his arm, her fingers resting in his dry palm.

"Thirty-three years tonight!" she said as they climbed the stairs to their flat at the head of the arcaded gardens. "The tenth of June."

"A celebration, then?"

"Chablis. A bottle of Chablis and a cake," said Rose. "But then we always have that."

"It's always a celebration."

She had been twenty-seven and he thirty-seven the night they had first met. Now she was sixty and he seventy, and he had never married her.

Entering the flat Rose went first to the basin to see that the cold water round the bottle of wine had not run out. She changed the water. Edouard sat down in his own leather chair and undid his patent-leather shoes. They were contemporaries, about to pass the kind of evening they were used to; getting into bed with a glass of wine on either bed-cupboard, talking side by side, careless of sleep, with noses pointing to the ceiling. Once the door was shut there was no one to see that they were old.

They were great night-birds. Rose slept late and Edouard did not mind how little he slept. The two hollow tops of the bedside lamp shades showed the ceiling in its lit patches to be rare and exquisite. Being part of the original palace it was painted with an orange cupid too big for the room (which had been subdivided), and near the far wall the cupid's foot, and the ball he was kicking, pursued the rose-pink bottom of another cupid who had gone into the wall. Round two sides of the ceiling (and across the cupid's back, as though thrown in mischief) were wreaths and swags of peculiar lilies, greenish, and in places embossed. An unseen lamp, down in the gardens, outlined the stubborn winebottle legs of the little balconade that fringed the windows, and on which Rose's geraniums would, in daylight, show vermilion on mole-grey.

"If I were a playwright's wife," said Rose, "it seems to me I would know when my husband should cease writing. But would one tell him?"

"I doubt it. Not when it's the only interest he has, the only thing he can do. And Cora left him—it must be twenty years ago. There was a baby, a son. But I never heard any more of him. Rudi is a working playwright. He gets no 'blick' on life outside himself. He'll die in harness. His only confidant's his dictaphone."

"Did you see, in the box opposite, that extraordinary yellow woman in white muslin? Was that Cora Holbein?"

"Opposite to Rudi's? Very likely. She's that sort of wordly celebrity who likes to test in public the name she has made for herself. Quite indifferent that it's the first night of her ex-husband. But hardly—surely—in white muslin?"

"The sort of muslin that costs a fortune. Is it hate, or kindness—or simply nothing—that's left over when a woman's divorced her husband? Or been divorced by him—which was it?"

"I think neither. She left him and they left it at that."

Rose shook out a shabby black lace nightdress. "To speak from the box like that after such a play!" she went on. "Lady Maclean must have flattered him and made him lose his head."

"Well, all that'll be settled in a few hours."

"How?"

"By the morning's papers. What Rudi thinks, poor old gentleman, won't be proof against them."

Rose, struck by something, said: "You don't mind realising that old men are the same age as you. Why is that?"

"I don't mind age, Rose."

"I wonder why." She took the bottle, screwed in the corkscrew and put it between her knees to pull.

"She must have told him a lot of nonsense," she said, and she pulled as though she were pulling a rival's neck.

"Perhaps.—Such a rash way to open a bottle!"

"I knew you would refuse to discuss her! Really, I become disheartened! Really," drawing out the cork, "in spite of what's happened to the world, to us all, why should she have everything? It comes of living in a clique. Round about that woman there's a myth. There's a determination that she should be unassailable. It used to be because of her beauty, but that can't go on forever, and now she's between fifty and sixty you are all so old yourselves that you don't notice your queen turning grey!"

"Yes, I do," he said. "I've noticed some ashy-looking hairs."

"Well, of course she's dyed, as we all are. I don't in the least hold that against her, but let's have the truth."

"And then . . ." (Edouard had got into bed and settling himself comfortably spoke with the utmost good humour) ". . . who is this set, this clique?"

"You. And your Marie-Innocence. And Rudi perhaps. And others. I don't move in your world."

"Rosie, pour that wine out for me and for yourself and come into bed."

She obeyed him. But when settled in bed she exclaimed, "I've forgotten the cake!" and springing out of bed like a girl she went back to her looking glass behind which she had placed the cake on a plate. She stooped and looked into the glass and turning from it she wailed to him: "I can't bear to see it, I can't bear to see it! One would think I drank! I *don't* drink, Edouard——"

"It's something I don't see," he said.

"Because your sight isn't good any more," she said, and continued to look in the glass.

What she saw, what everyone saw who approached her, was that all the dispositions of red in her face were in the wrong places. Flushes had established themselves so that they looked like swellings, and, not on cheeks but on either side of her nose, the skin was too rosy. She flushed even where her eyebrows had been—but they had gone, with too much plucking. It was all a slight readjustment, but most deeply unfortunate, for it is in such natural shadings and paintings that the face gives its impression. She turned her back on the glass and said in a low voice:

"I was so pretty. Nobody knows that now but you."

"Come into bed," he ordered. And when she got into bed he put his arm round her. "Your life is written inside my head," he said. "If your looks are exhausted it's I who have exhausted them. You must not complain of giving your life to a man if he values it."

"I hate to be sixty," she whispered.

"If I were not seventy that might be something," he said stoutly, "but your life is in relation to mine, Rosie. I'm here to put you into focus. And now you've still forgotten that cake!" And throwing back the bedclothes he in his turn went to the glass.

"What could they say of me, then!" he exclaimed. "A mean-looking, sneering old fellow. And with my collar off I have one of those necks I hate!"

"Swear to me that you've never loved her!"

"Who? Ruby? Wait while I find the knife. I'll discuss that in bed.

"And if I had?" he asked, carrying the plate carefully over to Rose. "Would it matter now?"

"I should never have thought when I was young," said Rose, "that at sixty I should still be jealous. We don't change, do we? But you are all I have, you have always been all I had. It's bad enough that I should have to share you with your sister."

"Well—believe this—I've never 'loved' Ruby Maclean."

"Ah! No? And now you change the subject again! This time it's Madame de Lison I'm not allowed to talk about!"

The Vicomte de Bas-Pouilly lived with his widowed younger sister in a large and well-regulated flat in the Avenue Matignon. He was exigent in his way of living, had a good cook, ate and drank with taste and entertained as much as any man of seventy wants to do. Every week-end he went to his cottage in the Forest of Bas-Pouilly. He was the fourteenth vicomte and hereditary owner of the forest and of the stone château (more like a station terminus than a home) that dominated the entrance to the forest. Since the State forbade the cutting of his trees, or the sale of any portion of his estate, he had to live with care. But he had always had to live with care and, though from time to time various depleted fortunes drifted in to him from the deaths of relatives, the taxes, duties and burdens kept his living much on the same scale. His cousin inherited after him, a young man of twenty-eight, not yet married, who had been all his life in the guardianship of his great-aunt, the Scottish Duchess of Nimours-Lardaigne. She was an arrogant old woman (much more arrogant since her widowhood), rich from her father's biscuits, with a gift for grim words, and radiantly successful as a gardener in her gardens near the Spanish border.

Young James Edouard Goethe de Bas-Pouilly had been eight years old when the duchess had stayed at Little Pouilly with Sir Gynt and Lady Maclean and had brought the heir to see his uncle.

"Don't you die, Edouard. Don't go and die," she had then said, stooping to pick up and examine a clod of earth. "I can't bear the soil here." Beyond that visit (when she had severely criticised Edouard for what she called his "sheds"—his beautifully organized workshops, for he was a happy week-end carpenter) he had not seen her again—though he had known her earlier as a young married woman. She was wrapped up in her gardens and rarely moved away from them.

The heir had seemed then to Edouard a sad, poetic little boy. The duchess, then fifty-three, was not at that time a widow.

"Why 'Goethe'?" Edouard had asked her, looking through the window at the boy on the lawn.

"My poor niece was romantic," said his great-aunt. " 'Edouard' is for the Pouillys, 'James' for home use, and 'Goethe' she used to say was her secret with the baby."

"Is he going to school?"

"Eventually to Eton," said the duchess grimly.

"Did you have a row over that?"

"Yes. We had a state meeting of Pouillys. But I got my way."

"Ah, you often get that."

"Much more often than is good for me. He's already in love," she added. "He can't take those dark eyes of his off Ruby Maclean. You should *clear* more. There are too many trees and too close. I hate a bosky garden."

"I'm not allowed to touch a tree," he replied, "as you'll find when you're regent."

Edouard, who loved his own repetitive habits, came always on Monday for the night to the Palais Royale, spent Tuesday, Wednesday and Thursday of each week in the Avenue Matignon, and on Friday night returned to Rose, driving down alone to his cottage in Pouilly on Saturday morning. Although the routine of his life in the Avenue Matignon was all that taste and good management could make it, some contrary streak in his nature accepted the haphazard conditions in the Palais Royale. High up, facing south, balconied, the two rooms and kitchenette-bathroom represented to Edouard the unresponsible laxity and repose one might find in an attic with a friend. The bedroom, being the first room approached from the stairs, was the only room they used. In it was their large bed (sitting on the side of which Rose spent her days), a walnut bookcase with some of Edouard's books, Rose's large dressing-table paint-table in one, its mirror hung with turbans—and turbans again were on the curled rosewood posts of the bed. Turbans were her stand-by. Stained and tired twists of gold and scarlet (many of them with a light toupee of waved brown hair attached to the front) were everywhere to her hand, or tossed down upon the tables. Her turbans were to Rose what false teeth might be to another old woman—to be reached for and put on before the first cigarette was lit. All her life her light, pretty hair had been insufficient; it had barely done its duty, had hardly lasted out. She had been used to wear it brushed up at the back off her neck and tilted over her brow like a forage cap. But now, if it must still reach the brow, it had to leave the back of the head bare. This she could not allow, so the old effect was maintained by devices and purchases.

Edouard kept a few suits with Rose and they were her pride and care, and the nearest approach she had to married life. What was left of her morning after she woke she spent in pressing and sponging, or mending—if there was a tiny point that wanted a needle.

The back room, beyond the front room, was as though they had never quite got there—arriving long ago at the front room with a sigh of relief, and there remaining for thirty-three years. The back room was so filled with what Rose could never unpack that the door hardly opened. Packing cases, trunks, easels, wicker baskets, cardboard hatboxes, were piled one on the other and sealed with spiders' webs. Long ago she had been one of a brood of almost starving children whom her poor father had supported by his indifferent brush. And she, and two of her sisters, had drifted at times from art student to model, and back, when the purse allowed, to art student again. Gradually she had had all the legacies, as one by one all her brothers and sisters had died. But they were legacies of nothing at all. Not one of the family had climbed out of poverty.

Sometimes, among the trunks, she plunged—bringing out a dress, but returning it again. She would remember a dress that she had worn when she had been a pretty girl. But she was no longer a pretty girl, and the dress, though it fitted, couldn't embellish.

"Ah!" Edouard would call out, seeing a green taffeta, "but you looked lovely in that!" Then Rose's eyes would fill with her ready tears.

The back room was a cemetery of the past, but in the front room they lived and talked, drank coffee out of bowls, cooked little dishes before the play, drank a bottle of wine on their return, and chatted in the old nest of their bed.

This had gone on for many many years. Rose was the petted, the tender attachment of his life. And his sister, who had mishandled her short, uncomfortable marriage, knew in some peculiar manner that this was so, and knowing it wished with resentment and anguish that she herself could be so loved. She was jealous. She was forced to accept that there was a long-established woman in her magnificent brother's life, whose surname she did not know, of whose whereabouts she had no idea, and she imagined the establishment kept for this woman to be sumptuous as she also imagined the magic qualities of this mistress to be just those of which her own personality was bare. Often she made Edouard frown by an innuendo, by a furtive or malicious allusion, but she had seldom the courage, in his presence, to aim straight.

Rose in her turn was kept in order.

"I'm not allowed to talk then," she complained, "of Madame de Lison!"

"If you knew her my sister Angel would not interest you."

"I'm not given the chance. She is your real life. At our age she's almost your wife. I'm more uncomfortable about her than about your Ruby."

"Would it make you happy to tell you that my sister has faults?"

"Very."

Edouard broke into a peal of laughter. "Listen. I've—very naturally—known my sister all my life. She hasn't a happy character but I love her. I love what belongs to me. She is all that remains of my boyhood, of our mother——"

"Every word you say makes it worse!"

"Wait! My love for Angel is a little candle, steady as a rock. Nothing can blow it out, it's small and cool, the candle you set in a window. But my love for Rose is like the fireside of an old man who was once young. It's his all, it's the place he wants to be, old as he is he knows its ways, and how to blow it up on a cold night."

She purred with comfort and the small face turned to him on the pillow took on its old expression of impertinence and triumph. She held her hand up to watch her rings flash.

"Yes, I know your birthday's coming!" he exclaimed. "You're going to have another ring."

"My hand isn't pretty any more," she said, but added quickly: "Never mind, we're well, aren't we! We're in health. It must be terrible to be ill. I keep thinking of that huge man—your Marie-Innocence—caught like that by the dropsy. It seems it's no use to be modern, fashionable, and a duke. That unrespectful illness catches him like a peasant's grandmother!"

"It's true. It's rare one hears of it in our class. Don't repeat it though. Alberti hasn't said anything to me himself. It mayn't be true."

Rose, while enjoying "in our class" which he had let fall, said only, "To whom should I repeat it! Is it Alberti he is usually called?

How dull when he has such pretty names! Alberti, Marie-Innocence, Duca di Roccafergolo . . . what more?"

"Italians have names which pay compliments to the histories of
their families. I'm very sorry for him. He's an old friend, and my
neighbour. In fact, of course, my tenant."

"Part of your country life," sighed Rose. "Part of tomorrow's
week-end that's forbidden to me. You go down tomorrow? I wonder
what you really do, Edouard?"

"I have a great deal of peace and happiness," he teased her.
"And I waste my time with ecstasy making stupid little objects,
things, alas, they also sell in the shops."

"But if they sell them in the shops?"

"They are never the same. What you make yourself is well-bred.
And then I see Alberti perhaps once a month. Occasionally I dine
with him. He has a very good cook. But all that you know, my dear.
You ask and I tell you a hundred times."

"He's been, hasn't he (if he isn't now), Lady Maclean's lover?"

"Alberti?"

"Yes."

"Did I say so?"

"You may have. Is it so? Was it so?"

"I promise you I couldn't tell you," he said. "One can't tell with
her or with him. They've both such a capacity for friendship. She's
very tender with him."

"If I were tender with a man . . ."

"She's not as wholly feminine as you are. She takes any amount
of trouble to please him. But then he's ill. And then too she's so
fond of men . . ."

Rose exploded with laughter.

Edouard laughed too, but he said: "It's true. She's kind to men
—as though she were sorry for them. And her life's very much
among them, except for her daughter. One has the sense with her
that she knows all about one. So much so that that seems the very
reason for her rapid, frivolous talk. She's like a palmist who sees
the lifeline end and cries quickly, 'Let's have a drink!' She spots

it all—the touch of fear, the lie, the moment when one chooses wrong, and with it she's no judge, she doesn't condemn. She has the magnanimity of a mistress and none of the reserves of a wife."

"That's enough, that's enough!" cried Rose comically. "You know I can't stand praise of other women. Is the daughter a beauty too? How much more luck have they down there at Pouilly?"

"The daughter is not there. She married."

"Ah, of course! That terrible marriage! The poor creature married a gigolo."

"Oh—not quite. A little better than that!"

"Not much. He had a gift, hadn't he? A sort of entertainer. For a short time I remember he was the thing. If I were the girl's mother I should die of fear for her, of rage, of anxiety. How did it turn out?"

"They went to Jamaica. There's a family estate there and they made him manager."

"She writes? What does she say when she writes? How old is she?"

"She's thirty-one."

"What? As much as that? One thinks of all brides as nineteen. It seemed the other day. But that's the war."

"Miranda was twenty-three when she married Tuxie. I've seen some of her letters home. They're like a schoolboy's, they get shorter and shorter. All about oranges and Negroes."

"Ah—if I were her mother—I should think it terrible that she should write only of oranges. I should travel out and see what was the matter! What sort of mother would I have made? Now we shall never know."

"You have been my mother," he said. "I know what sort of mother you have been."

"Edouard," she said, turning to him, "in the daytime I think so much of death."

"That you mustn't do. It will come when it comes. It won't be any better for thinking of it."

"But mustn't I prepare?"

"The Church says so," he said. "But I'm against it. You'll find all drops into place. No one makes a fuss when they get to the brink."

"Promise me one thing."

"Well?" (He knew what it was.)

"Bury me first. Manage it somehow for me. You know I can't stand loneliness."

"All right, Madame Egoïste," he said, as he had said before. And to divert her he asked her about a night long ago when he maintained that she had been unfaithful to him; and sometimes his joke was that it had been with Alberti, and that all her questions were intended to beguile him from the truth. The counter that she habitually made to this was never completely to reassure him. She had, actually, never met the Duca di Roccafergolo and at that time too he was too shy with women to have made any approach to her. There had been somebody, and some foundation for ancient suspicions that were now as dead as winter leaves, but they had both forgotten them, and remembered only the harmless shape of accusations and defences. It was their game. It had been played for twenty years. Like children they were able to listen to old jokes over and over again.


## CHAPTER TWO

The Duca Alberti Marie-Innocence di Roccafergolo was indeed a shy man. For one thing he was over life-size, a giant. For another he had been brought up, fatherless, with irritating anxiety, by a foolish woman, secluded, schooled by tutors, at the mercy always of his American mother's want of balance, the quirks of her ideas of food and health, mourned over by her as the frail orphan-bearer of great titles and estates, kept in bed a week for every cold in the nose, and, as he grew, subject to hay fever, and more and more fearfully shy. The third reason for his shyness was that he was involved in London in a scandal. But that was after his happy sojourn at Oxford.

That he became an Oxford undergraduate was luck for him, and due to some influence momentarily brought to bear upon his mother, some train of thought afterwards forgotten. At any rate there he went, remained three years, saw life for the first time relieved from oppression, and fell headlong in love with England. When he had been six months at Oxford and daily subject to the humour, the understatement, the casual manners, the code of his companions, the wind from ancient Greece that blows about the colleges, he felt as light-hearted as a huge spring starling on a chimney pot. The air that came up to his young nostrils was sweet as woodsmoke in a village, sweet as a bakery. All his life after he could hardly set eyes on an English man or woman without that early lightness returning to his heart. It was a gentle, diffident heart, and it was all the more damaging to him that he should have been caught, innocent, in a scandal, in the country whose good opinion he so valued.

The scandal came three years after he had left Oxford. He had returned from Rome to London and had taken a house in Brook Street with his mother for the season. He had by then long put on the fat which was the mild grief of his life, but with his immense height he moved with dignity, though a barrel-like appearance. His bearing, his silence, and his stature gave him a worldly look and made him seem much older than he was.

He gave a ring to his mother's hairdresser's young sister who looked like a violet on a bank, and who sued him for breach of promise. More than that she said, untruly, that she was to bear his child. His mother in her terror and shock changed her lawyer three times, then went behind the third lawyer's back and tried to buy off the girl, meanwhile talking, confiding, and weeping to everyone she knew—first saying that she thought Alberti guilty, then that she knew him to be innocent. Her conduct made fresh headlines every day. The huge young man was speechless with misery and shame.

All that he had done to the young girl was to write her three tender love letters. It had been his first time in love. In secret he had dreamt of marrying her, and had gone the length of giving her the fatal ring. No sooner had he done this than something about her set him thinking. His eyes slowly opened to her true character and he fled to Paris to think it over, from there writing her the letter that would have suggested breach of promise to a girl not already thinking of it. It so happened that at the very same moment she found herself to be with child by her sister's fiancé—that is to say in a temporary fix but with this bright way out.

The case was a nine days' pleasure and pain to his circle and he paid enormous damages. It was the size of the damages paid that made the size of the scandal. The house in Brook Street was shut up and he left with his mother for Italy. While still in London she had hourly repeated to him every word of shocked or surprised sympathy she had been able to rouse from people he knew by name. He had believed her to the extent that he thought himself ostracised. He felt that never in his life could he return, and that England was closed to him for ever.

Back in Italy, fabulously rich, a little celebrated, painfully silent, unnaturally buried in his library, a fascinating immorality was attached to his name. The Italian girls of his class gossiped in secret together, but the American girls, daughters of the friends of his mother, arrived at the palace excited and half in love.

At twenty-six, a secret virgin, though forced to wear the scarlet cape of the seducer, he was already going bald, but the blond hair that clung round his temples was as fine as a baby's, and his skin had the look of a rosy cherub. Seeming neither old nor young, and giving no hint of his mortal shyness, he would greet his mother's young guests (to whom she was always plotting to get him married), ask a formal question or two, and relapse again into silence. It was not difficult, as he sat, to imagine his mountain of flesh engarlanded naked in a glade—a stout and flushed young god painted by Rubens.

When he was thirty his mother died, and immediately he left Italy for ever, and finding among his possessions a house in Paris, and among his titles that of Conte di Melchiorre, he started a new life. He was not successful with the title for everyone called him the Duca Alberti, but the life suited him from the first, and in a moderate way he began to make friends. He still maintained his obsession, and avoided English people, adding to the obsession a new one—that he was too old to marry. At this time, at the height of her beauty and in the gay, brilliant middle stretches of her career, he met Ruby Maclean. Immediately the dear English breeze blew upon him from her. She was as casually English in her manner of talking as his lost Oxford companions. She looked then like a rose and a lily both and yet talked like a man at his club. She brought back the humour he had adored: she stared him in the eye with her Gainsborough face, and made him laugh. She opened for him her special gift for intimacy, automatically and unregardedly given to those whom she liked. To them she offered her mind undiluted, elliptical and without glossary, to take or leave. Alberti could take it. He was at once bound to her side. He saw (though he could never copy it) what it was to get the most out of friends. To her they brought their gayest disasters, and laughed, as she did, unsparingly at themselves. Mishaps that befell them were treated in friendly fashion, as though the best of life happens only on the side. They were a glittering band of untouchable philosophers who could not be discomfited.

She made enemies but did not know it. Anyone near her level was her friend. She did not notice the absence of the others. In Paris she moved from gathering to gathering, fetched, surrounded, attended. No one liked to be excluded. No one could afford to leave alone such a dispenser of life: everyone tried to feed at the spring. She seemed to develop, when in the company of those who enjoyed life as she did, a baker's yeast.

When she came into a room it was plain it was a spirited person who entered, a person with an extra dose of life. It was apparent on all sides how people were affected. They had a tendency to rise to their feet to be nearer her, not of course in her honour, but to be at the source of amusement, to be sure not to miss the exclamation, the personal comedy she might make of the moment of life just left behind.

Down at Pouilly—the eighteenth-century house bequeathed to Sir Gynt Maclean by his half-French mother, standing on the rise of an open meadow at the edge of Pouilly Forest and just outside the boundary of Edouard's possessions—the household came to life in her presence and missed her whenever she was away. There it seemed, in the twenty years that followed, an endless, rainless summer where no one grew any older. Each day, with its lively occupations, seemed to shake itself and leap awake with the freshness of a wild animal, each day was only another lucky chance to live.

Access could be had to the ruler of the household the moment she opened an eye. Naked or half-dressed or in her bath she began the life of the day in public. If she needed a private life she could take it in company. The servants made excuses to be in or out of her room, but though she was always in a hurry she was never out of humour.

Ideas involving activity sprang like a fountain in her mind. She made no distinctions. The enchanted flute played equally for friends or household. They rose, ran, followed, leaving their work and their distractions. The Scottish housemaid, the fat cook, Rosalba, the child Miranda and the dogs themselves, all were attracted to the bright bedroom and all invented reasons to be near her. The cook, receiving orders for a luncheon, would follow her to the edge of the bath, and argue energetically on the number of courses for a luncheon.

"We're in the country," came the determined voice. "We're simple people. Three."

"Four, madame."

"I won't have four. Out, out . . . move back . . . give me the towel . . ."

"But Madame hasn't used the soap!"

"Don't think," said the towelled figure, already crossing to the dressing-table, "that it's by numbers you spread your fame. Do your miracle again with the trout."

The gardener would look up, trailing his rake, and half catch an order from above that profoundly disturbed him. The lady who gave the orders from the window never explained herself twice or bent her language to suit her listeners. As with all her human relationships, people must spring to catch up with her, before with her brilliant humility she hurried out of sight. She would wave a suggestion, a floral idea like a carnival trailer into the garden airs, and usually the gardener only understood enough to grow upset. Then the black Jaamican maid Rosalba would return with the dogs from their walk in the garden and Miranda's name would ring down the wide landing, and the bustle and turbulence of the opening day would spread from the bedroom to the rooms below.

Miranda was ten in those days—at the time when Alberti first fell in love with her mother. That this had seriously happened did not occur to Ruby: she was never very sharp to recognise her victims.

"You've had half a life before we met," she said to him. "But by your frown you won't let me speak of this tremendous past of yours."

"No. I'm shy. At least about the heart I'm very shy."

"But one's love-life, as one gets older, is part of one's story."

"I have had no love-life," he said crossly. He sailed along beside her—they were walking in the forest—with the light gait of a fat man, his hat held in his hand, the wind stirring the tendrils that were left to him on his pink brow. If she could not see, he thought, that his true love-life began the day he met her, he would not tell her. He would keep that deep relief scrupulously out of sight, as out of sight as a church one never enters, but whose bells, at the wonted hours, ring behind the trees.

But his love rearranged his life for him, for Edouard de Bas-Pouilly—offering him at that moment a chance of renting a cottage in Pouilly Forest, he took it. He did not trouble to sell his Paris house (filled from cellar to attic with treasures brought from Rome) but settled himself more and more, and finally altogether, in his forest cottage. There, as he grew older (and in time more a Holbein than a Rubens) he became a gentle institution as a neighbour, a great dropper-in at Little Pouilly and even an honorary godfather to the small and stout Miranda.

Gynt had a theory that Miranda thought only in dog-language. "I wonder if we oughtn't to get rid of the dogs—just to force her to talk to us. Eliminate them, and see what she has left over to say."

"If I hadn't them as a morning introduction I couldn't find the way in to Miranda. It's how we begin. It's how her eye lights up. But she talks, doesn't she, to you?"

"She likes facts. I tell her facts. She listens."

"Birds?"

"Yes. Snow particles, stars, wolves, comets, the bottom of the sea. Oh, all the facts. She'll be clever, you'll see."

"She'll be bookish."

"Well, she'll be bookish. I want her well-educated."

"Don't make her your son, Gynt. It'll be too much to put on her shoulders."

"You must remember," he said, looking at his beautiful wife, "she's not going to be taking."

"Oh!"

"No, no she isn't. And she must be armed with other interests to make up."

"She's only ten."

"Young men are cruel. I took care only to know pretty women," he said. "And married the loveliest of all. But you and I, in our own nursery, have one of those others, those I left outside my hard heart. I saw how they got hurt (and this one's our own)."

"How can a small, soft child be so hard to understand?"

"She's setting up her walls already. I think we must be all prepared for a career."

"I'm all prepared for that."

"I mean—instead of the graces."

"But can't they be included?"

"She can only be second best, in this house, in the graces."

Next morning was Miranda's eleventh birthday.

At eight o'clock she walked into the bedroom, starched and clean, short and stout.

"Many happy returns, darling!"

"Thank you," said Miranda.

"Did you sleep well? Or did feeling eleven wake you early?"

Miranda couldn't answer two questions at once.

"I didn't sleep well," she stated.

"Why?"

"Sometimes people don't," said Miranda, and moving the talk immediately to the dog, "John hasn't wished me many happy returns."

In those days they had a fox terrier whose delicate front legs perpetually trembled.

"Do you wish me many happy returns, John?"

"He will—for a biscuit. They're in the silver box. Don't take them all. Papa comes in for them sometimes."

"When will he see me, Papa, to wish me . . ."

"It depends on whether he's sleeping on."

Immediately there was a shadow of offence on Miranda's face. She did not like to be cut short. Lady Maclean, in her gay hurry, cut everyone short. She tried to make amends.

"What would you like to do, that's special today?"

"To have an ordinary day."

"Oh, *why*, Miranda!"

It was perfect, the misunderstanding. It was delicately accurate. Nothing ever went right. Gynt came in his dressing gown.

"Hoi, Miranda!"

"Hoi then."

"The old thing's getting so old, her hair's greyish."

"It isn't then," said Miranda. And she went off into a shout of laughter, uproarious, awkward, almost hysterical. It was as though it was a relief to make a noise with her mouth.

Rosalba, who had brought up Miranda, said, "She better when she been away."

"But why should a little girl go away?"

"Some girls so. And some girls so. She better when she been away."

"Where to?"

"She like a schoolgirl already. That's where she better go."

But Miranda would not go to school. She did not only say she would not but she was able to produce a convincing illness every time it came to a head. She had appendicitis the first time there was an attempt, measles the next, and just when she was being measured for a reefer jacket she was diagnosed as having something glandular that required injections. What was so tiresome was that she was not really happy at home.

"Perhaps she can't be really happy," said Gynt. "Some people can't."

"What a failure then for me as a mother."

"People are different. Keep your eyes off her. She'll come round."

Miranda did not really come round. Not quite ever. Nobody knew, not even Miranda herself, that she envied her mother her beauty. She was not introspective and all trouble lay so deep below the surface it hardly rose into her mind. That was what made her so hard to make happy, so impossible to understand. She was outwardly intelligent, with a good memory, and, as Gynt had said, a love of facts.

Later on she said she thought she would like to be a lawyer.

"In England? Not here in Paris?"

"I should like to go to Oxford when I'm nineteen," she said.

"And your matriculation?"

"Miss Taylor will get me through that."

Miss Taylor came when Miranda was sixteen. She thought Miranda's mother frivolous. That she thought so, though she did not say so, was bad for Miranda. Miranda never blamed her mother for anything; she simply had no conception of her. She certainly thought her beautiful, but as that thought had some curious pain in it she put it away. She thought her also rather funny (and deeply loved her—of which fact neither of them was aware).

They still both laughed together over the dogs. That was rather cosy. But Miranda had got, one would have thought, too old for such passionate dog-life; still it went on. She had one definite criticism of her mother which did her good rather than otherwise. She thought she dressed her own round body with more skill than her mother dressed her lovely slim one. And in a way it was true. She was curiously neater, more compactly dressed, more integrated with herself in her clothes.

Miss Taylor stayed one year and got Miranda through her matriculation, then went away, satisfied that she had formed Miranda's character. She was an envious, competent woman, who in her teaching laid stress on solid qualities, and in some insidious manner implied that Miranda's mother was without them. Neither Ruby nor Gynt could bear her, but Gynt urged patience and the woman did what was needed for Miranda's Oxford life (which she never lived). For when Miranda had matriculated and letters had been exchanged with the principal of the chosen college Miranda made up her mind after all to stay at home. No one knew why. Ruby was delighted. Gynt was anxious.

"What's the matter with the girl? If she'd been a boy I'd have lost patience on the grand scale."

Actually the stolid, unconscious young woman, who came to few conclusions about herself, had come to one. She wanted to be married as soon as possible and she decided she would be wiser to tighten her suction on the sea-rock of home. Miss Taylor wrote her a long letter. Then a second. Miranda did not answer. Miss Taylor wrote a short note to Lady Maclean asking if Miranda were ill, and Ruby expostulated with Miranda.

"I'm not good at letters myself," she said, "but sometimes there are letters which not to answer is to be a brute."

"I'll have to be a brute," said Miranda (who was wearing a charming navy-blue dress and white collar). "It's much the best."

So Miss Taylor (who had after all taken much trouble) was

written to kindly and it was explained that for reasons not stated Miranda did not want to go to Oxford. Miss Taylor replied in such an involved and blaming manner that Ruby too had to be a brute.

At this time Miranda attempted to change her name to Alicia, but her parents, curiously outraged, behaved in unyielding unison, and Miranda, surprised, held her tongue.

"Your surname," said Gynt, "you'll probably change. But your first name belongs to us."

Miranda was secretly so pleased with the first half of the sentence that she said no more. Thus, in spirit, poor Miranda made ready for Tuxie.


## CHAPTER THREE

And Tuxie was nearing her. He was coming from quite far to fetch her. From the clubhouse in Rodzanbianca, penniless, born with a longing for pleasure, and full of gifts. When Miranda was twenty-one, a shy and silent twenty-one, he was there, in the same city, approaching and approaching, renting a dark room near Notre Dame, where he lay a great deal in the daytime on an unmade bed. He had some good clothes, and his only friend was a countess, dere-lict, haggard, painted, absurd, but good for an occasional party, and owning an acquaintance or two. She was writing her memoirs. He undertook to correct them. One of the most unaccountable of his gifts was a sense of words. It was perhaps his acute ear (which at Oxford, with mimicry, good looks, and musical deftness, had gath-ered him a circle). If he had only been able to play six kinds of musical instruments in a peculiar whispering manner of his own, that would have been enough; but as well as that he had early developed a specialty, a sort of topical recitative, fragmentary, witty, libellous, a thing quite of his own. The little sagas were daring, but too broken up to be dangerous, and he had a way of hinting, of allowing the guitar to drown the approaching innuendo, the awaited climax, the inference that was to be drawn. It was quite a gift. And while he sang his hard, enigmatic face moved the heart a little. The whole thing had glamour.

Here in Paris his acute ear helped him again. It fed on the French language and understood even a comb wrapped in lavatory paper and was at home when anyone asked him which of two sounds was the better. He had known a lot of French as a boy, spending all holidays in Rouen while his father and mother were in India: so when the countess read out her chapters he was able to tell her with authority where she had been redundant. She, looking at the handsome face, experienced what she had thought was gone for ever—love. He saw it and though appalled for the moment made capital of her. Through her he got to know the painter, Cora Holbein, whose nose for social life was as keen as her brush was brilliant.

"What a set of old guys!" he thought. But got to work.

He realised then that Parisian society was the paradise of elderly women. But they were no fools. He had to watch his step. One way and another he was asked about, invited here and there. He was astonished with what an assumption of power women of sixty could enter a drawing-room, with what a welcome, with what ludicrous kisses they were received if they had wit and confidence. "The pansies' molls"—he called them. But he had brains enough to realise that that wasn't fair and that it wasn't easy to reign: it must be done by personality, by achievement. His own achievement was nil and his personality did not inspire confidence. The little gifts he had must be dropped about negligently, as a woman drops her handkerchief. He listened, absorbed gossip, absorbed it so quick and close that it was red-hot, bone-new. Then one night, at a party to which Cora had taken him, when there had come that peculiar gap in the evening which may herald a movement to leave, he sauntered to a corner where he had left his guitar behind a sofa, and with a desperate, actor's courage, took up his instrument and leant against the door, the only door. No one could go. He tuned. His peculiar songs were not new to him, he had perfected them for years; in his exile they had been his only amusement. But now he was going to sing in French, he was going to put over the elliptical, dangerous quality of French gossip. First he sang a song in English, to clear his throat, to catch the room, and before anyone could move or applaud he had burst into his little French adventure; a gossip column set to music, with the names half said and the facts half indicated, bold, libellous, new as a new penny. Everyone was laughing. It was an amazing success.

Grimly smiling himself he opened the door and was gone, running down the marble staircase, ignoring the lift cage. His countess (of the memoirs) and Cora Holbein explained with pride that he was their own, their find.

So of course, after that, everyone spoke to him of Lady Maclean. He must meet her—she would adore him. It seemed curious to him that a Scotitsh woman could be so important, and then he remembered that when he was at Oxford he had cut a picture of her from the *Tatler*. He calculated. She must be over forty, but she might still be good-looking. It was Edouard de Bas-Pouilly who took him down to Little Pouilly, offering to drive him there to lunch. He didn't suggest putting him up for the night.

"I'm struck with the vintage of the women who matter in Paris. They're so extraordinarily old."

"Oh, we exaggerate," said Edouard briefly. "But our hostess is different."

They all remembered afterwards how they had gathered round the fatal luncheon. Gynt was absent, Edouard lunched, Alberti (not ill then, but majestic, and gay with a fat man's gaiety) was there.

Miranda was there, the cool and shy Miranda, who would still bend her head and speak to the dogs at the threat of any personal conversation.

The young James Goethe was there too, sixteen now and not yet handsome; long-nosed and melancholy and still in love with Lady Maclean. In his room at Eton her photograph was pinned above the mantelpiece. Now he was staying at Pouilly again and this time without the duchess to prod him back into the blushes of his early youth. He thought Miranda tiresome, with her silence and her occasional snubs. And he annoyed her with his eyes fixed like a baby calf upon her mother.

The hostess's own blue eyes considered the guest from Paris with that unintended insolence which was always her first expression, and sprang from an effort to focus.

Tuxie's physique was tremendous. Narrow-hipped, dark, immensely strong, well-dressed in his only country suit, master of himself, he sat still with bright dark eyes that watched. He took in everything. Above all he took in the atmosphere of the house, the ease, intimacy, sense of friendship, subtlety of talk, the direct effect on each guest of the hostess. These were civilised people who did not bore; this, he thought, was a house, a way of life, that he liked above all things. This was an exclusive corner that could not be bought or besieged. It was again his acute "ear" that made him know it.

After lunch, encouraged by Edouard, they urged him to sing, mimic, play. His mimicries were not set pieces, but a delicate ability to place upon his own features for a fleeting second the peculiar expression of a mutual friend, a flicker of the personal attitude towards life. It was quick, just, irrecoverable, controlled by timing and humour. Watching him Lady Maclean forgave him the faults that showed through like faint bruises as time wore on in his company. She was fogged by him. He was indeed fogging. He stayed for tea. So he burst into her circle, an alien creature from a nether world. Somebody said they had known his father: but in that gathering they did not ask credentials when the goods were delivered.

Suddenly, after tea, Miranda was at his side, speaking to him.

"I am going up to Paris," she said. "Can I drive you in my car?"

She had lately had a small Citröen for her birthday, and was going to a late party, but, as her mother had thought, after dinner. Tuxie, from the piano, showed no surprise. But he had taken in her freshness, the fine eyes and dark eyebrows, and orderly hair twisted tight to her head.

Nobody knew how the drive went off. If Tuxie took her out to dine in Paris before her party it must have been that he thought the little money he had left did after all need investing. He was very quick. He probably understood at once that under her calm air Miranda knew nothing of men. He came down to Pouilly twice after that day, when Miranda was absent. Twice again when she was there. Then the blow fell. Miranda said she was engaged.

In the staggered silence between Miranda and her parents Gynt was the first to speak.

"He's a cad, Miranda, and a cruel type. For God's sake . . . Miranda . . ."

"I love him."

"Your mother only had him here to amuse . . . to amuse . . . as one hires someone . . .

"Don't say it, Father. Don't! When we're married you'll be sorry."

"You're going to marry him?"

"Yes. I love him."

"Do you think I know anything about men?"

"I suppose you do. But I must judge for myself."

"Judge! Judge! You're in no condition to judge! You're hypnotised."

An obstinacy came then into Miranda's face that looked like strength. Neither Gynt nor Miranda knew the extent of the other's determination. Sometimes, with only children, this is never put to the proof. Gynt had no real power. The young creature had all the power. Gynt could shut his purse, but he knew his wife would not back him up in threatening to starve out Miranda and Tuxie. Who (he wondered) had done the encouraging? Was it the enigmatic Miranda? Or was it Tuxie, on the make? Tuxie had an interview with Ruby.

"Do you understand her, Tuxie?"

"I can't say I really do."

"But you love her? You do love her?"

"Yes. Yes indeed." It had an unsatisfactory note.

"But . . . You haven't a career?"

"I had one. I did ten years' coffee-planting. I went out when I was twenty-one. The trouble I had in my ear gave me blood poisoning and I was sent home. Since then . . ."

"Since then?"

He looked at her with his handsome, experienced face. "It's been difficult to get another job at thirty-three. I've done various things." (God knew, she thought, he looked as though he had.) "My mother died last year," he said, truthfully. "She left me three thousand pounds."

Ruby sensed at once that there was not much left of that. She felt Miranda was his life-buoy; but how convince Miranda?

In distress they found there was nothing to be done but gulp down the engagement, and, pretty soon, to arrange for the wedding. Some rumours that had come by letter about the manager of the estate in Jamaica were seized on by Miranda.

"That's what Tuxie knows how to do," she said. "And I should like it. I should love it. Start out there; perhaps come home later. I've always wanted to see where you lived when you were a child. We needn't stay for ever."

It was almost as though she wanted to hide her own feminine incompetence as far away from her mother as possible. Tuxie had no grounds for refusing the suggestion. He had no job and very little ready money. He thought he could work it that it was half a pleasure trip. Back on that unmade bed near Notre Dame he thought it over.

"But isn't it a mug's game going out to Jamaica when I've been all the rage in Paris?"

He might put it to himself like that, but he had been "all the rage" only as a breeze brushes over corn and dies again.

Tuxie really knew something about coffee and something about command, and even a little something about accounts. He had been sent abroad originally for that reason—trouble over his knowing about accounts. He was a dishonest man, not, as Gynt thought, seriously unkind. He simply did not wish to know right from wrong, and if Miranda could have joined him in this happy condition he could have been fond of her, and they could have got along. He could be very amusing too, but he had never, until after his marriage, noticed that Miranda had no sense of humour.

If she could have accepted his vulgarity she might have kept her feeling for him; but he had been a shock to her so soon after the marriage, dissolving as he did even on the voyage out, showing greyer as the gilt peeled off the statue. She remembered then her father's black look and oath of surprise, his silence, his lips pressed, the swallow in his thin throat; how he had looked at her mother, as though her mother could deal with it, and then after all spoken to her himself. For Ruby, watching the girl's stern young air, had been silenced with a caution that was rare to her. "Does she then know better?" she asked herself. "Do I suffer already from the vacillations, the hesitations of being older?" Miranda, who watched the world and said nothing, perhaps she knew better? For a moment the more complicated mind bowed before the inscrutable, firm girl. But the firmness was obstinacy, the inscrutability was self-defence, the bias to refuse help was the bias of a donkey at the cross roads.

Worsted by Miranda's obstinacy, baffled, Sir Gynt Maclean had stood in the church by her side wearing the dress of his clan, his heart black with anger and set within him like a jaw. As he stepped a pace back from the bridegroom, having given him his daughter, he was not able to stop thinking how he would have liked to have strangled the slippery thief. Pride choked him. He came of a race that would in its day have murdered the bridegroom and locked up the bride, and there had been a moment, he thought, when, if his wife had backed him up, he could have put a stop to it. But she had felt too strongly that it was Miranda's life and choice. He, Gynt, saw Tuxie clearly as a trickster on his beam-ends, but he had to go through with it, and with icy imprecations that never came up to his lips he put on his kilt and his medals and swished up the aisle with his flat, Scots step, and stood silent at the side of his stolen girl.

Then when it was over and the guests were gone that night he went out into the woods and spent the moonlit hours, as was often now his custom, on the track of some small night-bird. He had always had sporadic waves of emotion, difficult to control and very deep. On one of them he had married, and passionately loved his wife. He did not go into that: he loved her as ever, but he was not thinking about her. Walking down over his own land to the stream that flowed out of the ornamental water at the brink of the forest he stood watching the water under the moon as it mumbled and sucked at the bank. He was angry as he had never been angry in all his life.

The only thing that he and Ruby had bred was now wasted. A grandson by that bastard would not interest him. His family was stagnant. It had in it nothing that grew. His deep stiff pride ached in him and he thought, not of his wife, but of himself. He was fifty-six. His life was three parts over. Odd and haphazard things make people aware of age. The sponge-fringes in the belly of the stream wrinkled and breathed at the edge of his thought and he saw the shadow of a carp move like a question mark through moon-light into rock shade. There was only one thing now in front of him that he cared to make as perfect as possible—the ponderous un-wieldy chain of notes that stretched behind him, his half-finished book on night-birds, begun even in the sprawling hand of boyhood, his secret passion, one of those unassuming works to which men of leisure and means sometimes put a whole quiet life. He would redouble his energy now and make the labour answer for the rest of his existence. He would furnish the Mill Cottage in the forest and work there, secluded from the perpetual life that filled his home. He went on deep into the woods.

On the voyage, directly they were married, and Miranda alone with Tuxie in their cabin, he could not keep off the subject of her mother. "Is it she who really has the money? Or your father? Doesn't she enjoy her life . . . my word! If half the things they say about her are true . . . I suppose she has men friends? Well, obviously she has." He was determined to be cosy, to be at his ease, to be in his shirt sleeves with his wife.

"My word, you're a winner! If you hadn't been firm we'd never have pulled it off. Here we are, married. You've got a mind of your own!"

Miranda was startled to hear that it had all been due to her. She was listening to the real Tuxie for the first time.

"We ought to be fairly flush, you know, out there. What do you think? It's not an expensive island? We ought to be able to razzle a bit, if there's anywhere to razzle."

He looked fine, quiet and handsome as he spoke. For reassurance she looked again at his face. Then she hung another dress in the tiny cupboard.

"The old man," he said, "pushed it up. Did you know?"

"What did you say?"

"Given us a thousand. The last manager got eight hundred. I was surprised. Your father—if you don't mind my saying so—looked as though he could bite me when he increased the salary. A merry murderous look."

Miranda laughed. She had often seen him look like that at people.

"Your mother's a friend of that duke chap, Alberti, isn't she?" (Tuxie had felt cosier after Miranda had laughed.)

"Yes indeed," said Miranda warmly, "they're fond of each other. He's my godfather." Tuxie smiled a charming bony smile.

"I suppose now—your mother and he? Or you wouldn't know?"

"I wouldn't know," said Miranda gravely, a little frightened.

Tuxie reached out an arm and put his bride on his knee. "Don't go on unpacking, love," he said, "you look such a housewife." She kissed the hollow of his cheek.

"You've only to grow up like your mother! I could almost make love to her myself!"

Miranda, puzzled, smiling awkwardly, thought herself stupid. She could not understand, she well knew, a joke. And with the old bad habit of turning away from what alarmed her, from what was personal, she said inconsequentially:

"It was so sad, wasn't it, to leave the dogs . . ."

It was Tuxie's turn to stare.

"What have they got to do with it!" he said. "That was one thing I couldn't understand about Ruby" (Miranda's eyes grew wide)—"the way she messed about with them. Keep a dog—good heavens—I'd as soon keep a snake as a dog! I'll tell you what—" (he went on with the plans in his mind) "when we get out there we'll save like anything, be fearfully economical. So we can blow it when we come back next summer."

"Come back next summer?"

"Don't you want to?"

"I thought we were to stay for a year and then they'd come out and stay with us."

He gave a loud laugh, patted her on the knee, and lit another cigarette. Really it was better not to argue. She was a heavy little thing, quite presentable in her way, and he was prepared to be fond of her. For the moment he was magnanimous with success. That salary pushed up to a thousand, and then he'd two fifty and a little over left of his own money. He'd laid most of that aside for bets on the ship's run and had already stood a round of whiskies. Ahead of him was the old family house, stocked with silver and linen, and Victoria, Rosalba's niece, had been written to and asked to act as maid. It was all on a scale he had never thought he could wrench from life, and God Almighty, all done in six weeks! A little dizzy he returned to the same theme.

"Tell me some more about your mother, sweet. Has she always been such a gay bird? Or perhaps gayer?"

"Yes, I think always. Just the same."

"But one rather expects women to grow old."

"Perhaps she has a bit, only I haven't noticed."

"What are you going to wear tonight? It's the dance."

"I've got my . . . my Lanvin."

He was delighted that his wife had a Lanvin. He had not known it. They danced together that night, up the port side of the deck, under a tarpaulin festooned with coloured lights. Miranda looked very well. Dancing was one of Tuxie's top games. He looked a husband any woman would envy. People said, "They're just married. It's Lady Maclean's daughter."

Slowly, through pain and shock, through distaste and loneliness, Miranda grew up. She had never in her life had communion with a mind such as Tuxie's.

"Can we touch your father? Can you pull the wool over your mother?"

And his management of the estate she saw soon enough to be the fiddling of the petty thief. She did not know what to do. For pride forbade her to acknowledge her terrible mistake in her letters. The war had caught them, once arrived, and they could not return home. The double mastoid Tuxie had had prevented his being taken for service.

Jamaica was not, as Tuxie had imagined, the Bahamas. It was a poor island, and up near Newcastle, in the mountains, lonely. But he was quite a worker. Miranda was surprised at that. He did not spare himself, rising early, and constantly working with his own hands. His handsome, set face wore a look of purpose (as hers wore a look of withdrawal). But his purpose was the piling up of the nest egg he wished to hatch for himself.

He did, at the end of a year, a curious thing—making a will, leaving the monies he was already steadily placing in a private account back to his mother-in-law. When he signed the will in the lawyer's office in Kingston the lawyer reminded him uncomfortably that he had not mentioned his wife.

"Ah," said Tuxie very gently across the table, and considered the lawyer. After a pause he added, reasonably, that it was a family arrangement and that his wife was provided for. He had insisted that the will be simple, almost childish. "I leave all I possess to Lady Ruby Maclean, the wife of Sir Gynt Maclean . . ." without specifying. He could not specify as he had not yet amassed all that he intended to amass. Now that his mother, the only creature he had loved, was dead he had no one to whom he could leave his stolen monies, and he wanted to make sure that Miranda fully understood by this his disgust and displeasure at his bargain.

When the childish letters began at long intervals to come to
Pouilly from Miranda (letters containing brief descriptions and
briefer facts), Gynt wouldn't read them. Having read the first that
Ruby had given him he said, "Don't show me any more. She's
smashed herself. I wasn't allowed to stop it. Why should I be tortured if I can't help?"

"But we're alive, her father and mother. We're responsible."

"No, my responsibility has ended. There's no one coming after us.
I must look after myself now. I must see how I stand."


## CHAPTER FOUR

And now eight years had gone by and while the Duca di Roccafergolo was seventy, Lady Maclean had become in her turn fifty-
three, and the little Miranda had been eight years married to her
fortune-hunter.

Tuxie (whom Rose had gone too far in calling a gigolo) came to
know when it was done that he had married Miranda because of
her mother. That brilliant person had made her daughter seem to
shine and Tuxie had been confused. And indeed he had naturally
thought that, as a son-in-law, he would have basked in the amber
light, would have landed (after his terrible swimming) on a safe
and gay shore. That he had not done so, that by some deluded,
complaisant stupidity of his own (who was never stupid) he should
have become exiled to Jamaica, made him savage whenever he
thought of it. And just now, in that far island, three weeks before
the Holbein first night in Paris, he was thinking of it. He was down
in the banana grove before late tea below the coffee barbecues,
swinging his straight-bladed machete so that it raced through the
juicy stems of the bananas. His thoughts for the moment rose in
him so bright with indignation that he put down the heavy blade
and stood still in the shadow of the barbecue wall.

The sun was shifting away behind him and the cobalt shadow
ran down the hill like water. He looked across the coffee ravine to

the next hillside, the first of those hillsides that folded one behind the other as far as one could ride on a horse in a day. A shiny, monotonous, damn dull place with only the blacks and Miranda sitting in the house as plainly dressed as a school-teacher, and always reading, and the poorest company in the world. It would be tea-time in five minutes.

He got up and went towards the house, resolved to finish the bananas after tea. Each grove was cut down once in seven years. Their fibrous stems, half dry, half juicy, sliced easily under the swing of the big knife. He enjoyed cutting them. As they fell they crashed with a green-lettuce freshness. He had cut fifty. He had twenty-seven more to do.

Miranda sat in the old-fashioned drawing-room that Lady Maclean's father and mother had furnished fifty years before. The silver tray, fluted sugar bowl, and squat teapot with leaves around its base had come out of the safe—where they had been placed, wrapped up in green baize fitted covers, by Miranda's grandmother when she had sailed with her daughter in the fruit liner for England after the grandfather's death.

Miranda wore a neat white dress, rather surgical, and her skin too was white, for she seldom went out. She was dressed without adornment, neither was her hair allowed to help her face. She had thick, level black eyebrows over dark blue eyes. She looked up as Tuxie came in and had ready a remark.

"Would you ring the bell? Victoria will bring the scones."

One of her difficulties was to find things to say that would disguise their silence when they met. She had first thought of saying she had had a letter from her mother, but mention of her mother was sure to be amiss. Tuxie rang the bell, sat down on a chair, and looked at one of his boots stretched out in front of him. He seemed sullen and Miranda tightened up, ready for anything that might come. She was not afraid of him.

"If we're not careful," he said to his boot, "we'll be out here for ever. Do you realise that? I've written down to Kingston for dates."

Miranda too had written to the shipping office in Kingston, and had enclosed a plain stamped envelope. She had come to the end of their marriage long ago, but first the war, and then her pride and obstinacy, had delayed her.

"Yes," said she, for want of anything better to say.

"Yes what?" said Tuxie sharply. They looked at each other, and he saw a separate, secret steadiness in her face. They each drank from their cups of tea. It was hard to get through any meal.

Eight years ago Miranda too had realised that Tuxie had not got what he wanted when he married her. She did not know at first whose fault it was. Tuxie seemed to think it was her mother's, for when her mother's name came up he grew malevolent. Once, after a day of silence and depression, he sat down with her at table, conducting, without provocation, a terrible monologue.

"She palmed me off with you!" he ended by saying, driven beyond decency by Miranda's level brows and blue stare.

"What did you expect then—other than me?"

"Some sort of life that a man can live! How could I tell she'd turn her only daughter's husband into a remittance man!"

"A . . . ?"

"All right. Let's try to stop talking."

Miranda went on eating.

"How was I to tell," he began restlessly again, "that we'd be caught out here?"

And as she did not answer he said:

"Caught out here, I say! How was I to tell?"

"No one could tell. It was the war."

"The war! I bet Ruby's had fun—through the war!"

Miranda could let this pass—that he should always call her mother, whom he knew so little, by her first name. He had said worse things of her because he hung all his frustration upon her, and when Miranda had once broken out in indignation he had said:

"Much you know about life! You take it from me!"

At the end of that evening he held out his hand with a charming smile on his hard face.

"It's the gin. It does something to my temper. I don't mean it."
But she wouldn't take his hand.

On this day, after his tea (which he had swallowed in haste, refusing a scone from the dish), he got up and went out and nothing else passed between them—now, or ever, for, as it turned out, she never saw him again alive.

But he was thinking as he left her how extraordinary it was that such a mother should have such a child. Then it struck him, with pleasure, that now the mother must be getting on, losing those looks that were such an asset, getting stout perhaps. They'd soon see! He'd nearly got enough off the estate's monies tucked across into his own side of the account. His father-in-law must be now over sixty, beginning to lose that stuck-up look of his, and more ready for compromise. He'd be wanting to leave everything to Miranda one of these days. Better show up back home. They'd be glad enough to see Miranda on their doorstep. For his father-in-law he had a sort of sympathy. They had never been on terms and had hardly achieved speaking to each other. They had had some stammered conversation about Miranda. Gynt had said:

"Of course she can do as she likes."

Tuxie had said: "Well, then?"

Gynt had said: "No need to be rude."

Which had surprised Tuxie. In the days before the engagement when Tuxie had been a guest he had never heard his future father-in-law open his mouth. Usually he passed through rooms looking with his queer cross-eyes to see if people were in them, and passing on if they were. At the very end, after the wedding, when Tuxie and Miranda got into the car which was to take them to Marseilles, Gynt had thrust his dark face forwards like a man who is going to knock one down and had said: "You take care of her, by God." It was so like the threat of a punch in the face that Tuxie had stepped a pace backwards, and when he looked there was Gynt walking away. Though this conversation wasn't friendly, Tuxie was prepared to like Gynt better than he liked his mother-in-law, who, he felt, had swindled him. Just in what way she had swindled him he didn't analyse. Except that she had the freedom of the kind of life he had wanted to live, that she dispensed like a queen its pleasure and temperature, its pace, fever, and glamour, and had at the same time contrived to strike it all away from him, although he had married her daughter. Possibly he had taken it for granted that Sir Gynt and Lady Maclean would support him, living at their pitch. He had never quite acknowledged that to himself. But when —to give a son-in-law a job, since the man had nothing—Lady Maclean had suggested (and Miranda had eagerly backed her) that Tuxie and Miranda should go out and see into the trouble with the estate in Jamaica, it had seemed so pleasant and so temporary. A voyage, in fact. A month or two. The war had caught them and turned a temporary situation into a permanent one, and Tuxie had no one to blame; but he blamed. He blamed a woman who had brought up a daughter so unlike her, a daughter who didn't care for pleasure.

Thinking, thinking hard, he reached the banana grove. It was the time of day when men stopped work and drank. In the camp there was singing behind the shine of the coffee bushes. He picked up the machete where he had laid it down. Suddenly the figure he hadn't after all cut in the world maddened him. He was in full rage—which happened to him from time to time. He lifted the machete and struck out into a banana stem as though it were the Maclean family pushing him out of paradise, and the point of the blade, in passing, slipped between his legs and caught the back of his bent knee.

It was a terrible cut. The stem had been black-rotten on the further side: he had struck it with passion and it had offered no resistance. The artery that lay hidden behind his knee was severed and spouted. He needed immediate help. He shouted. But the voices sang on, blast and damn them, sang on, sang on, rising and falling. The house was too far away; Miranda could not hear him. He bent his leg over a branch, trying to improvise a tourniquet. The blood wouldn't stop and he fought against the dream that was coming on him; yet soon it didn't seem worth while trying. The loss of blood cut his will. It never occurred to him he was dying. He thought he was fainting. He died at the end of eight or ten long minutes, like a calf dies when the cord is badly severed. His pints gave out. There were only seven, and they ran away down the moss under the bananas.

Miranda was filling in her time between tea and dinner. She was somewhat of an organiser in small ways, and though she had nothing much to organise, the hours between meal-time and meal-time presented no great difficulty to her. For the first time in her life she read a great deal, conducting a postal traffic with the Kingston public library and taking the advice of the librarian. She mended her grandmother's fine fringed napkins, put buttons on the pillow-cases, feeling it to be a caretaker's job rather than wifely. She had taught herself to typewrite, and her writing desk was well arranged, neatly stacked with fresh envelopes of all sizes, sealing wax and stamps. But she wrote few letters. Now in the afternoons she was making a survey of the lumber room, typing an inventory of its contents, with carbon copies: but from time to time some object in the room arrested her attention and she lingered, vaguely aware of the house's past, regretful that nothing could be explained to her. Before tea she had carried into the drawing room an old box stereoscope, and a spidery hatbox containing cardboard slides with twin glazed photographs stuck upon them. She was pleased to have found this, for there had always been a stereoscope stand in the nursery at home and Gynt used to show her snowstorms, crystals, and rock and fish life under the sea. What she had found now would occupy her till dinner-time. Settling near her writing table she stared into the lacquered eyeholes and turned the wooden wheel. In deep focus Queen Victoria's white horses drew a splendid coach, cabs moved down Piccadilly, and, in a photographer's glade, a boy in a white sailor suit stood with his arm over a rock, his foot beside a cactus, wearing black kid gloves. A whole period that she had never known offered itself. There were twenty-four slides and she looked at them for a long time, soothed by a vanished life that could not hurt her. Then, putting them back in the hatbox, she saw that at the bottom there were more slides wrapped in a piece of black moiré silk. These were on thinner boards, and more amateur, taken no doubt by her grandfather. In the lumber room were his trays and jars, green paper hoods, velvet squares, his camera, his tripod, all packed in a tin uniform case marbled in red and black, with his name in gold letters.

Putting in the first slide she looked straight into the room in which she now sat. Standing by the window, holding the very curtain which still hung there, was a tall young officer, smiling a little, most gaily dressed in red, gold, and dark blue. She was, however, more interested in the furniture and how it was arranged. The cottage piano was covered as now in its spangled drapery with peacock's eyes of looking glass, the bird's heads sewn round in gold thread. It seemed, by the slant of the light and the sun, that the photograph was taken at this same hour, after tea.

She turned the wheel and the next picture also was taken in the same room; but on the sofa sat the child, her mother. The face was oval and looked back at her. She knew it was her mother because of the large blue eyes, full of light, with the small fold at each outer corner. It was her mother certainly: but the face plumper, and with the large eyes it was rather doll-like. She was about ten, dressed in *broderie anglaise,* a stiff, home-made dress, with a stand-up collar. Miranda did not recognise the beauty in the child's face; she thought it old-fashioned.

There were three photographs. The last one was of her grandmother, standing, with a spaniel at her feet. At this moment Miranda was widowed—unknown to Tuxie or to her. She looked at the photograph, and the dog's eyes perplexed her. She was not given to fancy, but the dog's eyes were alive, though the dog was so long dead. Poor Miranda could put nothing into words, but she had distinctly a sense of not understanding life. She withdrew her face from the eyeholes, and taking the three home-made slides in her hand, and reaching to her writing table, slipped them into a large envelope, sealed it, stamped it, addressed it to her mother, and then, thinking she might have put in a word, wrote small on the flap, "Writing later." At that moment a Negro boy ran shouting in at the doorway from the sun outside: "Massa bleed. Missee, come, come, he bleed." He beckoned. She ran unsteadily out after the boy. Directly she was gone, Victoria, coming in to fetch the letters for the horse-mail that was going down to Kingston, saw the stamped envelope, removed it, and it travelled home by sea.

Miranda sat down that night to write to her mother. "Tuxie is dead. It's been an accident. He cut his leg with a machete—that is a straight, heavy knife as sharp as an axe. He's lying in the house now. He bled to death. Dr. Nicholson came down from Newcastle and he said he probably fainted and knew nothing. I am coming home, of course. As soon as I can." But this letter was never posted, for Miranda packed it by mistake with the papers she took with her to England.

She had meant, when she sat down to write, to speak of the surprise and horror and pity. Suddenly she had been sorrier for Tuxie than she could express, but to her mother she could not write the words. As she lay face down on her bed she kept seeing the dog, whose eyes were alive though the dog was dead. She could make nothing of death, but in that she wasn't extraordinary.

Victoria came to her and said: "Someone must sit with Master."

"Oh . . ." Miranda sat up. "I can't, then! I CAN'T."

"We all frightened," said Victoria, pursily. "I—when my mother died. You must not leave him alone."

Miranda went obediently into Tuxie's room. If Victoria thought she could do any good to Tuxie, sitting, afraid, by his chalky corpse, she would do it. She saw his nose stuck up into the sheet.

"Stay with me, Victoria," she said.

"If a black woman stay," said Victoria, always complacently, "Master will be shy." She drifted out and shut the door.

"Mother . . ." whispered Miranda, "I'm such a fool. Must this be done? I don't know anything."

She went to the door and opened it.

"Victoria!" she called. (Victoria answered from the end of the corridor, where she was squatting whispering to the other house-servants.) "Get me Dr. Nicholson on the telephone."

When, in answer to her appeal, the old man came down from Newcastle in his car (where fifty years ago he had taken so much longer to come to Miranda's grandmother on a horse) and the cold, stand-offish young Mrs. Tuxie pulled him in at the door, her hand clutching his arm, her frightened eyes on his face, he realised he had a poor schoolgirl to comfort. He told her to leave Tuxie with his God and to come up home to his wife.

## CHAPTER FIVE

The doctor's old wife was crippled with arthritis and could never lie down. Nothing she liked better than to talk all night as she sat in her padded tip-chair, and put off as long as she could the little pill for the pain. The old man himself brought her tea if he had a night call; and tonight he showed Miranda the electric kettle and the canister in the cupboard.

"I could give you something to make you sleep," he said, "but you'll only wake up feeling as though you'd mislaid your grief. If you sit up and chat with my wife she'll tell you all about your grandmother and your grandfather. They had troubles too. It'll do you more good to hear about them. My wife's a little hazy nowadays on the present, but she's sharp enough on the past."

Mrs. Nicholson took very little account of Miranda's bereavement. "Married, were you?" she said when they were left alone. "And he's dead?" And without waiting for a reply she went on: "I always forget your name!"

"Miranda."

"It wasn't Miranda! It was the little girl who grew up and married the titled man. Your mother took her back to Europe."

"Ruby was her name," said Miranda, who had followed Mrs. Nicholson's mistakes.

"Didn't she go on the stage? Your grandfather wouldn't have

liked that! He used to get anxious about her. A wild, noisy girl—like a boy."

"My *mother!*" said Miranda incredulously.

"I remember the troopers when they came up the road. They'd just built the road. Before that it was a mule-path. She spat the rind of an orange she was eating down on to the sergeant-major's hat as he rode under the wall."

"My mother?" murmured Miranda again.

"Your grandfather beat her when the sergeant-major had ridden in at the gate and complained. Your grandmother cried. How did she turn out?"

Miranda had no words for how she had turned out. Could she say that she was beautiful, abrupt, famous, alarming, indescribable, not to everyone's taste? ("I'm a widow," thought Miranda. "Now I will go back and get to know her.")

"Was she very pretty?"

"Your dear grandmother?"

"My mother."

"The child? No. And as she was growing up she had a bad skin. Of course she had blue eyes. Your grandmother had such charming looks and golden hair. She was the toast of the camp. We had a white regiment up here then. It was nicer. Your grandmother used to sing at the Saturday evenings. 'Smokings' they called them. And your grandfather had a deep voice; he used to sing too."

"And my mother?"

"Your mother didn't come. She was a child. Your grandmother was a great hand at icing cakes: she used to give little parties down at your house. There was young Lieutenant Ussher. He adored your mother—your grandmother, I mean. He was lovesick. They used to tease him a little, and I did too. I had just married then and I was so glad to be able to say things I couldn't have said as a girl. You should get married, my dear . . ." The old lady dropped her head and slept a little.

"You'll have to go to the funeral!" she said severely, making Miranda jump. "I'll have you up here beforehand if you behave

yourself. Your dear mother won't want you with all there is to do."
Miranda stared at her, fascinated, but the old lady's eyes were fixed
on the opposite wall.

"Poor, poor man," said the old lady. "How your dear mother
adored him!"

The eyes travelled down from the wall and reached Miranda's
face. Mrs. Nicholson adjusted herself. "What could I have been
dreaming of! I was thinking it was your father's funeral."

"My grandfather's."

"Yes, of course. He had an immense funeral. All the natives
came from miles. He had done so much for them."

"What did he do?"

"He said he cured them with his medicines. I think he did, too."

"But he was a soldier!"

"Yes. But after he retired he took up medicine. He dabbled in it.
Dr. Nicholson used to laugh at him, but all with a good heart. He
was glad to have help, there was so much to do, and so few hands
to do it. Or legs to travel round."

"Why did my grandfather die?"

"He died of yellow fever. Your grandmother's heart was broken.
Then she took the child to England . . ." Mrs. Nicholson looked
at Miranda with a frown, wondering if she had still got it wrong.
But giving her head a little shake she said: "I was very surprised
she let her go on the stage. And she wasn't a success, was she? I
never heard she was a success."

"I don't *know!*" said Miranda somewhat desperately.

"Don't *know?*"

"Mother doesn't talk about the past . . ."

"Ha!"

". . . because she is so busy in the present, I think. She . . .
she . . . she does such a lot in every day."

"Gay and giddy."

"Gay. But not giddy. No. She used to say sometimes she's a little
melancholy, but I never saw it. People enjoy themselves so much
with her."

"Did you?"

"Yes," said Miranda, speaking up. "I did. But I didn't know I did. I haven't seen her for nearly eight years, but now I shall go back and see her."

"She's got a position, of course," said the old lady. "Money, I daresay. It's a pity your grandmother can't know that. It's a pity we can't pop back into the world to see how things go. But, after all, your grandmother was older than I. She would be over eighty if she were here, and I daresay she mightn't be so interested as one thinks. Come to that . . . your mother must be getting on. Past fifty. Grey-haired."

"No!" said Miranda sharply. The old lady gave her a malevolent look.

"We'll have some tea now," she said. "We're one third way through the night."

When Tuxie had had his funeral and the silver gone back into the green baize covers, and an overseer temporarily engaged by the solicitors, Miranda got her ship, and soon was well out to sea.

"Excuse me . . . I knew your mother!" said a grizzled ship's officer, halting beside her as she watched the return West Indian ship on the sea's horizon. "I think we shall be at Barbados in the morning . . ."

"You knew my mother?"

He was an elderly man with chestnut eyes and curling grey hair. "You're the young lady I took the dresses to, I take it. I'm the third officer."

"But . . . how . . ."

"Your name's on the list. I brought you out a parcel the first year before the war came. I had my own little ship then. I lost her. Banana trade. To Marseilles. Out of a job after that. Now I'm third officer. Your mother came down to Marseilles with that black maid of hers."

"Rosalba!"

"She had me to lunch at her hotel. Very kind of her. A handsome lady."

"It was very kind of you to bring the dresses. Mother wrote, of course, and told me."

"And did you wear them, now?" There was something very penetrating in his chestnut eye as he looked her over. "The idea was, you know, that I was taking them out for my daughter. I haven't got a daughter. They were packed among my kit."

(Now Miranda recognised the smell of tobacco.)

"Never met anyone like your mother," he said. "No, I did not."

"I haven't seen her for eight years," said Miranda. "How long ago did you see her?"

"Well, about that too," he said. "Eight years. Or maybe seven. Great pleasure to have known her. But she won't be much different now. Is she well, by your letters?"

"Oh, I think she's always well. I've never known her ill. How did you meet? How were you able . . . It was so kind of you," she finished lamely.

"Well now, where do you think? You'd never guess. We met in a cemetery. And she was wearing . . . trousers I'd call them. Slacks—don't you say?"

(The mysterious, mysterious life of her mother . . .)

"I was in an English war graves garden, small, set on a slope in a cornfield behind Dieppe. My son's buried there. Up came your mother, up the steepish slope, talking with another lady, and laid her hand on the gate of the garden and walked in. I think she thought I was the guardian. I had on my plain clothes. I'm about that respectable age. She asked me, rather sharply, why they'd put in little yews. She thought it morbid. 'Why have they done it!' she exclaimed. She seemed full of authority. And then she suddenly laughed. 'Perhaps you're not the guardian?' she said. I said, 'No, I'm not. I'm the father of one of these boys.' 'So you're all the more concerned with the garden,' she said, not a bit upset. (You know how people are when you tell them you've had a loss.) 'Those yews will grow and look as black as pitch and starve the ground for other things. Which is your son?' I showed her the cross. 'What age was he?' she asked. Then she saw writing on the cross. She got some big, outlandish-looking spectacles out of her bag and read the cross properly. 'Eighteen,' she said to herself. She made it seem as though she felt that was very young. So I said to her—what I've never said to a soul, for who is there to say it to? 'I used to think it was bad losing him. Now I don't think it so. It's a bitter world.' She looked at me. 'You know better than I,' she said. 'I've never lost a grown son.' She had a jerky way of saying true things. She had sandwiches, and the other lady and she and I sat down and shared them. I remember it so well. She didn't ask me to have food with them. She simply held out the sandwiches while she was talking, open in a paper, and said: 'Let's sit on the bank.'"

"Who was the other lady?"

"'Cora,' she called her. A little stout yellow lady, Japanese-looking. I told your mother I was a sea captain, sailing to Jamaica, and she turned and opened wide her eyes . . ."

"Yes?" said Miranda.

"I was only going to say it's her eyes, if you'll allow me to say so, that make her different-looking from other people. They open so wide you don't seem to get to the end of the colour, do you? It's as though it were that kind of blue right up inside her forehead. She was very excited and she said she had a daughter in Jamaica, a daughter who was fond of clothes. 'She's just married,' she said. 'That's the time you want to look a dazzler!' So we arranged it. She said she'd come down to Marseilles herself if I was to write and tell her when the voyage would be. 'Shall you come, Cora?' she said. But the other lady was looking at the setting sun, and didn't answer. So your mother did come to Marseilles that once, with that black maid of hers."

"She was my nurse."

"So she told me. It was funny to see them together, talking like two sisters, the one so golden, the other like a little black nut with fur on its head."

"When my grandmother had my mother—they lived in Jamaica

—Rosalba was the cook's baby. When I was born Mother sent for Rosalba. She looks like a nut because she's lost her teeth with the English food. So my mother came to Marseilles? Tell me?"

"She was to have come a second time. But when I lost my ship . . . And anyway the war came."

"How did you lose it?"

"The Admiralty said it was my fault. You have to take the rough with the smooth. I've learnt this in life . . . that nothing's ever strictly true."

"So you never heard anything from my mother after she came down to Marseilles?"

"When I lost my ship I wrote and told her. She wrote back and said: 'When next you are in Dieppe tell me and I'll drive down from Paris and we'll have lunch by your son and talk about it.'"

"And did you?"

"No," he said. "She would have come. She'd have done it like a shot. But I felt it was too much to ask. And the war came."

Miranda, as usual, was dumb.

Two passengers standing near them said: "Did you see that whale spout?" But the sea captain said softly: "Your mother was a woman to dream of."

He had been laid low by her mother, Miranda thought, sadly, and again she felt shut out.


## CHAPTER SIX

And eight years earlier, just after Miranda's wedding, when Lady Maclean had climbed to the hot yellow wall of the little cemetery on the hillside she had laid her hand on it and said:

"Let's rest here. I feel old."

"Old!" panted Cora Holbein, picking a thistle-head from her high sandal. "And my extra seven years?"

"Unlike me, you are indestructible," said Lady Maclean, and, looking over the wall, "Why have they planted yews?" she said to

Cora. "The beauty of these grave gardens is that they don't ever plant anything funereal." And seeing the dignified, elderly man standing among the crosses inside, she attacked him then in her bold manner, never shy with total strangers (more shy with friends). The sea captain, looking at her, answered her as he had described to Miranda. A seagoing man of sixty he had never seen such a lady, who spoke him so straight as though she knew him, and looked, so he thought, painted like an actress, and was not young, yet wore trousers as he had seen girls wear on the beaches. Whether she was really painted was something he wondered long afterwards. Her eyes, surely, were her own. He had never heard of an art that turned the colour of eyes. And they were very large, almost blank, not at all like her speech. She turned from the stout little lady (who sat down on the bank) and talked direct to him. He never could remember that the "ugly lady" (that's how he thought of her) did more than look at the points of her shoes, from which rose up plump, but shapely, legs. Finally, inside the cemetery, they all three sat on the inner bank, leaning against the wall. The actress (as he thought her—but later he learned better) sat next to him. They talked about Billy.

"Was he dark, like you? Eyes like you? Eyes, then, like chestnuts." (Only that he knew by instinct she wasn't making up to him, he might have thought this was something of a pass.)

"Billy was just like me." (So he thought: but what he remembered now was only the memory of a memory twenty-one years old.)

"Dying at eighteen," she frowned. "Do you think he had the best bit?"

"It's as you find life," he said. "I might give one answer and you another."

"Well, how have you found it?"

For some extraordinary reason, though he had never said so before, he answered, "I've found it depended for me entirely on women. Now it's all over I can see that. All the ups and downs, the happiness and upsets, they depended on them."

"Well, for me it doesn't now depend on men," she said decidedly.

"Nor for me either," murmured the ugly friend, but ruefully.

"Why do you feel that for you it depends on women?" insisted the actress, returning to what he had said.

"I'm built like it," he said. "So was he. He had that look. But I never knew, of course. That was what I was so sorry for when he died. I thought it hard luck he hadn't known women."

"Perhaps he had?" she asked.

The captain tried in his mind to bring back his son's face. "He was a child," he said. "What a long time ago it is! I'm getting old," he added. "I'm sixty. I don't remember."

"I'm forty-five," said the actress, half to herself, looking across the valley to the heavy ruin of Arques-la-Bataille.

"That's a good age for a man, I used to think," said the captain.

"And for a woman?" She smiled at him, and there was such a friendly intelligence in her smile that he was obliged to say what he thought.

"I should have said it was getting on—for a woman," he answered simply, with grave good manners.

"So it is," she agreed. "So it is. When I got here I was saying I felt old. I did feel it."

"I heard you," he said. "I was thinking, by his grave, I never heard any woman say it before."

"When you come here," she asked, "what is the good of coming? Do you feel it any good?"

"No," he said. "It's no good. I come sometimes when my ship is in here, but it means nothing. Of course I don't grieve any more. I just say 'hello' to him. But even for that it's more for a walk."

"We must be going," she said without getting up. "We've got to drive back to Paris, and then change our clothes, and dine out."

"Tonight? Dine out with your friends?"

"Yes."

"You'll be tired."

"No, I'm never tired. Sometimes, as you heard me say, I feel old. But that's another thing. The thing to do in life is to keep going."

"No, it isn't."

"It isn't?"

"You should come in ships."

"Alas, I should be bored. Alas, alas, I've wasted the possibilities of contemplation! And where do you sail next?" she asked.

As they then all three stood up he told her that he was going round to Marseilles, and then on to Jamaica, in three weeks.

"To Jamaica!" she cried. "My daughter's just on her way there now! Suppose, next spring, among the bananas . . . Could you not slip in a dress to take to her from me?"

"I take the bananas the other way," he smiled. Standing there in the afternoon sunshine at the top of the cornfield, on the deck, as it were, of the little cemetery, he had a giddy surge of worship— like a young man. Besides being beautiful she looked so much a woman, so confidently gay, as though she understood and could make plain the muddle of life.

"I'll take it," he said. "You give me your address and I'll take it. We're not supposed to, but what's the good of being king in your own ship if you daren't slip a law for a lady! It'll be my third voyage from now. Give me your address and I'll let you know the date to send it."

And when he saw written down that she was a ladyship he thought then that of course she couldn't be an actress.

Going about the world as he had done, and ready sometimes, when the mood took him, to talk, he had met people (very rarely) who were "different," who were, as he said to himself, "superior." He had this word from out of his youth, from his father, who once said to him (his father—a starving Welsh teacher, a burning classical scholar, a man full of learning)—"There are superior souls, Jim." It was on an evening, and he had looked up from his books, which lay under the lamp on the table. "They're about in the world. People better than we are. Keep a look-out for them. Living here like I do I've only met the one."

"Who was he then?" Jim had asked.

"He was a brewer," answered his father, glaring at him with his hollow-seated eyes, and Jim hadn't dared ask further.

The captain knew (as though his father had been at his elbow to nudge him) that this woman in her trousers and her paint was one of them.

They went down the cornfield and the man stared after them and remained in the cemetery. He saw the beautiful one hesitate at the top of the bank that sank into the road, and the ugly one, who being so short was nimble, hold out her hand from below to steady her. Now on the other side of the road he saw the open car. The beautiful one took the wheel. They disappeared.

He stood thinking. "I wonder if you did have a woman, Billy?" he casually asked the cross that was his. And such a question tinkled like a joke in eternity. Though he had said that Billy's eyes were like his own, and he remembered that in fact they were, he could not bring his son's expression before him; Billy was too long dead. And looking down at the cross before his walk back into Dieppe his father's haggard face was more real to him than his son's. It had bitten into him younger, when he was more soft.

"How I've chucked away," he thought—and he could still just see the car's dust—"the knowing of the nature of women! Raging so after them. It's only now that I'm quieter I'm getting a look at life." His eyes followed the now-empty, dun-coloured road running away to Paris from Dieppe, between the low hills, on which the two women had gone to join the life they led in towns, "supping and dining." "A woman of that age in my family," he thought, "would have looked put by, put away—not worth a glance. One would have thought that, with those looks, and that class, I'd have read of her in the papers. Missed it perhaps."

He always bought illustrated papers and read them on his voyages. He bought old numbers of the *Tatler,* and French and Spanish illustrated papers, tennis numbers, Christmas numbers, fashion numbers. He liked to read of a world in which he had no part. His cabin was piled with such things. "Lady Maclean," he read, looking at the used envelope she had given him. "Scotch, I suppose. What did she mean about—'for me it doesn't depend on men'? I should have thought it did."

And Cora, as they drove, asked the same thing.

"The last thing I'd expected you to say! Don't you feel what people feel for you? Are your conquests really unobserved? Is it a coquetry? Don't you feel these things?"

Lady Maclean seemed about to answer, but she looked so long into the distance as she drove that Cora went on impatiently.

"Oughtn't you to have some idea of your luck? It puts me in a rage to think you aren't grateful to God! If I could have one day of beauty, if the dear God in His kindness would let me change for one long day the impedimenta I've had to put up with for fifty conscious years! Can you faintly imagine what it is not to be well served by one's appearance, to have, at each new relationship, at each new meeting, to live it down? How struck I was at your effect on that man! You cut through him like a knife through cheese. Through butter. Without trying, without stretching out a hand. Not even, it seemed to me, troubling to exercise your charm as a woman. When you talk it's with the intimacy of a labourer in a bar. Or aren't they intimate? Like a man, then, who has known another man at school. Your conversation is quite unsexed. But down they go! Go down like . . . homosexuals!"

Lady Maclean laughed.

"Tell me," said Cora, who having been silent so long now couldn't stop talking, "what's the sensation, so peculiar, that I can never have, of melting a man, of seeing in a stranger's eyes such sudden subjugation?"

"You've been married, Cora."

"No, that was very different. And under special circumstances. Some day I may tell you, but dear me, we were then so obscure. And since I left him—so many years, another lifetime! And all this time the burden of this face of mine, this damned appearance . . . To be as plain as I am is to start life a cripple! When I look in the glass and see—when all's said and done—what I see, then I'm indignant. I have to accept my sallow skin, my horse's tail of black hair every morning that I live. I have to subdue them till they take a presentable, a palatable shape not once a day but before every meal, every encounter, to put up with my haphazard appearance throughout the only life I've been given! So it's not strange I'm burning with interest at a more triumphant passage—of a woman at whose mere sight men seem to grow kinder. Don't you feel it, savour it?" She pressed, with her aggressive intimacy, "Don't you take pleasure in these quick admirations that break out like bush fires in your path? Don't you? Do answer me."

"You know," said Lady Maclean at length, in her elliptical, embarrassed manner, "I'm not much—with life's experiences—for repetition."

"Pough!" said Cora disgustedly. "I feel like the poor man who hears the rich man say he's tired of being rich!"

"Why did you leave Rudi?"

"As a plant grows. Quite naturally. It's not even interesting."

"And the baby? I know there was once a baby."

"He's married, I hear. Comic, isn't it, to have been hostess, in that very intimate way, to a young Jew now married in New York!"

The car swept along (and at this remark even a little faster, as though the driver's foot betrayed an irritation) and the sun sank on their right hand, in the west. The spaces and fields of Normandy lay in squares and cubes, olive and dun, and the bland spears of the tree-shades made the road flash.

"When will you come down and see Gynt about the drawings?"

Part of the purpose of the visit to Dieppe had been to collect a number of drawings of birds which Gynt had thought he might persuade Cora to sell him for his book, and which she had left in a studio she had taken the previous summer. She was a woman for whom things were done and expeditions undertaken because she asked for what she wanted. Each morning as she woke and before she got to her painting she arranged on her bedside telephone that other people, as far as possible, should have all the bother. It was understood in her circle that Cora never rang up with any good news except for herself. Now that the day was over Ruby Maclean was only anxious to get it done with, and the car rushed towards Paris as the summer evening faded.

"Soon," answered Cora to the question about the drawings, "soon. How's Gynt taken the wedding?"

"Badly," said her companion. "He's been upset by it and the house seems empty."

"Your house is never empty. I know no one who has so many friends. How I remember you long ago when I first saw you! You were already then the loved and envied. Oh, you were out of my sphere! Rudi and I hadn't climbed into the precious stronghold (though he was already famous). We were in our way greatly in demand but not always asked quite where he wanted to be. Yes, even in those days when you arrived anywhere a certain pitch was immediately attained for the party. You were a magnet and an irritation—according to the freedom of admission to your circle! You brought your face to the gathering like a Louvre picture, with its expected, its assessed value . . ."

But Lady Maclean, who could be bold, could also be offended, and she broke in coldly—"But you were saying of Gynt?"

"No. Was I? How you change the conversation. One sees so little of him now. He was such a gay man. I hear he prowls like a cat in your local forest. Does it worry you that he's given up the world?"

"Not if it makes him happy."

"Ah—if it makes him happy. He used to have a look of pride and impatience, as though he expected a great deal. He was extremely male. I think the male confuses women. But they adored him: he was very much courted. And so quickly bored. That odd and barely imperceptible cast in his eye which gave the impression of inattention! Well, how we all change! Thank God, for I've grown out of Rudi's little housekeeper into a selfish and successful woman. It's you who've not changed. 'You have had'—I quote, it's not mine—'the advantage of beauty. For which Madame de Staël would have sacrificed everything.'"

But Lady Maclean's peculiar humility (as though her assets had been precariously lent to her) led her to exclaim—"Come, Cora! That's enough about the face. It's not lucky."

## CHAPTER SEVEN

Cora, who was dining late, went first on reaching Paris to a Russian dressmaker who would consent to see her after her salon was closed to the outer world. Here, between them, they invented the appearance that Cora presented, and wrangled like a pair of Arabs over the price. Cora, who was rich, hated paying. The Russian, also rich, naturally hated receiving less than her due. But they knew each other, and for fifteen years now Cora arrived regularly at seven o'clock in the evening once or twice a month, the tray of drinks was brought out of a cupboard, and Cora, standing in the centre of a mirrored room, would gaze upon the figure she made. Above her elegant dagger-legs a ninon garment—a butterfly's wing on granite—covered the mighty grasp of a corset that ground her body's features into a drum.

"We've never tried white," observed the dressmaker.

"With my skin?"

"But you had a brave theory, dear, that one didn't compromise."

Cora was silent a moment. "Dress me as you would an idol," she said. "If you think white looks fine on yellow clay send for it, for God's sake. Dress me like an outrage. I must be striking."

"I met a woman," said the dressmaker, pinning, pinning (when the workrooms were closed she loved to be her own fitter), "who knew you when you were first married."

"Who was that—mercy!"

"I forget her name. An American. But could it have been you she spoke of? Thin as a straw?"

"Thin as a straw. And as yellow. If I had understood clothes in those days life wouldn't have been the same."

"Life's not been bad for you."

"Splendid," said Cora reflectively, staring, straight at the dwarf in the looking glass. "Can you imagine how much it's broad-ened since I was a wife as good as gold, as loving as a dog? Things have bettered."

"If you'd had a child you might have been held back."

"I had a child. But I wasn't held."

Long ago, and newly married, after she had had a child a thickening had overrun Cora's physical body, and in doing so it had appeared to include her mind and her character as well. She had not so much slept before the baby's birth as been herself, like a cocoon, held in suspension. After the birth something coarsened and strengthened in her, and below the surface there was the wriggle and movement of a great talent.

Her intelligence in those days had stammered before the qualities that made her husband's successes: his clarity which condensed commonplace observations so that momentarily they seemed like discoveries; his wit, which was a trick of ellipse and inversion, very telling; his spectacular, lugubrious face, which had the success of a clown who tells a curious gay tale in tears; even his extraordinary height, above which the hatchet features hung like a street lamp no brighter than a moon, was again something much in his favour and to her ridicule. She was so painfully small then that it used to have an effect on her nerves. Her neck had ached as she looked at the man who should have stood nearer her level. All the Cora of those days could successfully do was to be on the level to fetch his slippers.

American, faintly Eurasian, tiny, bewildered by marriage, she had formed herself with all the understanding she could muster round her husband's idea of a wife. And from a wife he demanded above all things silence. She gave him silence. Silence and pliability.

Everything in that early time had been at stake. Rudi Holbein, though always a worker, had worked then with almost hysterical anxiety. He had known poverty and social darkness and Jewry, but he had known too, had always known, that the theatre for him was to be the gateway to a freer life. What he had not known was that the harness he put on so young was to be worn for ever and that the work he set himself even fame could not relax.

Long before he was twenty he had a gift for telling a story with a beginning, a middle, and an end. Almost without knowing it schemes for plays dropped from his tongue as he talked. Men and women whom he met were lit in his mind as characters. He never knew them deeply, and in the end he had no friends because people (who love to be well known) dimly felt themselves "used" and estranged in his hands. All this was natural to him, as a baby sucks its milk; it was so he saw all life, all problems. He could not hear of a divorce, a row, a murder, an elopement, a tension, a crisis, without automatically placing the strongest scene in its place, inventing a forerunner, and cascading the end. He was dramatically aware of Rise and Fall. There was really no moment at which he was not fit to be a successful playwright.

Although Cora came to him with money, success soon brought more money into his own hands. To do him justice this was a secondary pleasure. What was first with him was his passion for the theatre and its glamour. And, close behind glamour, that larger figure, fame.

His first play was produced, though not a success. In spite of that another management could not resist his second play. When his third play was financially good he already had his eye on doing without a management. He did not fancy being paid. He wanted to pay. Soon he had a play running in London and two in Paris and the German translation was in the making. About this time he formed a company to build his own theatre. The early plastics were making their appearance. He built a transparent dress circle, but he had to pull it down and replace it again, as people were embarrassed to sit in it.

All his burning ideas and activities required a quiet home. He got it from his wife, but gave nothing in return. He did not think Cora was happy because he did not think about her. He loved her, but no one, not Rudi himself, knew that. When the baby was born he remarked, "We shall have plenty of money for him." Harmless words, coming from a man who had known poverty, but they offended Cora, who was by now thrumming like a harp with offence. Deep in her silence she had erupted. She had begun to draw. And every day she drew better. She drew the skull-head of her husband on pieces of paper that were carefully hidden, drew the scenes she might have had with him if they had been allowed to take place, found that she could draw with heavenly ease and relief to herself rooms full of life, people of movement, expressions on faces that undid the bands round her heart. Her hate of Rudi was transmuted into wicked pleasure as she drew. She wondered about other people's drawings, wondered about her pencil, bought bunches of them, soft, hard, and sanguine, and brushes for sepia washes. She went to the Louvre, but found she could not yet understand how to learn from the Masters. The rush of creation started by physical conception was diverted into this new and thrilling power, and her skill spoke as plain as the written word that she was no longer the same woman. She wasn't interested in the baby. There was a good nurse and no difficulties and nothing made a call on her motherhood—if it existed.

When the baby was a few months old she made her first quarrel. It was her try-out. Rudi had been telephoning while she sat and read; often he telephoned for an hour on end, longer, discussing, planning, rearranging. When at length he put the telephone on its rest and turned round, weary, passing his lean fingers over the twin mounds on his skull, Cora said, not unpleasantly:

"How you bore me—telephoning!"

"I what?"

"Bore me when you telephone."

They had been married several years and she had never yet said a contrary word.

"That's not very nice," he said mildly. "You couldn't have meant it."

She looked up and met his eyes, those bovril-coloured orbs already well known to his public. But the telephone rang again and he forgot her. He had not noted the signal, and very soon his latest rehearsals broke over them. Rudi, working like a slave and a tyrant, took no notice of his wife, unless he fell over her. His secretary never left his side. A second girl came in to sit by the telephone. When Cora told him she didn't want to stay on for the supper-party he was giving in the theatre he looked at her as though he hardly heard her while the stage behind his eyes went on shifting and re-shaping. She arranged her evening therefore for herself and ordered the car to fetch her at the end of the play.

Making her way out through the hubbub and the comments of the audience she found standing by her chauffeur on the pavement an actress who had played in a former play of her husband's, and seeing that she had no car or taxi she offered to drop her on her own way home.

Suddenly, under the soft rug, as the car came to a stop by the given address, the woman, older than Cora, placed a hand, radiating and predatory, upon Cora's thigh. Cora stared straight in front of her, not able to believe her sensations. So they sat for a few minutes while the chauffeur pressed the concierge's button, and just before the heavy door of iron-strapped glass swung a few inches open Cora saw a new landscape and understood a second sex. The man opened the car door and the heavily scented, softly coated woman rose, stooped and left the car—wondering perhaps whether she had furthered her future chances with Rudi or retarded them. Cora remained stupefied.

Next day flowers were sent to Cora which she disregarded—as she disregarded the woman. But she pondered. Life had seemed so narrow, tedious, endless, and repetitive. She had had an almost sex-free life, and a great humility about her looks had prevented her from attempting any rearrangement in her relationship with men. She had not tried out any schemes, such as ugly women some-times light on, nor integrated her small yellow flattened face with a mode of dressing which might have made it positive. Just as Ruby, in her very great beauty, felt unlike her appearance, so Cora, daily humiliated and shocked, faced her mirror. The hand under the rug startled her like a telegram from the outside world—a telegram sent in code. There was room after all for everyone; there were tastes on strange palates; there was a world as new and wild as a jungle outside the way she lived. If the pencil in her hand traced the dark features, vacant and intent, of the actress on the broad cream margin of an art reproduction of theatrical designs, it was not because she gave her a thought. She piled the dry hair over the woman's forehead while thinking of other things, and what she thought of was not her husband, nor the nursery upstairs where her boy slept. She was fixing a date of departure. Not a date by the calendar but a date by endurance. When she had had enough (she knew what was enough) she would go. That she actually went in the early hours after a discussion about peaches and apricots was because Rudi struck her. That was unexpected and served to open the door to departure more generously. She did not actually mind the blow—being quite contented to know that she had deserved it. What lay between them now, unknown to him, was something that nothing could bridge. The sleeping steel had come to life. The implacable artist had risen like a phoenix from the wife. Rudi, brilliant, engrossed, shallow, unbending, understood nothing; never understood what had happened until real old age at length cracked up the crust of success. Then, his eyes dilating as he caught sight of his loneliness, he felt that Cora was the only person who had ever known him, and he must have her back.

They had been that night alone. They had eaten the soup and the sole and the *tournedos*. A gilt dish, half filled with syrup, held, floating, what seemed a dozen egg yolks. Somewhat greedily—he was greedy and this night he had forgotten to serve his wife first—he pulled the gilt dish sharply towards him so that the syrup slopped. Cora's eyes had narrowed.

He said: "I like these peaches," and Cora replied: "They aren't peaches, they're apricots."

"But I told you not to order apricots!" (His spoon in mid-air.) "I *hate* them!"

"You've just eaten four."

"I thought there was something wrong with them!"

"You couldn't have. You said the contrary."

"Ah . . . I couldn't have?"

"Well, no. You ate them and wanted more. You didn't know."

"I told you at the time there was something wrong with them."

"You think you did, but in fact you said, 'I like these peaches,' and pulled the dish towards you."

"No!"

"But you can't bear to be in the wrong. You will go to any length not to be in the wrong. You will perjure yourself under my nose that you may seem to yourself right."

"What are you talking of?"

"*You.* You who never give way to anyone. You who have never in your life said, 'I made a mistake.' Of you."

"You must be mad."

She had risen and stood now at her side of the small round dining table, holding her drawn-thread napkin in her hand, her black dress a little tight on her, her white unyielding neckband shaped like the porcelain base of a yellow china face.

"I am mad," she said. "With rage."

The giant Rudi sat hunched and listened.

"It's a long time now," she said, "since you've gone too far. I have no life in this house, I can't breathe. You teach me to be quiet and creep in felt slippers that you may sleep on in the mornings. You give yourself an importance that I can no longer put up with. Do you think a playwright comes before ordinary human existence? Are you a Messiah, or a prime minister (or even a poet!) that I must keep out of my own sitting room because it suits you at times to work in it, or that I'm unable to get into bed because the mood has taken you to spread your typewritten sheets across the eider-down, or that I must sit shivering in the cold chintz of my chair for the pleasure of watching the playwright correct his third act by my reading lamp? And that boy upstairs? Is he to be brought up in the same way? Not to breathe—lest he disturb God the Father!"

Rudi, half rising, reaching her easily, leant across the small table and hit her right cheek with his open palm. He walked round the table and towered over her.

"And another word," he said, his eyeballs ringed white like a man with glasses, "and I hit the other side."

She moved quickly, reached the door, looked at him, and went out.

He was very surprised. Both at himself and at her. First he sat down at the table and put the tinned fruit on his plate and lifted his spoon, for it seemed natural to continue with the small action that an earthquake had interrupted. But at the taste of the juice it came back to him that she had ordered the wrong fruit and he put down the spoon. Then, going to his dressing-room, he took blankets from the divan, and carrying them to his study threw them on the sofa. Now he would work. And when tired would sleep here. Let her come to him remorsefully in the middle of the night and he would perhaps have the pleasure of forgiving her.

It was three in the morning when he heard her light step on the stair. He sat listening, he held his breath, for the step went on down to the hall. He opened his door. At the bottom of the stair was Cora, dressed to go out, carrying a small case.

From that moment she had left him. Even though he hurried down to the door, looked up the street, saw the lit tail of her hired car; even though she returned, a stranger to him, at ten next morning, using Cora's key, wearing Cora's tailor-made, to look with a strange woman's critical eye at Cora's husband standing with the bony planes of his legs exposed.

He had turned from the glass to face the peculiar stranger who said to him: "Good morning, Rudi. I've not come for recriminations and I'm not open to argument."

"Then you'd better go," he said.

And she: "I'm going. I came in to give you my address for my letters."

"Get out!" he shouted suddenly, and dashed his spectacles on the floor in a rage.

At that she said: "I never ordered the second pair," and smiled. Then turned, and slipped out of the room and shut the door. It had never entered his head she would run upstairs and take the boy. She

didn't want him. He didn't want him either, but the nurse, afterwards, was set on getting the boy back. She would as soon, she said,
have given the little child to the stage doorkeeper as to his mother.

After she had gone he found his books, his whole library defaced.
Pictures of himself, oddly coarse, down the margins of bound volumes, his baby, naked, beside his own head; leering, wifely touches,
bedroom scenes—on the page in *Le Rouge et le Noir* where the
chapter heading is the remark which Cora so many years later
quoted to Ruby—"You have had the advantage of beauty for which
Madame de Staël would have sacrificed everything"—she had
drawn herself, her yellow skin touched in chalk, her bulbous eyes,
and the wiglike turban of black hair.

All his books, after she had left, became dangerous. He had to
burn them. His whole library was tainted with her hate.

So many years ago, so long ago. People, in one life, can change
so that there is nothing left of what they were. Cora, spreading her
hard wings, unhampered by the heart, drew and drew as if the
devil were after her. At the end of ten years she had the young in
one pocket and her contemporaries in the other. She was powerfully
astride her art like a male equestrian. Her spring and autumn exhi-
bitions were serious, important, and fashionable. By the time she
was fifty she was one of the ten foremost painters in France and
her reputation was European.

## CHAPTER EIGHT

And now tonight again was to be Rudi Holbein's First Night,
and all Paris, all Ruby's Paris, was soon to be dressing for it. Cora
too would dominate that horse's tail of hers and wear the cynical
white muslin that had cost a fortune. Poor Rose, distracted in the
Palais Royale, had long begun to fight with the rags of her appearance, and the bed was littered with the dresses she had thought
she could wear but could not.

Down in Pouilly the looking glass never gave Ruby trouble

(though sometimes she was puzzled by the unrelated look of her face). It was eight years since the day at Dieppe when she said she had felt old, but age had still withheld its hand.

"Alberti!" she called, hearing a noise in the sitting-room beyond the open door of her bedroom. "Is it you, Alberti? Come in while I dress." Always indifferent to privacy she continued her work of creaming her temples and cheekbones. The Duca di Roccafergolo moved into the doorway and watched her.

"Where's Gynt? Is he going?"

"He hates plays. He's working. He's got a camp bed now in the little Mill House in the Fantasia. Did Cacki put drinks in there?"

"I've helped myself." He was holding his glass in his hand. His voice had a clear, young, hollow quality. Always a tall and stout man he was now a monster in size, but, as gossip is so often wrong, he did not suffer from dropsy. Fifteen years before there had begun a glandular disturbance, which, in spite of treatments and an operation, had greatly increased the fat all over his person. The swollen lids of his blue eyes opened as though they were a burden. Fat, swelling from within, had ironed out the lines and creases on hands and visage, so that now he looked strangely young for his seventy years.

Coming into the room, carrying his glass carefully, he let himself down on to the ragged red silk of the Empire chair nearest the dressing table. Instantly against his knee, a little brown face with grey whiskers was pressed.

"You have the dog's chair," said Ruby.

"Must I move?"

"No. But I must remember to brush you."

"Isn't this the little dog Miranda has never seen? Or was it hers?"

"She bought it when she was engaged, thinking, poor Miranda, that Tuxie would let her take it with her. I've just had another of her letters. It's not worth while her writing them. It's as though she'd not said one word aloud to me for eight years. I want Gynt to write and suggest they come home but it's so hard to pin him down. He tries not to think of her."

"And I should have thought Miranda would have had a child."

"No child."

"You don't think so much is wrong?"

"Everything's wrong. She never mentions his name."

"But then your name would never have entered her letters either. Your little extrovert never did deal in persons."

"That's true."

He looked curiously round the room, at the beauty of the furniture, at the mixture of wealth and rags left now by the war. The staff of nine had become Rosalba: Cacki, the Chinese footman, was cook and butler in one. "If you'll allow me to say so, you wear very well," he said. "Only you are careless."

"If I wasn't careless," she said, "I shouldn't represent the point I had got to. I adapt myself to losses. For my face I perform the acts required, but I don't pay real attention." As she spoke, flicking her skin with powder, she turned a serious, chalky visage towards him, adding: "It's hardly absorbing now, you see."

"I see a clown," he said tenderly. "Now do the drawing. Draw in the features. I'm thrilled."

Obediently she drew the lips in red, the eyebrows in a soft ash, and stroked up the lashes with the brush dipped in blue.

"It seems to me each time I face the world I have to draw the whole thing from scratch. I know the plan so well I can put back things that time has disturbed. Like a housemaid in a drawing-room after a party."

"I'm fascinated," he said.

"But you've seen this countless times."

"No."

"No?"

"Other women haven't your Alpine courage."

The little brown and grey dog jumped on the duca's lap. He stroked him.

"That dog," said Ruby, "will be the only thing Miranda and I will be able to talk of when she gets back. He's still called the new dog. He was never even christened."

Alberti continued to stroke the dog in silence. Rosalba laid a dress of deep pink satin on the chair, and beside it a film of black lace.

"And the diamond daisies, Rosalba. Take the key of the safe."

"For Rudi's first night?" said Alberti. "Isn't that a dress for the opera? For Covent Garden?"

"I'm not French," she said. "And I have my own way of dressing. If I'm to sit in Rudi's box my job is to shine." She twirled a curl round a finger, leaning into the glass. "Have you ever thought— these easily lost faces—how one clings to them, how they have to represent everything that we are? Ever since I was a child I've been surprised to look as I look. Not—to tell you the truth—quite up to what I feel."

At this the big man laughed. "You don't do badly. If you'd wanted more I hardly think you could have got it! Did you expect to look . . ."

"I should have liked to have had more bite in my appearance. But one mustn't have been a beauty and grouse about it. Rudi did send you a ticket, I hope?"

"He did. I returned it. He has a supper party, I hear."

"He asked you to that too."

"I can't go to theatres any more. The seats are too narrow."

Rosalba handed the "daisies" on a little tray of velvet from the safe. They were eighteenth-century diamond tremblers.

"You look wonderful. Rudi's lucky. Have you eaten? You won't have anything till the supper afterwards."

"I've had my cocktail. Gin, in fact, for dinner. In my youth only people who wrote about the slums mentioned gin."

"Isn't it still early to start?"

"You've something to say to me?" she said quickly.

"Yes. I've sent my car round to the main road where the grass drive comes out, the one that goes round by the water. If you take me that way it won't be any longer and we can stop and talk for a short time on the way."

"I'm ready. We'll go now."

The little dog walked behind them down the stairs, treading on the satin dress or touching Alberti's trousers with his nose. They reached the stone-flagged hall lined with cream and gold bookshelves. Rosalba picked up the dog. "You take him?"

"Rosalba, *not* to the theatre."

"Even locked in the car he'll think it worth it."

Without answering, Ruby kissed Rosalba good night. Cacki had the engine running. He held the door open for her.

Alberti stuffed himself into the far side of the driving seat, drawing in his ebony stick after him.

"Cacki!"

"Iss, m'lady."

"Don't bolt me out. You remember last time."

"Aie . . ."

"And leave me that chicken leg . . ."

"Aie . . . aie . . ."

Cacki folded his hands across his breast—much as Rosalba did when she was vexed, ashamed, humiliated. The sophisticated Chinese and the little Negress had this gesture in common.

"Cold. Just as it is," she said, holding up her finger warningly. She slipped in the gear and they moved off.

"Has he eaten the chicken leg?" asked Alberti curiously.

"Oh, not at all," she said. "It's just an old battle in which I always lose. The chicken leg will turn into something unrecognisable. The suppers he leaves for me are his poems."

As she talked she had taken a grass drive that ran, skirting the ornamental waters beyond the water meadows, into the forest, where, in half a mile, a smaller overgrown track forked into deeper trees.

"Shall I drive into the Fantasia? If Gynt's there we'll say good night to him."

"If the grass isn't too long."

The car rocked gently in deep grass and burst into a small clearing where the fantasy of a dead duke rotted, uninhabited and alone. It was a mummified and foolish hamlet of four cottages never built for peasants. One was a mill which had never ground corn. The door was reached by a rotted plank put across a choked and unmoving ribbon of watercress. Up five richly decorated stair treads that wound round the wheel was a room on three sides of which blackened glass rectangles shone like coal in a seam. The forest leaves now pressed tight against them and inside the room it was green as a fish tank. Three white goats leapt out one after the other from a broken window of another cottage, where the dirty stories of antiquity were carved on door lintels and window frames. Two and two the four cottages faced each other across the clearing. A recent swapping had reduced the grass and weeds, and the clovery beheaded stuff lay smelling like Eastern tobacco on the ground. When the engine stopped the nightingales could be heard.

"Gynt's not been yet or the goats would have left already. Well, Bertie? And now—what?"

He looked at his watch.

"Don't hurry," she said. "Take your time."

"I have to tell you some news."

"Yes, so I see."

"First I must make my little preamble. To explain. People's lives, you know, are not what they seem. They have curious weaknesses, humdrum necessities, habits, contemptible lonelinesses, fears. Behind everything there's a bedrock personal life known only to one person, or, in a happy married life, to two. I'm not talking of sex."

He took a large and very clean white handkerchief out of his pocket and opened it slowly.

"There is always something that makes people old, at last. For me it's been this illness, this bore of bores, that I've fought for years. We don't mention it but it has to be taken into account. It's been a great shock."

"The illness?"

"No. The age that it has brought me to. Men, when age comes like this, will do things that may seem foolish. For women it's different: they are always glancing at age. They have thermometers behind their faces which they're accustomed to consult."

"You've done something silly, Bertie. You've not been near me for a fortnight. I see you're guilty. What are you preparing me against?"

His large face was grave. "My condition," he said, like someone reciting what he has learnt by heart, "makes demands and gives me a sick life that's very tedious."

"But you're no worse! I hate anticipation. I dread these prologues. Have you seen your doctor?"

"The moment you are outside the ordinary illnesses, believe me, it's a game of speculation. It's not magic, you know, seeing a doctor. They make fascinating guesses, but what's clear is that the fat is round my heart and the asthma round my lungs. No, it's nothing new. But there are the nights. There's no reason why a night should be short. It's long. *Je dors mal.* Things have to be done for me."

"But you've Celestine."

"I've had servant trouble," he said suddenly, looking full at her with a wry smile. "I've been obliged to marry her. Father Bonnie married us ten days ago."

"Good God."

"I did it quickly," he said. "Before a sensible word could stop me."

"But why, why? Have you been mad? Tied like that! *Married!* Could she have wanted it? You could have raised her wages. Better have given her a fortune!"

"But why?" he asked. "It's so simple to marry her. It amuses me."

"It does?"

"It's a good-luck story. I love them."

"I'm hearing aright? It's Celestine? Who lets one in at your door?"

"Yes."

"Might she be sixty?"

"Less. Fifty-three."

"My age. And you love her?"

"Don't think of it on those lines. An old man has to make provision for his last years. He may hanker after love and affection but for all that it's too late and he has no right to it. He may be full of self-pity but few people pity him. Before his situation becomes desperate . . . We are fond of our bodies and we grow sad to lose them. But mine has really behaved badly to me, for a healthy and well-living man. Disease is disgusting, but the fate of the body's disgusting and no one should dwell on it. I may become bedridden. It's humiliating. I am trying to make it as little humiliating as possible and I'll have every alleviation that money can buy. But I can't buy the human voice in the middle of the night. One could say I've been a selfish man, living only for myself. One has to pay. Why shouldn't I have to pay, now, when I want this special comfort?"

"But marriage? You haven't explained why it must be that!"

"She was restless," he said evasively.

"I don't marry my butler when he's restless."

"She suggested it. I didn't dare tell you. We've made a bargain. It's on special, very limited, terms. I don't think it'll make the slightest difference."

"But why under heaven should she want it?"

"It's for her good name. And for her son. He's illegitimate."

"Yours?"

"Oh no. No, good heavens. I've never even seen him. She adores him. What she wanted is that he could say he was the stepson of the Duca di Roccafergolo. I don't think he can pronounce a word of it. Of the Duca e Conte di Melchiorre . . . there's a lot more of it cascading downwards in noblesse. She has written it out. It was touching to see her labouring with a heavy violet pencil. I hadn't called it all up for thirty years. I had to look at my will to get it right for her."

"Has she a hand in your will too?"

"No. She's not avaricious. It's the title. She's a fanciful peasant and has this dream of being a duchess. You say why marriage? But nothing less would do, would it? If she had to be a duchess. Could you drive on? This place is giving me hay fever."

She backed up the track onto the soft drive that would finally come out on the main road. She was stunned with surprise.

"I knew you'd be astonished at first," she heard his voice continue beside her. "But what does it matter if you think of it? I'm ill. I'm seventy. When she first talked of leaving me I couldn't believe it: she's been with me twenty years and I'm so accustomed to her. Then I guessed it was the son."

"Is he a blackguard?"

"No, no. I say I've never seen him. I shouldn't think so."

"You should have seen him before you did it."

"Perhaps I should. From what she says he's a simple creature, handsome, childish, with grandiose ideas. She'd give him the moon."

"I daresay. But it's your moon you're giving him."

"At first I told her it was preposterous, and it is. But gradually I grew used to the absurdity. She's an old child herself—I know her so well and there's no harm in her—and she hankers to dazzle her village with my name. It's her fairy tale. And it won't be for long and why should I mind giving it to her if she will stay and see me out? My bedroom life will soon be all my life. I'm a sad, ridiculous, disfigured child. She's the nannie I lost when I was six—I need her. I need someone to open my shutters last thing at night and say 'Sleep well,' someone who'll come when I wake and say, 'Go to sleep again.'"

They turned into the road and his car and his man were waiting for him. "Old age can only finally be lived in one place and with one being," he said as he rumbled and heaved beside her, preparing to climb out. "Don't be angry with me, I wouldn't have risked asking your advice."

"Bertie——"

"Don't let's talk any more of it. It's done. And you're nearly late."

"What shall I do? Shall I come and see her?"

"Yes. Why not?"

"You will have to engage someone to let me in, to answer your door. Have you thought of that?"

"Oh, I think Celestine will do everything as usual," he said, a little astonished.

Driving away, the shocked tears still in her eyes, she turned round to wave; but the chauffeur stood by him, obscuring him, helping him to climb heavily back into his car.

## CHAPTER NINE

The Duca di Roccafergolo was not so sorry for himself as was his friend who drove away. He had got it over, his confession, and he thought of it with gentle approval. And about his marriage he was also not displeased. For a quiet man it had been an executive act, and this fond woman, this delicate cook, this clean, cosy creature of routine was now tied to him as his own. His routine had become for him of poetic importance. He had developed, in his solitary life, elegant habits that were dear to him. His reflective meals were a pleasure he would not have changed for the gayest party in Paris. Then he sat, dressed as for a ritual, his yellow cat beside him, his Greek philosophy, or the latest copy of *Nature* sent from England, propped open on the Dresden stand with the gold clips, and ate infinitely slowly, mouthful by mouthful, the river trout or the calves' liver in white wine that Celestine brought in from the kitchen and laid on a silver heater on the serving table at his side. He would drink burgundy or Chablis or Moselle according to the dish or the weather. Celestine, who had been with him twenty years, ministered like an acolyte. Even her faults amused him. For instance, she had always been a little wearingly romantic. She made festivals of his birthdays, working herself into anxiety about the sugar flowers for his cake. She kept an extraordinary book of keepsakes in the kitchen, with a piece cut from her mother's shroud pasted flat on the first page. She had teased him to get himself photographed, and when he saw that she had it on a sheet in the book stuck round with sugared violets he had burst out laughing and she had cried and put her apron to her eyes. She had great calm, but suddenly would come those unexpected side-channels of emotion. And then after all these years she had told him in the middle of the night when he had called her to him in a choking fit of asthma—had told him when the coughing had subsided and he was weak and propped up on many pillows—that she was going to leave him. He had been quite bewildered, speechless, half from lack of breath, and half because his mind was searching to understand hers.

They spent a wretched night. She stayed with him, sitting on a chair rocking herself and weeping, and unwilling to answer the questions he put from time to time.

"There's something behind this, Celestine. This doesn't come from you."

At last she told him the baker in her village ten miles away wanted to marry her.

"But do you want to marry him?"

"It's to make me respectable."

"And aren't you respectable?"

"I was never married. Zani is the son of a commercial traveller. They come in November," she sobbed. "They never stay very long."

"Now is Zani behind this idea of yours?"

"No, no, no, no."

Next day he was silent on the subject, he did not argue with her. In the daytime he felt indignant and that if needs must he could perhaps do without her. But it was in the nighttime he felt the break to be so unbearable. He had always been subject to a roving and unfathomable misery at night. For twenty years she had been to him in the day an automaton, but slowly, as his asthma grew worse together with his insomnia, and latterly the newer and more mysterious trouble that had made his limbs throb and ache, she had become his comfort of comforts, his night-nurse whenever he needed her. The subject of her marriage with the baker came up again a few nights later. He asked her many questions, but her method was to answer only those which were simple, and to sob whenever he pinned her in a corner.

"Do you love him?"

She shook her head. "Not at my age, Your Grace."

"It's purely then for marriage? Purely for respectability? Has this condition of yours been nagging at you then?" She sobbed annoyingly. Somehow he could not believe her.

"Is he well off?"

"A baker? And his father before him? It's a nice situation in a village."

(This extra consideration of the ridiculous rival he had left out of his talk with Ruby.)

It was on the third night that she suddenly lifted her pleasant, distressed face out of her apron and said, "Why doesn't Your Grace marry me himself then? All would be arranged." He was breathless from astonishment and coughed so much she had to prop him up and get him his asthma pipe. But afterwards she kept at it. He thought she had a bee in her bonnet. He could not conceive how her mind had reached to this idea.

"No, Celestine, no," he said. "A duchess is too much. It's greedy."

"What harm would it do Your Grace?" she said. "Then I would never leave you. Everything would be just the same, it would mean nothing, but I would have your beautiful name and my village would look up to me."

In the end it became a game: he grew amused. She was such a simpleton about it that he ended by getting her to paint the picture of her luck, of how she would go back, and stop at the forge and say: "Blacksmith, I'm a duchess!" How she would then reach the first shop, and finally the bakery, spreading her news. Of how the black-clothed women would cluster round her with their baskets, asking questions and astonished. He grew accustomed to this picture, but he asked for it over and over again. The long, empty nights were filled with the good-luck story. He began to grow fascinated with the idea himself. So it came about slowly that he glanced at what remained of his life and he looked full at her importance to him and he said the words to himself—"Whom does it hurt? Why not?" And one night he said to Celestine—"Now not a word more. I may talk to the priest. I will see. Now be quiet; go back to bed." And noting the change, the new note in his voice, she left him. So it came about that this very evening he had driven over to Little Pouilly and broken the news to his great friend that the knot was tied. He had ensured his death-bed.

Since the marriage Celestine had cooked for him as usual, and, as ever, eaten her meals in the kitchen. Many a rich farmer's wife will wait on her husband and take her meal when he is finished. Alberti, however, urged her to go back to her village and tell her friends her news. "Bring me back every word, Celestine," he said. "Every look on their faces. I want to hear everything. And especially how the baker takes it." But Celestine was curiously unwilling for this expedition. She put it off and put it off.

"Surely at least you want to tell your son?" he said. At that a peculiar look came on her face and she busied herself in silence about the room while he watched her.

Alberti's car now this night drew up at the edge of the grass by the garden of his house, and as he walked slowly between the double row of lavender he saw his wife standing dressed in the clothes she only wore on Sundays. For a moment he was surprised and then supposed her sister had come over to see her. "Well, Celestine," he said pleasantly, and passed on to mount the wide oak stairs to his room. But over the turn of the banister he caught sight of the table through the open door of the dining room laid with two places.

"Is Monsieur de Bas-Pouilly dining?" he called. For occasionally Edouard would pay him a surprise visit, carrying a pot of caviar.

"No," said the duchess from the hall below.

"Who then is dining?"

"I," she replied, made brave by the listener she knew was in the kitchen.

"Ah . . ." said Alberti, exhaling a long breath, and looked down at her. At the same moment his nose, sensitised by his asthma, caught the drift of a vile cigarette.

"Who is smoking?"

"No one."

"There is someone. Go and see."

"Do you order me?"

"Yes, of course."

"It is my son."

"Tell him to smoke in the garden," he said, and went heavily up the stairs. He must have time to think.

Gaining his room, he went to the window and leant on the sill, looking over the charming scene, the water meadows shining through the trees. His heart, for the first time, sank at what he had done. He saw well enough that she wished to consider herself his wife, as well as his duchess. What? Give up the evening hours? Never again to read Greek between the omelette and the trout? His sober Celestine, whom he had known these twenty years . . . His head swam. He saw himself as Ruby must have seen him, as a fool, a wild silly fool. He was suffocating, and turning back into the room he sank, coughing, into an armchair.

The door opened and Celestine came in.

"I am not well. I will dine here. Get me a tray."

So baleful was his small blue eye that she went, and presently returned with the tray ready laid.

"Where is the pepper?" he asked, looking the tray over. "And the paper-cutter?"

"The table downstairs was properly laid," she said, sullenly. "You can come down."

"I am not well enough."

"You were well enough when you went to Pouilly."

To his amazement he thought he heard jealousy in her voice. Did one marry an old woman to make her change overnight into a butterfly?

"It is my affair where I go. Or at what moment I feel ill."

"But it is now my affair."

"I shall suffocate," he said. "Take this tray off my knees."

She took it and he coughed again. At last when he recovered she drew a chair up and sat down opposite him.

"We are married now . . . husband," she said in an uncertain voice.

He said, "Those words aren't yours. Who has put you up to this? What's your son doing in my kitchen?"

"Your stepson."

"Have I ever seen him?"

"No. Never."

"What age is he?"

"Thirty-one."

"He's not in work?"

"No."

"Is he a bad lot? A good-for-nothing?"

She began to cry.

"He's a bad lot then."

"No. NO. NO."

"Did he suggest this marriage? This idea wasn't yours. Now I guess it."

She sobbed on.

His mind was full of anger. The panic vanished. Her deception, her wickedness, the knowledge that things had gone on behind his back, was not more to the forefront than the thought that she had intended he should never eat his evening meal alone again. He had no difficulty in making up his mind.

"I have been so foolish as to trust you," he said to the bowed head. "But I have not put myself into your power, as your son perhaps thinks. I have given in to your whim, not knowing you were egged on, and it may cost me a little money to turn you out, but turn you out I will. Until I see my lawyer tomorrow I will content myself with six months' wages. There happens to be money in that drawer and I will give it to you. You can sleep here tonight, for it's late. Tomorrow morning you are to be gone before I set eyes on you. You've been a good servant and for that I pay you. You have been a stupid and disloyal wife and for that I'll get rid of you. Do you understand?"

She cried loudly, her apron up to her face. There came a knock at the door.

"Who's there?"

A mumble was all the answer, but the duca smelt the cigarette again. He crossed the room surprisingly quickly and took from a drawer a small revolver. It was loaded, for in the village of Pouilly there had been recently two burglaries with violence.

"Come in," he said, concealing the revolver, and stood with his back to the chest of drawers, drawn up straight like a young man.

Zani, the son, came in, a dark coxcomb with a dash of Spanish blood, dressed in the cheap, tight clothes of the nearest town. He had had wine.

"Well, stepson?" said the duca.

"What are you doing to my mother? She's crying."

"She cries because I've given a servant the sack. Also I'm getting rid of a bad wife."

"A man can't send his wife out of the house."

"A man can do anything. He can also forbid his house to a menacing lout."

"What harm am I doing? I don't want my mother unhappy. You've married her. You owe something to a wife. Didn't they teach you that in Italy?"

But the duca was not listening. The hand behind his back lowered the revolver again into the open drawer, discarding it. With his other hand he lifted the telephone.

"*Gendarmerie*," he said.

"What are you doing!" said Zani, taking one uncertain step forward.

Alberti, his eye never leaving Zani's face, said into the telephone: "I've had an attempted burglary. But they've made off. They've taken nothing, I think. I saw a young man climb over the wall at the back——"

Zani gasped. "What are you saying . . ." he muttered, but the drunken courage was ebbing.

"Nothing's been disturbed, you understand," continued Alberti (still watching Zani). "Send someone to look us over, will you? Immediately. Yes, now, at once."

He put down the telephone and drew his heavy body upright.

"Call your mother and leave the room," he said. "She can sleep the night here as I've told her, but you leave the house and the neighbourhood at once."

"But it was a lie!" said Zani slowly. "I've done nothing."

"Even I can lie. You called on me with menaces. They'll believe me. It's a pity you're not educated to understand these things. Go!" he finished, and the small eyes in the large face (for the first time in his mild life) looked murderous.

Zani avoided those eyes. "Come, Mother," he said. And as she sobbed without moving, "Come, Mother, do you hear? Do you want to get me taken away?" At that she got up and went to him.

"Take the tray," said the duca. It was on the sofa. She took it.

"And now I want some dinner. These scenes make me hungry," he said. "Throw that away. It's cold. I'll have an omelette. And a tray won't do. I'll have a table. That small table that's at the end of the landing. Make sure it's properly laid. Naturally my book-stand. The book I'm reading is on my writing table, marked with the red leather marker. Stepson——"

"Yes . . . sir?"

"Warn your mother that my dinner must be without flaw. Return with her when she brings up the food. The table's too heavy for her."

Zani stood his ground for a moment, fingering his watch-chain. The oil shone blue on his curled hair.

"I can see," said the duca steadily, "the good-for-nothing that you are, dressed above your walk in life and with hands that have done no work, and that mixed blood that gives you a swollen head and no stomach. You might make a waiter. Your mother can give you your first lesson on my dining table. Wheel it in when it's ready."

Zani, with a last look at his stepfather, turned and left the room with Celestine.

Alberti, left alone, glanced down at the little revolver and gently closed the drawer. He had not known that he was such a man of wrath. He crossed to the window, actually humming with pleasure. He felt young and calm. Presently there came a knock on the door.

"Sir . . ." said Zani's voice. And then, "Your Grace!"

"Yes."

"Can my mother come in?"

"Yes. But bring in the table yourself." Celestine, swollen of face, held the door open while Zani wheeled the table through the door.

"Has it pepper?"

"Yes, Your Grace."

"And the paper-cutter? And the bookstand? Good. Here is your money, Celestine. Spend one more night under your husband's roof and be gone in the morning. And you, stepson, will leave now."

All was soon quiet in the house. Alberti had finished his dinner (eaten quite with his usual pleasure), and he rose and pushed the wheeled table himself through the door onto the corridor. He stood still to listen. There was not a sound. The quiet of the house sent a pleasant thrill along his marrow. He felt strangely well. He was pleased with himself and had known what to do. It is a very great pleasure in age, as at all times, to find one knows what to do.

But on turning back to bed, and as the night advanced, he fell prey to increasing depression. Twenty years is a long time to depend upon someone. If that someone fails, a quarter of a lifetime is lost. He lay thinking of Celestine and suffered a deep reaction, hearing first two and then three o'clock strike across the water meadows from the stable clock at Pouilly.

The door opened softly, and he knew that Celestine was in the room.

"Is Your Grace in pain?"

He rolled round to face the wall, so that when she put the light on, as was her habit, she should see only his back.

She put the light on.

"It is your old Celestine," she said with a sob in her voice.

Facing the wall, he growled: "It's not she. It's my fool of a wife, who thought she could get the better of me."

"I've been thinking, Your Grace. I love you better than my son. I did not know it."

"No more lies," he said. "Go to bed."

"I see that what I feel for Zani is natural affection."

"Very likely. And I shall soon die. He'll be with you longer. He's a young man. I wish you joy of him."

"But natural affection," she said patiently, as though she was not listening to him, "is only what the beasts feel."

There was a silence. Then Alberti rolled onto his back, looked at her and struggled up till he sat among his pillows, tousled but keen of eye.

She stood before him in the neat flannel dressing gown she always wore. "I believed," she said, "that one was always a mother. But it is not so."

"What's in your head?"

"I loved him," she said, "as one does, without thinking about it, beginning from the beginning. One loves one's baby. But now it's time he got away among new people. He has too many dreams. This was one of them."

"Was there no baker, then?"

"There was no baker," she said almost in wonder, as though she presumed that he knew everything. "It was all in his plan. How should I ever think of it? I admired him when I ought not to have. He was so good with talking and the priest thought him clever and when he was nearly grown he had ambitions, but I can see now that it was bad for him to have had such thoughts. Where he wanted to go was too far for him to get. All that doesn't concern Your Grace. But you're rich . . ."

"What's that?"

"It would not cost you much," she said, and he saw the straight-forward innocence in her eyes, "to arrange something interesting for him. He would not mind going to some other part of France. He is tired of his village, and they . . ."

". . . are tired of him? What do you call 'interesting'?"

"Zani will never work as peasants do. He is clever with money and ideas. Your Grace will know how to arrange it, and I shall stay here. I know your habits. Nothing like this will happen again."

Slowly he held out his left hand towards her. She fell on her knees beside the bed. After a moment he slipped lower on the pillows. He was exhausted. She saw it, and rising to her feet she drew his sheets across him, tilted the lamp shade, set the light screen across the window. Then, tiptoeing from the room, she went to her own bed like a dog that is at last patted and given his blanket.

## CHAPTER TEN

At the theatre Rudi had left a doorman to take her to his box.

Alberti's news, the light on his lonely condition, had so shaken her that when she caught sight of Edouard in the stalls and saw him bend his head to talk to his crumpled companion she felt for him too a tender and speculative compassion. All her men friends were getting older. The whole band, like a wagonette of picnickers, was driving towards the edge of the world. It was not so much the extreme edge, however, that gave her apprehension, as the pity she felt for hearts inwardly taken aback by the arrival of age. Contrary to what was supposed, it was easier for women.

There was Rudi now, who would soon come in and sit behind her, and watch once again the creatures made from his toil. She had known him a very long time and in his mute, extrovert manner he had shown that he was fond of her, but to her he remained a fresco-figure in society and she had no idea of the personal life of this famous old horse who pulled on in the shafts of his career. What could his relations have been long ago with his wife, what haphazard moment of attraction had once drawn him to Cora? Cora had the box opposite. It was bizarre that she should sit there. Did he send it to her? Did she demand it? If Rudi was to get little mercy from the press tomorrow, he would get none from Cora. She was present at every first performance of his to smack her lips, Ruby supposed, at how little she had lost. How unsparingly unkind was this world in which they all lived! She looked again round the stalls. The numbers of old people in the monied seats surprised her, faces full of spite and power. It was not really after all in Paris that the old were weaponless and to be pitied.

Rudi had not yet joined her; he was busy arranging the last moments of his morrow's doom. She knew he was outstaying his public acceptance but he could still command a fashionable audience, even if they came to scoff, and he had so harnessed his powers of work upon one thing that he wrote like a machine left running at the door while the master, the soul, was away on another errand. He had developed that trained eye that continued to see life in the sharpest drama, simplified to his uses, a beam that shone always upon the same furniture, the same arrangements, almost the same accidents —as though life grouped itself for him. Tonight—there she was to be—the woman who drugged and stole. Act One she was apprehended by the police. Acts Two and Three gave the reasons and the story since early childhood. Act Four brought it back to the present. That was how he saw it. It's a pity that the best you can do grows stale because you don't know when you've crossed the bar. Almost the way in which Rudi knew his job tired one. The suspension, awoken, soothed, then brought to life again by hammer-strokes—one, two, and three. She knew beforehand how the play would go.

People looked at her. Her curious blue stare, for which she was famous, took in the audience. If Rose was later, at the end of an act, to object that she presented a mask to the world, it was for the same reason that Ruby, looking into her glass, had said she felt a stranger to her face. In response it had an unmoving beauty, too classic for expression. And it was not tonight, absent-mindedly looking over the warm and moving crowd, on show for the aged Rudi's sake, that her intelligence, her understanding, the gusto of her amusement, should be allowed to break up the reproduced and photographed mask.

They were all there, as they had been so often before, the Freemasons of this compact upper world. The play was almost the old play. Her part on show was her old part. Rudi came into the box from the back, the old dramatist. He had an outsize carnation, and the largest silk facings. His yellow teeth showed as always where the pale lips were drawn back in that greeting that could not really be a smile and yet asked a smile in reply. He laid his surgeon's fingers lightly on her shoulder, watching the audience over her head, himself half in shadow yet well lit too by a small strip-light he had had put up in the box.

As she turned to greet him she saw that he was glittering with energy, staring with all the light of his eyeballs (eyeballs coffee-coloured and protruding that made one nervous).

A knock and a bell, premonitions of movement, more delay, and the curtain went up. The world went out and the theatrical sun rose on the woman who stole. Rudi settled behind her, as an eagle settles, long arms spread wide on unseen supports and cuffs alight. She could see one hand out of the corner of her eye, and the fingers crisping and relaxing. She pictured as she followed the play his coming disappointment, seeing each development through the bitter words of tomorrow's hostile critics. "Our Rudi," she read in words still unprinted, "hasn't yet learnt his place. In the dustbin." "It is impossible to sit through the Sixty-fourth Holbein confection without tears of boredom." "The machinery, loaded with dated sentiment, like moss on piston rods . . ." With her quick facility for tears, she felt them coming for him. She was upset at the thought of his courage and his pile of years. One tear in the eye nearer to Rudi got itself illumined from the stage and Rudi saw it. He had no idea of its origin and his acute anxiety lessened. She was moved, he thought, so all was going well. He knew he couldn't really tell by a first night, such a first night as this, but he could never learn that lesson. At any rate, if the second night told the truth (whatever that might be) this night was his party, his blessing, his reward for hard work. He couldn't himself follow the action on the stage; his mind kept branching off. He'd seen the action, built up, brick by brick, detail by detail, piled up, worked up, sweated up. He didn't at times even look. The little Jewess was all right. Lovely. Pretty. Pretty as a picture. Left him cold as mutton fat. He couldn't look at her. What had he got that was pleasure out of it? Not the work. That really indubitably was hell. Almost more laborious now that he knew the way so well. And the casting so frustrating and vexing. You never could get the man you wanted. Only the girls. They were easy enough. So pretty and such asses. But the clever young actors shied away. Then the work, work, work, right up to the ultimate moment —like a high tide against a wall. No, it was the sense of still being important that he got. To go to parties and for women to say, "Rudi's up to something!" And then he provided for them this (like a manager of a restaurant) First Night, Gala Supper, New Year's Eve— balloons. He shook himself and glanced again at the tear which he had seen like a gas-lamp on a blowy boulevard. But it was gone.

Four complete acts—she was thinking—they would all be there till midnight. She stared at a stage of Empire chairs, gilt console tables, and a seigneur's bookcase filled with identical bindings. The woman who stole was a guest in this mansion (from whose rooms footmen had no doubt removed any sign of life), unfolding her charms and hoodwinking the Innocents (all save the one man who saw through her, the fashionable doctor, as he lit his interminable cigarettes).

The woman who stole was now in the hands of the doctors. The play had gone back twenty years (she was ten)—always a tiresome technique. She was also invisible. Rudi was too wise to hire a little creature to lisp his lines. She was in the nursery, no doubt, at the top of this gilt house. But down in the frowning library (distinguished from the salon by more books, more alcoves, more oak doors) the fashionable doctor so addicted to cigarettes was himself young, and had got a gaunt friend (small part, old character actor) to help him. They were trying to explain to the father, a general, that the child of ten was liable one day to do what she should not. He was having none of it. "My daughter!" he shouted. "My little girl!" (It was a special form of illness; always so interesting on the stage. Rudi had got hold of it through much reading of the medical dictionary.)

In the crisis-third-act Rudi yawned: the lack of oxygen and a sudden, violent depression laid him waste. He was very tired, he was old; tired of himself and the world. It would beat him in the end. His spirit had been high, but in his relations with other people he had been too selfish, and he saw in a flash as he tried to watch his "crisis" on the stage that he had nobody. It is in this way when you are split in attention that truth pounces. His wife had run from him, his son hated him, and what had been done by him never could be now undone. There was no time to be kinder. This strange thought if externalised in black letters on his shirt front would have dumb-founded that audience. Rudi Holbein thinking, while his play moved onwards, "There is no time now to be kinder." He recovered. The play was over. The clapping pretty fair. It was then that he was guilty of the bad taste of making his speech of modesty and grati-tude from the box.

In the long studio at the back of the theatre the tables were covered with gold lamé and lilies, iced crayfish and plates of compli-cated sweets. Even Rudi's ideas of rich feeding had become old-fashioned. There was plenty of champagne and of whispering in corners, not of lovers but of elderly men and women with a laugh on their tongues. All Rudi's friends were levelled up in age. They wore decorations and a little grey about the ears. In a way it was a smart and powerful gathering, which to collect had given him much thought. He would like to have had younger men at his parties, but he did not know them. (The critics, of course, at this hour had gone hurrying off to plant their daggers.) The young actress for whom they all waited spent an hour getting herself dressed (though they would all have preferred to have seen her just as she came off the stage). Other principal actors came in one by one, including the "doctor," who had a name and was as vain as Rudi. He already knew he was playing in the wrong play and was dropping vinegar as he came through the corridor from the theatre.

Rudi, for the time being, felt no more anxiety. This was an inter-val before he opened the papers in the morning and took what was coming to him. Ah—his sixty-four first nights! He thought, "It isn't the triumph that has bounds but the ability to taste it. You can't burst the heart." He moved about, pleased, caressed by empty com-pliments. "I won't drink," he thought. "Nowadays I become sad when I drink."

Just then the "doctor" created a diversion.

"If it hadn't been for friendship for you, Rudi . . ." he was heard to say. There was a quarrel. The actor left.

At first Ruby put her hands over her ears. Then she said to her neighbour, "What did he say?"

"Didn't you hear? He said everything that could be said. There was nothing left out. How bad the play was—how dated . . . what harm it did him to be seen in it——"

"Was he drunk?"

"Let's hope for Rudi's sake he was drunk."

Rudi laughed his braying laugh and sat down by his actress and laid his bony fingers on her arm. Hours seemed to go by. No one wanted to be the first to move, for now it was important to side with Rudi. Loyalty had become canalised in crowd-form. Then suddenly everyone said good-bye and the dishevelled room was empty.

Ruby stood, her cloak on her arm, the last guest, the most loyal, if a little stunned.

"I can hardly stand," she said. "What a celebrated evening!"

"Don't go," said Rudi, opening the door through to his own flat.

"It's late. I've still to drive to Pouilly."

"Stay just a little." He drew her through the door into his own sitting-room, neat, dove-grey, bare after the broken lilies and the gold necks of the bottles. "Stay a few minutes. I want to ask you something."

But now it would not be what she used to be asked. Now all the giving came from her, to her old men, her children.

As she waited for Rudi to speak she sat on the arm of a chair, her long gloves in her hand. Rudi walked up and down. Was he going to ask her for the truth about his play? That, she thought, wouldn't be fair, for he had had all his local glory tonight. What he really got in the end was between him and the professionals.

"I've written to Cora," said Rudi, halting in front of her.

"Written to Cora?"

"Would she consider," said Rudi, searching for a word, "a re-union?"

"You've asked her that in a letter?"

"No. Only to meet me."

"She's sixty."

"What's that got to do with it?"

"You've been nearly thirty years apart."

"You know her," he said. "Sound her. Try the ground."

"But she's not the same woman. She'll make you unhappy! You'll be mad to want her."

He took no notice but walked up and down and said: "I know you'll do this. What I planned . . . She'll get the letter in the morning. I posted it tonight at five. See her before she has a chance of refusing. Press my claims for me. Tell her I'll write no more plays. I can't stand more of it. I can't stand the loneliness. When she left me I was furious, but then at the time I had a sense of liberation and thought life was all to come. But nothing has come. Nothing has happened to me in thirty years. Nothing. Except one play after the other. Although I deal in people all day long, on my sheets of paper, when it comes to intercourse, friendship, a little talk at night, a little sympathy, there's nothing, I can't get that. But be sure and tell her I'll write no more plays. This is the last one. I'm tired of the strain. It's not only to drag one's feet through four acts, but at the end, what I've been through these last weeks, it's like a gale at sea in a small boat. Yes, if anything will bring her back it's that news, that there'll be no more writing in the house, no more silence. We'll travel. I've seen nothing—after all—I've seen nothing of the world."

"But you've friends of your own in the theatre? You've somebody?"

"I? Not a soul! Nobody. The dramatist is the patron, but only so long as he can hold it down. At the slightest weakening one is betrayed. Did you hear what Dabencourt said to me tonight?"

"I put my fingers over my ears."

"I didn't. My ears were wide open like a donkey's. He said he played for me out of compassion."

"He was drunk."

"He hadn't had time to be drunk. He said it at once because he had already heard the way things will go. Haven't I learnt my craft then? For a play's a deep, ticklish craft, though they don't know it. I've spent a lifetime on it. He said I was an old man before the war. They date you by the war. They date a writer by the war. As though what he showed up in humanity had also its unfashionable moods. Like the heart—even what you feel gets outmoded! It's arbitrary. One daren't have been alive at that period: one's tainted. But I suffered by the war too. Didn't I suffer by it? But they want to make a corner in suffering, those severe, intellectually wounded, sensitised, allergic young men. Is their suffering sacred? But what do I feel? Did you see his eyes without pity or expression? Plum stones. Prune stones. He found himself in the wrong play (it's what they've told him). He'd heard the joints creaking, he said, as he spoke the lines. He said I would see tomorrow . . . It's three already! They'll bring in the newspapers at seven-fifteen." He sat down. Tears were on his yellow cheeks. "They hate me," he said. "All the lot are tired of me. I've held them too tight. It's on a night like this that a man wants his wife."

Tired though she was, one can't leave an accident, a casualty, even at three in the morning.

"It's overwork," she told him. "And Dabencourt drugs. I was told. You saw yourself the state of his eyes."

"I've no more to give," said Rudi. "It's plain as a pikestaff. What on earth shall I do with the rest of my life? My health's splendid. I'm fit for years of living. My doctor gives me a ticket for ninety. I've emptied the whole of my life to write plays, and now I'm as hollow as a drum. What have I left?"

"What all writers have. Your reputation."

"Nothing goes so fast as a playwright's reputation when his day is over."

"She was there tonight. You saw her, of course, in the box opposite?"

"I? No, I'm so short-sighted."

"She comes to all your opening nights. Don't you send her the boxes?"

"Not I. No. The box opposite mine, you say? I think you must be mistaken." He remained thoughtful a moment, then he said, as though all had been arranged, "So you'll go and see her?"

"I'll go. I shan't like doing it. Don't build on any results. She's got a life and a career that she cherishes. It's very difficult to think of her now as a married woman. She's more like a husband."

"Yes," he said, as though he were answering her, but he had not heard her. "And nowadays I know better how women like to live. She used to complain to me that she had no life. I took no notice of her, but we can remedy all that. I've had what I wanted. We might go to Spain for a little. She could paint—I shouldn't mind. Do you know when she left me she had drawn all over my books? After the first one that I found I pulled them one after the other out of the shelves. Indecencies. Caricatures." He frowned. "I was angry. It wasn't the value of the books (I had to burn them). They were bound volumes bought to fill the shelves. I was never a reader. One hasn't time when one writes, nor eyes left for reading. But all that's past and gone. I'll not mention it. I've learnt since that women sometimes have these rebellions."

"And in the end? How did you part in the end?"

He laughed shortly. "One has to part over something. In the end we parted over a dish of apricots."

"A dish of apricots?"

"A glass dish of them on the table. But how it happened I've no sort of recollection. I only know that much was said—and step by step——" He stopped. "Then I lost my breath, and hit her. Not hard, but afterwards I wished it had been harder. She left me that night. I don't know why, no, nor why it was so serious. Next day she took the baby away. She had a car waiting."

"And then?"

"There were letters and lawyers and negotiations and in the end I got the baby back."

"Did you want him?"

"No. I wanted to spite her. I kept the nurse. She brought him up till he was fifteen. It was then he started running away. He went to Dieppe once and across to England."

"Were you fond of him? Was he your companion in those years?"

"No," said Rudi in a low voice. "No. I wasn't a father who was much to him."

"Then he has been a victim of the separation?"

"I think he has."

"Where is he now?"

"I never see him. He hates me. He hates us both. He won't take money from me."

"You could pay him out for that—and feel more comfortable yourself too—by leaving him money in your will."

"I have made no will," said Rudi sulkily. "When I feel old I'll make a will. My son behaved badly. When I look back on my life Cora is the only person who knew me. That must count for something, don't you think? I mean with her. The whole of life's a closed book unless there's someone to open it with you. I would forgive her and I wouldn't mind saying that I thought myself to blame a little, if she wanted me to say it. It can't be a pleasure for a woman to live alone."

"Rudi, how can I explain to you! Cora's known throughout Europe. You who know what it is to be celebrated know it's like love, one wouldn't change it for anything. And then too, unlike love, one can enjoy it when one's old. She adores her life. But you've sent your letter. We'll see what comes of it. I'm not saying, good heavens, that I know the inner life of other people. There may be that in Cora that one can't guess. But to save you pain and disappointment I feel you can hardly have counted how much she's changed."

He looked at her and said, "She used to be silent and pale in those days. Very silent."

"Then she couldn't have changed more," said Ruby, "if she'd become an alligator."

## CHAPTER ELEVEN

When Tuxie died, the maid Victoria, feeling executive in the presence of tragedy, took it on herself to post the photographs in the long envelope, lying stamped and addressed to Lady Maclean. They caught that boat home that Miranda's later letter should also have caught—but that the later letter was never posted.

After the drive down from Paris, a drive during which she had opened the hood of her car and let the night air flow in, Ruby at length walked into her bedroom tired but filled with a dizzy vitality. She crossed to her window and stood looking out. Those stars which had leapt over her moving car like crickets now hung still. Their sudden light brought back her childhood and the Jamaican constellations which burnt like Bengal fires over the Blue Mountains. Across the meadows in the forest a mile away she could see an unusual beam shine from Alberti's window. She turned to speak to the little dog that had got off its chair, saw the envelope with Miranda's handwriting on her tray, and opening it pulled out some faded pictures mounted on cardboard. Now that it was so late she was in no hurry to sleep, and remembering at once the stereoscope stand put away on a shelf in the old nursery she fetched it and lay down on the bed, as she was in her stiff satin dress, and put her eyes to the dusty velvet holes. The first photograph was that of the young man's face. She exclaimed aloud (for the little dog sat up, startled)—

"That was love, wasn't it—Lieutenant Ussher!"

As a hook and line reaches the fish in deep water so instantly the past was struggling alive in her hand. She felt the movement of a light breeze: a curious sensation as though the hairs on the heart had moved, not the heart itself. The sun was on his cheek. His eyes knew her. His name that not once in forty years had occurred to her came straight back to her lips. So intense and violent had been the recalling that she thought that the bones of some old general must really tremble for a second in his grave—or the risen spirit of an army officer receive a sensation like pins and needles.

"It was love," she said, nodding to him. "And I know. I've had occasion to know since. But you couldn't have used my love. I was nine."

Somewhere in that room in the photograph her mother sat, towards whom past the child's head the young man smiled—her beautiful mother (who had no eyes for anyone but Ruby's father). She pulled out the card and slipped in the next, and there sat the child herself—dead without mourning or grief, whose departure as she grew no one had noticed. She could remember her own look now, in detail, like a character in a book, without identification. All that had made her since was there already, the oval of her face, the eyes —but at the time she had not liked her own appearance. Her mother had had a soft face, fair hair wound up in a bun high up on the back of her head and a happy fringe on her forehead. The child had never prayed in bed: "Make me like my mother," but, angrily, accusing, "God, why didn't you!"

If the two photographs were taken at the same time, then she who sat there with a dozen plaits, looking like a starfish, was already in love. The charm of the young man had struck like a dart, the starfish was already bleeding. She saw by the child's age how fantastic it would have seemed, but the love-heart was of course without age. The young man with his old-fashioned look had been without knowing it her first lover. Now at fifty-three she knew too who had been her last. Turning on the bed, she could see her face in the glass. There was, she thought, no similarity now with the child. What had been a famous appearance was in itself such a step from the child sitting in boots and *broderie anglaise* on the sofa, and what she now saw in the glass was a step too from the "famous appearance." She could have kept more had she chosen, as Alberti said, to be less "careless." But the carelessness came from explosion of living, from vigour, laughter, disregard of self. The only similarity between her and the child was that that traveller had not yet reached sex and this other had gone beyond it. She could see age in her face now as plainly as a friend. She did not shrink (it was a page she had written herself) but thought, "What a stretch I have had of it!" Soon the witnesses would be gone, the old men who had seen her young, and to Miranda any record of all this life of her mother's would be a book one reads for an hour. "One's life's written for oneself," she thought. "I'm its only heroine"; and she looked at the beginning of it with an interest not dry, but not too tender. Children are young, but not so young as people think.

She could see the little creature clearly now as she ran and played —intoxicating worships swinging in her heart like hops in the wind, like lanterns of ecstacy—for after the golden lieutenant she had invented other loves. She told nobody, but had chosen among her parents' friends heroes on whom to hang her adoration—stimulating her heartbeats, a little drug-taker; so that, playing alone among the coffee bushes, that spangled, olive bush-sea that surrounded the house, and called in at last at sunset, she would come tipsy with secrecy, as though she had taken alcohol. She remembered these premature emotions as she looked at the picture. Then threw the slides to one end of the bed and saw it was already dawn. "Once one has written oneself into one's name one can't look back," she said to herself, "except as an amusement. Youth's not a serious memory. The past is consumed. I'm here, I'm unconsumed. I'm what has happened."

When her father died, her mother sailed for England with a girl of fifteen who was sick of playing at love. She had grown thin and tall, and her eyes were discontented. If her face hadn't made her vain as a child of nine, at fifteen she liked it even less. She was tired of her imaginings and had nothing else to set in their place. The death of her father had woken her up from her nonsense, and with a shock she saw her mother's unhappiness, and felt ignorant, useless, unreal, and ready for change.

They were to be met by her aunt, her mother's younger sister, at Southampton.

"We've never had any photograph of Aunt Ursula. I've never

seen her. What does she look like?" she asked her mother as they sat on the deck of the ship. But her mother was always absent-minded nowadays and when Ruby asked a second time she only said briefly:

"She has something wrong with her face."

Aunt Ursula sat waiting for them in the ladies' drawing room of the hotel at Southampton. She was slim, upright, most fashionably dressed, wearing a hat with knots of velvet, a double veil, gauzy and spotted, and a sweeping dress to the ground. The sisters moved together into one of the long windows overlooking the street. Ruby, going to the other window and drawing back the coarse lace curtain, saw heavy traffic for the first time.

Presently they sent for tea. "Now, *now*," thought Ruby, "she'll put up her veil." But Aunt Ursula ate no cake and drank no tea.

Soon they went to the train, and at the end of the journey Aunt Ursula's horses and carriage met them at Waterloo. She seemed rich. Ruby had never been told she was rich. Perhaps nobody had known.

The house was dignified. There was a guest-room in which Ruby and her mother slept together. The big bath towels had muslin covers to keep the London specks from them, and the hip bath was carried in and placed before the open fire by a man in livery. The brass cans he poured from stood two foot high and held four gallons. When he had gone Aunt Ursula's old maid warmed something pink and thick at the fire and slipped it over the high back of the hip bath that Ruby might not feel the chill.

"It's fiddly doing it yourself when you're tired," said the old woman, holding out a hand for Ruby's foot, and binding the whole leg in a warm towel from the fender when she had finished. All the plumbing in America was not worth that hip bath at fifteen.

"I was your aunt's nurse," she said when Ruby was in bed. "I brought her up. She's coming to say good night to you presently." And as Ruby said nothing she added, "She has an affliction, but you won't notice much. Best say nothing." And then—"I haven't told you my name. It's Mackintosh. But your aunt calls me Piffle. You're too old to call me Nannie, I suppose?"

"Too old, yes," said Aunt Ursula suddenly, coming in. "Girls must go forward, Piffle, not back." Piffle stood up. Aunt Ursula looked at Ruby, one hand on Piffle's arm. Then she said abruptly, "Good night. Sleep well. Your mother's coming up," turned, and taking Piffle with her left the room.

Downstairs at dinner Ruby's mother had said to her sister with awe:

"So you really make it pay? Is that how you have this house, this food, these servants?"

"I refuse half London," her sister had replied. "I'm very much the fashion. Are you going to let me do a little for Ruby? She needs pulling together. She's gawky. She's anaemic."

"Is it right to tamper? And isn't she too young?"

When the butler had handed his last dish and they drank weak tea by the candles ("coffee discolours the skin") Ursula said, "I'm going up to see her. I want to look at her again. She's a handsome child."

"Really, we haven't particularly thought so," said Fanny humbly.

Bit by bit the young niece learnt the aunt's story. Ursula Smith had been born a monster. Her left ear, reversed, was spread over one side of her face, and embedded in the skin. It was larger than usual and looked like a sea-shell in flesh, coiled into the skin itself. With it too she had had a hare-lip and distended eyeballs. The hare-lip had been worked on, but not successfully. The coiled ear remained in all its cruel intricacy, a crest, a signature of misery.

Ursula's mother died directly of this trouble after five years. When the baby had been brought to her and she had looked at it and understood how little could be done she could not sleep. She lay through the hours of the night staring into the child's future. Slowly she grew more and more certain that there would be no old age, that a day would come when Ursula would kill herself. Trying to tell her husband he became severe with her and forbade such thoughts. But she could not forbid them. She was certified when Ursula was four, and died when she was five.

The young Nannie Piffle guided the poor baby's life. The father could not bear the sight of her, living in his office hours and dining at his club. Piffle, Ursula and Fanny lived closely together, lonely and somewhat backward (with only Piffle's stimulus from the grown-up world), but not unhappy—until Ursula was eleven. On her eleventh birthday, with no warning signs of special distress, out of the blue, she did what her mother had expected. She was found hanging from a hook at the back of the door, knotted up in her Jaeger dressing-gown cord, unconscious, but not dead. The ear had swollen under the pressure till it stood out in blue whorls on her cheek. She was lifted down in time.

Her father was very angry. If he could have brought himself to be angry with the dead mother, that is where his anger would have gone. He thought the cause mysteriously direct. Matter-of-fact man though he was, severe and cold, there were some things he believed, and that heavy thoughts remain round stick and stone was one of them. He sold the house and they went to live in Wimbledon.

Fanny never knew about the attempt Ursula had made on her own life. Ursula herself remained mute, and seemed to forget it. She had made her bid and muffed it and she accepted now that her life was to go on.

When Ursula was twenty and Fanny twenty-three their father died and left them six thousand pounds each. Fanny, already engaged, got married to her soldier. Ursula, taking Piffle with her, went to New York. Afterwards to India, China, and Japan. Later Berlin. They spent five hundred pounds each year and stayed away from England four years. Ursula, in travelling, had tried to find a cure for herself. She had ideas about skin-grafting; but no skin-grafting was done as yet at that time. She learnt a great deal about diseases of the face and the skin, and more still about women's reactions to them. She studied circulation. She did not put aside faith cures. She learnt from an Indian woman a half-mesmeric art of assuming beauty, and as it was impossible to remove or obliterate her ear, it was this that helped her most.

The hare-lip was again operated on, this time in New York, and much more successfully. The eyes gave way to treatment, not altogether, but sufficiently. The ear was wrapped up, and skill and investigation into strange stuffs, resins and plasters and silks made adhesive to the skin, helped her appearance. Her hair was beautiful, and her figure beautiful as well. She was tall and slight and moved with grace, unhurried.

"What sort of job have I made of myself, Piffle?" she asked at last.

"You have *looks,* darling," said Piffle. "And brave as a lion too!"

"But I shall never be able to walk anywhere without being stared at."

"But, dear, you are accustomed to that."

She was accustomed to that. It was not the frank stare that salutes beauty, but a glance, averted, and followed by a glance that stole back. The better arranged the silken cheek the more the eyes made bold to return to this curiosity.

As satisfied as she would ever be with herself, and certain that there was no more to be done, she now turned her attention to an occupation. Of the six thousand pounds there was less than four left. She was twenty-four, nearly twenty-five. She decided to open a beauty clinic and sell dearly the knowledge she had picked up in her painful travels.

There was something so sane about her advice, so authoritative about her manner, so genuine her belief in what she said that after she had got her first client others were recommended to her. She fixed her prices very high, but that was no deterrent to the fashionable women who came to her and to whom she was a tyrant, dictating their food and their hours of sleep, and refusing to receive those who would not keep to her rules. Her clients sometimes asked her about her own face. "No," she would say, "my trouble does not come into it. It's too unusual. It would be a lesson to no one." Once or twice Piffle had even been offered money to tell the secret.

When Fanny brought Ruby back to England, Ursula was rich, sought after, difficult of access. Twenty years had gone by, and she was forty-four. Ursula and Fanny, who had not seen each other for so long, slipped somewhat into the old relationship—yet with such a difference. Fanny was gentle, pliant, innocent. Ursula was hard from her bitter difficulties. Of love she had had no first-hand experience. No one had dared to love her. When she climbed the thick, carpeted stairs that night of her sister's arrival to look again at her niece she had a curious hope in her heart. This child of her own blood had to her knowledgeable eye the probability of beauty, like gold in the mine, pearls in the oyster, one of the desires of the world. She visualised, as she returned again down the staircase, the line of the cheekbone on the pillow in the room she had left. Even at fifteen the cheek had a droop of bone from ear to chin most classic at the turn of the jaw. As the face had moved round on the pillow, and turned away for a moment to watch the small yellow beam from a carriage pass over the blind, Ursula had seen what was lovely in Greuze, what in French is called the lost profile, the vase-shape of cheekbones which never change in age, and which support between their steady branches the sparkle and movement of the features. Standing still in thought at the turn of the staircase on the floor that led to her warm library, she said to herself—"What can I do for her?" But she knew she had Fanny to deal with. Fanny wanted for her only child a kind and happy future. But Ursula thought she could offer the owner of such a face a more remarkable life.

She moved into the library in the dark and passing over to the window pulled up the blind, and watched the lamplight gleaming on the horses' flanks in Birdcage Walk beyond her little garden. Tonight there was a party at Buckingham Palace. Her girls had worked hard all that day at the Clinic. She knew who would look well, what they would wear. Even from her dark window she saw a glint of faces she had in part created. After the terrible years of distress she was ready to live vicariously. If the niece could burn in the world like a marsh-fire to men the monstrous ear would be a little avenged. She had not known she would feel this sense of relationship. She had less feeling, she found, for Fanny than for Ruby. But perhaps she had "feeling" for neither of them, but in Ruby pride. What power could she achieve over her niece? What response would she find? Fanny, with her obstinate simplicity, her standards set by the dead, might well stand in the way of everything. Watching the lights of the crawling carriages she reviewed the world of society that walked on her clinic's soft carpets and lay down on the couches, quiescent and obedient, under her hands. She knew many of them intimately, but as a professional knows his clients. Almost she knew them as their spiritual adviser, for she was hard with them, expected much of them, she was the priestess of their appearance. But for all that, the intimacy ended in her clinic. It did not follow them to their homes. Ruby, for them, could be only an object of interest, a "sport," a spectacular beauty. No one of importance would invite her to important occasions. So in her own mind she decided on the stage.

She returned to Fanny in the drawing-room below.

"Have you any idea for Ruby's future?"

"Her future? No, none as yet. She is still a child."

Ursula, looking for a moment at her sister, was silent. She turned to her accounts at her desk. Fanny sat on by the fire. She found Ursula changed, secret, elegant, alarming.

"Go up to bed when you like," said Ursula. "I have accounts to check. You must be tired."

"Do you do all your own book-work?"

"I have a staff. But I keep my eye on them." And turning to smile at her sister—"I fill them with awe."

As Fanny in her turn mounted the stairs she felt lost. Her whole life had been built, since she married, round one personality. Now that he had gone she felt like a spiral of wound circles soughing with an empty wind.

Ursula's designs for Ruby were made possible ten weeks later, for Fanny died of pneumonia at the beginning of her first winter in England. Luckily for her peace of mind she slipped almost immediately beyond the power to worry; or she might have worried, leaving Ruby to her sister.

## CHAPTER TWELVE

So then began the burnishing of Ursula's candidate for fortune. Ruby, desolate, shocked, did what she was told. She went to a London day school for a year, worked hard through London summers and London fogs, school, dancing-class, elocution, a tedious hair treatment in Garrick Street, hours at a dentist in St. John's Wood, Piffle always at her side, in obedience to Ursula's plans. Ursula was enjoying herself. At last she had something to spend her money on, besides the fine plain clothes she ordered for herself. As yet she dressed Ruby plainly too and without particular thought. When she had rubbed and scrubbed the girl and made her shine, then quite finally it might be time to dress her.

Piffle represented Ursula as having a high sense of duty, so high as to make it urgent that Ruby should do her best. "She's a fine, a wonderful lady," said Piffle. "You don't understand her." Ruby felt no love for Ursula, though she respected her and was a little afraid. One day she asked suddenly about the property in Jamaica.

"Is it mine?"

This took Ursula by surprise and she allowed that it was—yet sorry that Ruby should have asked. She did not want any hook for independence.

When Ruby was not yet seventeen Piffle came in a cab to her school in the middle of the morning with a request that she might go at once to her aunt in the Clinic.

Ruby said, "What's she up to, Piffle?" Piffle pursed her lips.

"Aunt's up to something," said Ruby. "I have a feeling this is the beginning of good-bye to school." And as Piffle only rolled her eyes: "How I hate never knowing anything!"

Ursula's groundwork was done. Ruby was passed through the gate into beauty. Her appearance was now so charming that her face turned away wrath. This the glass might have told her, but she was not vain, and also Ursula was boring her with the stress laid on looks. She only felt that people behaved rather better to her than she behaved herself. Her temper was sweet and her small flashes of impatience only brightened her eyes and quite unfairly diverted offence.

"What am I going to the Clinic for?"

"I'm saying nothing."

"You're never on my side! Aunt Ursula wants to be a sphinx."

Up in the receiving room at the bend of the wide, soft stairway stood Ursula, waiting. She smiled at Ruby, pushed her hair to the side in a way that Ruby hated, and drew her after her into a small room where, on a sofa raised on a wooden platform, lay a muffled figure, her face covered with a gauze mask.

"Here she is," said Ursula.

"Well, little girl, well?" said a rich, soft voice. Ruby looked in front of her.

"So you want to go on the stage?"

"On the stage?" said Ruby, startled. "Is that what I'm to do?"

"That's what your aunt thinks."

Ruby, by her father's standards, had understood the stage to be a jungle where eyes of phosphorus glittered, legs hung from branches and a zebra of evil flashed in sun and shade. But she was ready to think she had misunderstood her father.

The hidden face was tilted back, covered with its wet gauze. The ringless hands were quietly folded and the rings glittered in a saucer on the side table. A lawn wrapper hid everything but slender shoes. Ruby could not easily discuss her future with this image. She turned to her aunt.

"If you want me to go on the stage," she said, "I'll do what I can."

"It isn't your own wish then?" persisted the rich voice.

"I've never thought about it," said Ruby. "Has one not to have a gift?"

"You have to work hard," said the voice, "as with everything else." And then, to Ursula, "And has she any talent?"

"Not that I know of," said Ursula smiling, as if to say, "Isn't that appearance enough to begin with?"

That her aunt and the stranger had already settled most things Ruby was sure, for the interview was so short. It had needed perhaps her assent. Aunt Ursula was cold but not oppressive and Ruby had no fear of being coerced.

. That evening after dinner Ursula turned round in her chair from her accounts and laying her arm on the chair back looked at Ruby, and Ruby too looked up at the movement.

"Are you fond of me, Ruby?" asked Aunt Ursula.

"No," stammered Ruby.

Both their eyes filled with tears at the shock. Ursula, smarting with pain, got up and sat by the lamp at the table, keeping her silk-covered cheek turned away. After a few minutes she said in a strained voice:

"I had taken it for granted. I hadn't thought enough about it!"

Ruby said nothing. Ursula had more to say but she waited till her voice was steady. "We have never spoken about my face," she went on. "I told Piffle to tell you I had a birthmark. Worse than a birthmark. There's no need to describe it. I was kept hidden as a child—Piffle always with me, Piffle knows everything. When I was much younger than you are I tried to hang myself." Ruby was staring, spellbound. "For years I travelled, and tried to cure myself. I couldn't entirely, but I learnt to make myself presentable. I'm hard. That's why I'm telling you this. I hadn't thought about it before you came—there was no one to be hurt by what I'd become—but when you tell me like that, out of your heart, 'No,' you are not fond of me, I feel, sweet-natured as you are, that you have a right to say it and that I've been a tyrant."

And now she stared at Ruby, for she saw that the tears ran in an odd way down the girl's still face. Tears moved down each cheek; others rose to the unblinking eyes, hung to the lashes and fell. Ursula had never seen a face which when it wept had no contractions.

"When I saw you, and saw that your appearance was everything that mine never could be, and that for want of my skill you might not be perfect, I wanted to do all I could for you. I wanted flesh of my own to enjoy life through beauty so that I myself could see it happen. You must remember that a face is," she faltered, "all that one can see—of the soul."

She put out her hand across the corner of the table and took the stuff of Ruby's sleeve in her fingers, kneading it, pinching it nervously. Not looking at her she said to her niece: "I'm ready, if you're not happy, to alter things. What would you like best then? What do you think you would like best?" And faintly she said a third time: "What would you like best?" She thought Ruby would say, "To leave you. To have some other way of living. To go somewhere else. To have a different life."

Ruby said, choking, "I should like a dog."

Ursula rose and went quickly out of the room. She could not afford to cry before another human being. The desolation and simplicity of Ruby's answer was not lost on her. She knew she had not acted as though she had charge of a child. Ruby sat on, staring at the table, wondering about the dog, and whether she should or should not have asked for it. The terrible things that Aunt Ursula had said so quickly in a handful of sentences passed by her. The Ursula whom she knew was powerful and successful. If there had been a child once, so different, Ruby had not known her. The child had passed away and everything except the living present was unreal to her.

Three weeks later they went to buy the dog. It had taken a little time to track down addresses. Ursula too had grown interested in the search. She remembered the dog they had had at Wimbledon when she and Fanny were children, and wondered she had never had a dog in her life since then.

Finally they drove out into the suburbs together on a day of winter sunshine, and stopped at a small house on a drive of gravel chips.

The lady of the house was a smart manly creature who called upstairs in a weather-beaten voice, "Are you about?"

"Yes, Mother."

"Bring those puppies down, will you." There was scuffling on the top landing and down the mean varnished stairs came a pale young man with an untrimmed blond moustache, carrying a heavy bull-mastiff puppy under each arm.

"Set them down carefully now," said the lady. "Mind their bones. It's my son Edmund. Fifteen. Looks older, doesn't he? It's that moustache." Edmund's pale face became scarlet. When he had set the two puppies gently on the floor he turned away and stood looking through the glass doorway into the back garden.

They chose the puppy, a dog puppy. Ursula paid for it in sovereigns and said to Edmund, "May I give this extra one to you? For looking after him."

"The boy doesn't need money," said his mother. "What he does for the dogs earns his keep."

"Ah, but it's my present," said Ursula in her highest manner.

They left the cold house with the shining puppy. At first Ruby could not speak. Then she touched Ursula's arm. "Thank you," she said softly.

"That was no boy!" said Ursula, pleased and embarrassed. "What was her idea—to pretend that he was fifteen?"

"She'll take your pound from him," said Ruby.

They called the puppy Duke. They tried it with Jonathan. They renamed it Hector. It was as difficult as naming a novel. Every morning Ruby lay in bed inventing names and trying them against their growing knowledge of its nature. Until it had a name the puppy's personality would not crystallise. Piffle made circles with a pencil and dropped her hand on pages of her Bible but only lighted on adjectives. At last out of fatigue they called him Tom. But he was too noble for Tom, and Duke he became again for his life.

He was full of ponderous jokes and heavy disobedience. His skin was so loose he seemed to walk forward inside it. Though built heroically he had humour. He liked to be told not to lie by the fire, so that he might move away, steal round in a circle and return again to the forbidden spot. Then in his melancholy face his eye was gay and he would repeat his joke again and again, the only joke he knew.

By so slight an incident as the buying of a mastiff puppy they were brought into the publicity of the trial of Edmund Hobble. Ruby became for one short afternoon witness for the prosecution, though she imagined it was for the defence.

The little maid in the villa behind the pantry door had heard Ursula insist that Edmund should have the sovereign. And as it was for the sovereign that he that night killed his mother with a chair it was only a few days later that a detective-sergeant called on Ursula and Ruby. As yet they had not read about the murder in the papers.

"I shall say, if they want me to, how badly she treated him!" exclaimed Ruby. Ursula looked at her. No good checking her: it was said now. That would have to be Ruby's contribution.

So long ago, now, that old murder, but remarkable in its day for being Ruby's own. Gynt had often said at a dinner party: "You know—when Ruby was implicated in a murder . . ." But the point, of course, was Beddoes Thomas and that Gynt had not known.

Given time, everything falls back into its place. Death, murder, lunacy (Edmund Hobble who turned out to be twenty was shut up for life) by constant telling lose their life-colours. Even seduction in the end need not exist. The past can be a sad story or a joke—the way you tell it.

Beddoes Thomas, prosecuting for the Crown, naturally noticed the girl witness, since he put her in the box to provide the motive. When the case was a few days over he asked Ursula and Ruby to luncheon, and very soon afterwards managed an invitation to Ruby alone and she found a way of accepting. Aunt Ursula never lunched at home. Piffle did not question some murmured explanation.

When they were seated opposite to one another at a small table Beddoes suddenly threw up his massive head, frowning. Ruby for a moment wondered what she had done wrong. With his head still tilted he looked at her down his cheek with his red-brown eyes. It was his big sex-look. Then lowering the angle of his face he faced her smiling and gave her back her confidence. (Nothing ever more misplaced.) When at the operational "third movement" he suddenly held across to her a strong white hand with a plain ring on it Ruby felt the old lift of Jamaican love. He on his side could hardly believe what he had found. When he heard further that she was just going on the stage it seemed handed to him on a golden tray. The lunch was followed by other luncheons, and not in public. It was a very private episode and when at the age of fifty-three you look back on such a thing it may or may not have happened. It is then of no account.

Beddoes Thomas was a first-rate lawyer, as clever as they are made, though perhaps without the best intelligence. Coming next after his work was his self-indulgence. But he loved his work and was on the highway to wealth and position. He was a man with kind movements of the heart, which were not allowed to cost him more than he could pay. In talk he easily passed into emotion and quoted Shakespeare. His voice, which was low and rich, his red-brown eyes, which could burn or grow chilly, his facial angles, which could give him the look of a bishop or a fox, were his armoury. Starting life with nothing he had found it as easy to cut as a cake. He was specially fitted to cut it. He had nothing too high in his make-up that undid or incommoded him.

Speaking of the pale Edmund who had at last gone out of the court, not to hang, but to a long routine, Beddoes said, at a later luncheon:

"I ought to have had his life. I've done badly." (The stage was to be a kindergarten after a few luncheons with Beddoes.) Ruby was decently older by the second luncheon, for she had had her seventeenth birthday. He was thirty-nine. He never made her love him, but she had her first sense of power, it was the first time she was even momentarily a miracle to someone else. He hoped, with his experience, that he had not let her see this, but she knew it. Himself a self-seeking but straight-looking man he set her right about many things, and while he treated her as a woman he talked to her as though she were a man. And stammeringly at first but firm, it was a man that answered back. She would ask him questions.

"What do people want most?"

"Not money," he said. "That's a great mistake. Money often comes as a surprise. Is thrown in too. They want to be important. It's the need above needs. It's the load on the ego perhaps of there being so many living creatures. It becomes unbearable. One wants to strike out. And often it's by crime. That's the terror and horror too of prison. That one's at once practically anonymous."

"And Edmund? Will he feel that where he's going?"

"Ah, there we're off the track. He's not normal. But all the same I think he killed his mother not for the pound, not in revenge for oppression, but to show that she had to mind him, that he was somebody. You aren't brooding on him, are you?"

"I? No." She was surprised.

"I don't think you'll make an actress," he said.

"Poor Aunt Ursula."

"How calm you are!" he said. "How sure of yourself. Why?"

She looked at him, surprised. She had never really as yet examined her own identity.

"I don't think about it," she answered. "What's the use? I don't govern my own life."

"But you will, I think. I should like to meet you in the middle of it."

"In the middle of my life?"

"Yes," he said slowly. "I can't see your not doing well for yourself. Or I'll put it differently. I can't see life not doing well by you. I think it will. We'll meet, a little later on. Shall we? And compare."

"Do let's," she said absently, as though she were thinking of something else (where another woman would have cried out, "But don't let's *part!*").

"She's not mad about me," he thought, and seeing how young she was he pretended to relief, but all the same he was astonished. He knew his powers with women and felt pique.

## CHAPTER THIRTEEN

Ursula started with terror, waking in bed one night, dreaming she had been visited by her sister, Fanny.

She had dreamed that Fanny stood by her bed and told her that Ruby had been seduced. The shock, the words used by Fanny, the solidarity of the dream woke her violently. She struck a match and lit her candle, wanting, as she leaned over it, to take instant action, run to the child's room, wake her, and ask for the truth. But as she sat up in bed limp still with sleep the quiet house-life of the candle told her to be still. She remembered how meagrely she knew men, warned herself that even by a child's questions in reply she could be floored. She waited until the strength of the dream grew less, but her heart beat with distress at the close, living look on Fanny's face. She, Ursula, now loved Ruby; but all the experience she had got from living was useless to her. She needed a special wisdom she knew she had not got.

Though it was two in the morning she thought nothing of ringing for Piffle, pressed and pressed the bell till the door opened and the old woman arrived, pale and shivering from her sleep.

"Light the gas fire. I've had a dream."

Piffle could not find the matches on the mantelpiece, groping among the ornaments: Ursula held out the box from her bedside.

"Sit down. Here by my bed. Do you see any change in Ruby?"

"Change in Ruby?"

"Don't repeat what I say. I'm upset. Is she seeing too much of that man?"

"That laywer? Mr. Thomas?"

"So you think so too! Do you think so? Why didn't you say so?"

Piffle's faded eyes became more acute. "I don't think so, Miss Ursula. But you've got to be careful with young girls that have no mother."

"I'm her mother. I'm her mother."

"No, no, no, dear. No."

"What are you saying? You are hurting me."

"There's no one to tell you but me. That loves and knows you. You're clever——"

"Don't wander, Piffle."

"I'm trying to say," said the old nurse soberly, "that you can't know, can you, about the ways of men."

"I didn't take the child. She was forced upon me. I didn't cause Fanny to die. She died. I can only do what I can. Who else is there? I dreamt Fanny stood there . . . there . . . by your chair . . . by your knee" (but the old woman kept her eye steady and would not look down) "and told me . . . that man . . . did her a wrong . . ."

"What are you saying!"

"That he took her in his arms . . ."

"NO. That little girl upstairs asleep now in her bed? Never! Never, Miss Ursula!"

"Piffle, Piffle . . ." sobbed Ursula, slipping down in her bed, and pushing her head on the pillow towards her nurse.

"You love her then?" Piffle put her small horny hands round the head, not afraid of either cheek.

"Yes. I love her. I want to do good to her."

"You shall do good to her. She'll come to no harm. You've been eating things. What did they give you for dinner? I can't remember."

Once again the old woman loosened the constricted heart, fondled the cold arm, warmed the milk that was kept in the painted safe in the bathroom, offered it in the rose-painted cup and saucer, sat by her afflicted child: and at last herself went up the small wooden stair the other side of the baize door on the landing to her own cold room, upset, tired, next day to be fretful.

"Miss Ursula wasn't well last night. What did you give her for dinner?" she asked the cook as she took her cup of tea mid-morning.

"It's the flaky pastry," said the cook shortly. "She likes it rolled out with half a pound of butter."

"Don't give it to her," said Piffle, sitting at the wooden table. "I'm worn out."

"What happened?"

"A lot of nonsense. It's her digestion. A lot of dreams. I've always made allowances. She's been my work. God calls all of us to do something."

"Draw your chair round to the oven, Miss Mackintosh. I'll open the door."

She threw open the iron door of the oven and the heat blazed round Piffle's knees and made rosy her pinched face. Soon she put out an elastic boot and gently pushed the door half-to.

"Miss Ursula lives like a man," said the cook. "She's easy to work for but not easy to say no to."

"Is she easy to work for?"

"She's strict. But she gives praise and she's never late. She runs an orderly household."

"Except when she rings for me in the middle of the night," grumbled Piffle.

"You like it," said the cook. "You're the mothering sort, though not married."

"I don't know anything of men," said Piffle. "But we'll have to learn, me and Miss Ursula, if we're to bring up Miss Ruby."

"Experience," said the cook, "is not as much use as sense. Miss Ruby'll be a plum for the men. Those that are plums for the men there's no keeping them out of hungry mouths." She bent down, put a casserole dish on the middle shelf of the oven, and shut the door. Piffle took the hint and carried her cup and saucer to the sink.

"You can leave it," said the cook. "I'll do it with the dinner things later."

"How such wicked visions can come to her!" said Piffle under her breath as the kitchen door closed behind her and she felt for the further door to mount the stairs, ". . . wicked, that is, if I didn't know her, and the life she's had."

Fatigue and dread had filled Piffle's mind all the morning, turning over and over Ursula's charge against Ruby's innocence, transmitted, if you please, from a ghost. She climbed the circular, uncarpeted stairs and paused for breath in the light of a webbed and dusty window. "I can only pray, then, she's not going back to her depressions." She remembered only too clearly the horrors of that nursery, when the little monster, playing with her toys, would drop them to stare stonily at Piffle, saying, "You wish I was dead. I can see it in your face." How the child had shed all that, had climbed to tolerable looks and sanity, Piffle hardly understood.

Sometimes, looking back, she could barely believe the travels were real, India, China, Japan, New York, Berlin, and home—that long search for a cure and the achievement of a compromise that had its private glory.

"But if she's going to see ghosts," said Piffle, disheartened, "then I'd sooner die and rest from it and be done with it. I'm too tired, I'm too old, ever to hold her up again: that is—if it was ever I who held her."

Never for a moment did she doubt Ruby. She would have cut off her sewing finger before she doubted Ruby. That night, however, when she saw them together, so much as usual, Ursula strong and calm, Ruby light-hearted, then she was glad to wind up the memory like a ball of wool. The ghost, knowing better, had not known how to convince.

The meetings ceased, the affair, which had hardly begun, lapsed, for Beddoes Thomas was called very suddenly by a rich client to New York and stayed six months away—which gave him time to remember the danger, to a rising man, of a connection with a girl so young. Ruby, whose life absorbed her, and who had a private and natural assessment of values (later to be called her "divine common sense"), came to the conclusion that the single act of brigandage which has been held for centuries to be a currency debasement did not matter very much.

## CHAPTER FOURTEEN

When Beddoes had gone to New York the young Ruby became more interested in her work and her life than in his memory. She had such a lucky shape of head and arrangement of features that she broached the world around her quite beyond competition and did not know what it was to want to be liked and to fail. She pleased as she spoke. There is no doubt that grief and failure are bad for the young. She was really no actress, but her days were warmed by pleasant encounters. She liked people as much as they instantly liked her, whether it was the old stage doorkeeper or the young woman behind the haberdashery counter at William Whiteley's.

Gynt saw her with her aunt as he was passing Gunter's in Berkeley Square. She was standing in the open doorway looking out across the pavement. When her aunt joined her and they crossed the street he tracked her home. He had never done such a thing in his life before. He was then twenty-nine. As he walked he saw her talk and smile. It was quite a long walk, for they were to meet Piffle and Duke in St. James's Park, and Gynt had half an hour as he wandered discreetly near them to be astonished at what can suddenly and violently happen to a spoilt and fortunate young man. When Ursula took her latch-key out of her bag at the front door of the house in Old Queen Street he walked rapidly back through the park. His mother, with whom, as his father had been dead ten years, he was on very close terms, was in the hall of the house in Charles Street as he let himself in.

"Gynt!" she said, pleased. "And lunch-time." He put his arm round her waist and moved her gently towards the little room at the side of the front door.

"What's the matter?" His face was serious as he closed the door behind them.

"Darling," he said. "Where's the street directory? Or do you by any chance know who lives at this address? I've fallen in love. Yes,

I mean it. Is it possible to see a girl in the street and feel you could love her for ever?"

"It's possible. I shouldn't have thought it was wise."

"I followed her home."

"Did you speak to her?"

"No, no. They were in the park with a golden bull mastiff. They walked, finally, to Old Queen Street."

"Then I know quite well who it is."

"You know!"

"I know the aunt, an awfully strange woman. She has a sort of beauty-parlour, but a serious place, very exclusive, very special. She makes a fortune. I've been there."

"But the girl? That girl?"

"It's her niece. I knew she had a niece whom she's wrapped up in. I've never seen her. She's on the stage."

Gynt's mother, half-French, worldly, observant, usually had some inkling when her son was in love. Sometimes she made a smiling half-allusion, but only when she was sure the affair was over. Their relationship was warm with affection but full of tact. He was aware that his own nature was oversecretive, and as far as he could he tried to remedy this towards her. But this time he had nothing to overcome, he came straight to her as though what he felt was a serious illness, and should be told at once. There was not room even for pleasantry. And she too found herself thinking immediately, though the girl of whom he was speaking had only just been met and in the street, "After all, he's twenty-nine. It must happen some day. But then is this in the least suitable? It can't be. No, it can't be." But her ears heard again the advice her husband used to give her, "Never get into opposition—try never to be in opposition before you must."

"Where is she acting?" Gynt was asking.

"I don't know, Gynt."

"But I don't want to meet her that way. If you know her aunt couldn't she be asked here? Couldn't they both be asked? Would it come naturally?"

"Have you thought that they aren't the people one asks to dine? And the aunt would never come, I feel sure." But the dark Celtic face of her son, that elegant and mystical face—with the curious cast in one eye that was so slight that it was an attraction, an enigma—showed no sign of either resenting or parrying her objections. It was the face of a man for whom she must do what he required.

Possibly if Gynt had first seen her on the stage Ruby's future would have been different. She was not incompetent, and her very small speaking part could not give much indication, but all that was original in Ruby, a sort of inspired common sense that she had towards life, was opposed to the art of interpretation. Or at all events within the limits she was given. As she spoke the few sentences allotted to her she knew she would have put the matter differently; she found it hard to believe in the type she was asked to reproduce. She was with a small company in a suburban theatre. Lady Maclean herself went to see her in the play, and wrote a note and sent it round to the back. "I know your aunt. Will you ask her from me if you may come to tea one day next week? I shall write separately, however, to her." Ursula made a curious move in replying to this advance. She wrote courteously refusing, having spent some time tapping her cheek with her pen, attempting to arrive at a pretext that would convince and not offend. She knew of Gynt's existence: she thought him too good a *parti* to be an honest one: she felt things must not move too fast with this flower that had unfolded in her home. She did not want Ruby admired or bespoke too soon. She did not yet know what her worth might win for her. There was at the moment no return of the anxiety she had felt over Beddoes Thomas. Ruby was engrossed in her work, and either Ursula or Piffle were for ever at her side when she was out of the theatre. Ruby, for the time being, liked the life that surrounded her, the corporate life, the friends she made, the jokes, the odd hours. She was not satisfied with her own performance but supposed that in time she would get better.

"She isn't coming, Gynt," said Lady Maclean, showing him Ursula's letter. He read it indifferently and dropped it on his mother's desk. He did things like a man with a fixed idea, without knowing they were unusual.

He went next day and called at the house in Old Queen Street, and without seeing Ruby again he asked Ursula if he might ask her to marry him.

"In the street? Last week?" said Ursula, a frown on her cold face. "You mean that? That you've only seen my niece once? Never spoken to her?"

Ursula's robot and dignified appearance puzzled him. She stood up and he was face to face with her look of wooden power, her sinister stillness and her veils. She had, he thought, a quite unclassable appearance. But nothing changed his determination.

Lady Maclean was moving home again to Scotland next day. No such "move" as hers could ever be changed or delayed. The housekeeper in Scotland was already walking round the hothouses with the head gardener; vases were standing in rows filled with soda and warm water; the white drill dust-covers for the London furniture lay in neat piles in Charles Street, chandelier bag-covers beside them. There was no question now of any invitation for Ruby less than an invitation to Scotland. This was made then and there—and seconded that night in a letter from Lady Maclean.

It so happened that the piece in which Ruby played her tiny part was coming to a close. Ursula thought over it all long into the night. Her own part would be finished—if anything came of this. The Svengali role she had enormously enjoyed would have lasted a very short time. She could retire on the money she had made from the Clinic, but she banished that thought at once. Was she, after all, to strip her life of interest? She cared for the Clinic. She would return to it more strongly, more devotedly than ever. On the whole Ruby had better go to Scotland, had better have this chance, though it came too early. She knew already that the stage had been a mistake, and without the stage she herself could offer no special platform.

Meanwhile Ruby knew nothing at all of Gynt's intentions, not even of his existence. Having received Lady Maclean's first letter she had replied to it, without interest, according to Ursula's direction. The second letter, inviting her to Scotland, did not come until after Ursula herself had been in communication with Lady Maclean and had made up her mind. "Look," said Ruby at breakfast, "this letter signed Marie Maclean again! It's extraordinary. She actually asks me to go to Scotland to stay with her."

Then Ursula had ready her adjusted story, a few sentences that made it natural that the invitation should be made, and might even be accepted. She ended—"It may be a house party. Or it may be quiet. But you must have some clothes."

Ursula, who usually never did anything unreasonable, who frowned on emphasis and extravagance of taste, ordered for Ruby two unfortunate and unsuitable evening dresses, each costing twenty-five pounds, a high sum at that time.

On the first night of Ruby's arrival at Gynt's home she wore a dress of green velvet, with a gold chain lent by her aunt, a dress more for Hamlet's mother than for Ophelia. On the second night the choice was worse. The dress was of black lace with white ostrich feathers curled round the bodice. Neither dress made the slightest difference to Ruby's confidence nor to Gynt's excessive admiration. Lady Maclean thought the aunt had made a fool of herself but did not visit the error on the niece. There were no guests but Ruby.

On the third night, as Ruby found it cold and had no evening wrap, Lady Maclean lent her a black dressing gown made of fine wool which closed round her like a glove over the bust and from the waist hung in fine pleats to the ground. Augustus John was drawing such skirts at that time on his Irish peasants. Gynt had not spoken to his mother about Ruby until the night of the black dressing gown. Then, about eleven, he went to her bedroom when Ruby had gone to bed. Lady Maclean was sitting at her dressing table. Gynt came in and stood beside her. She looked up at him.

"There's no question," he said, and drew up a small stool behind him, sitting down to be on a level with his mother's eyes, "is there? I must have her for life. I must have her for always. I want to ask her tomorrow."

"Are you sure?"

"Aren't you?"

"She's lovely," his mother said in a small voice. "Exceptional.— So very lovely."

"And good. And kind. And intelligent," insisted Gynt. "Doesn't she show the qualities you like?"

"I'm in a whirl," said Lady Maclean in her little sidelong manner.

"You don't look it."

"No, but think. You shouldn't ask me. Am I likely to give you a good answer? She's to be my successor, and meanwhile she's to stand between me and you, explaining each to the other when you're married. She's to be the one—this strange new girl whom I've just met—whom I must try to know as well as I know you—or the thing's lopsided. Don't ask me. I know you want to ask me. But do it, Gynt, if it's right."

"But with her," he urged, "you've only to look at her, she'd adore you, you'd love her."

"Yes, there speaks love. But I'm not in love, I can't share that confidence."

"Have you anything you want to say? I'll listen and think it well over. Oh, I promise I'll well consider what you say. Say it, darling."

"No. But if only there could be more time. Is that possible?"

He stood up by her and drew her head in against his hip with one hand, then bent and kissed her hair.

"It's not possible," he said. "I can't wait. I think of nothing else. I must know."

She looked up at him. "If I show a little jealousy," she said, picking up a diamond ring of her own from the table, "don't notice it."

"Jealousy!"

"Let it pass. In fact forgive it. I didn't even know I should feel it. You've allowed me to be so much to you and for the moment I feel the best part of being your mother is over. It all depends on her, and in a girl as beautiful and young I feel it's a lot for her to understand. But I should feel that in any case, with anyone. If she says

'yes' give her this. You can buy her another ring yourself afterwards, but give her this from me so she'll feel welcomed."

He took it slowly, looking at her. "But you'll get over it?" he said
anxiously.

"Yes," she said. "If I didn't tell you everything, I shouldn't have
told you this. I'm not jealous of her youth and beauty, you understand. Only jealous of being deposed with you."

So Gynt proposed to the young Ruby and was gaily accepted,
and they were married with pomp and splendour. The then Dowa-
ger Lady Maclean gave them the Château of Little Pouilly as a
wedding present, and there they went to spend their honeymoon.
They had been engaged three weeks and the torrent of events had
been so brisk that they could only strike out and swim. There had
been little time to feel. Ursula did not come to Scotland, although
she had been invited. Gynt was thankful, for she gave him a feeling
of horror. Ruby, after the visit, came back to London to her aunt,
and Lady Maclean also came back to Charles Street. Ruby was
driven visiting by the latter and to fittings by the former. Her future
mother-in-law was nervous (after the two evening dresses) as to
Ursula's taste. But the two dresses had been a single instance of
want of balance, a sop to Ursula's frustrated dreams. When she
settled down to the trousseau her choice was impeccable. Piffle
sewed underclothes all day and half the night, with a right hand
that shook a little until the needle met the silk.

"What shall I give her as a wedding present?" thought Ursula.
She smiled slightly as she felt she had given Ruby her flawless skin
and some of her self-confidence, but those were presents never mentioned. In Ruby's settlements was the estate in Jamaica. Lady Maclean found that a welcome surprise.

"What shall I give her, Piffle?" asked Ursula.

"You should give her Duke."

Ursula looked at the dog, who raised his head and looked at her.
He was full-grown now, beige in colour, with dark-ringed golden
eyes. He had not yet lost his fun, his mock-complaints, his simu-
lated disobediences.

"The dog is hers already," said Ursula. "Think again."

She spoke lightly, but was startled to think she might lose Duke as well as Ruby.

"She'll be lonely, Miss Ursula, with a strange man," insisted Piffle. "It's better she has the dog."

Ursula put out her hand and held the stiff white cuff and stopped its sewing.

"Would you like to come travelling with me again, Piffle?" Ursula asked, shelving the question of Duke. "After Ruby's married. Would you like to come?"

Piffle's glasses slipped a little down her nose and she looked over the top. "It was tiring, Miss Ursula. But it was a change. Only I don't want to take a chance and die away from England."

"Why not, Piffle? What's England to you?"

Piffle wiped her eyes. It had only been an idea. So they resolved there and then to go travelling, if only across the ocean to New York.

"I won't give her Duke," said Ursula. They both looked more cheerful. "I want Duke. We must keep something."

"What'll he do?"

"The maids will look after him. He'll be all right here. We shan't be more than six weeks. No, I won't give Duke. It's enough I give away Ruby, isn't it?"

"Then a jewel should she have? In her great position?"

"I think I will give her," said Ursula, her eyes fixed and thoughtful, "a Russian sable coat."

Piffle agreed, unimpressed. She had no idea what Russian sables would cost.

So it came about that all her life Ruby had Russian sables. For thirty years the soft furs, the furs of an empress, marked her as a woman treasured and apart.

Lady Maclean gasped when she saw what the cold aunt gave her niece. Directly the wedding was over Ursula and Piffle packed and the new car took them to Waterloo.

Duke was left in the care of the housemaid and the cook. He found them dull and spent a lot of time in the hall by the front door sitting in the hooded chair of black leather, the sentry-box of former footmen.

## CHAPTER FIFTEEN

Everything went well. The marriage was an unmarred enchantment. During the honeymoon at Pouilly the bride was admired by the French relations, and on the return to London, with a gayer world to live in, Ruby's aptitude for friendship and specialty for intimacy sprang into being. The mother-in-law found none of the difficulties she expected, and felt instead that this amused and amusing Ruby who became now the fashion was her own invention. The new-married social life began to blaze on levels of which Aunt Ursula knew the value.

So much so that after three months, when it was found that Ruby was to have a baby, Gynt thought it quieter for her to go back to Pouilly. Just as they were about to return again to London for the confinement the baby was born prematurely, lived one day, and died.

Ruby had the cot put beside her bed in the late afternoon and lay alone by it. She was still in the grip of that strange excitement that comes after a confinement and could not completely believe at first that she was going on into life while her little partner was fixed for all time at twelve hours old.

But she knew she wanted thoroughly to see the baby before it was taken away for ever. Gynt and she had called it Percival.

The French chambermaid came in with a taper to light the special candles in the wall sconces and the baby's face glittered as though it were alive. Ruby leaned over it and stared. Her life was too successful, his too monstrously empty! Her son was deprived of everything, he was lower than a beggar. He could not go on into eternity and say he remembered anything. Could he then exist? At that moment she looked up from staring at his face and saw her own. The cloudless, sea-blue gaze that looked back at her seemed calmly unrelated to her grief. It sickened her that she could look like that over the body of her baby.

Gynt came into the room.

"Don't, Ruby!" he exclaimed when he saw the cot. "Don't let him stay here. What's the good?" He looked at her. He could only see that in her shock and sorrow she looked more beautiful. She understood that her grief was an experience that he did not want to share.

They got over the death of Percival. Life piled its glitter on his grave. But from that day Ruby parted company from the face she tended in the glass. Behind it lived another woman, much more important to her. As she powdered her face in the evening or brushed its shining hair she was less astonished than at odd moments when she caught sight of it by chance in some wall mirror at the turn of a stair. Its expression then was such a surprise to her that her friends would note that she had broken off in the middle of a sentence to stare at herself. This gave her a reputation for vanity. Alberti, once seeing her thus halted on the way into dinner, said:

"What are you looking at?"

"What is supposed to be myself," she said. It took her a lifetime to make her face in the smallest degree her own.

Gynt fought in the war of 1914 and his young wife stayed in Scotland with her mother-in-law, bringing up a later baby, a little daughter with a cap of Gynt's dark hair—Miranda. Ruby saw her aunt when she went occasionally to London, and she wrote to her at first once a fortnight, and later less often. There might have been more to say had not Ursula's letters been so cold. Ursula, living now solely for her Clinic, did not want to speak of that in her letters, and beyond a mention of Piffle and Duke there seemed little else to say. She had vicariously enjoyed Ruby's beauty, and the success of her marriage; but she could not vicariously enjoy the married life. To that she had no key.

When Miranda was four Ruby suggested that she should stay

with Ursula for two nights, leaving the child with her grandmother. Her aunt was a little on her mind and on her conscience. When she arrived in Old Queen Street she found that a curious situation had grown up. Duke had taken her place.

Both Piffle's hands were palsied, and one of her feet shook also unless she crossed her knees. As she could do very little she now talked a great deal. It was her only amusement. She sat for hours in the drawing room with Ursula talking to Ursula's back while the latter did her accounts. Her talk was almost entirely of Duke, what he had done, eaten, and what she thought he had thought. To Ruby's surprise Ursula was not bored by this. It was their home life.

It would have amused Ruby too, except that Duke had changed so much for the worse. He had lost his humour and grown stout and pretentious. He caused the maximum of trouble, always wanting to have doors opened for him for no reason, and immediately wishing to return the way he had come. He was greedy to a point. He began to muse on his meal an hour before the meal was to take place, and long ropes of saliva would steal out and hang from his jaws.

"Look," shivered Piffle, "he knows it's twelve-thirty. Isn't he clever! He knows it will soon be one."

The young married Ruby had a sense of death-in-life from the house. She had broken into a home-life that was not meant to be opened again to her.

"Aunt Ursie," she said on the second night, their only night alone together, for on the first night Piffle would not go to bed in time for them to talk, "tell me about Mother." Ursula seemed taken aback. She did not at all want to talk about the past. Presently she said, "What is there to tell? She was a happy woman. She had a good life: she had all she wanted. Until she grew up I was her only sorrow. After she married and went away she had no sorrow."

"She lost my father."

"She'd *had* him."

Ursula now could see life only through her personal spectacles. Her mind, instead of expanding, had narrowed into a small focus. She, who had had such qualities, such courage, such tenacity, no longer looked towards change, achievement or success. There was a breakdown too in her former scrupulous elegance.

"How do you get on with your mother-in-law?" she asked. "People say it's so difficult."

"Come up and see," said Ruby. "Do come up and see. We ask you, you know!"

"I can't leave my work," said Ursula, aggravated. "And Piffle is so old."

"Bring her too. Of course."

"And there is Duke. Besides, to tell you the truth, Ruby, I don't want to see other people's lives. I know well enough there's a great deal that goes on elsewhere that I might want if I saw it. You might think that my own concerns here aren't very satisfactory, but then they never were. But they run well, they interlock. I mean here in the house. It's a small life but I've got accustomed to it, and Piffle and I are contented in our way. Besides, like a man, I like peace at night. My day's so full of adventure."

"Is it? Tell me."

"If I were a priest," said Ursula, "I couldn't listen to more extraordinary secrets. I know the strange, private lives of women, to whom I stand in a way in a relation. What I've never known is now thrust at me all day long, love, and suffering. I used to think I was maimed never to have had it." (Ruby was astonished by Ursula's exalted expression.) "What women will do for men," she went on hoarsely, "the lengths they'll go, the loss of decency!"

"You don't see the best women, I daresay."

"The best women? What do you mean? I see women in love. I've been spared that, Ruby. There they lie under my fingers with their piteous eyes and they're like the damned. They sink fighting, you know, long after they're beaten. They come to me always too late, when they're in despair, to see what I can save. But it's too late. I'm the high priestess of deterioration. Would you like some port? There's some very good port in that decanter!"

In the night Ruby could hear Piffle whimper through the wall of her bedroom. (Piffle slept now in the second-best visitor's bedroom.)

She put on her dressing gown, and tapped gently at the door. She was aware of Piffle's sudden silence, heard a movement, then opened the door.

"Piffle," she whispered.

"It's like a clock in my breast," the old woman sobbed. "Put on the light, dear."

The bedclothes were dropping away to the floor; the little flannel-clad body shivered and shook. Ruby lifted her into a sitting position, shocked at her lack of weight. She replaced the bedclothes and tucked them round her, and finding a box of matches on the table lit the gas fire.

"It's a sad way to go," wept Piffle.

"To go where, darling?"

"I'm dying, Ruby," said Piffle. "That's to say I'm on my way and it'll come. But what I mind is to leave her. She's lost all, poor, poor soul."

"Lost what?"

"Lost her self-respect—what she's taken all her life to gain. Living on their lives, she is, like a hungry animal. And not as natural as an animal. Ah, the poor soul. No one but me will ever know what a brave girl she was. I wish I could tell you, Ruby, before you go away back north. Perhaps I won't see you again. I'm a poor thing to be her only upholder, old, stupid, shaking like a jelly. If I could tell you—she's been more than a soldier—she's had such a life of it, and so much to put up with, and so stiff. And now to finish like this, and no one to say they know what she's been."

"Does she drink, Piffle?"

"Yes, poor soul, yes."

"Much?"

"Well—yes. And it'll be worse. I know the signs. My mother, bless her dear loving heart, she did the same. Here we live, Ruby, without anyone, and me knowing all the time, and no power on earth can stop her. Nothing ever did stop her, whether it was to brave her trouble, or just wanting the pastry that didn't suit her.

Nothing ever stopped Miss Ursula. Sometimes I think the dog knows."

"Piffle!" Ruby put her arm round the little shoulder.

"He sits and looks at her, does the dog, and he's the same himself."

"Don't tell me . . ."

"He don't drink, of course, but he only thinks of carnal things. I don't know what's come to the house. It's empty of God. There's no spirit about, no looking upwards. God's not here, Ruby. That's what makes me so low. Do you remember how Duke was? So gay and sweethearted?"

"Wasn't he! Yes, wasn't he!"

"Everything went wrong after we came back from New York."

"That's six years ago."

"Is it? I don't know how I stand in time. Not since I began to shake. It's upset me so to be a burden to her and not to be able to comfort her, to be shut out as she shuts me out. If only the dog'd be what he used to be . . . But it's the house. It's the house."

"You're fanciful. I've been talking to Aunt Ursula and she's more friendly than she used to be."

"The wrong kind of friendliness."

"You don't mean, do you . . . She's never the *worse*?"

"Stinking," said Piffle dreamily, using a word out of her long-forgotten childish past. Her eyes glazed a little and her head sank back. "I can sleep, Ruby, now, I do believe," she said, and Ruby saw that the tremors were less. She tucked the bedclothes around her, and leaving the fire on for company turned to the door.

"No!" said Piffle. "Can't waste gas." Ruby saw that her eyes were closing as the light faded from the fire.

Two months later Ruby heard from Ursula that Piffle was dead. Ursula wrote a short note, adding conventionally, "She was very fond of you."

"Darling Aunt," wrote Ruby, "I want to tell you that I know about the bottle. Piffle told me in the middle of the night. I tell you because I want you to know that somebody knows and cares and minds, and yet doesn't mind—if you know what I mean. It's me. I want you to know too that Piffle handed on your greatness. She told me (in her own little words) that she felt you had no biographer. She said to me that you were braver than a soldier. Now I know it too. Shall I come and see you?"

And Ursula never replied. Two years later, when Ursula too was dead, she left a jewel to Ruby. It was a jewel for which she had paid three thousand pounds, a Georgian "trembler" flower-cluster, of diamonds and rubies, and on a parchment label attached to it she had written in Indian ink with a mapping pen, shakily (Ruby never knew at what date)—"For Ruby . . . proud of her . . ."

She left her fortune (but it had dwindled to a very small sum) to her manageress, her secretary, and half a dozen of the head workers at her Clinic.

Ruby had not seen Ursula for those years between Piffle's death and her aunt's, because when the war was over Gynt had a strong fancy to live in Pouilly for a time (though neither of them realised then that they would make their life there). Old Lady Maclean also had died, and part of the Scottish estate and the cumbersome stone house on it had been sold.

The jealousy of which his mother had spoken to Gynt never wholly died down. She even admitted it; but all the same it only caught her occasionally unawares. She was delightful, charming, but grew less sincere as the years crowded on her. Even when she gave herself away it was for a purpose, and as she grew older her charm wore thinner and what she called her "bad character" showed through the cracks. She could name it, but couldn't do away with it. She was a rich-minded old woman, gay and sly, and Ruby understood her value and missed her.

How flat and labelled lie the dead, Fanny, Ursula, Piffle, and the dog Duke. He, the dog, must have had a reason for his carnal melancholy, and nobody now can unbury it. Nobody can say, nobody understands, why they did this, did that. The figures that one by one lay dead and were buried behind Ruby Maclean were less a memory than a soil. They were her roots. Tolstoi's Natasha, Madame de Renal, Madame Bovary were more real. But Fanny, Ursula, Piffle were the soil.

When she was given possession of the jewel left her by her aunt (it was sent over to the Bank in Paris and brought down to Pouilly by messenger) she opened the case for the second time when the messenger had gone—sitting on her dressing stool by the open window of her bedroom. The case, six inches by eight, rested on her knees, and the flowers on the black velvet, tied with a ribbon of diamonds, trembled in the morning sun. It was an ornament that could be worn only at a ceremonial moment, red and white roses in rubies and diamonds mounted on gold; leaves, stems, and ribbon solid, but the roses themselves raised on twisted spirals to shudder at a breath. Ruby had been told by the solicitor of the value of the ornament. Its date was about seventeen forty—a collector's rare piece, and its value still rising. She had never known what Ursula had paid for the Russian sable coat. She had not known what Ursula had suffered: she had not shared in the buried life of Ursula before the aunt and niece had met. "What was I to Aunt Ursula?" But she brought herself to admit it: she had in part consoled her. She understood that Ursula meant her to be sure of this, and the sables and the jewel were two princely statements that made it plain.

*Part Two*

## CHAPTER SIXTEEN

The second war had come and gone. The gap in common existence closed again. Everyone who had lived anywhere returned in
some manner to his roof. The friends in Pouilly and Paris resettled
themselves in depleted estates, and it was again that hot summer of
Rudi's theatrical failure, when Ruby had driven herself down
under the large stars to Pouilly, when Celestine had tried to share
her husband's evening ritual and Alberti had found himself to be
after all a man of action. And now, a few hours later, in full summer daylight, it was yet far too early for Cora to prise open other
people's mornings on the telephone.

"Have you seen the papers?" asked the dreaded voice, as Ruby
struggled out of sleep. "Are you not awake? My husband must be
weeping. Also I've had a letter from him and that's why I've rung
you. I've not had this honour, except through the lawyers, for
twenty years. You were in the box with him last night. Did he mention this to you?"

"Yes."

"Ah. And what's behind this invitation I've had to lunch with
him?"

"I told him I would come and see you."

"Read the papers. They're very amusing. When will you come?"

"Today?"

"And get it over! It must be something difficult he's asked you. I
paint till midday. Come at twelve. But not to lunch, for I don't

lunch when I paint. Come on the minute. There's no concierge. I'll open the door to you."

The two—so different—but abrupt voices ceased. Ruby lay still in her bed framing the useless question she had promised Rudi she would put, when all at once she remembered Alberti's beam of light in the night. He hated answering questions about his health on the telephone, so she got up deciding to visit him for a few moments on her way up to Paris to see Cora. And then too there was his duchess to be congratulated.

At ten o'clock her car drew up by his garden gate. But the duchess's eyes when she opened the front door in her humblest working clothes were so swollen with crying that the congratulation was abandoned in favour of a plain greeting. Alberti, she found as she went into his room, was gay and full of spirits.

"So you're well," she said. "I saw your light very late."

"I'm particularly well. I was reading in bed. I'm taking a holiday this morning from collar and studs in my dressing gown. But I'm shaved. Celestine!" he shouted loudly. She put in her head.

"Bring Russian tea." She withdrew.

"So all's as usual?" said Ruby.

"Certainly." She saw that he was pleased with himself.

"I was a little nervous. What am I to say to her? Does she know I'm in the secret?"

"Say nothing at all. Why should you? She wanted to be a duchess. But what she really loves is to have a master who's pleased with her."

"You're very high-handed."

"Tyrannical. I hardly know myself."

"And she's been crying."

"I made her cry," he said modestly. "And have you been reading what are almost Rudi's obituaries?"

"I glanced at them. I couldn't bear to read them. When you know the people who write such things . . . And then he's old. And as I'm getting old myself I'm all on his side. Cora wrenched me from my sleep this morning and I'm on my way to see her. It's

a long story that I won't tell you now, but last night, after the supper party, almost in tears Rudi begged me to reconcile him with
her."

"With that monster! You never know, do you, what things men
will do next when they're old!" His eyes met hers and he laughed
gaily.

Celestine came in, put the tea and some biscuits on the table and
left quietly.

"Your wife doesn't eat with you?"

"Certainly not," he said with spirit. She waited for more but he
said nothing. He thought as he looked at her that her beauty visited
and revisited her now. Was it the past or the present? One rubbed
one's eyes. There were days when she dropped twenty years and
others when she reshouldered them. But her life was at last, he
thought, elbowing its way through her face.

She was at the door, to go, when she said abruptly, "What's the
matter with Gynt, Bertie?"

"Don't you ever ask him?"

"I should be asking from too distant a point. I'm left behind.
When a man like Gynt has a Bible by his bed, is sometimes on his
knees when I think he is writing, looks . . . well . . . as he looks,
one can't just say, 'What's the matter?' One should have asked before."

"And why didn't you?"

"It's come so slowly, hasn't it? Bit by bit. All these years since
Miranda went, and long before that he had this absorption. It was
always his private interest and it's taken the place of and altered the
man I married, but then the sort of life we both led couldn't go on
for ever. A man who doesn't really like the world has to have something. There are men who play chess before breakfast—and pure
mathematicians, and people who look in Tibet for a cactus. I suppose he simply grew to like birds better than anything else. It all
happened naturally, and from keeping amateur notes as a boy he's
come to writing his book. That would have been fine—if something
else hadn't happened."

"What then?"

"So startling. I never could have guessed it. I think God caught him alone in the woods and told him to leave me and follow Him."

"God's above such tricks. But can't the Call be shared?"

"No. I'm an outsider. I'm unconscious of God. I haven't faith."

"My religion recognises the extreme difficulty of faith, you know. It's not supposed to be easy."

With the lightning visit of the mind to outlying horizons the wavelike past, at a far seaside, rolled up the image of Piffle—anxious, resigned, nervous, brave, passing away. "I don't understand it all, dear," she had said. "I only know you must be as good as you can." Ruby understood that. It was the short, bare creed in her own heart. But Piffle had that strange support behind her, the golden God whose bosom was to be her couch, whose promise had never been doubted, whose ways were wonderful; she had a future as firmly contracted as any papist's, for all she belonged to some grey sect as gloomy as her elephant-coloured gloves. For Ruby the absence of God had to be shouldered. She withdrew her eyes from the abyss.

"But my faith," she said, "—all I could decently expect—wouldn't get me where Gynt is." She looked at her watch. "And now for Cora. I must go. I've got to see what that heart's like, do a little operation. But I'm afraid of what she hasn't got. Wouldn't you be?"

"No, I should be afraid of what she had! But I was born nervous of people."

"You've got over it."

There are all kinds of friendship, and several kinds of love. Not a bad one, and little spoken of, is the friendship, in age, of two people who might have loved. For them what has never been said is a last elixir of youth, the only bottle on the shelf never taken down. But as it will not be said now, there is no danger of ridicule. It remains in the air, a secret, and because of it each feels younger. The Duca Alberti felt at this moment alive and full of importance, and whenever she came to see him joys and almost hopes flashed again over the sickbed of his body. She was to him Cleopatra missed by

inches, met too late. He knew he had got over his shyness since he
had loved her, but he only said:

"So you do this unpleasant job for Rudi? What a friend you are!"

"I'm sometimes sick of myself. I'm only good for friendship."

"Isn't that something?"

"It's so easily spent."

She drove on to Paris, reaching Cora's house (to which she had
never been) as the clocks were striking.

At the same moment, Rose, sixty, had come in from a little rare
shopping. She flung down her bag on the bed.

"I'm too ugly! It's obscene!" she said pettishly. "Even he would
say so if he saw me now." Edouard had left her early to spend his
week-end in the country, but before leaving he had wanted her to
choose a dress for her birthday, cajoled her, teased her, ordered her,
gone the length of ringing up a dressmaker whom he knew and who
would allow her to buy—if it fitted her—a model privately on a Saturday morning. To please him she had agreed, and, in trying to
choose the dress, had gone through her special miseries. Now she
took off her hat, so smart and out of date, and sat on the leather
chair and looked at her ringed hands (which gave her so much
pleasure). It would be her sixty-first birthday on Monday, and
Edouard on returning to her was going to bring with him the new
ring, for he knew all about the value she attached to the gages of
love.

She was haunted by the shop-windows and by the mirror in the
lift of the great house where she had tried (and failed) to buy the
dress. The mirrors in the fitting room itself had been different and
by some quality in the silvering had given back to her for an instant
a look of the Rose she had been. But in the lift and in the shop-
windows in the street she had seen again the sad coquettish old
woman junketing by.

"I'm in that army, that poor army at last—the army of ugly
women!"

After a length of street she had sat down in despair on the terrace of a café and giving a small order she concentrated on the women in the street. Some of the ugly ones had pride, she noticed. But then they had always been plain, had not fallen back to it as she had done. Her eyes sought out aged women but there were none. They stayed shaded and quiet at home, for the middle of the day was so hot. Then just as she was going to leave, an old woman took a seat beside her, a woman perhaps ten years older than she was.

"It's not much fun being our age in this heat," she said suddenly, smiling uncertainly and rising, so as to show she was not really going to talk. The other woman raised a soft, hay-coloured face, pleated and crumpled with lines. She was dressed in black, and wore black silk openwork gloves.

"That's one of the advantages of being old," she replied. "I don't feel the heat. I used to mind it very much."

"*One* of the advantages?" said Rose. "Are there others?"

"Not being so busy perhaps? Having more time to oneself." They looked at each other. "And then I get some consideration now," said the old lady, quite unhurried and rather intimate. "I have five grown-up sons. That's very nice."

"My case is quite different," said poor Rose, seeing at once how life ought to have gone (but then one doesn't map out one's whole life in preparation for age). "I've never had any children and I've never had anything at all to do." The other looked gently vacant, for she could not imagine such a life. Rose smiled at her and moved away. The word "consideration" rang in her ears. "If I had gone on with my painting now I might have had consideration." But she did not linger long over that. She knew from the life of studios how many aspirants went down, mown by lack of talent, by the dead weight of material life, by the passing of years. She did not really suppose she would have struck luck. But "consideration," respect. She had none—from anyone but Edouard. She could imagine it was the only cairn you could roll up for your time of age. Again the steel-dark glaze of a shop-window offered her pitiless eyes the picture of her climb-down, the "pile-up" at the back of her neck (though she was a thin little woman), the suspicion of a shuffle

coming in her walk when she was careless, the impacting of her
lower jaw with the upper and the grim look it gave her mouth in
repose. She straightened up but she knew it was no good, she was
too tired and forgetful to hold it. "To have been a mistress and not
a wife," she grumbled to herself, "is so unlucky after fifty. Why
couldn't Edouard have married me? He might have if it hadn't
been for his sister." She had never pressed for it, for she had always
been too respectful of Edouard's "smartness." He had been a fashionable and grand man when he had met her, a landowner, the
head of his important family. If she had known then that he loved
her enough to have stayed with her all his life she would have
looked at it in another light, she would not have been so humble.
And after all, even now, why shouldn't he marry her? It was no
longer a question as to who should be the mother of his sons, and
now he would only be an old man making his old love happy. It
would be a heavenly change to leave the little flat and the loneliness
and try being a wife at last. But there was his sister. Rose had many
spiky sides and never thought well of other women, but if there
was one woman who had earned her extreme spleen it was Madame
de Lison—who wore her grey curly hair short like a boy's, and the
whites of whose fine eyes were yellow (Rose had seen with satisfaction when she had passed her once in the street). They did not
know each other. Madame de Lison was aware of Rose's existence
and had her own attitude about her brother's mistress. She was
envious of her. She had never herself had the mysterious allure
and charm that she imagined to belong to Rose; but had been an
awkward boyish girl, and when she married, an unhandy wife. She
had a fine figure, fine eyes and a personal way of dressing, but there
was something gone out of the effect, it was not "related," she was
not really a woman, she did not know how to please, but remained
as she grew older some kind of stiff and difficult elderly boy. She
knew it. She knew that she lacked those secret confident graces,
and though she had had in her time her lovers (for there are always
men who like something), she had mourned that she must be on
such slippery terms with men, alienating them unless she was ex-

tremely careful. She had a fierce hold on Edouard—so Rose thought, but really it was a pitiful one. Brother and sister shared between them the importance they attached to their family and would often pass a whole evening discussing its ramifications, bulwarks and misfits, lawsuits, wine-growing, marital strains and tensions. Sometimes, in these conversations, Madame de Lison would throw in a regret that her brother had never married, and from this spring-board she would attempt to land in the country of Rose. But Edouard had a look and a moment of silence, a pause and dryness in his reply that kept her at bay. So with Rose too he would not allow her to go far on the subject of his sister.

Edouard by now wore the pictured face of a Pouilly in age. There were dozens such framed on the stone walls of the Château de Pouilly. His narrow-set observant eyes looked out over the drapery of his family sneer, and, now that he was so thin a seventy, two tented folds ran down from either nostril. Put him up beside the pictures and one could see what he had done to modify for his own use the family lineaments, slipping his magnanimity into their scowl, and sweetening their cold eyes with his own humour. He was proud, but also humble. About his life and the way he had lived it he regretted nothing. He had not married but he might well have had a worse son than James Goethe, his young cousin. His poor sister, Angel, was not quite as he would have liked her but he ruled her gently and successfully so that he got from her what pleased him and forbade the rest. Rose was his baby, his mistress and his love. Towards her he had the forbearance and pity of God. This charming man, so necessary to his sister, so vital to his mistress, well-loved by a few old friends, resourceful, quiet, occupied and normal in his way of life, had reached the end of it at eleven o'clock that morning. Just as Ruby had left Alberti's house in the forest, Edouard entered his a mile away. There as he bent to change his shoes in his bedroom the bag of tricks which is our life gave in some secret cranny. Without sign or warning he fell dying to the floor and there, dead, his servant found him.

The man telephoned to the doctor, to Madame de Lison in Paris, to Alberti, and in the course of the agonised morning the sister arrived in the cottage, dishevelled with distress. Alberti had driven over to meet her. The doctor had left and it was still only half-past twelve when an open letter was produced, addressed to Ruby, which Edouard's valet had known to lie always just inside the first volume of Montaigne on the bed table. It asked her to break the news of his death, if it should occur, to Rose, and gave the address.

Madame de Lison recognised that it would have been painful to her to carry the message, yet she felt a wave of vexation that once again she had been judged unfit for the important moments of life. She held out the letter uncertainly.

"There'll be time enough for this," she said, "later on." And at Alberti's questioning look she added, "She was his mistress."

"Do you know her?"

"I don't," said Madame de Lison, with a toss of her fine grey head.

"Ruby's now in Paris," said Alberti. "I know where I can telephone her. It would be cruel, wouldn't it, if his Rose were expecting him . . . And when I've telephoned I can't leave you here. It's too miserable. Will you come back to lunch with me?"

"Oh . . . one can't leave him!"

"That's, alas, what one feels. It seems so recent to be alone." Madame de Lison wept, and Alberti went to the telephone.

Cora had installed herself in such a way that her home was hardly "run." It stood still, receiving the minimum of impetus. Its mistress had had her experience as a housewife and wanted no more of it. When she did her entertaining she did it in a restaurant.

She had a fine bedroom on the ground floor of an old house, a cupboard with a gas ring, a terrace looking on a garden laid with gravel, and a studio built against the further garden wall. Ruby sat with her now on the terrace beside a trolley on which were oranges and an ice bucket with a bottle of champagne. Cora filled two glasses.

"Let me drink half a glass before I hear what's on his mind."

"He wants you to go back to him."

"Mercy!" She finished her glass and poured another. "I told him this would happen! But I told him so long ago that now I can't enjoy being right. What did he tell you? I should like to have heard it. Poor Rudi, for a playwright, knows nothing of human beings. His side of that ancient quarrel must be how the historians write history—all wrong."

"But right for him. It's how I suppose he saw it."

"I daresay. He saw things so flat. Did he talk at all of a little wife you wouldn't recognise? How one changes! The house was so silent—I was so silent in it that the mice could be heard in the walls in those days. Go back to him? I couldn't find my way back. It was a narrow, airless life into which only a small woman fitted. So when I saw him stoop and talk to you . . ."

"No, it was afterwards. After the supper party. He told me particularly to tell you he would write no more plays."

"Then he must be at the end! The very end. And I'm the only woman he can think of to nurse him. No thank you. He never knew anything, poor Rudi! It's why his plays are so empty. I doubt if he even knew why I left him, or why we parted."

"He told me the story of a dish of apricots."

"Yes. The last word in the last quarrel, the only quarrel he heard, the only one he thought existed."

"And that he hit you."

"He was welcome to. That made no difference."

"Was he cruel?"

"Oh no. Cruelty's a live thing. It's I who was cruel. I had a strange, abnormal upbringing. Rudi was a waiter and I ran away with him. I'm sure he didn't tell you that? Did you know I was an American? There's no trace of it now. How we change! There's nothing left of what I was. Neither my father, nor Rudi, nor I myself . . ."

"Your father?"

"My father had a fixation, a terrible fantasy about me. He invented my delicacy, he persuaded my mother of it. For me they were afraid of the sun, of air, of microbes, of human beings. It was supposed to be quite certain I would die. I never dressed before eleven. The doctor saw me once a week."

"What was the matter with you?"

"Nothing. How could there have been anything the matter with me when it has never reappeared since? I was eighteen when we came to Paris—as Americans do. I was always dressed in white or pale grey. When I walked I took my father's arm. On the broad carpeted stairs of the hotel I rested at every turn. In those days, as I never saw men except at a distance, though I was ugly I didn't know it or bother about it. Let me fill your glass."

"Tell me how you met Rudi."

"Pass me your glass. One day for a change I dressed and came down to breakfast and Rudi was the waiter at the table. I'd never spoken to a man alone without my father. He told me he was really a playwright, getting material. So he was. It was how one looked at it. He didn't tell me he was on his beam-ends, and it wouldn't have made any difference to me if he had. I didn't know anything about beam-ends. I had hardly ever put my hand in my own purse— if I had a purse. I slipped down every morning, and at the end of four days he asked me to marry him. Immediately I knew that my illness had all been bunkum, that I was now going to live. Rudi wasn't to me a lover, he was Christ raising the dead."

"So you loved him?"

"Did I say so? I never loved anybody. But I was almost killed with hope. I told my father at once."

"What was that like?"

"Terrible." Something indeed altered in Cora's face. She seemed to flinch as she spoke.

"My father acted a scene with me that grew like a tempest, clasping his hands together and shouting up through the ceiling to God. We moved out that day to another hotel. But I was born again and nothing could stop me. In the evening I ran away. Rudi hadn't the money to get a license but enough for a room for one night together. I didn't know what it meant but I obeyed him. He seemed to know everything. The night wasn't pleasant—but it was life. Then we told my father what we had done. Rudi came with me."

"And that scene? Worse?"

"No. My father was exhausted. He could strike once but not again. He seemed no longer to know what to do, so Rudi told him. He told him to whom to apply to get us married and what lawyer to go to to make settlements, and Father did all as he was told. Mother cried all the time. She ceased to be able to speak."

"Weren't you conscience-stricken?"

"No. We got married. Father gave me an allowance. They went back to America. He died a year later."

"Did it kill him?"

"It didn't kill him. He died of pneumonia. But I've exhausted my love of the past. I had some reason for telling you but I can't remember it. I meant to speak of my married life but it would bore us both. All that talk of art I had to put up with—it's not amounted to much. Rudi had something in the beginning, but he turned it into money. That mouse of a wife of his had the best fun in the end."

"I'm going now," said Ruby. "And who's to tell him?"

"Tell him what?"

"Whatever you have to tell him. The answer to what he asks you."

Cora's eye was glazed. "Painting's like love," she said sententiously, "but a man can't enjoy that. He can't go to bed with rose madder or chrome yellow."

"I don't think it's bed with Rudi, I think it's the grave. But it'll hurt him less, I daresay, if I tell him. On the other hand he'll only believe it if he has it from you."

They walked back together through the large bedroom which had once been the drawing-room of the old house. The further wall was covered with mirror, to reflect the garden. Over the bed was thrown a white fur rug and on one corner slept a yellowing Pekinese which, like the rug, looked as if it had been to the cleaners too often. A quiet parrot hung in a cage. This was the home that suited its mistress, which certainly nothing would make her leave.

"Have you ever thought," said Cora, as they halted together at the looking glass, "what a film it would make if an ugly woman could make a bargain with the devil? I would sell my soul, like Faust, if I could walk out now into the street and look as you do."

"You're absurd. Make your pact at least for what I used to be."

"The devil's about!" said Cora. She went nearer to the glass. "He's heard me! The terrible black, I see for the first time, has a thread of white, and I may become a blonde at last. Who knows whether old age, after what I've gone through, won't be more like beauty? Devil—give me a break! Ugly women can have love but what I want to feel is admiration. I should go mad with pleasure to make a conquest of a sheer stranger. It's why I like to be with you. I could watch you for ever and your effect on other people. I'm not a sad old Lesbian by nature so much as from envy. I'm forced to make my meal off women who have better luck. Write, won't you, to Rudi for me. I really can't be bothered. Tell him I never lunch out when I'm painting. I can't waste the light."

At that moment the telephone rang. It was Alberti. Ten minutes later Ruby was climbing the stairs of the Palais Royale.

And as she climbed Rose sat on her bed full of the idea of marrying Edouard. The more she thought of it the more she saw it might be possible. The castle in her mind went up into the sky. The hated sister would remain in Paris, and she, Rose, installed in the forbidden country cottage, visiting and visited by . . . She would dine, as he did, with Lady Maclean. The country air, the happiness of being married, the change in situation—all this would modify age.

Her toupee, damp with the heat, had been taken off and hung as usual on the bedpost when someone pressed the bell. She walked softly across the room with her shoes off and opened the door. She was taken dreadfully off her guard. Lady Maclean herself stood, hatless, in the doorway. Oh—this was a shabby trick! Rose, indignant, clasped her ringed hands round her undressed forehead and glared at Ruby beneath glittering badges.

"I'm ashamed——" she said, backing away. "But do come in. I

know you. I've often seen you. Will you go over to the window while I get tidy? I wasn't expecting anyone." And Ruby, glad of the respite, walked towards the grey balcony and looked across the roofs due south into the sun. Rose, behind her, brushed the powder from her dress, slipped the elastic of the false hair over her head, and felt better. She heard Ruby say, "Come and stand by me, come into the window," and when she went to her she felt a hand on her elbow and a voice which said, "I've come to tell you what is terrible. Edouard de Bas-Pouilly has had an accident."

"In fact he's dead?" asked Rose.

"Yes."

"I must be brave," said Rose conventionally.

They both turned from the window back into the room.

"Won't you sit down?"

Ruby sat on a chair. Rose sat on the bed.

"How did it happen?" Ruby saw by the wearing of the toupee that it was the same woman who had been with Edouard at the theatre, and whom she had taken for an old relative.

"A friend telephoned me. I was in Paris. He left a letter for me."

"Edouard? For you? Why?"

"To tell me to come to you—if this ever happened—as it's happened this morning. So that you should know. It was found by his bedside. He had only just reached his cottage and fell down in his bedroom. The doctor says he had a haemorrhage of the brain in stooping to take off his shoe."

"And knew nothing, of course?"

"And knew nothing."

"How sudden to die like that," said Rose, and looked round the room like a new tenant who inspects a property. She even looked up at the cornice and at the cherubs on the ceiling. Then she said, "If you hadn't come I should be sitting here without knowing."

"Were you just going out?"

"I had just come in." And then, with a tone that seemed like a reproach, she said a little louder: "No, if you hadn't come I shouldn't have known."

Ruby said patiently, "One has to know some time," knowing it didn't matter what she said. She sat waiting, beginning in a leisurely way to undo the small buttons that fastened her linen coat. Rose got up and went to a curtain by the wall, drew it back and showed Ruby Edouard's suits, a town morning suit, two evening suits, and a black coat.

"He kept them here," she said. "I was good with his clothes. Nobody pressed them like I did. He had a valet at his house but I could see he didn't give them proper attention. I expect him on Monday because it is my birthday . . ." She stopped suddenly. In the strange, subdued sub-light of her shock she found herself thinking of the ring. She stood, her arm still holding the curtain, rather struck by that.

"How long have you known him?" asked Ruby. (Any question would do.) But Rose only answered, "I shall be sixty-one on Monday."

"Would you like to see him? Do you feel like that about death? I could drive you down if that would be any good, if you would like to see him."

"Oh dear no!" said Rose, almost gaily. "Though of course I could do things now that he forbade to me! He never let me go to his cottage. But I could go now, of course. Or do you think, lying there, so close to what happened this morning, he would know?"

"What about your lunch? You must eat. It's lunch-time. Where do you have it?"

"Different places," said Rose. "Sometimes I don't want any. I'm a cake-eater. But sometimes I go out. I feel much older in the streets."

"Will you put on your hat again? Will you come and have some food with me?"

"Thank you very much," said Rose. "No."

"But I'm so hungry," said Ruby, to get her to come.

Suddenly Rose looked sharply at her. "Don't leave this room," she said urgently. "Don't leave me alone. I've a lot to tell you. A great deal about Edouard and me. It's only I can't begin." Just as she said this she gave a choking cry and lay down on the bed. Ruby got up and pulled her chair to the bed's side, took Rose's hand firmly and sat still. The total and irreparable loss of Edouard that moment made itself known to Rose as she lay, and turning itself into bodily pain there came through her closed lips and through her nostrils a low animal sound with each breath, like a woman in labour. Soon this noise had an almost narcotic effect on the two women. They listened to it, Ruby holding the wrist, and Rose not recognising that the sound came from herself. She was like someone who groans and breathes after an operation when the anaesthetic is wearing thin. Behind the noise, in an inner chamber, her thoughts were still and hardly clothed in words. Ruby knew that all that was taking place on the bed was normal and that she had no further duty than to keep contact with the hand and wait. "This is the heart," she thought, "bleeding from a death-wound. She can never recover. She can only tidy herself up a little and learn to walk and eat." And her own thoughts went to herself and to Gynt and how she was losing him not by death but by a slow remorseless chilling. His heart was growing colder. But she would not say it was worse than death. What Rose was soon to feel could not be exceeded. The twin brews had to be drunk, death, and grief for death. Edouard had swallowed the one this morning: Rose would be drinking the other from now onwards.

But Rose had suddenly fallen asleep, and the rings on the still fingers shone in the shadow of the sheet. One of them Ruby was sure she had seen in Cartier's in the last year. What secrets men have! How Edouard must have cherished this old woman in this disordered room. Edouard, a little dry, she had thought, so self-contained, ironic, invulnerable and quiet. What value had he set upon her? She looked round the room, taking in the disorder, the easels, saucepans, books, face creams, canvases propped against the walls, and wondered what she should do for this bit of salvage, this dried rose.

"I said good-bye this morning," said Rose, waking suddenly.

"Yes, Rose."

" 'Rose,' did you say? I saw you at the theatre and I was jealous. I never dreamt he'd die. It never crossed my mind. Was he ill? Should he have warned me?"

"It's a thing that can come without warning, once you are old."

"Edouard wasn't old."

"He was seventy."

"Yes," said Rose, "he was seventy. It's all been so short. I shall have nothing to do now. I shall be so bored I can't wait to die. But I might all the same have done a lot of other things. I might have married a man I once knew and had children. I might have made my living as a painter." She waited, looking a little over her shoulder at the empty side of the bed from where the gentle voice should have mocked her grumbling. But no one spoke. Then she sighed, one of those shattering sighs of which we hear only the echo when we have drawn them. Tears ran down her face in silence.

Ruby made up her mind. They could not sit there for ever. "I shall take you home with me," she said resolutely. "You can't stay here." Rose opened her eyes wide at this. "To stay with you?" She gave in easily. "How astonished Edouard would have been," she said. But it was another matter finding a small case for her clothes. Ruby went into the back room to look.

"Have you never used this room?" she asked, astonished.

"Never," said Rose. And with a laugh she said, "It's too full, isn't it?" She was amused and pleased to go to Pouilly and exerted herself, like someone who tries to walk without knowing that all her bones are broken. Her sorrow flickered up and down and she was sometimes for whole minutes without the thought of Edouard. As they drove down to Pouilly she was eager to see the cottage where he lived but it was too far off the road and Ruby could only show her the direction. "I've really been too long in those rooms," she said once. "Thirty-three years. I should have had a change." In these remarks, and many others like them, which were a criticism of Edouard, she tried to keep him alive. If she should stop grumbling then he must die completely. It was a little artifice, and after a while Ruby understood it. Ruby put her to bed in a room at the end of a passage, with a pearwood door. Rosalba came and looked at her and took away and washed and mended the tattered black lace nightgowns.

"Is the poor lady to die?" she said.

"She's not ill."

"She going to die," nodded Rosalba. But Rosalba was often confident about nothing.

## CHAPTER SEVENTEEN

Edouard's funeral set off from the house in Paris, and his body, at the end of a long day's ritual, was lodged in the vault behind the private chapel of the monster château at Pouilly. He took back to the Pouilly gathering ground the little differences and specialties he had been able to weave away from their common blood. James de Bas-Pouilly, the heir, came up from Lardaigne and stayed with Ruby and Gynt. But the Duchess Alice had an attack of lumbago and could not do the journey until it had passed. She meant, however, to put in an appearance and make one of her rare journeys away from her home.

Ruby would have liked to have taken Rose to the funeral and Rose felt almost a wife at the suggestion when it was put to her, but she wasn't, in the end, able to go. She felt, when she left her bed, that the only thing that now embraced her was taken away from her. She cowered back and got among the pillows again, touching her rings with her thin fingers and shutting her eyes. It was Angel de Lison's day as chief mourner, but she was very miserable. It was not lost on her that in the gathering of Edouard's friends in remembrance of him there was not a close word of comfort said to her. Nobody had ever known her well enough for such words except the brother she had lost. It is not always remembered—(but nothing can be done about it)—that unpleasant people are unhappy.

When James arrived at Little Pouilly he had not seen Ruby for years. Not since he had left Eton, and he was now twenty-eight. He

had been sent to Harvard for two years after he had left Oxford.
The Pouilly clan, who hated this foreign education, had had to put
up with a lot of interference with their heir. But the Scottish great-
aunt was obstinate.

James had felt all the way coming up from Lardaigne in the train
as he had felt when he went to his first theatre, extravagant, high-
lifted feelings, all of them gilded, expectant. He was in love with
Lady Maclean before he arrived, the result of his boyish adoration
of her, larded with the legends and the shine of her reputation.
When he was at length by her side she seemed the only fully grown
woman he had ever known. He had felt up till now that beautiful
young women were heady and divine, but as companions for life
they made nonsense. This woman made sense. Now that he was
here at last he felt her fascination come straight back to him from
his own past. She was the Lily Elsie of his boyhood. But now—and
he had had his love affairs—he was grown up and a man and face
to face with her. He did not try on his fingers how old she might be.
What he bathed in was the blue look in her eyes that he had loved
as a boy, the ambience, the face which hardly was faulted by age.
She upset, surprised him. She was wasted, wasted on anyone but
himself. Wasted on that scowling monk for ever striding into the
forest.

"When I was a boy here," he said to Ruby, "don't I remember
Sir Gynt as a very gay man? That was my impression."

"In our time we've been whales for pleasure," replied Ruby, in
that quick language of hers so easily mistaken by those whose ear
heard only the light tones. "But now he's taken aback by growing
old."

"Good God, does that happen?"

"What?"

"That it doesn't come naturally? That it doesn't feel all right?"
She laughed.

"It's too extraordinary to explain, dear Goethe. It's a whole landscape."

"But, you—I wasn't asking you!"

"Well, you could ask me. I have to think of it. I think it over. But not as much as Gynt. For him it's that he——"

"Yes?"

"He watches eternity as though it were a sea to cross and he Columbus. And I, you see, never lift my eyes from the island we live on together. I hardly know it's an island. That makes a barrier."

"Between you and him?"

"Yes."

Ruby spoke her thoughts in her abrupt and uncalculating way, as she would to man or child, always curiously unaffected by her listener, gambling, if she thought of it at all, that she would be understood. But to James it seemed an intimate and significant confidence. He thought it over. Everything she said had a meaning vibrating to his manhood. He was blinded. He did not know that she had ceased to send out the fine golden puffs of seed powder upon the breeze. This thing that bursts all over the room like a pollen had gone. She knew it was gone, and she always faced facts. But for him the motes of love drilled up and down before his eyes like gnats on a fine day and wherever he walked his head was in a cloud of them.

She became in a short time aware of his love. He hardly left her side, lounged in her bedroom, savoured her make-up, was fascinated by her pots of cream, by her fingers stroking her temples, by the blue of her eyelid. As the whole household shared her bedroom life neither was he forbidden. But as she looked at herself in the glass, listening to his talk as he moved restlessly about the room, she thought that the aids she used were now part of her dressing, her habit, like her gloves or her hat. They were her civilisation. In no way done to attract James Goethe. He leaned over her shoulder and kissed her. She recoiled as immediately as a virgin.

"What's the matter?"

"I don't like wearing something too young for me!" she said uncertainly. "It's like the shame of the schoolboy dressed in a sailor suit. He can't hold up his head." He leant his hands on her shoulders and they both looked into the glass.

"Don't give me love, Goethe," she said, nodding at her reflected face. "It's too late. You can't see it. But I can feel it."

"You look wonderful."

"Yes. Perhaps. I have what they call 'looks that wear well.' But now it upsets me to inspire love. It humiliates me."

He gave an exclamation of pain.

She rose quickly and called Rosalba in her nervousness. When he had kissed her she had missed her own magnetism but knew that James was unaware that it was gone. As Rosalba came into the room carrying her dress she said, quickly, tenderly, "It is that I can't bear to swindle the Young."

Although he did not fully understand her the pain was smoothed from his face.

Ruby had said nothing explicit to James about Rose and her special relationship to Edouard, though he knew there was a visitor upstairs who never left her room. He had taken it for granted through a chance allusion that some relation, invited for the funeral by Ruby's kindness, had fallen ill during her visit. But as Ruby constantly left him to go to the invalid he asked, almost in irritation—"Then who is she? And what's the matter?"

"Grief."

"For Edouard's death?"

"She was his mistress."

She saw surprise on his face.

"You hadn't thought then that a man's mistress can die of missing him?"

"She hasn't died."

"Rosalba says she will."

"And does Rosalba know?"

"Poor Rosalba has instincts that let her down. There's nothing medically the matter. I've had the doctor. But Rose has nothing to live for. Would you go and talk to her one day for half an hour?"

"What can I talk about?"

"About Edouard. What you remember of him when you were a

little boy. How you came here and how he taught you to work his lathe. She's easy. She would so love to hear that."

"I'll go any minute."

"Now?"

"Of course."

So she walked with him to the end of the passage where the magnolia had one branch across a landing window. The little pear-wood door on the left was narrower than the others. She knocked.

"I've brought you the heir, the new Bas-Pouilly," said she, pushing James past her. "Tell him all about Edouard; he knew him so little. He ought to know more."

The young man needed all his fortitude to go and stand by the bed. "How do you do?" he said, holding out his hand, and from the sheets he received a little claw. On the bed table lay a heap of rings and brooches. Rose adjusted her toupee, which had slipped back, and put on her rings.

"Sit down. What are you called?" she asked.

"James Edouard, Goethe de Bas-Pouilly." He sat down.

"Edouard? Really? Edouard?"

"The Pouillys wanted that."

"I never knew any of them. I was only, you know, his little friend."

The expression was grotesque. He thought her seventy, and that she was really sixty made no difference. It was difficult to find answers without knowing how far he might go.

"You had known my cousin long?" The manner in which he said "my cousin" delighted her. It had a family-including air. She sat up and reached for her dressing jacket, and at the sight through her thin nightgown of the shadow of her body to the waist he was shocked by her dilapidation, offended for himself, upset for her, and above all anxious to hide such thoughts from his face.

"Since I was twenty-seven. Oh, don't think I looked like this then! You see me now—we all come to it. But it's only now that he's gone that I see myself what everyone sees. While Edouard lived the girl remained alive—though I grumbled and teased him every time

I looked in the glass. It's only these last few days, these very few days, that there is no one to deny how unutterably old I am, that I can look up and see—Rose as she is now—lost, lost to all resemblance. Did you know how kind he was? Did you meet him?"

"Only when I was fourteen. He was kind to me. He showed me his workshop."

A shadow passed over her face. "I didn't know his life here," she said, and picked at the quilting of the counterpane with her ringed finger and its red nail. "He was a heavenly man," she said at length. "A man of heaven. He had no temper at all. I suffer all the time, ALL THE TIME."

Poor Goethe, it was hard on him. But he took her hand in his as it lay on the counterpane, and he thought that it felt like a packet of drills that you buy at the tool-shop. She had no fat under her skin at all.

"He was a nice man. I was old enough to know that. Had you a house together?"

She brightened a little and told him about their perch. "We never got further than the one room," she said. "We had another. But we didn't use it. Oh, if only I could get rid of this remorse, this remorse!"

"Why do you have it?"

"Because I was so bad to him. I wasted him."

"I don't believe that. I can see you loved him very much. I am sure he didn't think you were bad to him."

"No. He didn't think it. He spoilt me. He would let me get cross and smile and smile at me. Then he knew better than I about everything. I'm lost. Old and lost. He said I would die first."

"That's not a promise he could keep, is it!"

"I thought he could. I had such confidence. I'm a silly little thing. And the worst is that I always grumbled; because I thought it was I who was wasted."

"How? Wasted?"

"I used to paint. My father was a painter. A bad one. But I thought I had talent. And long after I never touched a brush I went on imagining it was Edouard's fault that I never painted, and never made something of myself. It was why I grumbled so much. I even dreamt that if I were without him I should have been a fine painter and have had my circle. I didn't know then what it was to be without him. Now I know." The tears ran slowly down the tinted parchment face, not fast, but perpetually. Now there was a tear caught in a crease, now another at the ledge of a nostril. She had cried so many tears that they found their way without effort, and had their channels like water on mountain paths. But she was able to brighten.

"He kept his clothes with me." She explained all that to him, with her sense that he had allowed her a touch of home. "I did nothing, you know, all those years but wait for him. I had no other life. When he came, we talked through the night, sometimes right through it. When he wasn't there I waited. So now I don't know what to do with the day. I hope I shall die. Do you know his sister?"

"I've met her."

"What is she like?"

James considered. "She wasn't young any more," he said, "when I saw her. It was three years ago in London, at a party at the French Embassy."

"She is my age," said Rose, "and I've seen her in the street, out walking. She was jealous of me. Sometimes she prevented Edouard from coming. Then I was angry. But when I said so he would stop me. He was fond of her."

"Then you were jealous too?"

"Oh, I was always jealous," she said, casually. "It's my bad character—and that couldn't be mended. And Edouard had a way of saying, 'My sister . . .' I was specially jealous of her because she was his home, his respectability, and she shared his position. Though you mustn't think it was position I wanted—only when it's the man you love you want to see him among his friends. When I was a girl I was fond of people. I'm not shy, as you see. I love to talk. I was brought up in a world where there was no difficulty in having friends. So when I was with Edouard all those years I was often thinking, 'If we could have friends of our own together . . .' But perhaps it wasn't possible. His friends were different. I daresay I wasn't fitted for them. I used to say that living with Edouard was like spending one's life at a junction, waiting for the train to come in. But I was born discontented."

"Couldn't you have painted during all the hours that you waited?"

"I daresay I hadn't after all the talent. It doesn't matter now. It only matters that I should have thought it mattered. It matters to have been so wrong about everything, and so wasteful. There are people born to grumble, I was so pretty once I don't think he minded: he took it as just my trick. He would tease me and I would come round, so I never learnt any better. Oh dear young man, what can I do with myself?"

He thought—"Is Rosalba right? No wonder Ruby brought me here! She's lost." And aloud he stammered—"Should you lie here all day? Isn't it doing nothing that makes it worse? So much worse?"

"What can I do?" she said, astonished. He did not know. What do old women do at the end of their lives when they have lost all? No, he could not say. But she broke in, with her easy thoughts, which even in her grief sprang up as light as blades of grass. She had been so much alone that her little thoughts were her novelettes.

"Isn't it strange I should be here? Isn't it wonderful that she should be the one person to come to me, she of whom I've also been more than jealous!" (James, at this, had a pang of surprise.) "I wasn't allowed to meet her. They kept her to themselves, Edouard and all his friends. They seemed to make out she was on a different planet. It used to make me mad to hear him talk."

"My cousin?"

"Edouard swore he didn't love her. I do believe him. I really believed him then, but I wouldn't admit it. If I knew her as I do now, perhaps I shouldn't have minded. Imagine what life does to different people! She is only seven years younger than I am."

"That's not . . ." He stopped.

"Not possible, you think? Are you in love with her too? I wouldn't be surprised. How lovely she is! I always told Edouard the secret of her youth was in her jaw and her cheekbones. We talked of it when he took me to the theatre and of how she sat so straight in Rudi's box, and dazzling in her diamonds. I thought it unfair. That's how I am—I think things are unfair. What an idiot. Edouard put his hand on my knee and I shook it off."

"Just because Lady Maclean looked beautiful?"

"Just because of that, dear."

"Have you told her?"

"I tell her everything. She doesn't mind what I tell her. She listens and laughs. It's such a relief if people can laugh at one's sorrow. She isn't afraid of it. I can see now what Edouard meant—that with her to be beautiful is an extra."

"My cousin knew her well?"

"You're jealous, poor young man."

"Please don't say that. And don't say it to her."

"I won't. Though it's no use trusting me. My thoughts run about, and some are outside and some in; I never know which. And I forget. The only thing I am sure of is the pain. If he could walk into the room . . ."

"Hush."

"What can you tell me? Do you believe in God?"

"Yes, I do," said James. "But I'm no use to you. The way one believes is according to the time one has lived and what one has gone through. My believing's too easy and wouldn't convince you. I take God on trust. You should ask Sir Gynt."

"Sir Gynt?" said Rose. "He hasn't come to see me!"

"Shall I ask him to come? But he's very shy."

"No one is shy with me," said Rose. "I'm in too much pain."

As James closed Rose's little door softly behind him he saw at the end of the landing Gynt on a low chair in his bedroom pulling at a shoelace. He crossed the landing and stood in the open doorway. Gynt, with his unwillingness to make contact, fumbled at the knotted tie.

"I've been calling on Ruby's little visitor," said James. "I think she'd like to see you." Gynt looked up startled.

"What can I say to her!"

"She asked me about God. I said I was so ignorant."

"And I!" said Gynt explosively. His face closed down darkly. He reached out his long arm and took the Bible from the table by his bed.

"It's all there," he said. "The trouble is how to take it." The book was held in such a way that James had to accept it into his hands.

"That is the trouble," he said, and took it. He waited. Then, as he went, he put the Bible back by the bed.


## CHAPTER EIGHTEEN

The forest was deep green and flecked with sun. At eleven in the morning Alberti in his handsome dressing gown sat like a Roman emperor in his solid chair in the french window reading the papers. He looked up and saw Miranda walk down the path between the privet hedges.

"You're not a ghost, girl!" he called. "It's you?"

"It's me, Godfather."

"But nobody's heard anything! Your mother, she hasn't heard of this! You just arrive, no luggage—you're flesh and blood? There's nothing the matter? Come in and tell me everything. Where's your husband? Have you come from your mother?"

"I haven't been to her yet."

"Not been to her! You're crazy." He rose heavily to his feet. "I'll get some coffee . . . Celestine!"

Celestine appeared. It did not occur to him to say, "This is my wife," nor did it strike Celestine. She took his command for the coffee, and Miranda looked so cold in spirit she did not even greet her though she well knew who she was.

"Now, why haven't you been to your mother? And why are you here?"

"It wasn't far out of my way . . ."

"I'm not asking . . . great heavens . . . how you got here. Why to me? Why has nobody heard?"

"Mother has heard, surely, that Tuxie is dead?"

"Not a word."

"But by now?"

"Not last night, for I phoned her. Dead—is he? What am I to say?"

"I'm not grieving. But I was sorry for him. We've had a frightful life. I am glad not to have him, but I wish it hadn't been by death."

"Of course. One wishes that. How did it happen?"

"He cut himself with an axe."

"And was poisoned?"

"He bled to death." Alberti recoiled.

"How is my mother?"

"Well. And beautiful."

"Beautiful. Tuxie was in love with her."

"Don't tell me these things. Go and see her, at once, at once. Don't stay here."

But she did not move. Celestine put the coffee tray softly beside her.

"Yes. That's what I must do. Go and see her. I have his will."

"Tuxie's will? Had he anything to leave?"

"He had several thousand pounds. All left to Mother. How is my father?"

"He is well too," said Alberti. "But he's changed. You'll find him very changed."

Miranda clasped her gloved hands nervously. "He has never written to me. Never. Has he never forgiven me? What is the difference in him?"

"He's gone in on himself. He doesn't speak much. I don't think even your mother knows what's happened to him."

"He was always serious."

"Was he? No, not that I remember."

"He was. It's from him I get my——"

"Your what?"

"Perhaps my difficulties. But he's well? He's not ill?"

"He seems perfectly well."

"That's why I came here first. It would have been too much—to go straight back and know nothing. Letters tell one so little. And now that I know that for some reason Mother hasn't had my letter . . . And then . . . Godfather Alberti . . ."

"Aren't you old enough to call me by my name?"

"So I am. I'm thirty-one. Alberti."

"Go on."

"I don't want to fall into the old troubles. I'm most anxious not to fall into the old troubles. That's why I came to you."

"What can I explain to you?"

"Everything, I think. I've thought over it all enough. I've had nothing else to do and no one to talk to."

"Tuxie?"

"We weren't on speaking terms."

"The whole eight years?"

"Except for rows. And that's not conversation. I want to know why I'm half afraid of Mother, half suspicious of her. I've never been able to explain myself, but this is so very important. She is the most important person in my life, but I don't know who she is or what she is. I want to know that. I want to know how she seems to other people, what sort of woman, what sort of woman . . . You can tell me."

The old man flicked with his fingers at his lower lip, looking at Miranda, who sat with her eyes on her hands, ashamed and determined.

"That's an extraordinary question," he said at length. "You ask who your mother is, and what people think of her. But surely what you think of her is what matters?"

"I don't know, I tell you!" she cried impatiently. "I was her little girl, her daughter. I was too close. But I loved her!" she said sharply. "Don't think that's in question. I love her. I've half forgotten her. See—how I can talk to you! I could never in my life say the word 'love.' I'm like my father."

"He could say the word 'love.'"

"Could he? Then perhaps I don't know him either: but with him I never was bothered by not understanding. What frightens me is that I'm going back, going home, and unless I understand better I shall fall straight into the old difficulties. I shall miss her, I shall lose her, I shall waste her all over again. How does she seem to you, Alberti?" she pleaded. "You love her?"

He started and turned his large face and his voice trembled. "Yes. Always," he said.

Miranda had asked her question in her awkward innocence, her stupid innocence, on a different key. At the tremble, at the tone, she knew with sharp disappointment that once again here was a spellbound man, a man joined in this league against her, an old Atlas whose shoulders supported the hidden paradise from which she, the young woman with rights, was shut out, and of which her mother, even through so many years, had the freedom.

"If it's any help to you," said Alberti slowly, "your mother also feels guilty. In her humility she feels responsible that you've never enjoyed each other. But I think she doesn't know why. She doesn't analyse things but comes somehow to her conclusions, and they make her sad, for she's helpless to change. She would exclaim long ago when you were a child in the nursery that she talked you to death, didn't give you a chance, was too gay for you. She made her little jokes about it, but she minded and tried to alter. But she can't alter herself. What she is, she is. She's too strong. You must understand her as she is."

Miranda seemed not to listen to him.

"Tuxie used to say dreadful things," she said.

"And did you believe him?"

"No. But I can't bear men being in love with my mother. That's what it is, Alberti. I cannot bear it. Are they still? She's not young now."

Alberti sighed. Neither could he bear to explain to this "girl of fifteen," even though he saw she suffered.

"Are they still, Alberti?"

"Yes," he said a little crossly, "and you must put up with it. A woman like your mother doesn't get old. She still has her great fascination, and as she is witty and generous as well, of course men like her. What's the matter with you? She's been an honorable man and a beautiful woman and perhaps that's confused you? Or is it jealousy?"

Miranda looked at him sadly and shook her head. "I'm a sort of cripple," she said. "I've never felt love at all."

"Not with Tuxie? When you insisted so wildly on marrying him?"

"No," she said, "not with Tuxie. I've come home to hope for a second chance."

She was standing now, picking up the gloves she had lately taken off and the bag she had laid on a chair in her neat, meticulous manner. She had the desolate air of a secretary who has been interviewed and dismissed. He took her to his garden gate, sailing like a great ship beside her in his dressing gown.

"It seems so simple," he said. "You've been very unhappy. When you meet your mother tell her all that. It wouldn't surprise me that she loved you better than anyone. Crÿ, if you feel like it."

"Ah, I couldn't," said Miranda. "I don't cry now. It doesn't happen."

She walked away from him through the trees without looking back.


## CHAPTER NINETEEN

Outside the forest in the sunlight a young man was looking at a statue. He stood in the damp yellow grass of the water meadows looking up at the poet's face. The old-fashioned head was cloudy with birdlime and looked noble and forgotten and the poet was indeed nowadays rather unknown. The young man, turning, looked at Miranda and remembered her.

"Miranda!"

The poor young woman stared. He thought she looked frosty.

"I came here when I was a boy. I'm staying with your mother. Don't you remember me? My cousin has died, you know. My cousin Edouard. I'm James, whom your mother called Goethe. But you're supposed to be in Jamaica!"

"Yes, I've just heard I'm not expected. It's so strange my letter never came. I wrote it."

"And no luggage! Just walking home like this as though you had been living in the bole of a tree——"

"The hotel people in Paris are sending my luggage down this afternoon."

"You stayed the night in Paris! And never telephoned. And your mother talks of you as being thousands of miles away! But where have you come from? I mean now, this minute?"

She didn't answer. He thought her odd, and walked beside her. He started to talk again.

"I can't imagine her surprise, I can't imagine her pleasure. Shall I stay to see it? Perhaps not. Yet I'd adore to see her look so suddenly happy. She's in the dining room doing the flowers. She was when I came out."

To Miranda it seemed as though he talked like a son of the house.

"And she asked me to bring some leaves in and I haven't got any. Wait while I break this birch branch. It's my great-aunt. She's arriving tomorrow. The house is all being keyed up. We've had the funeral."

"Funeral!" Miranda stopped dead.

"Edouard. My cousin. I told you. Edouard de Bas-Pouilly. You haven't got a knife? This branch is so tough. No, why should you? That poor chap on his pedestal made me feel gloomy till I saw you. It's a lovely day though. Do say something, Miranda."

"I can't."

"What?"

"I'm thinking about getting home. We shall be there in a minute. Could we sit down on this grass for a bit? It's dry."

"Yes, if you want to. Aren't you dying to be home?"

"Oh, please don't ask so many questions!"

She sat down, neatly putting her small feet out in front of her, her bag on the grass. That almost surgical neatness, as of a nurse, that used always to repel him, was on her still. Yet she wasn't bad-looking. "She must be over thirty," he thought, "but she looks twenty-two." He stood, looking down at her. She looked up at him.

"Sit down, too," she said.

"I keep thinking how your mother . . ."

"It isn't your affair," said Miranda tartly. "Everyone hurries me home. It's my business how fast I go."

"Everyone?"

But as he got no answer, he sat down. He thought her as difficult as he used to think her, when he was a boy of sixteen. She had always had a snubbing way of talking, and certainly hadn't lost it. Then it struck him that there was something set and apprehensive in her face, and he wondered if she had bad news to tell. As she did not talk he went on (he really could not sit there silent):

"You'll find your mother just as you left her. Perhaps more beautiful. You might be afraid she would have grey hair, but her hair's golden, and yet each hair seems to have silver. I can't think she'll ever be what's called 'grey.'"

"Somebody asked me in Jamaica if she dyed it."

"I don't think she does, but if she does, why not? Lots of women tint their hair even when they are very young. What a funny thing to ask . . . in Jamaica."

"It was an old woman who knew her as a child. How you've changed, James."

"Well, I should hope so. I'm twenty-eight. It was time to change. But you haven't . . . much. You look so young. Really, you look twenty."

She turned her white face and dark blue eyes up to him. "No, I don't seem to change," she said.

"Would you like to?"

"Very much." She got up. "Now we'll go on. It was only a moment's grace that I wanted."

As they walked the house across the meadow came in sight and there was someone on the terrace.

"I think she's there," said James, and Miranda glanced at him. They went across the last field.

Ruby saw them coming. It was Goethe, she saw, but he'd picked up a girl. So he should, she thought. That was what he must do soon. He was too young for this passion he offered her; and she was too old. She stood and watched them. As soon as she understood that it looked like Miranda her heart pounded. It could not be Miranda, so why should it look like her? Then Goethe took the girl's arm, and made her run. "If it's Miranda, she'll hate that!" Miranda did hate it. She shook him off and walked. So it was Miranda. What could have happened? How was this possible? Where was Gynt?

When she held her in her arms, it was the old stiff, white-faced Miranda, not changed a day—the stiff resisting body and the old strain. A sob of love was in her throat; a tenderness that was unspeakable. "Go away, dear Goethe," she said, "it's too much for me." The little dog ran barking out of the French window. Miranda was about to stoop, and Ruby caught her hands. "No! Not the dog, Miranda!" and kissed her on both her eyes.

## CHAPTER TWENTY

James then remembered Miranda as a monster of a nuisance. Always in the way. When he had been looking at the stone poet he had been thinking entirely of his love, of his happy unhappiness. And suddenly there was Miranda beside him, sulky and struggling with herself, white and irascible, as of old. And when he had brought her across the last field to the terrace Ruby had said: "Go away, Goethe." And although she said "dear," she said it like an aunt. He had gone round the corner of the house on to the gravel and stirred the carriage marks with his foot, and on to his bedroom.

Whatever her resolves, the tired and sad and tense Miranda could

not get through the first half hour of welcome without an antago-
nism which hid her aching love. She managed to deflect it a little
upon Rosalba chattering and weeping, instead of on her mother.
She managed to say to Ruby with a smile in her dark blue eyes:
"You know what I am. Let's be practical. I'm awfully bad at wel-
comes. I'll tell you everything bit by bit, but let's pretend just now
that I've been here all the time. Where's Father?" And Ruby said,
as Alberti had said, "He's changed."

"To look at?"

"Yes, that too. Don't exclaim when you see him. I mean he's very
grey."

But Miranda thought she knew best how to speak to her father.

She walked down before lunch over the fields again and through
the forest to see if he were writing in the Fantasia. During this walk
the pain of eight years was eased in an extraordinary way. She'd
come home and the wild homesickness she had borne, the stiff lip
she had kept with herself as she daily faced the enemy, her husband, all this was wiped out, and she felt life might be opened
again, if only someone would help her. Help her with her ignorance
—to hide which she could not but clamp down this mutinous and
obstinate mask.

When she reached the clearing she saw the mill door propped
open. She set her foot on the short stair.

"Who's that?" called her father's voice.

"Miranda." There was silence. She walked into the room and
saw him, turned in his chair, watching for her—thin, evaporated,
changed. Now she believed her mother and Alberti.

"Father," she said. Her voice was warm with him because she
had to overcome him. He got up.

"I wish I'd had warning," he said querulously. "I'd have shaved."

"Oh," she said, "I'm not that a lady!" She ran to him and put her
arms round him and felt in them the stiff unwillingness that she
had shown to her mother's arms. "Tuxie's dead. I've come back. I
wrote a letter but no one got it. I've been to Mother. I've only been
back an hour."

"Oh . . ." he said and sat down.

"Why are you so thin?" she asked. "What's all this writing everywhere? Tables and tables of it. Is this all your work? You look like a monk. Are you an author now?"

"Yes," he said. "I'm an author. It's the old book, you know."

"Not the one when I was a child? The bits you used to read to me?"

"Yes, but in those days we both liked facts, didn't we, and nothing was so difficult. In the last ten years I've begun to think about writing. And when you begin to think about that you wish you hadn't. It's the dickens. First one sees how one can do better. Then there's no end to it. I'm slowed down to such a standstill I turn my commas round and try them upside down." (He was smiling now. She had won: they weren't going to talk about Tuxie.)

"I'm old," he said. "I suppose that strikes you?"

"You look careworn. And much graver." Then she caught sight of the large Bible, propped open with his empty pipe. To show him that she had seen it, she smoothed the dog-ear of the left page a little with her hand. She was still standing. "Have my chair, Miranda. I'll sit on the box." He got up again.

"Is there only one? I'll sit on the box. Why is there only one chair?"

"No one comes here. One is enough for me."

"Doesn't Mother come?"

"I see her at home. This is where I work."

"I must ask it," said Miranda anxiously, "I must ask it, Father. I've been gone so long. It's been so dreadful. Nothing's happened between you and her?"

She saw his stony eyes soften, and the hint of the old smile come back. "Nothing," he said. "Poor child. Nothing. It's I who've failed, not she. I've grown peculiar and I know it. Nothing could be more rare, more noble, than your mother. Tell her I said that when I'm gone. Not dead, you understand, but I've made up my mind to go a journey. I'm going away."

"Does she know?"

"Not yet. I tell you because I trust you. I've not been able to write to you because I couldn't forgive you. But now I don't know why. And that man's dead. You said he was dead?"

"Yes. An accident."

"I don't want to know. If he's dead it's finished with. You must marry now. A proper man."

"If I could. If I could."

"Your mother will help you."

"I don't think she will. I mean I don't think she can."

"You must get over this trouble of yours. It's all your fault. It was never hers. You must have a boy. I shall come back to see him."

"But where are you going, and why?"

He put out his thin hand and laid it on the Bible as though it was a comfortable place.

"When I've finished the book," he said, "and done the birds justice, I want time to myself."

"You have it here."

"No," he said. "And you'll keep your mouth shut, Miranda, till I'm ready to speak." It was the old expression he had always used to her. They had always chuckled about it, for she was born with her mouth shut. She felt that even in his trancelike state he held on to what had been familiar between them. She was home again, dear Father, even with what remained of him.

"Get on now back to your mother," he said. "I'll be happier while I work thinking that you're in your home."

"You'll be back tonight?"

"I may be."

"But my first night home!"

"Don't tamper," he said with his faint warm smile. "Let well enough alone. People don't change their ways because other people come home."

She was satisfied. Even as she left him she saw him turn back to his desk.

It was a household on thin ice for the rest of the day. The emotion was too great for the people who had to handle it. James was sulky. Miranda had a startled and resentful eye upon him. Gynt came in in the evening but the returned traveller could not tell her tales. When the great-aunt was there (Ruby thought) Goethe had better be careful. The duchess was sharp and knew him well. She would soon see whom his dark eyes were following. "If I'm humiliated to myself I shall be still more before her." And now too there was Miranda. To ease things she became as of old the talker, and told the traveller the tales of home, of Alberti, of Edouard's death, and of what remained of him, his Rose. And as she talked over her table, looking occasionally at the stiff, the pale, the hardly-changed Miranda, missing none of the difficulties, she was filled with a strong feeling that had no content mixed with it. It was joy. She had her child: she had a second chance to fulfill her task.

It was the arrival of the Duchess Alice next day which pulled them all together.

## CHAPTER TWENTY-ONE

At five in the afternoon the heavy, crested car arrived, drawing its luggage trailer in which were packed straw baskets such as peasants use. The duchess herself with her maid beside her, both wedged with cushions, had rocked slowly over the long roads from the Spanish Alps. She was now seventy and though she had acquired a rugged magnificence of appearance spiritually she had deteriorated with age. Her Scotch cheekbones jutted high: she had a tired black eye and a Roman nose: her iron-grey hair, knotted in hoops and plaits, was tied and joined with black taffeta bows. Her powder was many shades too light for her brown skin and she had rubbed red paste on to the lobes of her ears. These apparently scalded lobes glowed like rubies—a strange decoration, due to some chance remark or advice lost half a century earlier.

Her clothes were not countrified, though they were not Parisian. They were romantic. She got out stiffly from her car, trailing a double-decked black cape from one shoulder and corseleted with some sort of red waistcoat. Her maid handed her her stick; the chauffeur gave her an arm. "It's taken a great deal to get me here—though I'm glad of it," she said to Ruby, peering close with her short-sighted hollow eyes. "But you're older!"

"Does that cry out at you right on my doorstep?"

"I feel for your face," said the old woman (who had prepared this backhanded passage in the car as she bumped over the roads), "as I feel for the national treasures. I'm indignant at a speck of dust."

Turning to her chauffeur and her maid, who had begun the unloading of her baggage, she resumed her natural voice and began to advise them; but neither took any notice of her, the man because he was deaf, and the maid, a peasant woman from Lardaigne, because she always treated her mistress with a minimum of deference.

Before the duchess would leave the hall for the drawing-room she insisted that the luggage should be checked by a crumpled list she held in her hand. "Organisation is my weakness," she said, while she tapped her maid's arm and tried to get her attention. She had brought enough luggage for a voyage to Australia, but later Ruby understood that it was the size of each garment and not the number that required so much housing, for each dress was long to the ground and very full, and each had a coat to go with it. One of the straw cases was packed with cashmere rugs, and another with the letters it was proposed to answer. A third had literary notes and a rubber cushion and a fourth contained the luggage for the dog. That the duchess should have brought a dog at all was a surprise. "I don't like my poor dog," she explained, "but she's used to me and I couldn't leave her behind."

"How awkward to have a dog one doesn't like."

"It can't be helped," said the duchess. "I never liked her from the start."

The great-aunt, like everyone else, was not wholly a comic character. She was shrewd and observant, and if she had not acted her emotions so that they seemed unreal she would have passed for a better woman. There was so much knowledge mixed with so much pretence that she did herself an injustice. She had never outgrown her desire to impress, and was often rude in her wish to seem forth-right, attempting to repair her rudeness with heavy compliments. After tea (at which she asked suddenly for toast—the only thing missing from the loaded table) she went round the garden. Here she was at her best. Her instant forgetfulness of self was delightful, her garden wisdom subdued her selfishness and she was full of un-derstanding of failures and successes.

"You've got your man still?" she said, turning suddenly on Ruby.

"My gardener?"

"Your husband. But no, I should have heard. Naturally I should have heard. I do my ten-year stretches buried down there and I often come back to find people dead. Gynt's well, is he?"

"Perfectly."

"I used to say of him that he had a secret religion. 'Gynt worships in an odd church, you'll find!'—I remember saying to poor Edouard. But nothing's come of that? He's not become peculiar?"

"Except that he's writing a book on his birds."

"Book-writing, for unsuitable people, is very disappointing. But it might be worse than that. It's good you still have the head of the house. When he goes there's a great change. A woman loses caste for a long time and only regains it in very old age. And by then she's neither man nor woman. You can't grow that bush in that position. It looks as if it had rickets."

"No, it doesn't do well."

"Don't grow things that don't do well. It may be dull to stick your soil but for an amateur it's more effective. Gardening is more difficult than cooking. There are so many coincidental factors. And don't grow bachelor's buttons close to the lawn: you'll be sorry for it. I was once in love with Gynt."

"I remember it."

"I hope it didn't cause you anxiety. I used to call him my 'cat' because he was unstrokable. But you didn't find that, I daresay. He very much preferred my dear Henri. Well, now I've forgotten about love, and how it feels."

"So you don't miss it."

"One can't miss what one's forgotten. That's the answer to age and why it's bearable. I was certainly a romantic girl but I've got over that as I've got over most things. How fresh it is to look at someone else's garden and see the chances there are!"

"If anything occurs to you give me advice."

"Everything occurs to me. But it's too tedious: I'm too old. And the things I know, what good are they? Come and see my garden one of these days. But you won't. And I've got over pride. I grew flowers at first because I was proud of my skill, but later because I loved them. It's a relief. There's so much desk-work in old age. It's an odd thing that the older you get the more you have to write. Do you find that?"

"Gynt . . ."

"Wait till you're a widow! It's endless. My maid follows me with a picnic basket of letters from which I only skim the top. God knows what lies at the bottom. I shall find out while I'm here."

"Don't you have a man of affairs?"

"I don't trust anybody. That's another thing about getting older; you try to do everything yourself, and you do it so slowly. Yes, I have a man of affairs, but he's afraid of me. My maid's the only person who's not. She's been with me twenty-five years."

"Are you fond of her?"

"Alas, no."

But the duchess in the garden was different from the duchess indoors. She was so accustomed to isolation among her dependents that now when staying once again among her equals she was unable to allow for other people's perceptions and continued to act as though her wishes and her comfort were a known general anxiety. She spent her time writing notes to Ruby altering the hours for dinner, or wanting to see old friends in Paris who had no telephone number. Fresh flowers had to be sent in every morning from the garden but at night she threw them into her wastepaper basket—an odd trick for a flower lover. Ruby saw the basket full of still-dewy roses mingled with envelopes, matches and corks. She bristled with spiky habits, carrying on a warfare with her maid, who, proud of her mistress, but proud of her own domination, ran her down with muttered ejaculations and asides. It was a relationship intimate, dry and strong, and though each irked the other the annoyance was in itself a dear preoccupation.

"What a noise on the landing!" said Rose—with her quick intimacy—to Miranda, whom Ruby had pressed to come and see her.

"It's James's great-aunt," said Miranda. "She's just arrived with her maid and her dog. I believe we didn't expect the dog."

"Oh, it's all too late, and I should have enjoyed it so!"

"Too late?"

"Staying here. Being in things. Hearing a duchess arrive. And now when it's only the end for me."

Miranda wasn't as easy to talk to as James had been, but Rose took no notice. She no longer wanted response.

"But then if Edouard had been alive still it wouldn't have happened, would it? But nothing can be changed now. Do be happy while you're young."

Miranda stiffened. Then said: "I'm not a gay character. I don't seem ever to have been one. But of course now . . ."

"Oh, I forgot. You're a widow. But your mother said it wasn't like my trouble: you didn't care for him so much."

Miranda had not been prepared to be immediately on such close terms, but she had not the readiness to escape. "I didn't care for my husband very much," she said, serving up her mechanical answer, "but I was sorry that he died."

"Death is the worst thing in the world," said Rose. "It's the only thing you can't alter. But you'll marry again. What a smooth young face you have! Do you look in the glass? It seems that one's face will last for ever, but it doesn't, and it hurts so much when it goes. I used to say to him: 'I'm an old thing now!' And he always answered: 'Not to me.' You are not, of course, like your mother. But she's at last getting old."

"Oh no!" said Miranda involuntarily.

"Well, I see it. And I'm an expert. I see where everything begins. That young man . . ."

"James?"

"Your mother calls him something else."

"She always called him Goethe. It's one of his names. His mother was romantic."

"He thinks your mother is the queen of the world. What a run she's had!"

"A run?"

"Well, she's between fifty and sixty and still the only woman in the room that anyone looks at. And yet she isn't at all what I thought she was. She isn't a flirt, for instance. Except for her wonderful face she's more like a man. And she seems sad, almost melancholy, in spite of her being so gay." Rose was lying flat on her back, talking and looking at the ceiling. She had forgotten Miranda. "Ah, she knows she's on the edge of the end of it all, yes and I know it too. She's proud; she doesn't like prolonging it. She doesn't want anything twice. I'm different. I'm grateful for anything left over. I can't live now that I can't have admiration, and there was only one person left to give it to me. But your mother—— There's a peculiar look comes to a woman at the end of her beauty. As though the edges melted, but the eyes begged to be left where they are. Beautiful women look sadder than plain ones. But of course I, for instance, was never like your mother, though I was pretty too. I was a chic little thing, full of cheek, and cross, pretty ways. I met Edouard when I was twenty-seven and he was kind and had a great name. I thought I was lucky, but I didn't know how lucky and I didn't know it was for life. Funny meeting a man and then you find you spend your life with him!"

"That's what one does when one marries."

"But we didn't marry. How casually we first met—and then he took the rooms that were our home. And now I'm sixty-one and he's dead. If I could have one minute, one minute of it back again. If I could tell him those things one can't say." She turned energetically on Miranda. "You must get married. That young man would do very well. Your mother doesn't want him. He's got charm. He's got quite a look. He's good too. He would make you happy."

"Why do you say my mother doesn't want him?"

"I'm sure she doesn't," said Rose. "Look at my rings. Edouard gave them all to me. When a man spends money on you it's a guarantee he loves you. It's peculiarly tender. It made me melt to think that Edouard had paid away so much to put those rings on my finger and to make me happy with them. I would like to be buried with them but I suppose that's a waste, considering what one becomes."

"Does James like my mother?"

"What did I say?" asked Rose, now looking at Miranda, who with mounting colour was looking out of the window. "What were the words?"

"That you said?"

"Yes. What did I say? About your mother and the young man?" Miranda was dumb, but she was scarlet.

"Of course I never had a daughter," said Rose, considering her. "I say things I shouldn't say, and that's because no one's ever checked me and I've been alone a great deal. But you're old enough to understand, aren't you, that young men fall in love with women like your mother, even though she isn't young. But she's absentminded: she seems all the time to be thinking of something else. She doesn't value a young man and his love. She's tired of that."

"And I've never had it at all," said Miranda, with sudden anger. "I've never been in love."

"I was never out of it," said Rose listlessly. "Didn't you sleep with your husband?"

"No."

"What was the matter with him?"

"If I talk of him I shall say cruel things. I don't want to now that he can't answer back."

"Oh, he's gone!" said Rose. "I'm sure he doesn't care! People don't stay earth-bound. I wish they did. I only think of death now, you know, and I get quite an idea of it now that I'm so up against the edge. You know how water brims to the very top of a glass, almost lifted, and doesn't fall over. I am like that fold of water. If I took a real sigh I should go. I used to take for granted all my life (but I didn't think about it) that we blew out and went. But now I think that we change into something very strange. So strange that it's no good talking about it. It hasn't a name. Oh, do listen to that! Open the door a little and see what it is."

Miranda obeyed, putting her eye to the crack in the door.

"It's the duchess scolding her maid."

"Oh, what is she saying?"

"They are unpacking. She is walking after the maid, backwards and forwards, and trying to get her to listen to her."

"And won't the maid listen?"

"It doesn't look like it," said Miranda, closing the door. "The maid looks very firm."

"Tell me everything that happens at dinner. Perhaps she will come and see me? I shall ask your mother to bring her."

And so next morning the old duchess came rustling along the passage to the little pearwood door, mentally arranging her phrases. She had been told by Lady Maclean of Rose's long connection with Edouard de Bas-Pouilly and of the thirty-three years' devotion. This she thought interesting and romantic but she was shocked to see an old woman just like herself. As she sat down in the chair placed ready for her she thought Edouard a fool not to have arranged to be devoted to a younger mistress.

"I am told we have a link," (she had this ready), "in my cousin, Monsieur de Bas-Pouilly. I am glad, as a very old friend, to meet someone who made him happy."

"I hope I did," said Rose. "I hope I did."

"Without a doubt."

"But if I had it over again I would be different. Now it's over it seems hardly to have begun. And his face has gone away out of my mind: I can't remember it. Edouard knows nothing of me now, not now."

The duchess did not feel like contradicting her. She could not, as the doyenne of the family, answer for it that Edouard took an interest now in his mistress. Yet at Rose's words she remembered her own pain. She was selfish, but her duke had not found her so. He had been a great tease and a great Anglophile: he knew his English like an Englishman but he liked to use his words with the licence of a foreigner. "Alice is very decent," he would say, "if she only cared to permit herself." And this would irritate and enrapture her: she knew what he meant. There had been nobody after he died to play games with the stones in her character: no one in fact had ever known her well again. But though she remembered pain she could not bring herself to include Rose. This small, frivolous old creature was not to feel what she had felt. The sight of the passing of a whole generation had made her heart grow colder.

"It takes time to get over it," she answered evasively.

Yet Rose had a way of going to the truth: she had the clear eyes of the dying.

"Did you never feel remorse?"

The duchess was taken aback. Yet in her heart she was on well-known ground, and unlike Miranda she was always happy to move into a philosophic field.

"Death and remorse are cousins," she gave out, dilating her nostrils. "It's a natural regret for the imperfections of relationships. It's not unique to die, and one must remember that everyone takes his turn."

Rose, who lay looking at the ruby lobes, took no interest in the sentence. As soon as the ducal lips had stopped moving she broke in restlessly: "Did you know him when he was young?"

"What did you ask?"

"When he was a young man did you know Edouard?"

The duchess, irritated, replied, "Yes. When I first married and came to France."

"Did all the young women run after him? How did he seem? Very brilliant?"

"It was thought a great pity he never married."

"I was the reason!" cried Rose with her colour flying up. "Should he have married? Did you all speak of it then? Did his relations discuss it?"

"Isn't it always better if a man marries?" said the duchess, secretly ashamed of herself. "But he was a man who knew his own mind and no one would have dared advise him. What has been has been. And now you must get better." But she felt cross with Rose and got up, thinking that her hostess had made a great fuss about a little woman nobody knew anything about.

"I shan't get better."

"Ah, that's what people think. But you mustn't lack courage. Courage must be kept for the last ounce of breath."

"Whatever for?"

"Because," said the duchess, heavily (for she did not know), "our common human nature demands it. I am leaving you now to rest. But tomorrow we may meet in the garden. I think some fresh air would be good for you." On this gracious note she was able to turn and get out of the room.

"I suppose you are quite sure," she said to Ruby, "that your invalid was really such a great friend of Edouard's? Have we only her word for it?"

"How did the meeting go off?"

"I was astounded at her looks. Does that little red damask face speak perhaps of the bottle? She seems much older than Edouard."

"She's sixty."

"I don't think so."

Instead of taking the air as the duchess counselled Rose died next morning from heart failure. She had had her breakfast, but at eleven Rosalba found her very still. She ran frightened for her mistress and Ruby came at once and stood looking down at her. She felt immense relief. Hearing a footstep in the corridor she saw Gynt passing and called him in.

"She's dead," she said softly, holding his arm. But Gynt drew sharply back.

"Dear God," she heard him whisper, "how it comes!"

## CHAPTER TWENTY-TWO

No relations could be found, and Father Bonnie, the parish priest and Alberti's confessor, gave permission to bury Rose in Pouilly churchyard.

The Duchess Alice, having heard with amazement of the marriage of the Duca di Roccafergolo, occupied her morning before the funeral by paying a call. Though seventy she was a fine walker and she set off alone down the grass slope of the water meadows, remembering the way. She took note of the forestry as she walked, the neglected clearing of the undergrowth, the clogged streams. She stood still and wrote down a remark about the condition of a bridge.

When Celestine opened the door to her (and dropped her a little curtsey) the duchess, like Ruby, deferred her words of congratulation in favour of verification: but shown in to the duca she heard him say (almost before he could rise, so that there should be no misunderstanding), "You have met my wife?" The wife, however, vanished so quickly that the old duchess could only glance back at a closed door.

"I came to pay my respects," she said grimly. "So long as it's been a success. This call is really paid upon your wife."

"It's been a charming success," smiled Alberti. "But she's shy. She's busy in the kitchen. Were you surprised?" He offered her a deep cretonne chair.

"I'm no longer made to bend in the middle," she said, taking an upright one. "No, I'm never surprised at the things old bachelors will do. You should have married long ago. And so should Edouard. When men don't marry they always regret it. As you've shown. We've had a funeral this morning."

"Yes, they're burying Edouard's Rose. I'm not well enough myself to go to any funeral but my own. Ruby says she died of a broken heart."

"She had heart failure. It's hardly the same thing. And I don't know—though it's not tactful to criticise the dead—what proof there is of all this devotion to Edouard."

"There's seldom proof," said Alberti. "These things are so private. I suppose if he'd wished he could have married her. But then we should have had her here as his widow. That is to say if she had lived. And now, Duchess, since I've a change of landlord—I'm an old man—how about my tenancy?"

"It's my great-nephew's affair. But nobody in the world's going to dispossess you. And talking of James have you noticed his great preoccupation?"

Alberti set his nerves in order, guessing what was coming.

"I'm pleased," said the great-aunt, proceeding with her intention to speak plain, "to see that he's fallen in love with his hostess. It will keep him out of mischief."

"So you think he has?"

"Don't you? He has eyes for no one else. Certainly, I'm glad to see, not for that girl Miranda. A cold, stiff girl. Most curious—as Ruby's daughter—but paralysed, I daresay, by her mother's ease with life. I've seen it before. But then one's seen everything before. I've a great regard for Ruby. James is safe for a year's infatuation. He's a romantic or he would notice she's looking older. She has, of course, the same fault she always had—a lack of dignity."

"But it's one of her virtues!" exclaimed Alberti, caught out.

The duchess laughed her short cackle. "On the defence! The usual reaction. But I only mean that at her age she might look more restful. I know it's the fashion in Paris to remain with the same appearance. There's really no such thing now as age. Women fade a little and grow a little tiresome. Beyond that, nothing. I'm old-fashioned, but I live a long way away and very much in the country. Twenty years ago I was fifty, and really I see now that I needn't have placed myself, as I did then, in a category. Still, at fifty-three (as she is) I wouldn't have inspired love, nor expected it. And if I had, I shouldn't have known what to do with it. I daresay our beautiful friend knows very well, and I don't disapprove. It's a fashion, like everything else. There's a certain want of calm: it provokes, I think, a look of anxiety. But perhaps only to my eyes. Of course if one keeps something of one's looks—and she has kept so much—then experience of life adds a fascination, and especially to young men. And not everyone goes mad over freshness. You don't mind my dog?"

"Your dog?"

She abstracted the little dog from the folds of her cloak and set it on the floor.

"Have you carried it all the way?"

"She managed half a mile. I can't leave off her exercise altogether."

"You must be very fond of her."

"No. And my maid unfortunately less, or she would walk her. What do you think yourself of the girl?"

"Miranda? I'm her godfather." And changing the conversation he asked:

"Will James live here now?"

"I imagine," she said, "James will let the cottage. I shall certainly suggest for occasional use a flat in the château itself: the Institut could well arrange that, and the sight-seers keep only to the main apartments. Mercifully he still comes a great deal to me."

"You are very fond of him?"

"To tell you the truth——"

"Yes?"

"It's only for him I can feel anything. Don't you find that as you get older the heart dries up?"

"No," said Alberti.

"Ah—I've been a widow too long, with no one from whom I now accept reproof. Too late to alter that, but it's done me no good. I like my own way. Except for James it's the only thing I do like."

"I hear your garden's a miracle."

"It's my bit of life," she said. "But a poor substitute for a family. The seasons go round too often. It becomes shocking how soon the spring bulbs come again."

On the whole Alberti liked her better than Ruby did—since he saw her only as a caller. He was fascinated by her appearance. Under her black cloak she wore today again her scarlet waistcoat, but as her maid was careless a bar of emeralds and diamonds closed the gap where a gilt button was missing. She had a black summer hat, long out of fashion, which lifted on one side to show fine eyes, blue lips, and coral ears. She looked this way and that round the room, feeling that there was more to say. But there was no more to say, at all events not what she could say sitting. So she got up as though to go, and, less easily, so did he.

"I thought you would notice," she said with her old woman's reiterative mischief, "how James is in love," and passed through the door he held open for her. "I think you said you noticed it."

"I didn't say so," he smiled back at her. "I only notice that he has the same delight we all have in Ruby. She's so gay."

The duchess reached the garden before her irritation found words.

"Such a capacity for gaiety is feverish at her age. I find it frivolous." She was cross.

"Such a pretty word," said Alberti, walking with her down to his garden gate, "to frivol. Especially when it is a philosopher who frivols, and a beautiful philosopher, and one who knows the value of gaiety."

"Well, you're in love with her too, as I thought. What extraordinary people you are who live near Paris! In my part of the country we get over the measles earlier. It must be tiring to have these emotions—so prolonged. There's no mystery, no permanence about the human relationship. I've got to the end of the heart—and a dry one's a comfort in old age. I'll see that James leaves you in peace."

She pretended to find comfort in her drying heart, did she?—he thought, as he watched her walk away, carrying the little dog. For persons who must drop off the world within a given number of years was it, after all, a relief to find the hooks already unfastening? What did she then make of life? Had she any retrospective view? Did she conclude anything? No, he thought, she depended, as she always had done, on living in the moment, on shutting out pain with her vitality. When these protestants took that path, he thought, they had no one to remind them. But God knows what a risk they took! He turned back into the house.

A faint and savoury smell from the kitchen reminded him of his wife. This was one of the moments when he needed homely companionship. Seldom in the daytime. Chiefly when he woke at night and saw the stars shine in a black, enormous heaven. His own heart, he thought, showed no signs of drying.

"Celestine," he said, standing at the kitchen door, "come and talk to me."

She looked round from the stove, smiling, one hand gently shaking a frying-pan in which fresh butter was melting, strewn with a few fragments of bacon. From this came the particular scent, which was, in its manner, first class.

"Will Your Grace wait?" she said. He watched her while she tenderly browned four slim slices of breast of chicken, took them out with a draining spoon, and set them on a sieve to cool. She came round the kitchen table towards him and sat, with the smiling assurance of a privileged person, on her wooden rocking chair with its faded cotton seat. She knew when her lord wanted to talk that he had restless thoughts that needed calming. He had not always anything particular to talk about.

"Well," he said, smiling down at her, "Duchess?" He called her "Duchess" as one calls one's cat "Princess, Prince, Duke."

And to that she replied comfortably, like one who repeats a Penitence, "I pray to God every morning to forgive my fault."

"Yes, you were a bad Celestine. But you were influenced. You are a weak woman."

"Yes. It was my motherhood. But I have been thinking——"

"What have you been thinking?"

"That, like the animals, when a son is grown the ties are loosened."

"Do you think like that when you lie in bed?"

"No, I sleep. But when I cook, I think."

"But you love your Zani still?"

"I love good men," said Celestine simply. "But I think often of Zani and hope he will behave and grow rich."

"Have you heard from him?"

"He does not write," she said. "I thought perhaps you had had news?"

Zani had been sent to work in a large racing stables near Bagnoles de L'Orne, as a buyer of grain.

"It is the nearest I can place him to a black market," Alberti had thought. "To be happy and successful he must be placed where it is possible to make illegal gains, and the buying and selling of grain for racehorses will give him a start. If he is bottled up in righteousness he will explode again in my face."

"No news is good news," said Alberti, who had learned Celestine's language of proverbs. "I think perhaps you won't hear very often. He is probably interested in what he is doing. I think he will get on."

"I have to thank you," said Celestine primly, bobbing her head a little.

A frown was knitting itself in the rosy muscles of Alberti's forehead. Now he remembered he had, after all, something to say, and something better said in the kitchen in the mid-morning than in the empty night.

"Which reminds me," he said. "That old woman and I—you know she is another duchess, but an older one—we mentioned death. When I go, Celestine, I want to be with you alone."

She looked at him.

"You alone, you understand."

Her soft brown eyes looked obstinate.

"What are you thinking of then?"

"Of milady. If such a thing should happen she will think I keep her out."

"But she must be kept out. Let me explain to you, I don't know yet whether I am a brave man. Nobody knows till the end. I want to be alone with the woman who has looked after all my weaknesses. Do you understand now?"

"I understand how much you love her."

"Yes," he said absently. "And I depend on you. Is it a promise? When it comes, and when I say the word, we go through it alone."

They said no more, and Celestine, remaining in her kitchen, thought of this superior love, this marvellous love which she did not grudge. In some way it was a proof to her of the value of the master who had been good to her. She respected it as a gift, fine and bodiless, the private life of archangels. She did not really think she could keep his great friend out of the door when the duca was on the point of death, but she had promised to do her best and she would try to carry it out. She was herself unafraid of that moment and would know what to do. Since her husband had definitely told her he must die, she accepted it from him. It was a heavy weight on her heart, but not to be questioned.

As the duchess set out to walk slowly back across the fields Edouard's sister drove up to the front door of Little Pouilly. The hearse had not yet arrived.

It was common knowledge that Edouard had been overgood to a tiresome sister. Ruby knew Madame de Lison as an acquaintance but had never troubled to think about her. Now as she stood in the sun on the terrace waiting she realised with a shock that she had not told this woman one word of the Rose-story. She had totally forgotten all about her, and it was all the worse since Angel de Lison was so easily forgotten.

The visitor came quickly through the drawing-room with her uncertain look, having today given up her bareheaded custom for a black hat with an embroidered veil. Through it her handsome, insecure eyes were fixed on Ruby. She put out her hand and began to talk in her rushing, emphatic manner.

"I would have come before," she exclaimed, "to thank you for what you did for me in Paris. I've been killed, literally killed, by these legal men. Edouard seems to have kept all his most difficult documents here at Pouilly. If you're free for a few minutes—I shan't keep you, I'm on my way up to Paris—but what sort of woman—I

want so much to know—did you find? You saw her? She made no
trouble about anything?" As she talked she was all the time manœu-
vring that she and Ruby return to the shade of the drawing-room,
as though she hated the light of the sun. Ruby understood at once
that Angel de Lison had been burning to know more about her
brother's mistress and she felt guilty at the situation that had arisen.

There might have been time to close the drawing-room door. But
it stood wide open. Neither of them heard the shuffle of feet on the
landing above. "I ought to have told you," Ruby began unsteadily,
"I should have rung you. She's been here. I've had her here . . ."

"Not this Rose! Not in this house!"

At that moment, facing the open door together, they both saw the
coffin as it was carried downstairs at an angle into the hall. Madame
de Lison grasped Ruby's arm with a cry—

"You are burying someone!"

"She died on Wednesday. I brought her down. I couldn't leave
her by herself."

"In that coffin? She! Not in that coffin!"

"Yes. Rose. Three days ago."

"Rose! His Rose?" Madame de Lison was fighting with her veil,
hunting desperately for the pins that held it. "But I wanted to see
her! I've wanted for years to see her but he never would let me. To
have missed—— You should have told me! Oh, it's not too late!"

"It's too late, isn't it?"

"No, no, no. Before you bury her open the coffin! How could you
not have told me!"

She leant against the piano and got off her veil. Two men had
passed ahead of the coffin to stand the trestles in the hall. One of
them signed to Ruby, who went to the door to speak to him. The
hearse still had not arrived.

The voice from the piano called shrill behind her. "I must ask
you," it said, shaking, "to have the lid unscrewed."

"Unscrewed?" Ruby turned around. "Whatever for?"

"I want to see her. Those men can unscrew it. I must see her. I
ask. I insist." Edouard's sister stood now with her hat in her hand

and the thick grey hair tufted upright on her forehead. Her eyes shone with a sort of liquid. Her salved lips were pressed into a thin line before they opened again to cry in a sincere desperation:

"I shall choke if I don't see her! I shall choke if I don't!"

At that moment the hearse arrived, but Ruby overcame the undertaker's objections and two men began to undo the lid with their screwdrivers. Madame de Lison, breathing hard, took a step forward and another till she reached the door. When the lid was lifted Rose, pale at last, appeared again among the legendary white ruchings.

"But she's OLD!" cried Edouard's sister in a loud voice of disbelief across the coffin to Ruby.

"Women get old," said Ruby. "Put this by her hand." She took a magnolia bud from a glass dish on a table near her.

Madame de Lison took the bud mechanically and dropped it where she was told. Staring down she rested her hands on the sides of the coffin.

"His 'Rose,'" she said. "This! So all these years I need never have worried myself. It's all been for nothing. Not even beauty . . . Then what do men want?" (Ruby wondered that Rose could lie so calm.) "What could have bound him to her?"

"I imagine—love."

"Love!" cried Angel de Lison, so sharply that the trestle tilted on the uneven floor. She started back, for Rose had nodded in the filtered light.

"And do you suppose," she asked in tones that fear made ringing, "she could once have been pretty?"

James came down the stairs, his coat over his arm, and stood still with a look of horror.

"What did you expect then?" he heard Ruby exclaim. "That one's pretty looks would last for ever? How do you think, Madame de Lison, you will look yourself one day, tucked up in white satin and carried in a box like an old doll?"

He saw Madame de Lison raise her head and stare, and he had just time to spring to the hall door and hold it open as Edouard's sister, with a shocked look, went quickly out to her car.

Ruby snatched the bud from the coffin and put it back in the dish. Two men lifted the lid gently back over Rose's appearance.

The old duchess, walking in at the door, and nearly knocked over by her distant relation, had missed a scene she would dearly like to have watched.

## CHAPTER TWENTY-THREE

"Ceremony!" exclaimed the Duchess Alice, just dressed and down at last after her tremendous morning at her papers (as Cacki moved the decanters, bottles, glasses which were usually left in the outer hall near to the drawing-room window). "Who's coming?" (It was two days after Rose's funeral.)

"Gynt's bringing one of his bird men down from the Travellers. An old gentleman with a Hebridean island. Gynt, you know, corresponds all over Europe. It's like the centre of a spy system." (Letters arrived in peculiar, foreign, crabbed handwriting, filled with secret passwords—"white-rumped wheatears, black-tailed godwits, spotted redshanks . . .")

The guest was tall and bent, a tired, keen old man of the world with sunken eyes and an impersonal quarter-smile, wearing the kind of pale suit, a shade natty, that one chooses for Paris in the summer.

Gynt, saying something that Ruby could not distinguish, went over to fetch him sherry.

"Beddoes Thomas," said the guest more clearly.

"And we used to know each other," said Ruby pleasantly.

"It's a long time ago," agreed the guest. She introduced him to the duchess—"Mr. Beddoes Thomas."

"Sir Beddoes," corrected Gynt, handing him his glass. Luncheon was announced immediately, for Gynt and the guest had been late.

"But there's no hurry," said Ruby. "Cacki always bustles us."

But the duchess, who never drank anything unless, rarely, it was champagne, and who knew, because she had asked, that the first course was omelette with asparagus, would not let them stay long with their sherry. "I'm always starving in other people's houses," she said, "carry in your glass"; and she took him herself into the dining-room, starting at once a Scottish conversation. She even knew his particular island.

"Though those Gulf-stream islands are morbid, I seem to remember. Hot in the centre and depressing, growing shrubs they ought not to, given the latitude. And too windy to breathe at the edge. And the men who live there—I don't mean the peasants but the rich owners like yourself—fall into trances. Don't you go into trances?"

"A trance of love," he said. "Heavenly, happy inertia. But my wife shares your feelings. She goes there when I go because she's good to me, and to spoil me and see my shoes are dry, but generally we live near Oban."

"Now have I met your wife?" said Ruby. It was the gold ring that fascinated her. Certainly the same one. A man's plain ring of that sort is practically a birthmark.

"I married late," he said. "Ten years ago." His eyes rested on her.

"She's not here with you in Paris?"

"No. She's an abandoned, shameless stay-at-home. We've cattle, a small dairy, dogs she won't leave. To drag her up you have to excavate her like a tree stump."

"Ah—a tree stump!" said the duchess. "A good simile. We old women get rooted like that, all the more when there are no branches above. And we require a—what is that prehistoric instrument that's quite modern?"

"A bulldozer?"

"These American words carry no European picture with them, do you notice? That's why one forgets them. When there's a garden it's hard to leave it, but it's not only the bulbs, apple blossoms, lilac, roses, the engagement-book of high points like a society season, it's the habits in the house from morning to night—that go round like a prayer-wheel when you get old and tie you down."

"But one can break through the ties by fresh plans, fresh hopes."

"Old people may plan but they don't hope. They simply live. While you still hope you waste time. Is your wife younger?"

"Than I am? Oh, much, much. Thirty-five years."

"You mustn't let her get like I am. Like your tree stump."

"And do you too take excavating?" asked Ruby.

"I'm nearly as bad since I married. And since I became old. I'm seventy-five," he said with a little pride, for he knew he looked much younger.

But to his surprise she replied thoughtfully, "You must be." At that he laughed and said:

"I'm in the habit of expecting compliments. I'm supposed to be a very well-kept, deceptive old man."

"Oh, you are," she said. "But I was calculating on facts. Of course I realise now—Gynt, you know, only labels people on bird-levels— who you are. So I know, more or less, your age, as one knows that of a building. Gynt—" she said, "don't you know who he is—what he was to me?" The guest did not flicker by an eyelid. "He was the Public Prosecutor."

"Ruby's murder!" said Gynt. "Ruby's famous murder? She always thought, you know (but I expect you've forgotten it), that she testified for the murderer! It was years before I discovered that you put her in for the Crown."

"Edmund Hobble." (Ruby helped him.) "He killed his mother. She was a dog breeder. I gave evidence. I'd seen them both a few hours before it happened. He killed her with a chair."

"Didn't they hang him?" frowned Sir Beddoes Thomas. But he never forgot a murder. "No, I remember. A long time ago. He slid out from under my hand."

"One's story is one's story," said Ruby. "What you tell for so long becomes true. I saved Edmund Hobble. I stuck to it that his mother was a brute."

"That wouldn't have saved him. That was motive. You can't escape because you don't like your mother." He wore suddenly his little stagey smile, and the red-brown fox's eyes were slanting at her —as he slipped into court again and felt the warmth of his wig.

"But there was more," she said. "My line should have been that he was sane; your office did a little coaching. But when I heard them badgering him I saw that I should say with all my might that he'd struck us as daft, wanting . . ."

"Even after all these years I can be shocked at perjury," he said. "But it would have made no difference. It lay with the doctors." He turned as the door opened and James came in.

"I've had lunch," said James. "With Madame de Lison. Only so terribly early. Are you having coffee?"

But they decided to move onto the terrace for their coffee. James took his great-aunt to the writing table in the drawing-room to witness a signature for Madame de Lison.

"Bring your port," said Gynt to the guest. "I want to show you Cora Holbein's drawings for my book. And then I'm going to take you down to the Fantasia."

"Give him five minutes here with me," said Ruby. "I'll send him in to you. I want to know—I want him to tell me—what will have happened by now to my murderer."

"It all depends, of course." Beddoes turned his glass slowly. "It's according to their condition. If they come out it's naturally kept dark. The police know. Some small tobacconist's shop perhaps. He's probably a quiet man whom everybody trusts. One way and another . . ." he said absently, losing the thread of what he was saying, for something was warning him, a *banderilla* planted in his skin—and how she reminded him of someone! The stare of the celebrated turquoise eyes, the tales he had heard of her, the pictures he had seen of her, accounted, he supposed, for this. And Gynt's port had made him sleepy. He was vexed that he had taken it. But he broke so many rules since he was seventy. "One way and another," he called back his wandering sentence, "there must be murderers who are good neighbours."

And then, touched like a boat by a gusty air, his mind listed. A rainbow of surprise and regret stood in his sky. He was all of a sudden sure that he had been in love with her. But he didn't know when or where or to what degree or whether they had ruptured in vexation or through circumstances, or how important they had been to one another, nor to what lengths they had gone—for physical loves differ so little and are so easily forgotten—and it was impossible to take and handle and speak of something that might have happened in any capital in Europe or in any year. It certainly couldn't have happened at the time of the case—she was too young. "But she must have been *lovely!*" he thought, upset. And felt, what he seldom felt now (since he married his brown-haired Camilla), the shock that life was spent.

And Ruby, watching him, saw the mouth that had kissed her and had been—how many times renewed? (If skin changes every seven years? But everything changes every seven years. Time washes over the beach and nothing is left. You can't leave your sand-castle or forget your sand-shoe.)—There was the plain ring she had seized and kissed so feverishly. But a kiss so long ago is a thin picture. There were scenes in literature more real.

Gynt, impatient, came back to them from the library window and joined them. "Well—go!" Ruby said. "Still—I must spoil your afternoon by telling you that you once took me out to lunch and that you've forgotten me."

But he was not going to be afraid of her. "That's what it is to be old," he said easily. "One forgets very important things and remembers trivialities. I hope we were nice to each other?"

"You were charming. You said to me—one of the things you said to me was that you hoped, when I was a middle-aged woman, we'd meet again!"

"No, no. What an unpleasant word! Besides, I couldn't have calculated that by then I myself should cut a pretty figure, that I should be seventy-five!"

She watched them walk back into the library. Everything in the day for a moment changed its aspect, disfigured for her by the indifference she felt for the past. One of those spasms of melancholy which specially assail gay people was upon her. James came out again with his great-aunt.

"Gynt's well-dressed friend," said the old duchess, "made me homesick for the way people mellow in England. Possibly not originally what we used to call a gentleman, but so long, isn't he, turned into one by success! Here in France people who have got anywhere protect their importance by growing stiffer. But when a man in England's reached the upper levels his mind grows more and more informal. It was a pleasure to talk to him. A lucky old man. I doubt if he's even been a good one. Where was Miranda?"

"She lunched with her godfather. With Alberti."

"You should send her over to London for the season."

"Tuxie's hardly been dead six weeks."

"I don't look on her as a widow. I'm going up to my room now and shan't be down till tea-time. I'm leaving you the day after to-morrow. If I don't I shall lose the habit of being alone."

"How stimulated she becomes by meeting people," said Ruby to James when the duchess had gone in. "Walk down with me towards the hamlet. We'll pass Sir Beddoes on the way back with Gynt. I never said good-bye to him. Will she really go the day after tomorrow? The first word she's said to me about it."

"My poor old aunt has so enjoyed herself. She's afraid, as she says, of taking hardly again to her rocky isolation. She was a clever woman once and when she meets other people her wits come back to her and she knows it. At Lardaigne it's bad for her, she's such a despot. It's an indulgence here but she thinks she shouldn't have too much of it. She's her own law. She's been hinting since this morning that I go with her."

"But you won't?" she said quickly—and his longing heart had the impression of a momentary ascendency. "You still have a lot to do here. But how she loves you!"

"It's a responsibility," he said. "It's so terribly unequal—to give pleasure to the old. Great-aunt Alice has been father and mother to me. I'm even her heir, which was quite unnecessary. Not of course to the title but to all the Scottish money."

"You will be very rich. Much richer than Edouard was. I should think she has her father's understanding of how to keep money."

"She does everything herself," he said. "But nobody really knows how well. She has a man of business, but she tortures him. He's lost his nerve with her and says things you can see he immediately wishes he hadn't. The poor man sweats at the thought of a second's silence. In her attitude to people she's become like an old man. She hasn't lost her vanity but it's not the vanity now of a woman. She's delighted to make an impression but she ignores failures. She's vain but not sensitive, and I find that a blessing. I'm sensitive for her perhaps.

"The time that I dread when I'm there is dinner at night. I go there a lot now and the country's lovely and by day there's a great deal to do. But at night we sit together, following the pomp and ritual I can remember since I was a child, and she's tired and silent and I suffer for her, reading into her silence thoughts that perhaps don't exist. Then in the morning I ask her—" (and he laughed) "—'How have you slept, Great-aunt?' and she says, 'From one end of the night to the other, as I always do.'"

"The old are a bit sad," said Ruby, "but it's like rheumatism—one can do nothing about it and they grow used to it. And then it's not unique. We shall all be there soon. What did you think of the guest—Gynt's friend?"

"I took a dislike to him. I'm so unfair to old men. That look they wear of outlived successes, the complacent and papery worldliness— but it isn't so much I blame them as I wriggle at what's to happen to me! Life's so horribly serious, and then to come to the end of it in a suit of pale stuff and a knowing old smile! But my aunt thought quite differently."

"She enjoyed him."

"Old people like talking lightly. It's a sort of manners."

"It's more than manners. Life really becomes a little lighter. The emotions have been found by then to be not all they are cracked up to be. But though they don't 'love' they remain loving. And the complacence that annoys you isn't very deep."

"If my father had lived I could have forgiven them. But I've been brought up by women and perhaps I drank their intolerances when I milked my porridge."

"Dear, dear," said his companion, "you should have been brought up by me. My life is spent with old men now. But I always loved them."

"Not that one, I hope!" And Ruby, tired of enjoying the joke of her day alone, said deliberately:

"Yes. Yes, that one."

"I'm speaking of Thomas."

"I knew you weren't speaking of Gynt."

"Good God. You can't—you don't mean it?"

"But I do. Don't be absurd. That's the generation I passed my youth with. Obviously he was once younger. Did you see a gold ring he wore? You did? Long ago I kissed it. I was sixteen. He was the first man who ever kissed me."

"Yes, I hear what you say. I hear the words," said James impatiently. "I'm busy taking them in. But even though everything was long ago—as you call it—there's some discrepancy. If you were sixteen."

"To save your arithmetic, he was thirty-eight."

"You didn't *love* him?"

"Yes, I must have." (But the link now with the elderly guest at luncheon seemed laughably indecorous.)

"It's terrible to me, even if it sounds ridiculous, that you should have been in love before I was born."

"Is it?" she said, sorry for him, but really she couldn't play at being his age. "Well, that's not reasonable."

"How does one meet after so many years? How does one touch on such a thing? I came in late to your luncheon, when everything, I suppose, was adjusted. How can one meet? Is it pain? What's taken for granted? Or is nothing mentioned?"

"I need someone, you know, my own age to laugh it over. I see you're not able. Beddoes Thomas—— By the way, we've missed them, we've missed him——"

"Thank God!" said poor James.

"—couldn't remember me. He was my first lover but he'd forgotten it. Does that give you a sense of proportion? I've really, you know, had my day."

"I'm very unhappy," he said squarely, walking by her side.

"I know you are. I don't belittle it. And if I hurt you with chance words it is that, like Rose, I am beginning to let them escape me. They come from a source of speculation where nothing's as sacred as it was, and love, though it's not a perfect stranger to me, takes its place in the past with the other troubles. There's nothing now on those lines in front of me. I've had all I want. I don't mean I'm contented, nor do I understand how to face old age. But a last love won't solve that. It isn't that, with all its anxieties, that I want."

"But you—to fear old age! Or even think of it!"

"It's not so much age I fear as becoming insensitive. It's the ignorant shrinking before the anaesthetic. One looks so silly half asleep."

"The whole thing's mad!" he burst out. "I won't listen to the way you talk! There's some horrible mistake—looking as you do! Do you take all chance and hope away from me? Ruby—I won't ask much! Two months? Three months?"

"As my lover? No. Oh no."

"Oh . . ."

"I've finished. I'm folded up. I've done my packing."

"I could put back what you think's gone! What you're reckless enough to think's gone!"

"Stop begging like a child for chocolate. It would be nothing to give you the whole box, but it's empty. You're too young for me."

"I bore you."

"Yes, if you like. I only want men now when they can look backward. As Alberti can. I want—I'm even eager—to explore the age I really am."

"How can that be? How can that possibly be?"

"You can't believe it can happen?"

"No. I could believe it of my great-aunt. Not of you. Not of you with your gaiety and your vitality."

"She may be a handful of years older. But I'm in her class."

"How old then?"

"Fifty-three."

She watched him thinking, calculating. She knew he knew now

that he could easily have been her baby in its cradle. She could have carried him, put on his bibs and his rompers, dressed him in grey flannel for his first school.

"I knew you must be that," he said at length, "for, after all, Miranda is over thirty. But you are all I want, all I want, all I want."

And all the time she was thinking: "If my child had this young man!" She was almost afraid to think, lest the word "Miranda" should escape and run like a hare through the trees and he should see it.

"I have nothing that you want," she said with determination.

"Don't speak," he exclaimed, "if everything you say must set and harden words that shouldn't be said! You think I am romantic. You call me young. That's because you've known me as a child and it's unfortunate for me that I worshipped you then in my small-boy way, for now you take it all on that footing. I was sixteen when last you saw me. It's hard for me to undo that. But now after twelve years away I've become a man and I come back to find you a woman without equal. I could tell you your face isn't as beautiful as it was if it hadn't changed into something I love better. I'm in love both with what you were and with what Time is putting in every day. The civilization of your appearance, your reddened lips that make the truth sound as I've never heard it, the beauty of your careless clothes, the way you're at home with life . . . If I had you, if I had the luck to have you . . ."

"In what sense?"

He held out his hands emptily. "I don't know. I'm in despair. Of course I want you as my wife. How could I not want that?"

She overlooked this wild expression of his folly and contented herself by saying:

"It's a pity it's me, isn't it? So many women would feel you guaranteed what they mustn't lose above all things. But I never was like that. I hate outstaying. I'm all for the heart, but I really only trust the old heart of affection . . ."

"But I . . ."

"You're going to say you can give me that too. I shouldn't believe you. I only care now for human beings who are as they are: not changed by wild and temporary feelings. My looks aren't solid enough to sustain them. They would vanish under the load. I like to be what I am. I like sober, solid relationship. For instance, Alberti . . ."

"He adores you."

"Yes, once. But he's an old man now. The fires are sunk. It's candlelight in his neighbourhood. All my old men are seventy. That suits me, you see."

For a quarter of a century Ruby had been more fun than anyone else. Age seemed to have by-passed her. She was prepared, like Titian, to die of the plague at ninety. But she was tired of the circus-circle, nor did she want to hear daily reports of Goethe's heart. And he, walking at her side, unhappy and bewildered, had a slow sense of offence (as she meant him to), offence and wounded pride spreading at a low level like a bruise. They were nearing the brink of the wood and could see the house beyond the water a quarter of a mile away. Soon they were out of the forest into the full light.

"Must I never talk again as I've talked?" he said abruptly.

"I don't make unnatural commands," she replied. "But you'll find you can't do all the loving by yourself." He tried to tell himself that now in the light he could certainly catch sight of the age she spoke of (wanting to press hard on the wound she had made). But whatever was in her face it bewitched him. They climbed the rising field to the house.

Miranda, who had returned, leaned on her window, watching her mother and James. And as they came up the last slope she saw how they talked to one another, and it was from this intimacy that she by her ignorance and clumsiness was shut out. What did they say? On what lines did a woman speak who had so much behind her as her mother—who walked in admiration and ease of friendship as though there was no other way of living? If she could but listen once to such a conversation she might understand.

And while she watched, half hidden by the magnolia, she heard James say:

"But you aren't like me. You never think of yourself."

And to her surprise her mother's voice said: "I think of myself, alas, without stopping. It's a shame and a scandal and an humiliation!"

She could not believe her ears. On what conundrum in her own life could her mother possibly puzzle?

## CHAPTER TWENTY-FOUR

It was Miranda's thirty-second birthday.

The duchess had been playing them off all day about her departure. She would not totally commit herself. She was one of those people who, having given all the trouble necessary to get her own way, thinks no one has really noticed it.

Her chauffeur, who stayed at the inn, was now warned. Her maid had worked on the packing since the morning. But at luncheon the duchess asked to have a new bedroom got ready for her so that if she fully decided to leave the maid could continue packing after she herself was asleep. This she said would be a convenience for everyone.

Finally, as she dressed for dinner, she made up her mind to leave at seven next morning, and scribbled a note to her hostess in which she asked fancifully—she always believed that a fine phrase could cloak an offence—if she might be "called by starlight." Ruby replied in another scribble from her bedroom: "Is that poetry? Or is it the name of an hour?" Yet another message went back—"Is five too early?"—getting from Ruby the magnificent reply, "Oh, not at all."

Ready and dressed well before the hour for dinner, the duchess sent her maid for James to come and see her. According to the habits of the household, he was sitting in Ruby's bedroom while she dressed. Miranda was there too, and the little dog, now nine, was coiled up on the ragged silk of the old Empire chair. The maid, told to come into the room, stared at them astonished. The young master, in a dressing gown, was in the window seat, and the young lady, looking very well, was fully dressed. But the lady (who, she had learnt from Rosalba, was old Rosalba's own age) sat before her looking glass painting her lashes with a brush. If the peasant's yellow skin could have responded it would have reddened when Ruby turned to speak to her, for there she was in the room with a young man, and wore a lace garment that hardly concealed her breasts.

James rose to go to his great-aunt. "I shall be late," he said. "I've not even bathed yet," and hurried after the maid.

The duchess wished to get her nephew to return to the South with her in the morning. He explained to her as he had before, but gently, that the legal work connected with his succession was not over.

"You can come back," she grumbled, a little under her breath. "Of course you can come back. But I wanted to discuss your final intentions. I know, of course, James, that you won't live in Pouilly, though eventually one might get the Institut to let you have a few rooms in the château . . ."

"I'd sooner live in St. Pancras!"

"And Edouard's cottage should be let and those workshops of his pulled down. Who's going to take a cottage with the garden looking like a factory? I've long planned a good garden where they stand. I used to try to persuade Edouard. See how much there is to talk about! If you come with me tomorrow we shall have all the day and part of the next to talk as we travel."

As a small boy he had been taken such journeys. In those days, sitting beside his great-aunt, and wedged as she was with rugs and cushions, the butler used at the moment of starting to hand him a little Dresden basin wrapped in a towel. The nausea of those journeys was almost the only bad memory in the childhood he had spent with her. To please her, for he could not resist pleasing her, he said:

"I believe there's an air service. In fact I know it. I'll stay two more days and be there very soon after you arrive."

He thought she might frown on this but to his surprise she said:

"I've wanted to fly myself." And he saw her glance go to the kneeling maid and the straw cases piled in the bathroom. For a moment she considered abandoning her departure: but the thought passed.

"Well, you won't come with me," she said without vexation. She respected him and never pressed him too far. "Go and dress. I wanted to say—" (she spoke in English as she always spoke to him) "—take it well, from an old woman not as wise as she thinks she is—be careful. That strange husband may want to be free."

James became breathless as he took in her meaning.

His great-aunt continued to look at him. In his upset he started counting the black taffeta bows on her head, each pinned with a diamond. She seemed to have announced to him that she had seen everything, so there was no point in concealment.

"She won't have anything to do with me," he finally said aloud. The duchess at that on her side ran through a great many thoughts. She didn't believe him—or Ruby was playing a deep game—she was loth to make herself clearer—she had said enough.

"You had better dress," she said again.

"But I must know!" he exclaimed, rising. "What can you mean about Gynt?"

"We're the same age," she said. "We are all the same age here, Gynt, and the Duca de Roccafergolo and I, or at least on the same shelf. We have all had our much earlier relationships. I know things that are hidden from you. I know pages that were written then more clear. Gynt's a mystic. When I was a young woman I had a weakness for him. And then he's my countryman. He comes from restless people, and I've often seen that after fifty a man changes and his ancestors begin to get him back into their arms. It's ten years since I was here and I find him very different. Watch him as he sits at table. Watch his non-participation. He used to say he wanted to spend his old age in travel. He's nearing seventy, he's getting in a panic. He'll be off one of these days, I think. Though it's late in the day I think you'll find he'll be off."

"But what can you mean when it's said as a warning to me? Do you imagine . . . What can you imagine?"

"Nothing at any rate that I disapprove of. But if he goes away and you are here people will talk. I only say be careful. The Pouillys are not Parisian. You are heir to a country name."

That was what she had to say to him. He then went in a hurry to dress by dinner-time—(though Ruby attached little importance to her guests' punctuality, and Cacki nightly worked a miracle over the delay of his first course). The duchess, left sitting alone, and with nothing to do, called to her maid.

"We wake at five," she said. "The wheels must turn at seven."

"And who's to wake us?" said the maid, turning round from the floor on her knees. "I don't wake till I'm shaken."

"I will shake you. That's arranged."

"How is it arranged? It's not for me to tell the servants."

"I've arranged it, I say!"

"But if your arrangements, Grace, aren't carried out?"

"Oh dear, how you argue! Her ladyship writes me a note to say it's understood, it's all right."

"For us perhaps. We understand each other. But these people in this house don't live like that, obeying an order just because it's given. They are different, in this house, as foreigners. Milady, to-night, when you sent me with the letter, was naked in front of the young master."

"Nonsense! Were they alone then?"

"No, there was the young lady."

"Then what you say is exaggerated, as usual. You are so easily astonished. Now we have to think of tips. Who has looked after me?"

"I have."

"The good people of this house must all the same have their present. Tell them I will see them after dinner. Bring my purse."

The purse was found to contain too little.

"Very well. You have the petty-cash purse. How much have you in that?"

"That's overdue."

"There you are, leaving things till the last minute! You should have made it up and given it to me before. Tell them in any case that I shall see them after dinner."

"Where will you see them, Grace?"

"They had better come and stand up on the landing."

"At what hour?"

"Don't pin me down. How can I tell?"

"But if they go to bed! They'll be tired. There are only the two here."

"Then they will lose their money." The duchess resolved to be very late with her tipping. "You understand—I am sleeping in the room opposite. I did that to make it easier for you. For tonight you had better have Medallion."

"Your Grace knows," said the maid with satisfaction, "that she howls when she is not on your bed."

"It's time I went downstairs." The duchess got up and the maid opened the bedroom door. "My mauve sleeping draught; the light one. I don't want to oversleep. Five senna pods only. And the toast-water was too strong last night."

"Then I can pack the photographs?"

"How can I sleep in a strange room without them! Why should you pack them? You can slip them in in the morning." Part of her bed-equipment, which grew more and more complicated as she aged, was a folding table set out with silver photograph frames. The maid put them out: the mistress did not look at them. They were the likenesses of the duke, her living sister in Scotland, her dead niece (James's mother), her own father and mother, and the dog before Medallion.

In the large room at the far end of the landing a tired gay face was being doctored and decorated: skilled but bored fingers were shaping the curls, and Ruby, on one of the thousand, thousand evenings of her life, worked over the short life of the appearance and the traces of beauty with accustomed hands. Beauty fades like the go and return of a pulse. She had been less beautiful before and had recovered. The tide would pull round and what was called for and expected would return again and again to her face. Again and again but with its limits. Slowly, slowly the sense of power had weakened. Men's bondage to her was undermined. She could still hold up her head and glitter, but the candle of her power was sinking. Just so had she perceived the eclipsing of other women's faces, the beauty that would hang still like the banner of an old regiment, the desultory, the intermittent movement in its folds, those moments in the last period, like marsh-fires beckoning and false, before the old woman, taking up again the freshness of her age, attends to her wits and her honesty, and the charade is over.

She leant nearer to the glass, oblivious of her daughter, and the eyes looking back at her, blue eyes made of perishable stuff, saw everything, saw the map of the future.

"How unexpected that when it comes to the point one shouldn't mind!" she thought, as she looked. "As though one knew the road. As though one had been led that way before. Like childbirth, getting older is only unpleasant if one resists!" Aloud her bold voice said suddenly:

"I wonder if it's plain sailing when you're seventy? Then you know where you are, don't you? Then one knows better where one is."

Miranda had always found such remarks difficult to answer. She was nervous of the nebulous-implicatory, of the elliptical, of her mother's habit of speaking in shorthand. But now, wanting to please, wanting to understand, she searched for an answer. So at last she said:

"You mean the age of the duchess? Would you like to be that?"

"And yet do you think it's really much different?" asked her mother. "Some little thing drops away at every stage and one hardly notices it. It's only, for a woman, so very striking when the face ceases to get you anywhere, ceases to come to your aid as you speak."

Then the young voice behind her said with a break in it: "Why does everybody love you? And no one loves me."

So now it was said—what Miranda had suffered beside her mother. Even in the death of Percival, the baby, Ruby had never felt so keen a pain. Yet with the pain there was sudden keen excitement that Miranda at last had found an honest voice, that the hare was at the break of the wood looking into the light; and the hand that wound the curl in the glass took care not to abandon its action.

"Why, you must be mad, darling," she said.

"Tuxie loved you," said Miranda patiently. As there was no answer she said: "And James too loves you."

"No," said Ruby instantly, "that's a mistake! Young men are tremendously affected by their hostesses. Haven't you noticed? It's the admiration of power, the hero-worship of power, of a power that's delightful and doesn't go down with the death of a woman's looks. I'm a Napoleon of hostesses to Goethe, because—you know—the house is fun. Especially after living with his great-aunt . . ." (Oh that Miranda should have got this disastrous idea into her head!) "Pride, you know—" (she went on, knowing that Miranda was earnestly listening)—"girls don't always know how much—plays a big part with a young man. That they should know, can be with, can count as a companion a woman admired, a woman of consideration, a woman—let's say it—like me——" (She was labouring, but there was truth in what she had found to say.) "To be me, you know, Miranda, is like being the star actress, who, though she may be aging, is still the thing, the captivating centre, and has long been worth her pay. They don't love me, but they love to be with me. It's the secret of an elderly woman's power, and when a woman's too old for love, as I am, it's what's left, darling. It's what's left."

"Oh."

The little cold word was like a drop of water: it had no identity.

Ruby turned on the dressing stool. She had gained confidence. She could look at her daughter.

"Take me as you find me," she said. "You have been away so long. Don't analyse what you may believe about me, nor think of what lies Tuxie may have told you. Take it from me, if you can believe it—I ask you to believe me—that there comes a time when one's had enough. I am speaking the truth. Haven't you noticed what's missing in me, Miranda? What is missing you have. It's

youth. But youth must be gaiety—joy. If you haven't joy you have
nothing better than I have. Don't imagine wisdom can supplant it.
Not even beauty. I have had that." She turned back to the glass
and raised her hands again to her hair. "If you wonder at me
equipping myself, if one goes on paying careful attention, it's become a habit. And to make oneself agreeable and acceptable is a
very deep habit. It outlives its logic. And then too one has at last got
skill! I don't like grey. It's dusty. But," she said, turning round on
the stool again to look at Miranda, "I may turn grey one of these
days if there's going to be too much confusion."

She sat for a moment, her fine hands hanging just inside her
knees denting the silk of the wrapper, and stared at Miranda absently. Then she got up, went to the dog and touched it, not thinking what she was doing.

Miranda spoke, looking at the floor.

"How do you make a man love you?"

And the reply came fast, as though now in a moment her mother
had detected quite clearly the fault.

"In your case—*smile*, Miranda! Laugh. You don't laugh, so you've
nothing to give."

"What?"

"Men want treasure. Not poverty. They want to share a contented fastness. They want to climb in where they aren't wanted,
where a person is merry without them. They're contrary. And most
of them are searching for secret glory. They want the extravagant,
the transformation, the unknown. The way you look, Miranda, is
hungry, is fatal. You must have a secret life! Then they want to
share it; then they want to rob you of it. Smile—as though you had a
lover already! Pride. It makes them envious to see you proud!"

A light tap at the door let in the heaviest of men. It was as well,
for in her gay way she had said all she wanted to say to Miranda—
in the first confidence they had had in their lives. Alberti had
climbed, wheezing and breathless, to the bedroom to pay his call
before dinner. Miranda pulled up a heavy chair for him and Ruby
slipped her hand into his coat pocket and drew out what he called

his "little remedy," his asthma pipe. When he had inhaled it he recovered, and smiling at Miranda he held out what was in his hand. He had for Miranda's birthday his father's emerald tiepin.

"It's for your manly scarves, God-daughter," he said.

She was pleased and gay and the white of her navy-blue eyes was like birds' eggs, he thought, and the dark hair sprouted from a round ivory forehead.

"What a pretty dress!"

"Father paid the bill—for my birthday."

She did not look tonight like the "hospital's pride," the brilliant young surgical assistant in the operating theatre. Her birthday dress was in striped silk muslin, long and cloudy, a Renoir-thought of a summer girl on a beach. Usually she was so afraid to go outside the narrow lines she laid down for herself, but clung to her uncomfortable rock of severity, just as she clung to her cold silences. She could not make her inner life flow into her talk to enrich it, and before her lips would move at all she had to invent words that would serve, words that had never been inside the house of her heart but had been picked up off the doorstep. The poor heart, which was real, was wordless. But tonight something had at last burst from her, a cry for help, to which her mother had instantly replied. She had a sense of relief, and seeing herself in the glass as they went down to dinner she thought with surprise that she looked charming.

Now, down at dinner, his grey face offered to the bright table with as little reflection as a stone, Gynt sat in his place. Alberti, opposite to him, expanded, rosy and bland. The duchess, on Gynt's right, had hold of the conversation. It was her last night before her feudal hibernation and she allowed herself liberties, impatient of any talk that did not bear directly upon herself. With the black bows nodding and the diamonds at the bows' roots winking, a little drunk with candor and gay for an old woman, she broke into a story recalling her far past. Fastening Alberti with her blackened eyes she said:

"I knew your mother. Yes, and did you ever know that I was once a candidate to be your wife!"

Alberti raised to meet hers his ruminative face with its pale eyes and waited placidly for her to go on.

"I was submitted to you on approval. But you don't remember. Ah, how very long ago."

"Then we met?"

"My dear mother was determined on a duke for me. She was a friend of your mother. I was a catch. (And so were you.) We were tremendously rich. My father made biscuits. But I was nervous and romantic. I wanted to be a writer. Your mother asked me to tea."

Yes, he had been the catch of catches. And now a whole generation had disappeared and young catches had grown into old men, and he was there alive like a stray elephant lost to the herd.

"Was I polite?"

She did not listen to his question. Her eyes were fixed on the girl in Rome. After tonight she would be gone and perhaps she would never return. They would remember that she had talked of her youth. Everyone saw that the look on her face carried in it for a moment the girl she had been.

"I got out of it on your scandal. Fortunately you had a scandal. You were thought romantically dreadful and I got wind of it. Although it was the one thing—the one thing in those days—that might have melted me. But when I saw you you were so cold, so alarming, Duca. Why was that?"

"I was equally alarmed. Of all the young ladies."

"Ah, I didn't know that! No young girl knows that. A man puts up such a face, doesn't he? Such a front. And I was an only child, arrogant and fond of my own way. So I told my mother I would prefer to marry a common man. That's how we spoke in those days. Nowadays one doesn't say such a word."

"Yet in spite of wanting the common man you still became a duchess?"

"My dear mother was too much for me," she said, smiling. "When you wouldn't do she found me my kind Henri."

It was as though, giddy with her farewell moment, she put out buds of memory, as an old tree about to be felled bursts into small greenery around the trunk. James whispered to Miranda as he went round with the champagne: "Never in my life heard her talk like that! Never, never. Can my dear great-aunt have had too much to drink?" And Miranda, looking up, laughing in his face, the champagne ran over her fingers; and they laughed at that too.

Asking for more savoury rice the duchess was suddenly silent and depressed by the laughter. The brief wind had gone out of her and she saw that the future was really going to go on by itself in spite of her. But Alberti would not leave her to eat. "And when you married how soon did you accustom yourself to France?"

"Where I live," she said, looking at him with a grain of rice on her lip, "so very far south, it isn't the France you know. It's kinder."

"Then you think the French cruel?"

"With us they're cruel," she said, "but generous. We're half Spanish. But the France that centres round Paris is not cruel, it's unkind. It's the most unkind nation in the world. Don't you think so?" She looked at Ruby.

"Ruby doesn't know," answered Alberti for her. "Wherever Ruby lives it's her own brand of England. People become English in this house."

But the duchess was preoccupied; she wanted a toothpick. She was also thinking: "That girl looks gayer. What's the reason?"

Gynt, while his fingers pushed this way and that a small tray of almonds, sat imagining how he would vanish. Half absently he heard the duchess speaking of her youth. He raised his eyes to her face and he too remembered her, older than he was, spoilt, tyrannical, handsome; scheming when he dined with them (for he had been fond of the witty, sweet-tempered duke) to find a reason to be alone with him. He looked at the caverns of the once-imperious eyes and remembered that he had kissed her. It deepened his understanding of decay, and set going again the angry hurry in his heart.

He had come late to the study of himself and now that he was old he was struck that he had thought so little through his life about his reason for living. He had been like a thrown ball which while it rolls is satisfied, but, when at the end of its movement it lay still,

wondered what it was doing on the ground. That there was a reason
for his personal existence the mysticism and belief of his forefathers
insisted on, and their cloak was now on him. He was not a man of
doubts: only a puzzled man. And he was determined that the
second-bestness of old age was not the answer: there must be a better reply, and he would find it. (No wonder, he thought, looking at
his wife, that she could not feel the pull of the tides. Not a hair of
her head seemed yet to be affected, and, to her husband's eyes, not
a line of her face. It was almost, he thought, sad that she had not
grown old. It was almost alarming.)

He too had seen the smile Miranda gave to James, and he
thought—"While she lives I live! While her child can say 'My
grandfather—' while her grandchild can speak of 'My grandfather,
Sir Gynt Maclean'—I live. But after that I'm swept back out of
sight. My times are lost, my habits, my tricks of living." He looked
round the living heads at his table. "Chilled into antiquity," he
muttered. "Unrecognisable as a man." The duchess thought he
spoke to her, but turning her head heard nothing.

Then with surprise he remembered that he had no grandchild,
and that the train of thought had been started only by Miranda's
smile.

If there had been the smallest grain of new life in his circle, a
boy to teach, to whose eyes he could have opened the forest, transmitted the lore he had acquired, for whose future he could plan, it
would have been an opiate to the pain he suffered. But here, in this
present life that ran on about him, he had lost the taste for the passing of his days.

He wondered what Alberti, older than himself, made of age. But
then he was a Catholic, and his Church took responsibility even
for its bad Catholics. Alberti no doubt thought he had a pass for the
grandstand. Yet looking at Alberti's face he doubted that Alberti
would allow himself short cuts to peace of mind. And James? Young
men, if they think of it at all, imagine old men to have arrived at a
conclusion. But old men could tell them that age contains nothing
new in it, no new powers, no new discoveries, no arrivals at tri-

umphs. The country of the old is like a moorland, with long nights, short days, and a sunset one does not want to see.

He was going away. While there was still time he would search for something better than the European resignation to age. He would go to the East, where he could track out the triumphs in its long history, little-known and magnificent victories in spiritual life and death, where some old men, emptying their days from the torture of the present, had attained in the idea of God the relief for insignificance. And now Ruby must be told. He dreaded it. How much idea had she already of his restless misery? Why had he not warned her long ago of the path his feet were on, and allowed her to watch the growth of his trouble so that she could have known how she stood with him, and what she was up against? But it was done now. His old secretive nature had closed over his wounds. Life seemed no trouble to her. She was not light but she had this divine gaiety. She had common sense. The way she had it made the word seem of first importance. This world of human beings that was so unsatisfactory to him was her whole life, yet its shallow present and its terrible fate did not sadden her. She was not even impatient with it. He had hardly ever seen her out of temper. Every situation interested her, even disaster. She knew how to turn defeat into a triumph. Except Miranda.

That was the one defeat he knew his wife felt. That she had not, with all her gifts for other people, been able to make her daughter a happy woman. "That's me!" thought Gynt grimly. "That's my part of the bargain. Poor Ruby can't undo what I've given to the child." He sighed. Well—tomorrow morning it had to be said. Or tonight? Or tomorrow morning or the next day. Soon anyway. He'd even got his tickets.

## CHAPTER TWENTY-FIVE

Later in the evening—it was when they were going to bed—(Miranda indeed had gone up to bed but had come down again—still dressed—to fetch Alberti's tiepin which had been taken to the pantry on the coffee tray)—later in the evening Miranda was for a moment alone. She looked at herself in the mirror at the turn of the hall between the two bookcases. It was a mirror (with its two candle-sconces) that had shone back at her mother's face for thirty-five years. It reflected a vase of green branches.

Above the branches Miranda's face watched itself with a look a little severe.

James said from behind her—

"What are you looking at?"

She drew back as though found out. "I? I was looking——"

"It looked very pretty, between the candles."

"Looked pretty?"

"Your face."

Miranda blushed like a child of sixteen that has been kissed. Such a blush that there was nothing else to do but accept it.

He knew her well without loving her at all, without much liking her, and said:

"But you look guilty to have been found pretty! Do you like to hide it?"

With an effort Miranda said:

"I long so much to be thought pretty that when it happens I'm winded." The colour that had been hounded up into her cheeks made her brilliant. She smiled and looked at him steadily without flinching. He had a curious moment of fear.

"You see I'm recovered," she said. "I'm quite capable of taking a compliment. I was only surprised."

He followed her as she went through the hall into the pantry. The tiepin lay on the corner of the table.

"What did I disturb? What were you thinking of when you looked at your face?" he said, watching her pick up the pin and hold open the door into the hall.

"I was thinking that it was the only thing that makes one woman's life different from another's—the sort of face that she has. And I was wondering whether any corner of my face looked like my mother. Some corner I hadn't yet found."

"And did you find it?"

"No, I never have."

They were silent. They had too many secrets. Then she said with an effort:

"What is it that my mother gives out? What is it she has?"

He said, half laughing, "She's simply Helen of Troy."

"To you?"

"To all her friends." And, watching her:

"Is that hard to bear?"

"Very."

So that was it! And even on her birthday! So he added, sorry for her, "But it's so different, Miranda. Her life is made. Yours is to come. For her, she says, it's finished. So she insists."

"Insists?"

He saw he had made a mistake. "I mean she won't permit that we talk in the same breath of each other—the old and the young. She won't allow there's the same outlook. I should have thought, with a mother who felt like that, who had that idea, it wouldn't be difficult for a young woman to live beside her."

"Oh, it's not her fault," said Miranda, still smiling, "it's not as complicated as that. It's just that people don't look at anybody else. And all the time I'm here. I'm the invisible woman."

"And you need admiration?"

"Oh yes. It's the only confirmation I have that I'm not a young man like the rest of you. It's . . . it's my right. It's the only way I understand love."

"That you should be admired?"

"That I should be admired."

"Isn't that vanity? I'm not against vanity but it isn't love."

"You could never understand what for me it is to be a woman. For Mother it's different. She's fuller. She has more sides. For me I've only the one thing. I'm the one, of us two, who's really feminine, with all its limitations."

He looked at her with surprise and considered this claim.

"In any case you're more really the sphinx," he conceded.

"The sphinx? Because I can't or don't speak? I'm only inscrutable because I have to be. All I can do is watch and wait. I get so impatient. I must have admiration or the wind won't spread my sails. I can't begin to live. I can't set foot. I wish you could understand. I never can speak as a rule, but like your great-aunt I think it must be the champagne."

"It's a pity they don't give you champagne oftener. You ought to ask for it."

"Oh, if I talked much I'd have nothing to talk about. For it's all on the one subject."

"Of men? Of love? I had no idea you thought these things."

He was struck by how definite she was, how much she had decided about herself, this fresh, young-looking girl who went about all day sulking.

"Hadn't you? I seldom think. But I feel. And I see how short a time I have to be a woman. You've all your life to be a man. If you caught me looking at my face in the glass it's because I was examining my capital."

"Once you get talking, Miranda, you're a surprise."

She was a surprise to herself when she found herself saying:

"It's my birthday. You haven't given me a present." She held the emerald tiepin towards him.

"I will tomorrow."

"That'll be too late."

"Well, what can I do?"

"You can give me confidence. That'll be more valuable than Alberti's tiepin."

"I'd love to give it to you. In what form?"

The navy-blue eyes shone. They leant forward as her face bent. He thought suddenly that Miranda was a deep woman, extrovert but executive. Shy, but when released from shyness quite able. So James found himself kissing her. And when they had kissed she said, shining:

"Don't worry. That's only a birthday present. You'll owe me another when I'm thirty-four. (I'll let you off at Christmas—but a birthday's so personal.) And don't arm yourself with a tiepin or I shall be offended!" Her mother wouldn't have recognised her.

Gynt, coming through from the garden, called, "Is that you, Miranda?"

"I'm going to bed," she said. "I was just talking to James." And ran upstairs.

James felt very peculiar. And very surprised. The thought came to him suddenly that Miranda might be right about her mother, who wasn't out-and-out feminine—if that's what one wanted women to be. Or one didn't, according to one's particular masculine nature. The talk in the forest had done some underground work in him, and the bruise had spread. He was deeply angry with Ruby that she didn't want him, but his anger was undefined and uncomfortable. Miranda's kiss had not relieved or affected it—he took it as she made it, as her birthday joke—but the remark about her mother eased him and he felt again his self-respect. That was it! Women went back out of their womanhood on to neutral ground. All women probably felt that way, but most wouldn't admit it. Lady Maclean had eyes which saw where her feet were walking and she was too curious about living ever to lie. She found the facts as they were more surprising. She found it more exciting to have a grey hair than to dye it. Once she had said about death, "I'm sure it goes easily. One mustn't fuss. The important thing is to get reasonably exhausted by life, and avoid this hankering for repetition. What you've had you've had."

As, for instance, what she had said about love. She was "reasonably exhausted" by it. (He was still angry.) But he couldn't in his mind accuse her of losing her palate. Her eyes never missed anything and blazed as easily as ever with delight, or at the comedy of faults, at the cock of ambitious ears, at the little pushes people give to their days and their claims. He followed Gynt into the library to say good night to him.

"Making a night of it, sir?" he asked from the doorway, for Gynt had already sat down and pulled a portfolio of papers towards him. Gynt often worked all night and slept in the day.

"I'm adding a note," Gynt said, "to my will. If you don't mind waiting five minutes I'll get you to put your name here—to witness it."

James sat down and lit a cigarette.

Gynt turned in his chair at last. "'If Miranda,'" he read aloud, "'should have a child I want it to have my portrait by Blanche, my personal jewellery, my Court uniform, and two copies of my book on Night Birds. The copies and the uniform to be kept together in the camphorwood box in which my uniform now lies.'"

"Read it for yourself," he said and passed James the sheet.

James thought Gynt a little mad, but it was a harmless request and he signed his name.

"We ought to have a second name," said Gynt, "but we can get it in the morning. No one's going to dispute such a small thing. Miranda isn't even married. It's idiotic, isn't it?" He leant back. "I thought of it at dinner tonight. The idea is to give a child some picture of his ancestor. Of me. If it plays with my uniform, sees my portrait, reads a little here and there in my book—some boys are fascinated by birds—and has as well, as it grows up, the responsibility, the pride of my dress jewels, my links in its first shirt cuff and so on . . . it's possible it might say 'My grandfather, Sir Gynt Maclean' with a little warmth."

"I think it might. But you never know. It's so difficult to imagine."

"Isn't it! But it's the best I can do. I had a fancy at dinner that I objected to total disappearance. But then Miranda's not married! And when she marries she may not have a child."

"And if she had a girl?"

"D'you know, I think she wouldn't! She's a boy's mother."

"Is she like you, Sir Gynt, in her nature?"

"Oh, she's very Scottish. What we call black Scottish."

"She's hard to know."

"So am I," said Gynt, smiling.

James went up to bed. . . .

At five next morning Ruby walked into the darkened room herself to wake the duchess.

"You! Ruby?"

"You are *my* guest, dear Alice. I couldn't ask Rosalba, could I, to get up at five?"

So the departure had the ghost of a sting in it.

"I couldn't resist it," said Ruby to James as they walked up and down outside on the terrace in their dressing gowns. The trailer was being packed with its straw baskets and two stars were still in the sky. "But one should resist those things. It's undone, perhaps, the goodwill of the visit, and I'm sorry, for the goodwill's been great."

"Oh, she can take punishment!" said James. "And part of her vitality is that she forgets everything, disregards things, and therefore forgives. I've so often said I was sorry and she has only stared at me. I've seen she's totally forgotten. It's rather grand. Here she comes."

"Well, Ruby," said the old lady, who was hidden under dark glasses and a veil, "this is the end of my visit. It's done me good to see how other people live. But the lesson's too late, I dare say. Come and stay with me. You'll find me at my most selfish, but the country there is lovely and I should like you to see it. We are feudal, aren't we, James? She ought to see that before it goes. Is that Gynt I see trailing up over the grass so early?"

Ruby turned. "He's been in the mill or the woods all night. He's coming back to bed."

The old lady was now in her seat and the cushions tucked round her. "I'll drive away before he comes," she said. "Make my goodbyes for me. He was rather a young man of mine once, as I told you, and quite suddenly one becomes aware of one's deplorable old looks."

She went; and Gynt, arriving on the terrace, stood with James and Ruby watching the cautiously driven conveyance turn the corner of the drive towards the stone gates.

"Come and have breakfast," Ruby said to Gynt, her arm in his.

"Have you had yours?"

"Not yet."

"In your room then. I only want coffee." And he went on in up the stairs.

Standing by her window a quarter of an hour later, he put his cup slowly back into the saucer on the window seat.

"I don't need to tell you," he said, "that I'm restless. Nothing escapes you. Should you mind if I went away for a time?"

She looked up quickly. Now it had come.

"Where?"

"To India. First. Then to China."

"That can't be called a short journey."

"No. And it's to be more than that. It's a journey I must make into myself. I had to tell you sometime and it's so difficult to begin. At whatever stage I tell you, it's got its first shocking moments. I've put it off, and put it off, out of cowardice, until everything's done, everything's arranged."

"Arranged? Everything's arranged?"

"I must go soon. I must go very soon. I'm in a panic that I shan't be able to accomplish it, that something will happen to stop it. I can't go on as I am. I'm unhappy, and more than unhappy. Life doesn't offer me what it gives to you. I'm a sombre creature. At all events I've become one. I haven't the genius to like people. I like them less and less. People have only to open their mouths for my heart to sink. That can't be altered, though it may be unfortunate. In any case all revision at my age is impossible. What I want to do is to be clear about the time that is left."

As she made no answer he said after a moment:

"Can you be on my side—Ruby?"

She said with difficulty, "Not all at once. Tell me first about your book. Is it done?"

"I should have told you before. It's finished."

"But if I've not asked," she exclaimed, distressed, "it's because I've felt a delicacy! You haven't mistaken that?"

"No, I understand that. But I've been ashamed and afraid about it. Afraid that after all it's not been worth these years I've given to it. All these years that it's been my opium and my soothing syrup. While I held the final door, the last chapter, open it's seemed a part of my immortality (if I ought to use such a word), the thing that excused my want of living. But now it's shut, and the last chapter finished, and it's only a book. To stand up on a shelf against other books. Well—we'll see when it comes out."

"But is anyone . . . Is there a publisher?"

"No. May I leave it all to you? It's part of my cowardice that I don't even want to hear of the machinery. It's finished. I've given it the best I could do, but for a man of my sort to attempt to use words on paper is very hard. The more so as I've become aware as I went on how much better one could do. And now—it comes to this—when life no longer nags with its demand to be lived I want to prepare to live without time. To be finished with plans, palliatives and side issues."

"And with me. With me too. And our life here together. How long must you be away if this is what you must do to make you happier?"

"I can't tell."

"And when? When?"

"At once. Quickly. There's no sense in waiting."

"And I'm to be almost a widow," she burst out, "for this bloodless, this fantastic reason! I'm to accept what isn't death, what isn't an illness, what isn't a betrayal? And give God my husband! If it had been a woman—to make you happy, Gynt—I'd have given you to her."

"I know. I know."

"It's the death of the heart. Your heart. Not mine. It's something most terrible you ask me. You want to go alone?"

"That's the essence of it. I could have had no idea this would happen to us. You say this isn't an illness. I think it is. I think most men accept a sort of melancholy compromise. But me—have pity on me—I'm tortured. I seem to burn. I'm haunted with a need to set things straight between me . . ." He stopped, frowning.

She looked at him with tears.

". . . and my reason for living!" he finished with anger. "My right to be here. I can't take things on trust to the very end. I must do God the civility to try and find out!"

"Then I know you must go," she said quickly. "I know what's right between us. Help me, help me, Gynt, not to think it's my fault."

"Your fault?" he said, surprised (she noticed) that she could think she had anything to do with his anguish. "No, it's violently personal. It's all within me. I would have shared it if I could, oh long ago, but it wasn't possible. Your fault?" He stared at her as though through his pain he now took her into account.

"How in your magnificence could it be your fault?" he said and took her hands. "I haven't always known what you are. I've been a worldly man. We've both lived in a gay world of close friends, where everything's been first-class, particularly sincerity. Yet I haven't made friends with the best of you. I've missed it. I've dwelt so on the worldly side. I've been proud of you as a woman, of your looks, of all you've made of life. Your beloved face" (and he smiled at her with some tender reflection from a light that had gone down) "has never been worthy of you. It's been too beautiful. It's blinded one. There's something rare behind it, but it's no longer for me. I'm too distraught a creature. If I find peace . . . if I find peace I'll come back."

"You'll find me old. I'm on the edge of it."

"Sometimes I think," he said in his hallucinated, unregarding way, "it's a misfortune not to grow old. The spine, I think, should bend, and the eyes fail, and the legs tire. The world needs blotting out and our vigour is so hampering. But no one grows old," he added, "at the same pace. And neither, you'll find, is one the same age all day long. It's really handsome of God to give one so much warning. I'm going to ask you a hard thing."

"Another?"

"Don't write to me for a year. Don't expect to hear. Think of me as dead without the pain of death. I shan't be dead. But try to forget me: don't attempt to remember me. It will be easier than you think, much easier. Set your face against that curious remorse that attacks one in absence—one from the other. Free yourself. And free me too in thought."

"Oh, you ask a lot."

"Yes," he said absently. "And then there is Miranda. She must make another marriage. It struck me last night at dinner—that young man—might he not like her? Think it over."

From then on, dumb with astonishment at the total change that had burst on her, she allowed everything to take place. Gynt, she found, had arranged the last details already. Banker, trustees, a plan of travel, all had been attended to before he told his wife. Perhaps he had expected more opposition than he found. Now that he had broken his news to her his last obstacle was removed and something of an earlier happier look returned to him. At length he placed in her hands the heavy bundle of manuscript, blotted, pasted, and corrected. "If I had my life over again," he said, "I'd have thought more about words. And thought about them earlier."

But Ruby doubted it—remembering the man she had married.

Two days later he was gone.

"When I'm out of sight," he said, "go and see Alberti." It was the only small sign he had shown of thinking of her pain. But she said not a word now to weaken him. She forced herself to see this companion of all her grown-up life turn away on his own odd terms. She did not know that he had said to Miranda: "Good-bye, Miranda. Look after your mother. And don't be squeamish. Put out your hand and get that young man. He's worth getting."

Somehow he suited Miranda. She was able to nod. It swelled her self-confidence.

## CHAPTER TWENTY-SIX

When the old despot down in her castle in Lardaigne heard that Gynt had actually set out for China she was divided between pleasure at having been right and doubts as to whether she had been wise. It had not been wisdom but jealousy that had made her try to warn James. It had irked and annoyed her that a woman less than twenty years younger than herself should be what she called "in the racket" (forgetting that after all it took her more than an hour every day to erect her own appearance). But on the other hand, by his infatuation for Ruby Maclean, her darling—the last darling she would have on earth—was kept from "those girls." Theoretically she wanted him to marry and had made complicated provisions in her will for every child he should have, but all the same she hoped she would be allowed to die before it happened, or rather (a little different) that it would not happen until after her death.

James now, using the air service, went constantly backwards and forwards between Lardaigne and Pouilly, and his arrivals delighted and gratified his great-aunt as much as his departures upset her.

"And Miranda?" asked the duchess. "What does she do with her time?"

James looked blank. "I wonder what she does. She's there. She's about. What do young women do with their time?"

"In my day there was plenty to do. One was either courting or breaking things off. It seemed to take all day, when you consider the clothes that had to be made for it. But Miranda seems a sexless sort of young woman."

"I wonder."

"At all events she doesn't do what most young woman do—she doesn't set out to attract. She doesn't take trouble with women either. She was hardly civil to me."

"Perhaps she isn't happy."

"She's her own worst enemy," said the duchess sharply.

"Oh yes," he agreed readily. "I think she is." With this answer his great-aunt was more than satisfied.

"Is Ruby missing Gynt? She must be."

To this question James gave much deeper consideration.

"She doesn't talk about it," he said. "Or hardly. Or at all events only once. My own feeling is that she cares for him so much that she has a sense of relief. He's doing what he wants to do and she's let him do it. From what she said the only time she spoke of it, it's been a far greater pain for her to see him grow so spectral, so unhappy."

"Does she know," said the duchess, "that it's hereditary? That his grandfather did it before him? His father died early, so we don't know what he would have done."

"What happened to his grandfather? It might help Ruby to know."

"No, don't tell her. Every woman likes to think her husband is an individual. It wouldn't help her to bear her semi-widowhood because those old Scots devils were beckoning him through his blood. His grandfather, a very handsome man, much richer of course than Gynt ever was, a gay figure in Victorian society, married and had nine children. Then he walked out one day, just like Gynt, and he died in an hotel in Cairo. He wrote one letter, the only letter, home when he was dying, saying, 'I'm sorry for this. I'd meant to come home and see Edward.' And Edward was one of the nine children and not one towards whom he'd ever paid particular attention. Not a word to his wife, with whom he'd been on affectionate, if tyrannical, terms."

"But how do you know all this so closely, Great-aunt? It's so long ago."

"My grandmother was the young under-governess to the children," she said dryly.

"Really women's friendships," exclaimed Ruby one late afternoon to Alberti, "only consist of confidences! They think that in the name of friendship one can do all the talking and the other listen. I've had visitors all day, one after the other. Ending with Cora. But were you asleep when I came in?"

"In a way. When I was young and looked on age with astonishment the old seemed always to be falling asleep. One vacates the house on trial. It's not unpleasant. Is Cora going back to torture Rudi? Is that her answer to his letter?"

"She's found a better answer. She's painting him."

"But that doesn't give him a wife!"

"Her theory is that, like children, the old never want things for long. That a substitution is just as interesting. She telephoned to him and offered to paint him and they've had their first sitting. She finds him entrancingly vain and easy to please."

"What a portrait she'll make of the old Scaffolding! He's magnificent, with his jointed layers of height and his sad, clown's face at the top."

"It's made her gay. Anything may come of it. She finds the old relationship completely reversed and every moment's a triumph. What he used to extort she now insists on. His vanity's at her mercy, he's full of respect and agog with excitement. If he could die at the end of twelve sittings he'd die happy!"

Alberti rested much latterly. The summer tried him. He lay now with his yellow cat beside him and watched her from the sofa.

"Have you heard from Gynt?" he asked.

"Oh no," she said, surprised. "Didn't I tell you? That's part of the pact—that we don't write."

"Ruby!"

"He wanted us to be free from that kind of deification, that false remorse, that follows a separation. Free from the thought of each other."

"And is that possible?"

"It's more possible than I'd supposed. At any rate it's got to be borne. I had felt calm, you know, about age. I thought I was to have had my life's companion. It's not the party of life in the end that's important. It's the comment in the bedroom. He's gone—on his great adventure. And I feel he's had great courage."

"Do you?" Alberti only felt that he had had great selfishness. "The man of the world gone monk. The too-late repentance. It's you who have the courage. You look, as you always looked, as though you had a bold plan for the rest of your life!"

"None at all," she said. "What plan can I have? What plan is there? We shall see."

"Alas, I shan't. How can we watch these animals under our nose"—he stroked his large cat—"and not be startled at the difference?"

"At the difference?"

"They don't apprehend death."

"Oh, they understand it."

"They don't apprehend disappearance." He glanced down at his bulk on the sofa. "Have you ever thought that there's a benefit in dying fat? One doesn't catch sight of the skeleton-to-be!"

"That's the password," she said, "to gin-time. It's evening. At our age we are allowed alcoholic escapes." She poured out a cocktail for him.

"How can I grieve," she exclaimed, "as I know you all think I'm grieving, over this Herculean effort of Gynt's to put things right! Could things go on in the state he was in? It was like an illness when no one calls in a doctor. No, if you see shadows on my face it's because of Miranda. If I could pray, it would be that she should marry James."

"He's your young man."

"He's a surfeit," she said slowly, "that I can hardly bear to consider. It's too unfair. I never had these problems. I never dreamt a girl could be denied her birthright. I'm too blunt an adviser for a young woman. I'm not feminine enough."

"Very beautiful women are seldom feminine," said Alberti. "And then it was too plain-sailing for you. You entered by right into the savage state where man pursues. It's what Miranda suspects. She thinks your advice—on her difficulties—worthless. God knows I've had my adolescent troubles, but if I were born again I'd still be born a man! But you know one can't hurry another human being. Miranda's an oyster. A soft little piece, no doubt, but with a hard shell."

"I can see—oh dear—it's been appalling to have had a known beauty for a mother!"

"I didn't know you knew it. That has been the trouble."

"Did she tell you?"

"Yes. When she first came home. It was not so much the beauty as the love and admiration with which you are surrounded. She didn't know how it was done."

"No more did I. It was luck. I hold my breath to think of it. I was a humble girl, Bertie. But my Lucky Star wasn't a snob, and God had painted my face the right colours."

He looked at that face, hand-painted now, but so commanding in its disregard of self. She wore her face, he thought, as though she stood like an intelligent soldier behind it, holding a shield. She was milky and gold. And if the milk was powder and the gold was ashes and gilt, to him it was the same beauty, she was the same wonder, but age now had put them on a level together. He was happy in this ungotten woman: nothing had been spilled.

"Tell me, I wonder if you can, what it's really been like to you to have been a woman?"

"Well, I know now, by the absence of it, what I lit."

"No short cuts! Better than that. Describe it."

"Alberti. Dear Alberti."

"Try."

"It's been witchcraft," said Rudy. "Life's fallen into my hand. I've had love freely offered to me and I've been grateful, but inwardly amazed what a face can do. It gives one, all the time, the something more than one asks, and I shall have now to grow used to the little bit less, the equivalent, that will in future be given on demand. As you force me, quite impersonally, to say it—to have been a beautiful young woman was really like possessing genius. There have been times when you couldn't have threatened me with death: I shouldn't have believed in it! But now I can only glimmer like a sinking candle, and the extraordinary moments are over, and the gay sense of power. One has to learn something stiffer. The sun already doesn't warm my back as it did."

"But one doesn't know that!"

"Well, I know it. But I don't really mind. I take it as a sign of progress. But towards what, heaven knows! I have an instinct to spend everything and get beyond spending. Of having gone through a schooling and getting ready for some world. But first—to lay the ghost of everything!"

"Then when one's laid the ghost can you tell me what's left?"

"A small something. A high-quality nugget of truth."

"And what can one do with this truth—if one's on the point of going out? I speak for your point of view—of being something less than a poor Protestant."

"They say one takes nothing into heaven. But my nugget gets by the Customs. I think it goes too. And don't ask me what world or what heaven, for I've no idea. I can't conceive of life after death in magic hints. All I see is a small arc of a gigantic circle. One really has to cast loose to get the rest. My relationship with my eternal future is of the most trivial nature. What connection can death have with being alive! But lasting annihilation is too profound for me. I can't believe in it, and as every tooth, every hair falls I feel in decay a dogged pride of qualification."

"Are you speaking seriously?"

"Seriously, but not clearly. It's a curious desire—I who adore individuality—to want to finish with it. The differences between people don't appear to be sufficiently great."

Alberti rubbed his hands together—

"Ah, ah!" he said, as though Celestine had laid a good trout before him. "I lie here sick and come to the same conclusions. But when I hear you too, who live in the world, corroborate me, I'm pleased. I'm always suspecting myself of making it easier for Alberti. I think we're put here, my dearest, to lay this ghost of becoming individuals. It's our temporary destruction. It's why we hate, and fight, and, among nations, why we die. Oh, remember childhood. The misery, the pain of what grows within one, the ignorant ache to catch attention, the longing for fame (which is the revolt from anonymity), the shivering ego that can't bear laughter or sneers, that fights when slighted, that denigrates its neighbour, that won't admire, that can only envy. But it has to run its course. It's only now when we're old that the armaments race within ourselves can slow up and we see how we're situated, and we have the permission to allow the individual to give up its fight. It hasn't amounted, as you say, to much. But it was meant, it was meant. It's part of the vast, terrible design. And in the end comes joy."

"What joy? And at what end?"

"Liberation from envy. The Greek, the liberal creed among the angels." He gave his shake of laughter. "Oxford. But in heaven. And now about Miranda. She's proud, and difficult. And she makes bad choices. And then over all her mistakes she insists on drawing this unattractive mantle of primness and makes even her clothes conform to it. Paint my portrait to her! Tell her what I say. We must dress her differently."

"If I were as wise as Solomon and as beautiful as Sheba it wouldn't do. It couldn't come from me. I am the person who loves her most and I may even be the one she loves best. But her instinct to oppose my experience is deep. She won't let me help."

"It's only because I love you," said Alberti ruefully, "that I can put up with my pigheaded god-daughter. Send her to me. Send her to me. I'll offer my advice."


Alberti said to Miranda, who paid him a visit next morning, "May I give you a dress?"

"Alberti, I have dresses."

"But I've never had a daughter."

"You mean you would like to give me one?"

"Yes, that's what I meant."

"Dear Godfather! In what sense, in what way do you want to choose it? A day dress? A dress for the evening?"

"Say over to me the names of the dressmakers."

"The great names? But they——"

"I must remind you that I'm a rich old man. Begin. Mainbocher, Worth, Schiaparelli."

"Christian Dior. Jacques Fath. Lewis Afric."

"Yes, I've heard of him. Go on."

She had always been dress-conscious and she knew the names, the old ones as well as the newest. In Jamaica her mother had sent her *Vogue.* In it she had looked, though she had never raised a finger to copy (preferring her aggravating "uniform").

"Would he come out to see me?" asked Alberti, when they had settled on Afric the pederast, a leader of the world.

"Out here, to see you?"

"Doesn't he go somewhere for his Sundays? I don't see why he shouldn't lunch with a rich bachelor."

It was then easily arranged through Ruby. And Celestine, who loved a visitor, selected her trout for *truite au bleu* and her lamb for the *noisettes*. Alberti liked his *noisettes* served with a branch of lettuce on the plate and no other vegetable. The lamb was followed by six kinds of local cheeses on a straw tray and that fine butter that Celestine found if she took a bus home to her village. Alberti would pick at his cheeses with the tip of his knife as he talked, and he liked to eat cheese and drink coffee till four o'clock.

"These perverts are such gossips," he said to Ruby. "I don't want him trotting about saying that Miranda is an old man's keep. How shall we prevent that?"

"Shall I come to lunch then?"

"No, no. For he'll want to dress *you!*"

"I don't think I should bother what he relays," she said. "One never gets it back. Think—in my life—what must have been said about me."

"But if one ever hears, dear me, how it upsets one!"

"Perhaps. But one doesn't hear."

The famous young man came to lunch, easy and simple as a king. Alberti took to him. He had always got on well with homosexuals. They quarrelled to tears among themselves but were deferential to him, and then so quick to take small points. When, at the trout, Alberti mentioned the dress he also said: ". . . those pages in Proust about the girls on the beaches . . ." and they were off on Proust with pleasure, picking over their fancies. The young man was not so young in a strong light; he looked worn. Alberti was entranced by his beautiful drawing. He had a notebook with him

filled with a paper that was like wax and on it he drew dresses for
Miranda as light as beaten egg.

"But you mustn't imagine her so pretty nor so light," protested
Alberti. "When she comes in you'll see. She's almost stocky. It's you
who must put in the lightness. Can one still buy muslin?"

"Organdie."

"She's stubborn and neat. Neat is all very well but we must undo
it a little. It's a change in her character I'm looking for. What one
sees in the glass reforms more than the appearance. If I had been
a thin man it would have made a difference even to my soul."

Miranda came in, wearing navy blue and a white collar. Lewis
Afric saw at once what was the matter. In integrating her clothes
with herself she had been far too successful: had allowed nothing
accidental to suggest itself. Every time she saw herself in the glass
her character, confirmed by the image, conformed towards it. He
felt her stubborn insecurity; noted the mulish, cool good looks, saw
what was hidden, saw everything at once, as they do these wonderful observers. She did not stay long. She knew by his eyes that a
few minutes was enough and she was embarrassed.

After she went Afric returned to his talk of Proust—whom he
had once met.

"You *met* him?"

"I was taken by a friend. Alas, he said then nothing I can remember. Just the room, and the eyes. The 'sad-dog' eyes."

Alberti began to see that Afric was nearer fifty. The whole afternoon went by and there was no talk of going. They looked together
at Alberti's library. At last the dressmaker said: "Am I to see the
mother?"

"Had we talked of it?"

"No."

"Don't see her. You'll lose interest in the daughter."

"That's not likely, for the mother's reputation is herself. What
she wears makes no one turn round. But the girl is someone to
rescue."

Alberti's large face shone with pleasure. "Girls were so beautiful when I was young," said Alberti. "I remember girls who seemed to have fallen on the ground like blossoms. Too beautiful to touch."

"There never were girls like that," said Lewis Afric. "But I'll see to it that this young woman looks a good deal better. If she'll be patient and good I'll make her more mysterious. Then we must find a romantic."

"I have one in my eye," said the conspirator. "Try what you can do."

"Warn her then to have patience with me."

"She'll do it for me," said Alberti. "I don't irritate her."

"Who does then?"

"Her unique, her beautiful mother."

It was the Armenian's lack of nonsense that had its effect on Miranda when she went to see him in Paris. He told her hard news.

"Don't think I say that you dress badly," he said to her. "You dress well enough to force attention on your dullest qualities. You underline what's wrong, and make it all too clear."

Miranda winced.

"Nothing I say ought to upset you. Try to understand. No one, if you see what I mean, wants to count on how trim his wife is going to be when he marries her." He talked with his mouth full of pins like the humblest dressmaker, fastening the toile about her. "Men want just about the same things they've always wanted. Nothing changes. How can there be anything called 'modern' when time never gets out of the melting pot?" He pinned and cut and sat back to look, half thinking of what he was doing, half of what he was saying. She stood and turned obediently and after a while she felt "taken over," comforted and young. He was as dateless and impersonal as an antique minor god.

"You've only to do what every animal does," he told her. "It's made so easy with silks and scents. It's so straightforward. There are the men, and alas they want the women. What's the trouble?"

"It's not easy," she said.

"Those poor impatient victims? Not easy? You've only to set it

going and it can be done as quickly with muslin as with flesh—
thank God, for it fills my pocket. It makes me mad to see what
child's-play it is for you women. You are standing on the scissors."

"But you can't imagine how unhandy, how stupid——"

He sat back again on the floor and looked up at her.

"Do you think I can't? Don't I see every day how you've all lost
your instincts? If only you could do with yourselves what I can do
with your appearance! In fact, you've only—when I've done it—to
let well alone! I redressed my mother when she was sixty and she
was so sweet. But it was too late. She'd had a lifetime of darling
black widowhood and no fun. Do you want me?" He spoke to a
respectful, grey-haired woman who stood in the doorway.

"The silk for the Queen of Egypt's cloak has come out the wrong
colour. The bolt isn't the same."

He collected his pins, scissors and sketch and put them on a table,
ran a chair swiftly up with one hand for Miranda and left the room.
His delicacy and good temper fascinated her. In the hurly-burly of
his splendid establishment he kept, by his efficient organisation, a
central stillness for himself. He was never impatient, never hustled.
Queens could do no good by urging. He was observant, relentless,
perfectly natural and perfectly sure of himself. Miranda almost
loved this restful man.

Sitting on the chair, half pinned, straight-backed, thoughtful, she
put her questions in order, and decided to ask him how he thought
then that a man is attracted. He was a friend for straight advice.

He was soon back, pins in his lips again, silk cuffs turned back,
fingers pleating or turning in the canvas.

"Well, mine's guesswork as much as yours . . . my answer. But
there's a safe recipe. Don't go into it too much. Rely on the appearance, and don't spoil the impression when made. Why do men fall
in love with actresses? And how often is the love killed dead in the
dressing-room? That's the answer. Keep quiet. *Look* right: keep
quiet. Look like a packet of mystery done up for a birthday and
don't spoil it by being silly. It's too easy. They don't want to know
what your mind's like. Keep that surprise for when you're married.

But you all go too far. See, when I've done this to you and that to you, brought out your femininity, held in your waist, given you a look as though your clothes would fall off you if they weren't held by one buckle, told you to sit in the shade in white and in the sun in yellow, made you simply edible, like Turkish delight . . . what then, my dear, have you to do but keep quiet? I see my dresses rendered useless every day, and my beauties being such donkeys. If you could know that you have only to start it, and the yeast rises! Don't let a draught blow. You poor poor things, it's draughts you are all creating. Turn round then! Turn round."

He was pinning and unpinning, narrowing his tired eyes, standing and kneeling. And a young girl helper, innocent and pale, a schoolgirl, held the pins and scissors beside him. Her eyes were dreamy and she did not seem to listen. Miranda wondered what she was taking in of the talk that pottered gently from her chief's lips. Or were his ways and words so well known that no one paid attention?

"It's kind of you to help me," Miranda said.

"I adore it," he replied. "I adore making . . ." He stopped, for he had meant "I adore making something out of nothing." But still, she was enigmatic, he thought. She had that. She was cool and silent, and softly plump so that she need never really look unfeminine, if it were not for those eternal navy clothes that lay over a chair.

"What led you to dress like a housekeeper educated at Girton?" he grumbled at her. She did not reply, for she always felt cross at criticism of her way of dressing, though she was now willing to change it. She had a tiny waist and her eyes were the colour of a fresh thunder-storm.

"How easily you fall silent," he said. "Do you sulk?"

"I have so little to talk about."

"Make it less," he jibed.

"That's all very fine," said poor Miranda, at bay, "but if it's to men you mean, don't they want to be amused? Don't they?"

"Not the kind I mean. Not the kind you want to marry. Keep

going out of the room till the ring's on! That is, if you can't be yourself."

"Oh . . ."

"Well, look how you are with me! Can't you be like that? But no, I'll swear you put on a manner you've invented."

"Oh, but with you, you're . . ."

"I'm not a man! That's my cosy fascination."

"I didn't mean that."

He laughed like an old friend.

## CHAPTER TWENTY-SEVEN

James took to looking at Miranda. She became a pretty sight. She hardly took any notice of him, but would walk through the forest to see Alberti in a dress that had cost more than a hundred pounds. Not that it looked unsuitable for a morning's walk. It always looked the very thing. As she went about her daily life she grew much gayer; she seemed to have a secret arrangement with pleasure. Ruby was puzzled and said to James, "Can she be having an affair with someone? She looks like it." She felt for the first time that there was someone young in the house. She knew of course about the dresses from Alberti, but Miranda looked as though more was going on than dressmaking.

She had known of girls who fell in love with homosexuals and all at once she thought Miranda just the person to make that mistake. Miranda would be so struck with the easy intimacy, the lack of fencing, so soothed in her disquiets by the Proustian "convolvulus" hidden in the success-splendour of Lewis Afric. And above all, Miranda could be so silly about life, and so silent while she was being silly.

"Does Miranda talk to you, Goethe?"

"Occasionally. Not very much." He had hidden the tiepin evening from her.

"Don't you think she looks preoccupied?"

"I think she looks happy."

"Could it be this Afric? This dressmaker?"

"He's doing his job well. She's looking charming."

"Not too well? That doesn't strike you?" He looked at her.

"She's always with him," said Ruby a little impatiently. "She sails in and out of the house on a ship of excitement. Is it possible? There are girls as idiotic as that. You're her age. Don't you get a hint, Goethe?"

"From Miranda? Not a hint."

"These people take wives. It's part of their bluff. That would be a disaster."

For the first time he felt antagonistic to her mood. He had a sense of his youth and liberty—and of Miranda's. He found he was no longer in love. Ruby was too removed from him: his pride was unable to stand it. He thought she looked older now. Now he could see it. Since Gynt had gone she had suffered. And now talking to her he felt lonely. She was preoccupied, changed, she lifted her eyes all the time beyond him. He felt sulky, damaged, sorry for himself. He had been down to Lardaigne and had returned again, spending time with the lawyers, and walking daily through the meadows and forest to Edouard's cottage.

Angel de Lison was a great deal there too. It had crossed her mind . . . But really she hadn't the courage and she was too old. Yet it's wonderful what old women dare to think of. This morning she drove herself down the road from Paris to Pouilly, her thoughts on her young cousin. He was helping to sort her brother's private papers and letters. The letters from Rose, tied in bundles with white tape, were found in a tin box. Rose's writing coiled across the page like rope, looped and feminine, unpunctuated, conversational, with every now and then a Rose-cry, firm and clear as though she were alive. James was shocked that Angel insisted on reading them. But she would. "And then there's nothing in them that Edouard would mind!" she said. "They're so empty. But I must and will know what it was they felt."

A great part of the letters was occupied by Rose's grumbling.

"She seems really odious. He must have been under her thumb."

"No. He understood her," said James.

"However do you know!"

James himself was surprised at knowing. "She told me so," he replied. Angel snorted.

"Don't read them. I wouldn't," he said seriously. "You can never know what happened, can you? It's closed and finished. It's true that I only had that one talk with her, but from it I got such an impression——"

"Of what?"

"Of love," he said, looking at her firmly, as though he insisted she should accurately know. "Of real love. It was like a condition. As definite as an enlarged liver. If you cut into a rabbit you see what's hidden behind the grey and brown fur, you see the scarlet life that no one dreams of. So in talking for one hour with Rose I saw the heart that's never seen in daily life. She couldn't keep still on the bed. She loved him, in agony. She loved your brother. She died of it. I'm sure she did."

Angel burst into tears. She put her hands over her face, and turned in her chair so that he could not see her.

"Madame de Lison," he said unhappily.

She found in her bag a pair of sun spectacles and put them on, holding a little handkerchief for a time over her lips. He continued to make notes on a sheet of paper, describing the documents and letters he was slowly taking out of a box. At last she spoke. "Everything has missed me and gone by me," she said. "I may as well tell you, to explain. I have never once in my life been in love with someone who loved me. Perhaps you didn't know that could happen? One sees so many women on the pavements, and there are all these marriages in the newspapers, and one's friends—they have children and to do that all must have taken place. And yet there are women like me who have never loved and been loved in return at the same moment. When you say it was not so with my brother and Rose—when you say that all this took place out of my knowledge and my grasp, yet under my nose, then I feel over again the crippling disappointments of my life. Now I must be resigned to die without it, like someone born deaf or blind. But I am not resigned. You heard what I said when you stood on the stairs the day Rose was buried. You were shocked and we've none of us spoken about it. I was shocked at myself too and I've regretted it. But you don't know the provocation. My brother, without intending it, teased me with the bare idea of that woman. I wounded myself with the thought of her, and it went on so long." She looked at James's bent head. She did not know what he thought: she never knew what men thought. Even when she had been his age she had been just as much at sea.

"There are women," she said slowly, "who don't, by nature, know what's expected of them. They don't know what place they ought to fill in men's regard. I'm like that. I wouldn't know how to remedy it if I had my girlhood again. For thirty years this Rose of Seduction has stood for me for all I've not got. You see me old now but it's always been the same. I'm without what cannot be described to me, what's not taught, and that to me doesn't come naturally. And it has ruined my life."

James was drawing a church tower and putting three dots for the cross on the top—but thinking of Miranda. He thought she was another such helpless and clumsy woman. But she wasn't sixty.

As Angel looked at James, who drew on with bent head, her heart ached over her losses, and she knew that nothing could be retrieved and that for her all time was lost. She had been herself with him, but she was never happy when she offered no more than herself. It wasn't enough.

"He will marry some girl to whom all will come so easily that she won't know what she's getting, won't see him as I do, as a rarity."

And self-pity, the constantly permitted flood, invaded her, like town-water rising through the cellar-trap of the soul.

James, who could not imagine this desperate water, these self-inflicted exclamations, could not banish Miranda's peril from his mind even when he listened to Madame de Lison. With his gift for sympathy, he did not think about himself nor wonder why he was given such confidences. But he could not keep his full attention on her while he was thinking that much of what Miranda had said to him on the night of the tiepin was now clear. As he did not know how to say anything to Madame de Lison on the subject of that heart of hers which had misfired through life (for wasn't it too late—surely she assumed that?) he said after an interval:

"I'm now the landlord. Are you sure you don't want to come and live here, at least for week-ends, before I offer it up to be let?"

"I haven't the resources," she said, "for the country. There would be too much leisure."

"I think all the same you would make a good countrywoman."

"It may be. I'm a very moderate Parisienne."

"But you don't want to try it?"

"Where," she said under her breath, and she put her hand out towards him and laid it on the table, "are you going to live?"

There was something terrible and appealing about the nervous, charged softness. What she had meant she said aloud with her hand. He became instantly aware of her in a personal relation to himself, and, conquering his shiver, called all his strength to deal gently with her.

"With my aunt," he said. "She is over seventy and very dependent on me for company." He took the poor hand (that did not know how to withdraw itself) in both of his and looking calmly across the table at her he said:

"I think I shall be a good deal with her—until I marry."

"You are going to marry?"

"Yes, I think so."

"Do I know her?"

"I am going to ask Miranda Maclean tonight."

It was the wildest, rashest piece of instinctive swimming he had ever done. He had made up his mind without thinking of it. He could hardly believe he had said it. It was one of those tranced executive moves which bring corporals to fame and turn them into generals.

"Does she not know?" breathed Madame de Lison.

"No."

"So you'll be engaged tomorrow?"

"Only if she agrees." He got up quickly. He had to recover from his own choking surprise. He had done something that could only be justified by success. He had to stop Madame de Lison at all costs from another word, from any comment. He went to her side and put his hand on her shoulder. "I've told you what I didn't know myself, what I haven't even made up my mind till now to do! God knows how much you'll help me by assuming I haven't said it! You'll help me for ever by being gay and talking about everything in the world through our lunch together. By anaesthetising me from this minute, by doing your best with me. I shall never forget it and we two will be friends. You must be clever and act at once and start now. Tell me all about yourself and what life is like for a little girl and for a young woman. I never had a sister, and no cousins to play with. There's sherry in the cupboard . . . no, it's here, and with glasses! I'll bring it to you."

At last a man had asked Madame de Lison to do something real for him. She would show him what she was made of. Striking out any jealous fire that might be catching above the tears in her heart she plunged into action. James stood holding the sherry, looking like a beloved brother (as though—she thought—he could never have laughed at women with other men).

"I must do up my face for self-revelation!" she said, crossing to a mirror which hung up on the wall. But the mirror was shaded and she held up her own little glass. These little glasses magnify, and the yellow in her eyeball was like the yolk in an egg, so putting on her rather harsh lipsalve she replaced the sunglasses, and at that moment Edouard's man summoned them to luncheon.

Edouard's little dining room was the gayest room in the cottage, hung with curtains of striped lemon and white and with a faded crimson armchair on either side of a dining table for two. The room smelt of black butter and vinegar. The sun was shining. Madame de Lison did not stop for a moment to collect her thoughts but plunged at once into her life story as though the devil were after her. As James drew out her chair she said, "My mother was adorable." And unfolding her napkin, "My father was harsh, unpredictable and fond." When the man had served the first dish she went on, "I could not understand him. When he stormed at my mother I thought the marriage was on the point of breaking up. I was nervous and always tried to put on a good front. My mother had a sentimental taste in children's clothes. She dressed me in frills and old-fashioned embroideries and I had fifty little dresses hanging in my wardrobe all at the same time. I don't know whether we were so much richer in those days but we lived as though we were. I was a very indignant child: always expostulating. Even at nine I was sure the clothes she made me wear were not suited to those day-dreams that were to be the prop of my personality."

(James was delighted with her. He could see that she had long had it all pat. He was not only protected from himself but was giving her extreme pleasure.)

"And was Edouard at home then? Or at school? But I suppose he had a tutor."

"He had a tutor. Edouard was seven years older than I and away a great deal, but he had a tutor in the holidays. Edouard was my salvation. He was my humour and my philosophy. When I raged he could say something flattering and soothing to me and yet flattering and amusing also to my mother. Whatever he said made us both feel better pleased with ourselves. My wrangles with my beloved mother would dissolve in laughter when he was in the room."

"Were your wrangles then all about your clothes?"

"I wanted my personality," she said earnestly, "more than anyone has ever wanted theirs—to help me. It seemed mislaid. I had to try and find my way towards it through a thousand impalpable obstacles that my mother placed before me. She loved me so much that she had invented another personality for me and everything she did and said caused confusion and rebellion in my heart. The clothes made the plainest arguments. In them her attitude and mine was crystallised. I would not know it now so clearly had not

Edouard explained it almost every day. He would laugh and say, 'You are a potter, Mother! And Angel doesn't want to go on the wheel! She won't be potted. Between the two of you you're getting the crockery crooked!' And we would all three laugh, but that didn't prevent it beginning again. I think I had no common sense. I have none still. In our family circle Edouard had taken it all."

She talked well and so fast that the word "Miranda" only sat like a sparrow on a statue's head. He could feel the light feet on his brow but no more. Madame de Lison had a wonderful luncheon, one of the happiest of her life. She took him rushing through her childhood, swept him into her dreadful moments with society, introduced him to her wedding day, left out her wedding night (for the sun was shining too brightly), divorced Monsieur de Lison and settled for good with her brother. But through everything it was apparent that only her mother and her brother had ever counted in her life. All other human relationships had been unsatisfactory, nebulous, mismanaged. It remained to be seen whether at the end of lunch she could say good-bye without a finger to her lips, without a wink. Without payment. She could not.

Her wink was a ring for Miranda. It was a very "knowing" gesture. She had counted the cost in her head while she talked—over the coffee. It was one of Monsieur de Lison's presents and so had no loving significance. It was a pretty emerald. She held it out to him as she was driving away—as she sat behind her sunglasses in the shadow cast by her car and looking for that minute forty years younger. It was a good gesture for her but it was awkward for James as he stood holding it and watching the departure of the car. He did not like Madame de Lison enough to make her ring his first present to Miranda: and he was sure Miranda did not. He was not at all a person who judged others hardly and he was glad the little drama of the gift had pleased the giver. But he was not going to give it all the same.

He had exhausted his love for miracle upon her mother. He knew he would always hide that from Miranda for her own sake. He would lie to her, he thought, without conscience, and tell her it hadn't been the real thing. It had, but things blow over. He would make her his child for a while until slowly she mended. Miranda would be his creation, and not her mother's. He wanted a young creature whom he could hold as his own, whom he could turn into his heart, who would suffer with him, who would never leave him at night. "Do you remember," he heard himself say in the far future, "what a wrong-headed little idiot you were, my darling?" And she would not remember. She would be surprised—and perhaps offended.

Poor Miranda. Oh, poor, poor Miranda. He loved her. She was full of faults. Perhaps she was trying to mend her pride with this pansy who was dressing her. What an enemy she was of her own life! Obstinate, stubborn, and suddenly as dear as his right hand. He laughed. He began to walk across through the woods to Little Pouilly.

## CHAPTER TWENTY-EIGHT

Now Miranda was to have two proposals on one day: and to accept the first.

At the end of a "fitting" morning in Paris, Lewis Afric took her out to lunch. He ordered food without fuss. He ate very little, preferring boiled fish and stewed apple, to find which he went to the most expensive restaurants. He did not insist that Miranda should eat the same. As soon as the waiter had left them Lewis Afric said to Miranda:

"I have an important conversation on hand with you. Shall we begin it now or shall we wait for coffee? On the other hand I really prefer to talk while I'm still hungry." Miranda said he could start when he chose.

She half turned on the velvet wall-seat and removed from behind her a small green velvet bolster and dropped it on the floor. It was not her habit to lean or sit slackly. Everything she did was neat and upright, although she now wore clothes to contradict this side of her character. Her creamy neck rose from a wide collar of blue-white organdie, a huge eruption of shadows and snow as fresh as the birth of Venus. Alberti's tiepin was stuck through the knot the organdie made where it was drawn together at the division of her breasts. Afric glanced at her as a chef might glance at a soufflé. But he was grave.

"I want you to know where you stand," he said. "Listen carefully. For I am going to suggest that we get married. Wait! I'll put my side at once. I have ideas on your side too. I am not selfish: I think your point of view should be well gone into. I'm a man, as you've probably heard, who has—delicacies—well, a difference of taste. I'm not at all male. I detest it. I'm not the man you are supposed to be coupled with, but then I don't personally find you are a typical woman. I really don't want to force myself to be clearer, if you tell me you understand?"

"I understand," said Miranda, quite cool, and listening.

"Very well. I'm lonely. I've met in you someone who can conform to what the world thinks should exist (a household, a woman at the head of it) and yet who will not upset me, who—doesn't require—— In fact, if you married me you'd get no husband in the understood sense, the crass stupid sense, but you'd get a great deal all the same, affection, loyal affection (I know myself), sympathy, a directional tyranny that's good for you. I'm fifty-one, my dear. Rich and busy. Those are my credentials. On the other hand there is a young man who, when he comes back from the East . . . the only strain, the only tension you would have to put up with. If there was anything else it would be hidden from you. But you needn't, except in the case of my Charles, whom you would like for himself—he's charming—you needn't trouble with that side of my life. You will be the unique, the deeply important creature to me, the being I can build my affection on. I wish my mother were alive. She could reassure you."

Miranda heard all this with inward amazement. She understood that he thought her unsexed—she who considered herself as far more a woman than her mother. At the same time she saw her future spring alive even if with a strange light. This was a chance.

But if she "confessed" herself the chance would be taken from her. Lewis Afric understood everything, excepting of course that she was all the time a perfectly simple woman. She said cautiously—she went so far as to say—"Suppose at some time I were to fall in love with someone?"

"I understand that," he said. "I should understand that, but you mustn't tell me about it. You must hide it with great care. I couldn't endure the actual knowledge at the moment. But in principle, so long as I don't know—if you understand that, don't let's talk about it."

"And this friend? This Charles?"

"You'll like him. I haven't any doubt that you'll like him. He will never be much in England. He's in the Anglo-Iranian Service. They think a great deal of him, I'm told. To me he's an ideal. He's the nobleness of youth. You'll come, when you know me better, to realise there's nothing sordid about it. I couldn't give him up as a friend, but I shouldn't care about hiding him. There is nothing furtive about Charles. You will see. I can promise it won't be possible not to respect him."

"Am I allowed to think . . . to think it all over?"

"Good heavens, yes! Think all you can. It's not every woman's idea of bliss, Miranda. There are advantages for you, and great disadvantages. I can offer you a platform that needn't be discreditable for you. People will talk and laugh at first and one can imagine how they'll say, 'She's married to a pansy!' But if there's one thing people settle down to it's a married couple who steadfastly dispense money and taste. I've money enough and taste to conquer anything. In two months from now, if you'll marry me, you can begin your life as you've never begun it. We'll have a quiet, an almost secret wedding, and then break upon Paris with a famous party. If you marry me it will be a compromise: you must face that. But I can get you going, I can give you a career, I know everyone's weakness. I know what they'll take and what they'll admire. With me behind you I can turn you into an enigmatic, a sought-after, a delightful hostess. Would you like that—Miranda?"

"And children?"

There was a pause. "Eventually," he said coldly.

Miranda looked as cool as a cucumber but she was in a panic. She was offered a golden chance to sell her birthright. What a sad thing that life couldn't go simply for her! Afric went on eating as though he had suggested a merger between the houses of Afric and Christian Dior.

"Can I ask you any questions I want to?"

"Of course."

"Since you are not in love with me——"

"But I am."

"I thought——"

He laid down his fork and looked at her. "We couldn't live in the same house unless I was drawn to you by romantic feelings. I will look after you with tender care."

"Shall I know the difference?"

He did not know whether she would know the difference. He felt a great deal for women, but he did not know what men felt. He loved women, as women love each other, with irritation and a deep enjoyment of their company; yet not quite as women love each other, for he was more chivalrous, more selfish, harder, and more capable of pain. He did not know if she would know the difference. He looked at her, and after a moment she said a little helplessly:

"What do you advise, Lewis?"

"I think you ought to marry me. I'm not stupid. I can see to it that you are not unhappy. Materially everything will be done, and you have it in you to make full use of money. But all that would be barren if I wasn't sure that we can be something important to each other. One always misses something in life, Miranda, and you don't want to lay your finger only on what you are missing."

"What's your—is Afric your real name?"

"I'm an Armenian," he said shortly. "Whenever you don't know what a man is and you suspect he's not very proud of it, he's an Armenian. New York has them. They know them. I was born in

New York, but I came here to Paris with my parents when I was seven. My father died then and my mother died last year. My name's Snosvic and so will yours be on your passport. You were quite right to ask." He pushed his plate an inch away, he looked hard and defeated; for the moment he looked a very real man.

Miranda took one of her swift decisions, making up her mind, as with Tuxie, rapidly and wrongly.

"All right," was all she said.

"All right?" he asked, not quite understanding: and met the dark blue eyes smiling so sweetly at him that the tears came into his own. He was very emotional and very lonely: he missed his mother almost every hour of his life. She had been a little woman with an American air about her, witty, proud of him, and in her last years very well dressed. He had bought an exquisite old house for her and furnished her bedroom like a girl's. And she had always laughed at him and humoured him and even sometimes let him cry over his love affairs upon her shoulder.

"You are shocked!" she said to an old crony, a bosom-friend of her girlhood. "Yes, his father too, he would have been shocked. But I, you know, find all suffering is respectable."

Lewis and Miranda went to Cartier for a ring immediately after lunch. He longed to begin again his acts of generosity. Though in his love-life he belonged to the sad, accursed race it was to women that he was fond of giving presents. It was distasteful to him to give presents to men. He flinched at their gratitude.

And at Cartier he let himself go. He got a trade discount, naturally, but even so he spent a sum that upset Miranda. It was such an overweighted seal on her consent.

They had walked from the restaurant to Cartier. Lewis telephoned from the jeweller's to his chauffeur and told him to leave the long sports Delage in the trade yard at the back of Afric. He told him to take a day off. (He would have to get rid of him immediately.) "I'm driving myself down to Pouilly," he said to Miranda. "We'll just go back to the workroom and see that nobody wants me." The commissionaire called them a taxi.

In the taxi Miranda said, "I'm afraid of breaking this to my mother."

"That's all right," said Lewis. "I'm breaking it to her. That's what I'm coming down for. Everything difficult in life is, from now on, to be done by me."

There could have been no words spoken that could have seemed more manly to Miranda. Now she had her own champion.

It was five when she got out of the car near Alberti's cottage (they had made a detour for this reason). She was to talk with Alberti while Lewis went on to Little Pouilly to break the news to Ruby. Miranda could tell Alberti or not, as she decided on the spot. Sometimes he was not well enough for worry. She would stay half an hour and then walk home over the water meadows.

Lewis drove off slowly under the trees in the shining car. She watched him. While she yet had heard no arguments to the contrary, while she was still unshaken, she ran over the points in his favour, prepared to brace herself. But she found there was not much need for bracing. It seemed not credible to her that he belonged to the Race; his whole manner was so protective and tender. "He's just what I need!" she exclaimed almost aloud. She put the ring inside her bag so that Alberti should not see it, and opened the gate of his garden. And as she walked up the little path she had time to feel proud and excited and expectant—as though life was at last opening to her—and very determined. At the thought of argument and disapproval all her obstinacy crept through the fibres of her spirit like chalk which hardens the arteries. "I have my own life to solve," she said. And there was Alberti lying in the window. "Goddaughter!" he called. She smiled. She was looking very pretty. He was immensely satisfied with his idea about the clothes. He looked so cheerful that she decided she would tell him. It would be good to practise resistance before she met her mother. Out of his sight, while she was walking through the door into the room where he lay, she slipped on the ring again, the immense sapphire, navy blue like her eyes. He saw it even as she crossed the room, as she pulled out a chair to sit beside him.

"That ring!" he exclaimed.

"From Lewis Afric. This afternoon."

"The scoundrel!" he said energetically. "So that's what he's made of my order for your clothes! You've not been fool enough—— Good God, Miranda!"

"We're engaged. He has gone to tell Mother."

"You can't know about him!"

"Yes I do. He told me. He has told me everything. He's also an Armenian and my name is to be Snosvic."

"Snosvic? What's that? But he's one of those unhappy creatures! Has he told you that?"

"Yes. At once. He told me that first. It's no use, Alberti. I am absolutely resolved."

"What will your mother feel!"

"She's feeling it now. He's telling her."

"You'll be the laughing-stock of Paris."

"Don't let's exaggerate, Alberti. He's famous, and . . ."

"A dressmaker!"

"And very rich," she went on patiently. "If there is one thing my mother's friends like, it's money."

"That's an injustice to your mother, and you know it! If she lives in a light world she does it with a splendour of spirit!"

"I don't say it of Mother. But I've seen enough to know that money . . . what's the word—exculpates. If you are rich enough you become out of reach. I shall be very rich."

"But that's not what you are doing it for!"

"No. But it's part of what I get. The other part is his friendship. His protection."

"Protection! What from?"

"From miserable thoughts. From being lonely. From despising myself."

"Won't you be lonely still? Won't you still despise yourself? This isn't a marriage! You'll never be happy. I've known you since you were a small child. You've always been obstinate. I want you, before you dig your toes in, to realise how much obstinacy counts in your nature. You may think you act on free will but you're quite wrong. When you married Tuxie you made just this same mistake. One would have thought you wouldn't do it twice, and the only explanation is that you first make bad decisions and second you stick to them. For God's sake don't look on this as a battle in which it's important that you win. Look at it freely. Let me help you to look at it. I won't be your enemy. I won't be antagonistic. I'm an old man. What have I to gain except that I want to set things right? Why should I have thought of the dresses—I an old man lying here thinking of things that aren't cheerful—except that I want to do all in my power to make my nearest friends happy?"

"Alberti," she said earnestly, "please don't be angry if I say that when you think of your nearest friends you think of my mother. And when you want to make them happy it is she whom you want to make happy. I am only in it as a cog, as a machinery to that end. And that's why it's important for me that I don't listen to your advice. It's not given to me. It's given to her. There is no one to think for me but myself. And now Lewis. He will think for me. Yes, now I have Lewis, who will think for me!"

"You have always had your mother."

"She is too old for me."

"What, what?"

"Yes, too old for me. She is not only another generation——"

"—about four years older than your rogue-dressmaker!"

"—but of a romantic generation when women were courted. I've grown up in a white-blue neon light of most unsatisfactory equality."

"Miranda, men don't change. And women are the same. No one at home here has ever told you the truth. Your father has gone God knows where gallivanting after God! Evading his responsibilities. The attractive women get the men. The others have to work hard to make up for it. They achieve it sometimes to an extraordinary degree. They grow clever, and they see that they must be sympathetic. Men are not dragons but human beings. But what have you done? At the first touch of failure you've turned sullen. And at the first touch of flattery from a man on the make you've gone under. You must be one of those silly women whom flattery takes in at the first word. You must be praise-hungry. I lie here telling you hard things about yourself and I don't pretend I say it for your good. I say it out of revenge for your mother. I am tired of hearing about your problem. But I'm wrong to try. You aren't worth so much discussion. Perhaps if you marry your pansy you'll be right. You'll be at least settled!"

He turned heavily away from her and closed his eyes. Miranda was white and still. No one but Tuxie had ever spoken so to her. She got to her feet and stared at his back which panted a little like a tired whale. She left the house and began to walk back through the woods.

## CHAPTER TWENTY-NINE

Lewis Afric was sitting with her mother on the terrace. Cacki had put the cocktails near them but neither of them had drunk anything. As Miranda walked off the grass slope onto the terrace James also moved out from the drawing-room and joined them. All four were suddenly together.

Ruby said, "Miranda!"

And added, "But bring a chair. Have you come from Alberti? Have you told him?"

James said from behind, "Told him what?"

Lewis said (to Miranda), "Your mother is very angry." Miranda felt calm. She had her champion: she had only to remain silent.

"Your mother is very angry, but I tell her it's no good. I bear no grudge for anything she has said. When her anger is over we shall be friends. We shall forget everything. But we are determined. Aren't we, Miranda?"

"Determined."

"To get married?" asked James, looking at the ring.

"James de Bas-Pouilly," said Ruby briefly to Lewis. "Staying here. But he'd better go. You'd better go, James."

"No, no," said Lewis Afric. "I don't care at all. I don't mind. Really." He got up and shook hands with James. "It's a very old situation," he said easily to James. "Lady Maclean doesn't want me to marry her daughter. I am so sorry she doesn't, but we are both determined, as you heard."

"Ah, but I'm going to marry her," said James, as easily and pleasantly, still standing. (So all Ruby's prayers were answered in this way and then thrown back in her face.)

"I'm afraid that's not possible," said Lewis. "We're engaged. She has just promised me."

"I saw you'd given her a ring," said James, and he fetched a folded garden chair and placed it, open, by Ruby's side. But then he did not sit on it. He said, "Miranda, will you chuck him and marry me? I know I'm rather late. But I don't want to be later still. I didn't mean to ask in this public way, of course, but now I think any delay will seem like agreeing to your engagement—which I don't do for one minute. I must explain," he said, "that I meant to say this today. It was unfortunate that Miranda was in Paris."

"Very," said Lewis Afric.

"Yes, but it's got to be undone," said James. "You aren't going to be obstinate, I hope, Miranda?"

"You're mad," said Miranda. "We're engaged. I wear his ring."

"Ring! Ring!" said James impatiently. "Don't be an idiot, Miranda! It's for life! All our lives, till we're dead. It's for our children, it's for when you're an old woman and I'm an old man. Don't be fatheaded, Miranda. You're a conceited girl besides being a humble one. You've got a habit of pretending you're right even when you know you are in the wrong. You're not right now, you're dead wrong. Afric has his own ways of living and ideals, and I daresay he's a good chap but he won't suit you. It's very tiresome to have to say all this in public but there's no other way. We are all tremendously concerned in it and here we are together and we shan't be again, so I know I'm right in telling you. Miranda, here it is straight. I love you. I want to marry you. I'll look after you till . . . till my bones crumble. I'm just going back into the house. I'll be in the library so as not to embarrass you." He slipped back into the draw-ing-room.

Miranda looked at her mother and then she went and sat beside Ruby in the chair James had opened. She dropped her forehead onto her hand. Afric came closer.

"I can't do anything. I can't do anything, Mother. You must tell him. He mustn't speak to me again."

"Who mustn't, Miranda?"

"James mustn't."

"It's for life," said Ruby. "You've had two jobs offered you."

"I've taken one."

"Not while I'm here," said Ruby. "Not while I'm beside you. You've had enough mistakes in your life. I've been vain, wanting to be agreeable, to make you fond of me, to be tactful, considerate, civilised—rather than to speak the truth. I've wanted your ad-miration."

"As well?"

"As well," said Ruby grimly. "And now more, much more, than anyone else's. But I've been soft in order to get it. That was a mis-take. I'd have done better if I'd beaten you when you were small. Better that than be a mother whose word counts for nothing. When you wanted to marry Tuxie your father wanted to throw him out. He was right. But it was I who stopped him. You," she said, looking up at Afric, "know it's better she marries the young man!"

"Well, it's better," said Afric. "But only if she loves him. She's not doing this blindly, you know. She and I have talked it over."

"How can you have talked it over! Miranda can't imagine what she's going to pay out. She has no imagination."

"I've made it plain to her."

"Are you going to give her children? Tell me that, and tell her that."

"She asked me. I said yes."

"But you said it grudgingly! She'll have no children! Miranda, you'll never have a child! Miranda, don't stick to the letter of your silly promise. Chuck him. I see he'll suffer. I can't help it. He'll recover. He's used to blows and buffets. Don't be a fool and don't be a coward, Miranda! This poor man of fifty has had half his life and he's damaged. I say it in front of him because like James I'm desperate. You did it as a compromise because you thought, my darling darling, that you were, in the language of the day, a failure. You wanted to get started. But now you've got love to start with and a young man who loves you. Stop it. Drop it. Be brave enough. Say what you want out loud, Miranda."

"Miranda!" said Afric anxiously, bending over her.

"I'm so ashamed, Lewis."

"So you ought to be. If this is really going to be true? I can't believe it. Can't you wait and speak to me alone?"

"It's only happened since lunch today. Will it be very bad to undo it?"

"Not if you want to. It can be done. But is this all *not* so sudden, not so unpremeditated? What's been going on beforehand?"

"I loved him," whispered Miranda. "But I thought he loved you, Mother, so I thought there was no chance for me."

Ruby took the unresisting left hand and drew off the sapphire.

"Post it to Cartier," said Lewis Afric. "I don't feel like carrying it back with me," and he turned and walked round the house to his car at the front door.

Ruby's impulse was to go with him, but there are some things you must leave alone. You can't eat your cake and keep it.

Miranda got up and went to the library.

James crossed the room and put his arms round her.

"Wasn't it awful for him?" said Miranda.

"Why ever did you do it?"

"I did the best I could for myself. I thought I did. I had to do something."

"You'd better be advised by me in life, Miranda," he said. "You really are an awful fool." She felt safe as he kissed and kissed her. She felt soothed for all she had suffered in perpetually doing the wrong thing.

## CHAPTER THIRTY

The duchess, down in Lardaigne, when she heard from James, would like to have lashed out. But she sat still a little first at her walnut desk with the Dresden cupids supporting the pigeonholes and gave herself time to think it over. She had dipped her pen in ink but she let it dry. Miranda was a dull, cold girl but it would be wise not to say so, if one could keep it to oneself. No old woman could break a young man's marriage, if the young man were worth anything. James would marry Miranda. She felt physical pain. It had made her older in this hour since she had had the letter at breakfast. Something placating mingled for the first time with her reckless nature and she stared, unseeing, into the pigeonholes which were solid with listed packets and folded documents held in rubber bands. She took the pen again and dipped it. James had asked her to write a word to Miranda. She must do so. But what could she force herself not to say?

"My dear Miranda," she began. "I congratulate you." (That she could both write and mean.) "Your mother must be happy," she wrote on slowly, and on that the pen dried again as she pondered the meanings the words could carry. Ruby was losing her lover to her daughter, so how could she be happy? Or it might read, "At last your mother has got you settled—be it even to her own lover!"

"They say the old," she thought, "should find pleasure in the happiness of the young. But that's easy to say, and nonsense. How tiring it is to see everything happening over again! What hypocrisy to think one can be glad to look at what one has lost. One has to have all the courage and strength to support the heat of life and then, by a miracle, turn all at once into a selfless onlooker!" She thought of the old women she knew down in the village, sitting in their doorways, nuisances, most of them, of course they were nuisances! Life with its slow pressure had built them up strong and wary. There was no arrangement made about this gift for abdication that was supposed to be their evening coronet. The truth is—as she had said to Alberti—one must empty one's heart. Empty one's heart and look after oneself all along the last lap, for the next generation, forcing the pace onwards, caused one such pain in passing.

The longing to re-become young and cherished rushed upon her. She spread out unwieldy hands beside the pen and, as with Rose, the half-embedded rings told her the duke had loved her. And as with Angel, all now was gone, but she had a different grief. She had stood like a rock that divided the head of a river and streams of kind water had embraced and cooled and softened her. Now the water had left its source. Its glitter had all run down and its bed had dried and she was left like grey slate and shale—"the old duchess." She hated her loneliness.

She did not at all times hate it. There were long stretches when she enjoyed despotism. But sometimes she knew that in the eyes of God she grew less worth saving. And it was done now. Whatever she had made of her time, it was done. Henri would not have interpreted it that way, but he was dead, and his was the only voice that spoke up for her. She sat, dumbly furious. Furious that she had grown old, furious that she must write and pat this girl on the shoulder for stealing the last affection of her heart. It seemed so short a time since Henri was putting the rings on her fingers and now, to James and Miranda, she was imprisoned in her generation as some curious insect is packed in ice for transport to a collector. They expected her to write this letter easily, as an old woman writes, strewing blessings from her basket! They expected her to say things that became her grey hair. But she was out of sympathy with the renewal of life. She did not want to hear of or bless marriages. Sitting in the orange velvet dressing gown, shabby, ferocious and sombre, she clenched her hands with longing for the only companion proper to her, the commentator living at the same rate and to the same distance and on with her into the same indifference. "Do you find you care now about other people?" she could have said to him. "Not a bean!" he would have answered, meeting her eyes and smiling. (Ah, that ambition of her mother's to make her a duchess, that "arranged marriage"—what a happy marriage it had been!)

She pulled the best ducal paper, thick as cardboard, out of a drawer. She must presently copy her letter onto that paper, when it was written. If only James had been a Catholic, as he ought to have been, she could have made delays and troubles on that score, she might cynically have invoked the family opposition against this marriage with a Protestant. No, there was nothing to be done, and he would marry Miranda. He didn't pay more than light and loving attention to the heartbreaks of old women. And James too (she burst out to herself again) younger than Miranda! And who might with his wealth, good character, his charm and his looks . . . Her man of affairs came in after his second knock. He had a long walk up the shining boards of her business room. She turned and watched him so that under her silent waiting he lost confidence, almost to the use of his legs. He stumbled on a rug. When he arrived at her side she told him of the engagement, but in a manner that forbade congratulations. She asked for her jewels from her safe, intending to choose and send to Miranda the handsomest bracelet so that she could write the coldest letter. She would do rather more than her duty, and less than a heart should do.

"You can go to the safe while I am in the garden." She rose, treading on the hem of the velvet folds.

"Your Grace, if you would first sign these papers for the leases of the cottages . . ."

"Tomorrow."

He rattled the papers he held in his hand unhappily.

"Tomorrow. Tomorrow. Put them down. Go down now to the safe. Ah . . . I've dropped my stick!"

He picked up her black stick and watched her go through the old-fashioned conservatory doors that led from the business room into the garden. She wore the duke's leather hunting belt round her broad waist, and from a hook on the wall she took a basket as she passed. It was a vintage autumn, as yellow as summer, though colder in the mornings. Not a mauve plume moved as she passed down her border of Michaelmas daisies. She snipped, cleaned the stalks, and filled her basket as she had done in flower-season after flower-season for fifty-one years. But now she had done it too often. There was a limit set to everything that she could feel. The crystal air did not cool the heat of her eyes, her feet no longer loved the spongy autumn grass. She was heavy, smoky, tired like an old city. James had failed her. The garden could not prop her. Only the duke could have said to her—"I too, Alice. Hold my hand."

But when she got to the bottom of the border and turned—wonder of wonders—that must be James coming down the path from the house! He waved to her. Slowly she stood upright from her bending position and waited for him.

"It's not my ghost!" he called out as he neared her. "I flew down. I got a plane at eight this morning. I wasn't going to let you brood over my letter all alone." (No matter whom he was going to marry he loved her! He could take this ardent trouble for an old woman!) But she stood, unrelenting, in his path, black lace over her head, her lips set, the orange gown spotted and faded in the sun.

"I thought you didn't care for her!" she cried obstinately, hiding the winelike happiness. James took the basket, set it on the path, and kissed her. "You said you didn't care for her."

"She's full of faults," he assented. "Where shall we sit and talk? On this seat?"

"It's dewy. It's October."

He put his coat on the wet stone and sat in his shirt sleeves, the sun shining every moment hotter. She sat down slowly beside him.

"If there was one girl . . ." she began.

"But you wouldn't have liked any girl, would you?"

"Have you had breakfast?"

"No, and we'll go in in a few minutes. I told them to get me coffee. It won't yet be ready."

"But you were in love with her mother, James! How can you change like this? How can this have happened?"

"Hush. It must never be said. Poor Miranda has such a history of jealousy. We must cure all that. But you must never bring it up."

"But were you?"

"I was. But it's over. What I felt for Ruby was too high to live on. And she felt nothing in return. She's wonderful, a divine woman. But tired of love."

"Don't you believe it!"

"She is, Great-aunt. You'd better believe it. It's far more interesting to accept the truth. She's on fire to get old."

"What? To this? To this terrible condition! To my condition! How these beautiful women twiddle you round their fingers! She can make you believe anything. Did Miranda know about it?"

"She hasn't spoken of it."

"And if she does? Shall you deny it?"

"Absolutely."

"Ah, so you've thought it all well over."

"I know how to treat Miranda. She's got to be remade. We've got to begin again with her. We've quite a job. When you have your tussles, Great-aunt, I may not always side with Miranda."

"I? What am I going to have to do with it? If you really are going to marry you'll live at Pouilly and Miranda can make a muddle of Edouard's garden."

"I shan't give her the chance. Have you thought about a wedding present?"

She looked at him questioningly. He got up.

"The wet's coming through," he said.

"Your coat's soaking. I'm sending Miranda a very fine bracelet. It's being taken now out of the safe."

"I shouldn't. Not till you feel better. Wait till you can send her some very small thing, with your love."

She thought Miranda would have to wait a long time for that. They walked together down the path to the house, James carrying the basket.

"You asked me about a wedding present?"

"If I've been in love with Ruby," he said gently, "wouldn't it be better to have the first years down here? I may keep Edouard's cottage so that we can go back whenever Miranda wants to see her mother. But I thought, Great-aunt, you would give us a house?"

The rocky face turned to him was so lit with hope that James felt tears in his eyes.

"I'd give you the castle," she muttered.

"No," he said, smiling at her. "We're going to have a few small healthy rows. Miranda's sometimes going to be tear-stained. We must be a couple of fields away from you. I adore women, but they have to be women I know very well, and they have to be under my thumb. I've got my eye on the white house down by the arm of the river. It'll be a handsome present, for you'll find it wants a new roof." She was hunting for her handkerchief.

"There's a bog garden," she said with a sound like a sob of happiness. "What'll her mother feel?"

James, who had at first thought, like Tuxie, that to be a son-in-law might be the perfect relationship, was already full of the natural treachery one generation feels for another. His chin rose a little.

"Ruby's too much for Miranda," he said. "I really think she knows it."

## CHAPTER THIRTY-ONE

Ruby had the utmost feelings of relief. Relief so sweeping, so melting that she understood how tense had been the anxiety. To see Miranda carried into the harbour of James was like the third day after a serious operation in which life and death had been at stake. "The patient will live now." No doctor ever says that: but it is what the wife or mother understands he would mean to be understood. James had taken the little child who had evaded her, assumed full responsibility, found her worthy of love, and from now on he would woo and seduce Miranda into speech and happiness, disarming that angry and defended heart. She guessed Miranda had had suspicious and jealous feelings but now she shrugged her shoulders. Miranda must get over that, and that was James's affair. Miranda would do silly things, would purse her lips at the wrong moment, but James

knew her and knew it all and had this curious attitude of pleasure
in her faults. He pounced on them, and Miranda, quivering a little,
a little white about the lips, shone almost through tears. One evening in her bedroom Ruby said, "Would you have gone on with it?
With Afric? Would you have gone on to a marriage?"

"If you hadn't been there?"

"If I hadn't been there."

"There's no knowing," said Miranda. "I don't know. When I
want to change my mind it's so very hard. You have no idea what
it's like to be obstinate. Do I get it from Father?"

"Perhaps. Not from me."

"I wish he knew about this. About James. When we go down to
Lardaigne what shall you do? Will he ever come back, do you
think?"

"Do you think it's a strange thing to have happened, Miranda?"

"No, no, no I don't. But if it should happen to me—with James—
I should die."

"Do you blame me then? He didn't."

"No, it's entirely in Father. It lies in him. You've always been
yourself."

"But a woman who is a wife shouldn't be herself."

Though Ruby didn't see it, Miranda pursed those lips. She was
particular never to take advice from her mother. Her own life was
to be different. Changing the subject, she said:

"I'm absolutely out of scent. My bottle is empty. I forgot last time
I was in Paris."

"Take mine." Ruby held out a bottle. "I also forgot."

"But it's your last drop."

"Why should I hang out my flag, darling? I've nothing to sell."
How Miranda hated that way of talking.

Just before the wedding Alberti became seriously ill. He was not
sure that it was going to be death but he talked with Ruby of it.

"After seventy," he said, "every illness is a strange one. It's no
longer a case of colds and measles. One thinks one has control, but
I've noticed the moment is gone in a flash. I may be in full control

now and in the night it may be changed. Have you sat with someone who died? With a dying man or woman?"

"No."

"Not your mother? Or your father?"

"No. I was a small child when my father died and still a child
when my mother died. Her sister was with her."

"I've been with people very ill," said Alberti, "but never at the
end. This is going to be first-hand."

"Are you afraid, Bertie?"

"A little. I had not expected to be."

"Are you going to have the priest?"

"Well, yes."

"How alone I am."

"Yes. I think of that. You are alone because you have no religion,
and also practically. The family you have built up is dispersed. Even
Edouard is dead, and now I am to go very likely. With women
usually it is faith that takes over."

"And also apparently with men."

"I'm a bad Catholic. But I must believe that it's possible to be
taken back."

"You have a swell's soul to save, Duke. The Church is human."
Alberti shook a little with his own brand of laughter.

"But what," he said after a moment, "will God decide?"

"One must suppose it will be a real examination. But if He judges
fairly He'll say you've been good."

"You think so?"

"I know no one as good," she said. "I'm prepared to say 'noble.' "

"I thought of leaving you my fortune. I've had my lawyer down.
What I own has been a surprise to me."

"I wouldn't do that! No, I wouldn't do that. Let me think!"

He was silent.

"I don't want to re-enter the world. I'm almost taking my vows.
Did you know that James—I mean before Miranda came (this has
a bearing on what you've said)——"

"I know. I knew he loved you."

"I only say it to show you that it was because of that I had to search my soul. I found myself older than I thought. Now I want something new, not the old life. Your fortune, Bertie, would bring the world buzzing back."

"Yes, I see," he said tranquilly. "To whom then shall I leave it?"

"Do you ask me?"

"Yes. If you won't undertake it. For then I really don't know. I'd had my secret plan for your life. It's perhaps the only time I should have been allowed to influence it. And it touched me—I can't find the word——" She sat waiting.

"It comforted me," he resumed, not looking at her, "to leave a little monument to you at the end of my road. Like those roadside niches in Austria. I would sooner it had been a poem, but I'm not a poet."

"Have you jewels?"

"Any quantity."

"Leave me them." She said it to please him. He smiled. He knew that the jewels in Italy alone were worth a fortune. He was pleased with the idea too. It was a pretty thing to leave her jewels.

"How secret we've allowed you to be about yourself! Is there no heir? I suppose, as usual, all our lives I've done the talking. Have you no heir? Who takes the title after you?"

"It lapses. I'm to be totally wiped out. I leave only my duchess."

"Well, then, it's very serious about your money. You really have to do something."

She thought a moment or two.

"On what sort of scale? Houses? Land in Italy?"

"Land in Italy, a palace in Venice, another in Rome, my house in Paris, my collection of modern painters. And besides that I'm worth three million. The equivalent of three million English pounds."

"Bertie! But you've always known?"

"I'd forgotten. Yes, I knew of course. But I'm bad at counting scrip. Part of the income came in direct to me, but I had a second, accumulating account. And it's accumulated! And you really don't want it? Or any of it? I mean besides the jewels. Celestine of course is provided for. I've bought a house for her in her village, though she doesn't know it, and she will have five hundred a year."

"For your widow you might make it a thousand!"

"No. I know what I'm doing. She's not to be sponged upon. I know her weakness."

"And these houses, palaces. Sold up?"

"Sold up. And now, do you see, if you do this to me I really don't know what to do." As he lay placidly in bed, with, even at seventy, traces of pale curling hair on either temple, while the mound of his large Dürer face stared up at the ceiling, there was something knowing, something amused and sparkling in his prominent eyes.

"I had really in my mind swung the whole thing on to your shoulders. There is a great deal to be done that I have never done. A great deal to be expiated."

After a silence the voice spoke again.

"You must do as you think right. I'm too tired to arrange again. I thought I'd said good-bye to my lawyer."

She crossed the room to lean on the window sill.

"There are Miranda and James," he went on, speaking to her back as she leant out, "but James has really enough and the great-aunt will leave him the Scottish fortune. And Miranda—dear Ruby —I don't like Miranda enough to leave all my things to her," he complained. She turned from the window and came back to his bed. "You must forgive me," he said penitently, "I don't like jealous people." He was smiling and she held his hand, accepting what he said.

Her love for Miranda did not depend upon Miranda's virtues and wasn't altered by her faults. It didn't ask for corroboration.

"All the same, Alberti, 'name her,' as they say, in your will."

"Of course, of course," he said. "I've done that. Oh, it's quite handsome!"

"If I become," she said, "a millionairess, with all it means, its responsibilities, its lands, houses, taxes, consultations with lawyers, bailiffs . . ."

"Yes!" he said eagerly, "just that!"

"Its journeys."

"Exactly."

"Why do you think that must be good for me?"

"You'll have to postpone those bedroom slippers you are on the point of taking out of the cupboard. I'm not for your leaving the world. It's your gift and your burden. Through my responsibilities you'll get in touch with unfamiliar people. You'll be arbiter for many poor. There's half a slum in the collection. There's a picture gallery. There are five votes for a cardinal. But those they won't let you keep."

"You would have asked me to marry you if we had met early?"

"Yes, of course."

"Instead of which you want to make me your widow!"

"Yes. And I think you should learn Italian."

He lay still, relishing what he had done, and her way of taking it. He knew she had the whole picture now in her mind. A little bubble of laughter crept about in his chest. But he looked very tired, and over his protruding blue eyes the red eyelids sank. "In living so moderately," he said, with closed eyes, "I suppose I've lived selfishly. I could have given more pleasure, but that will all have to be worked out with God. If I've done wrong on a major scale, I've done quite well on a minor one. And there's been a good man of business. I see you're cross with me." She sat down by the bed and picked up the fat, rosy hand. "I told Celestine to turn you out if I got bad. But I should like to die chattering to you. Should you be afraid?"

"Not if you talked."

"Do you feel I've trapped you? If you really feel that, I suppose you can shift it somewhere. Something like the Nobel prize. Or perhaps when Gynt writes to you . . . but no, I shouldn't care for that! If you won't administer it I don't want Gynt bolstering up some Yogi university. Take my advice! I think I see extremely clearly. Try not to waste your magnificent strength in hankering after Gynt. I think you must accept that he vanished, that your married life was over before he went. He was a mystic long before he knew it. Who was I ever to give you advice? But this folding up you've been lately inclined to speak of, it's the folding up of your life as a woman. Now I ask you to accept the life of a man. My fortune's my last and only prescription for you. There will be things to set right—many things in Italy—that I should have done. And with the money—there's so much of it—you might really (why not?) endow a college to teach children philosophy. It's as you like. It's only a dream of mine. I've always thought we ought to know more about the rules of . . . sagesse . . . when we are young. Knock out geography and mathematics and Latin. Two hours, instead, a day on the few rules people have proved—maxims—well, why not call it philosophy? One of the lesser manifestations of philosophy is to learn to be philosophic (for instance), which isn't at all the same thing. There are simple virtues that aren't mentioned in church. Give and take. Insistence on common sense. When virtue is advised from within the Church it's veiled in such chloroforming language the senses don't take it in. The details of how to get on with one's fellows. Magnanimity. Patience. A sense of proportion. To be good, in fact. Serious lay lessons on the practical value of being good. High marks for wise behaviour. Such a large part of my life was spoilt by being silly. One might admit pupils from fifteen. That's a terrible, a sickening age. How I remember it! When I was fifteen I was so sad that my poor mother had such faults. Later I got used to it. Could you call Celestine?"

But Celestine was just coming in with a small tray. His eyes were tight shut: the fine linen bed-cover was sculptured over his large body, and his face was inclined back on a low pillow.

"Celestine!"

"Your Grace."

"I feel ill tonight. One never knows. But milady's not to be put out."

"Not? Well. So much the better." She stood near him with a steaming bowl."

"I smell the soup," he said.

"It's good."

"I won't have any."

"Is it the pain? Shall I rub you?"

"No, it's more uncanny."

"What about the doctor?"

He opened his eyes. Ruby was startled to see how the blue in them was faded.

"How about the priest?" he said gently.

"I'll go for him," said his wife. She left the room, putting the tray of soup on the table. Her eyes met Ruby's as she went, and Ruby felt that, with Celestine, a calm animal strength went out of the room.

"She knows her place," said the lips. "It's a place quite near me. She knows that too. Is that soup still in the room?"

"Yes. Shall I give it to you?"

"Put it outside. I can smell it. I don't want to eat again. I may drink water. Father Bonnie will know when he comes."

"Will know what?"

"Whether this is going to be death. If so, God's arranged the arc of life very well. I'm glad to be sinking. I'm immensely tired of being alert. I don't want to open my eyes for fear you should see them, but what time is it?"

It was seven in the evening.

"If Father Bonnie doesn't make it—but they usually do, it's curious—Catholic priests are so at home with death. They even know when to hurry. They leave messages about, as a doctor leaves them, saying where they can be found. I woke up this morning and breakfasted in the usual way. It's bizarre that the day of a man's death should open like other mornings."

He lay silent while she sat holding his hand. She wondered at this certainty that seemed to have come on him in the last hour that he was dying. He seemed to disregard the idea of the doctor, and she did not interfere. These hours had been planned by him before with a certain sequence and ceremony. Celestine, she felt, knew his wishes. She could not yet think of him as dying and she thought instead of this extraordinary responsibility he had planned that she should undertake. Argument was past: he was too ill. She thought, should he die, that she would say nothing at all about the will until James and Miranda had gone to Scotland on their honeymoon four days from now. She felt wryly that somehow Miranda would see it as one more instance of how her mother had a habit of stepping into the landscape. Ruby knew well that Miranda couldn't stop such thoughts and she marvelled at the love she knew they bore each other and which never had had any expression and perhaps never would. Miranda's soul belonged to her, and if it was a patchy one she and James were cheerfully ready to do their best with the dark spots.

Her thoughts escaped her, running about in the still room. She thought of Celestine. Was she considering in her practical way the urgent and dismal arrangements which might have to be made for tomorrow? That is what it was to be alive. And then, at her age, and Celestine's (which she remembered to be the same), death could not be felt with the same shocked pity as in youth—as something one would never have to endure. She watched his face, wondering what was going on behind the closed eyes in that bony chamber where sat the little pilot. Celestine opened the door. She had telephoned the priest, who lived quite near, and had found him in. He stood behind her, holding a tray with various objects wrapped in holland covers.

"You see!" said Alberti suddenly, knowing his presence at once, and speaking gaily from behind his shuttered face. "He was more than ready! He's like a shark round a ship!"

Ruby looked up at this and saw a direct and confident smile on the curiously worldly face of the priest.

"You must go, Ruby," said Alberti. "You're an outsider. I'm to be dressed for God. Come back afterwards. Read in the library."

Ruby went slowly down the stairs to the library, the living-room of this princely and humble man. The first thing was not to fail Alberti. She agreed with him that he was going to die. That she was to be named in a few weeks the owner of millions was now inevitable and there could be no more discussion: it was too late. Probably even to reject the fortune would mean a year of work. She could not merely thrust it from her. She sat down in his high, stiff chair and thought.

With Miranda's happiness she had an enormous sense of liberation. For Gynt she could not remain responsible. He himself had taken what remained of his life from her.

James and his offered love had opened her eyes. Instinctively she had recoiled, as though to accept love at that turn in her life would be unnatural, stupid, a marking time, a falling back. That was what was the matter with those women friends who surrounded her. They would not accept this and paraded their ghostly womanhood like the detached and tired wrapper of a novel. She who had been love's exciter, which, as Cora had guessed, is rarer than to love, was nearing the large period of the wise woman, when, having been a woman to men, she now remained a woman only for herself.

But with Miranda's return an unfinished task had halted her journey inwards. Suddenly agonised, and accepting full responsibility, she had waited by Miranda's side, holding tight to a hand that was restless in her own. She and Miranda, useless to each other, had held their breaths. Then James had opened the door to Miranda's happiness and to her descendants.

The deep emotion she felt surprised and enlightened her. Miranda would have children. She would never herself have first-rate interest in the second-rate job of being a grandmother, but something tremendous in her blood and Miranda's, no matter what trivial dissensions were between them, was released together into the future. "I am her history," she said. "She can't escape me. I'm only authentic now in my daughter's heart."

She had said to Alberti:

"One lays the ghost of everything." But at fifty-four it had been too soon to be so sweeping, and his reply was to give her an immense job to do. She would take on Alberti's job. She felt ten years younger. She had mistaken the dying womanhood as too wholesale a warning. She still had herself: there was to be no folding up in

the final sense. She knew that, given work, she might live to eighty.
Somehow she must tell him before he went.

Celestine came in and sat quietly beside her, in her stiff practical
manner, as though library chairs were not her custom.

"Is it certain, do you think?"

"What, my lady?"

"That he's going to die."

"He says he is. He is usually right. He's a great man."

"You've made him happy, Celestine. That must help you."

"I nagged at him to marry me. That was wrong."

"Did you? He never told me. But I think it's forgiven."

"I think it is. I have often thought I wanted you to know it was
my fault. I didn't know if you knew it, my lady."

"Don't call me that."

"It suits me. I don't want to change anything. I should much like
to know if after he's gone he has made arrangements for me? Has
he said so? It worries me. I'm not young."

"I'm sure of it." Ruby was at first surprised, but then thought,
"It's her simplicity."

"A little money is important. It's terrible to be without it. But I
know he would not like me to be anxious. I think he must have
thought of that."

"How you'll miss him."

"Oh . . ." She raised her hands and dropped them in her lap.
"While I have been near him I have lived a life I can never live
again. Every day has something to make one think."

"What do you talk about?"

"We are not much together. I like to be in the kitchen. But sometimes he comes to me and says, 'What do you think of this or that?'
And I say what I think. I never have any difficulty because of course
as you get older life becomes quite plain. He listens to me as though
he thought what I say would be useful to him. That I don't understand, but with him everything's easy and one doesn't need to
understand. Generally, in everyone, there is something one must
fight against. In him never. I don't wish to be impertinent . . ."

"What?"

". . . but I should like to say to you, my lady, that you are the light of his life. I have found there is much remorse after death. One doesn't always know how much one has been loved. While he still breathes and when you go up to him I wanted to make sure . . . But there's the bell."

"But you're coming up?"

"I shall sit on the chair on the landing. Better not linger," and she hastened to the door.

Ruby went quickly upstairs. Father Bonnie was on the landing.

"Will he die tonight, Father?"

"I think so. He is ready."

She would like to have asked more, but the priest seemed to wish to leave her and his eyes were impersonal. She opened the bedroom door. The big man lay heavy and quiet, his eyes still closed, the pink cheeks paler, hands turned formally, palm upwards, at either side of his hips. The priest seemed to have made a change in the room and yet all was as it was before. She sat down by the bed, not hiding the noise of her movement, so that Alberti should know she was there.

"My sin was the sin of idolatry," he said, very suddenly.

His only crime sat beside him, unwilling to touch his hand.

"Take my hand again," said the firm voice, with the same edge of smiles on it as it had always had. "These things must be weighed up in heaven. They've all the evidence. I've been a very large man with a small soul, and I shall need an enormous mercy—not justice."

"Are you no longer afraid?"

"No. I believe."

She leant nearer to him and said: "Bertie, you've been wise for me. It's all fine. All arranged in my head."

He only smiled at her, and nodded.

"Celestine is outside the door."

"Tell her to come in. I've no more secrets."

Celestine came in and sat in a chair on the opposite side of the bed. The dying duke breathed quietly on, fresh-looking and absorbed. Each breath seemed to have a value, as when one sets a clock very near the moment to ring the alarm. Ruby could not think for counting. It seemed important to count each intake and expulsion that meant he still had life. She held his hand, and after a while he put out the other hand for Celestine to hold also. After that everything was still. Presently his lips moved, but all one could hear was, "I think so." And again, something which might be Latin or Italian. The apparatus of thought was still in movement. Celestine, holding his hand, had her eyes fixed on a picture on the wall, as though no word of his belonged to her private ear. It grew rather dark. Suddenly Alberti said, clear and loud:

"Pull. Pull on my arms." Celestine nodded and stood up. Both of them, holding his hands, pulled firmly. Ruby too got up. His shoulders came up a little way, and, without opening his eyes, without a gasp or a catch in his throat, he seemed to change. They laid him back and put his arms on the bed. Celestine put her hand quickly over his eyes. She crossed herself with her other hand and said a peasant's prayer, the one she had said for her mother, her father, and a little sister who had died. Ruby did not kiss the face on the pillow. She said after a moment:

"What's to be done?"

"You must go home. It's your dinner hour."

"But you're sure?"

Celestine smiled. "I've seen it so often," she said. "I'll telephone to the doctor. Yes, the good duke is dead. I should think he will be much welcomed in heaven."